GOODBYE TO ROMANCE

GOODBYE TO ROMANCE

Stories by Australian and New Zealand Women
1930s–1980s

Edited by Elizabeth Webby
and Lydia Wevers

Allen & Unwin
Port Nicholson Press

First published in 1989
by Allen & Unwin New Zealand Limited in association with
the Port Nicholson Press, Private Bag, Wellington, New Zealand.

Allen & Unwin Australia Pty Ltd, NCR House, 8 Napier St, North Sydney,
NSW 2059, Australia.

Unwin Hyman Ltd, Broadwick House,
15–17 Broadwick St, London W1, England.

Allen & Unwin Inc., 8 Winchester Place, Winchester,
Massachusetts 01890, USA.

ISBN 0 04614 019 0

Cover painting: 'Summer Head' by Sally Burton
Cover design by Belinda Ellis, Lindsay Missen Design
Typeset by SRM Production Services
Printed by Australian Print Group

Contents

Introduction *by Elizabeth Webby and Lydia Wevers* 1

Christina Stead The Triskelion *1934* 5
Helen Simpson A Posteriori *1935* 19
Robin Hyde America Won the War *1937* 26
Isobel Andrews Every Saturday Night *1940* 33
Marjorie Barnard The Party *1943* 40
Ruth Park Regatta Day *1944* 45
Lyndahl Chapple Gee Double Unit *1945* 52
Margaret Trist The Bridesmaids *1951–52* 60
Greville Texidor An Annual Affair *1952* 67
Sarah Campion Amble *1953* 79
J. C. Sturm Where to, Lady? *1950s* 84
Ethel Anderson The Rector's Wife Tempts the Bishop with a Brew of Nyppe *1956* 93
Helen Shaw Singeing the Cockerel *1957* 110
Eleanor Dark Serpents *1959* 114
Janet Frame Jan Godfrey *1961* 122
A. E. Batistich A Place called Sarajevo *1963* 127
Judith Wright The Nature of Love *1964* 133
Thelma Forshaw The Grand Passion *1966* 148
Lyndall Hadow Act of God *1967* 155
Kylie Tennant The Case of the Blond Beast *1967* 163
Gwen Kelly Country Show *1970* 176
Oodgeroo Noonuccal Mumma's Pet *1972* 181
Vicki Viidikas The Snowman in the Dutch Masterpiece *1974* 185
Margaret Sutherland A Servant of the People *1974* 195
Finola Moorhead Where are you, Ellen Spalding? *1976* 200
Glenda Adams Wedding *1976* 208
Marion Campbell Peepshow *1977* 215
Elizabeth Jolley Woman in a Lampshade *1979* 219
Patricia Grace It Used to be Green Once *1980* 231
Joy Cowley Apple Wine *1980* 237
Ania Walwicz Big Tease *1981* 250
Ania Walwicz Big Red *1981* 251

Anna Couani Xmas in the Bush *1981* 253
Anna Couani The Train *1981* 255
Bub Bridger A Wedding *1982* 256
Olga Masters On the Train *1982* 264
Kerryn Goldsworthy Female Friends *1982* 268
Helen Garner Postcards from Surfers *1983* 274
Kate Grenville No Such Thing as a Free Lunch *1984* 287
Sue Reidy Alexandra and the Lion *1985* 291
Beverley Farmer Home Time *1985* 307
Yvonne du Fresne Christmas (Shirley Temple is a Wife and Mother) *1985* 316
Joan London The Girls Love Each Other *1986* 327
Anne Kennedy The Road to Damascus *1986* 336
Keri Hulme The Knife and the Stone *1986* 344
Marion Halligan Blood Relations *1986* 353
Shonagh Koea The Dancing Master *1986* 365
Jessica Anderson The Late Sunlight *1987* 374
Fiona Farrell Poole Footnote *1987* 389
Carmel Bird Buff Orpington and the Disasters of Middle Life *1987* 397
Barbara Hanrahan Lily *1987* 403
Thea Astley Right off the Map *1987* 407
Wendy Pond Journal of a Hanger-On *1988* 415
Janette Turner Hospital Isobars *1988* 424
Fiona Kidman The Tennis Player *1988* 431
Rosa Safransky A 'Happy Little Vegemite' *1988* 442
Jennifer Paynter The Sad Heart of Ruth *1988* 445
Stephanie Johnson The Glass Whittler *1988* 453
Jan Hutchinson Romance, Gardening and Feminist Theory *1988* 457
Barbara Anderson Up the River with Mrs Gallant *1989* 468

Notes on Authors 476

Acknowledgements 487

Introduction

In Christina Stead's story 'The Triskelion', the mother of one of the narrators remarks: 'I hate nature: it is full of cries and tears like a female madhouse.' Stead's story, one of *The Salzburg Tales*, was published in 1934. In its gothic darkness, its severing of the connection between landscape and the fulfilled human (female) spirit, and its concentration on the deterministic and deforming patterns of family relationships imaged in the three-legged triskelion, 'bound together at the ankles to form a wheel', Stead's story signifies the shift that occurs in the writing of women from the nineteenth century to the twentieth.

The dominant and dominating story form of women writers up until the 1920s and 1930s, is the romance, a form which made the short story predominantly a vehicle for reassurance, a reaffirmation of life's great pattern ending at the church door. In the 1920s and 1930s, a more experimental use of the short story by modernist writers began to enlarge its formal possibilities. Cultural locations in the work of women writers also began to shift: from in front of the church door to after the wedding; from romance of the unmarried to the distances and separations of the married; from the defining binary oppositions of heterosexual identity to postfeminist lesbian romance. *Goodbye to Romance* offers a sampling of these movements. From Christina Stead to Barbara Anderson and across the boundary of the Tasman Sea, its stories suggest some of the re-writings and re-inventions of the female subject by Australian and New Zealand women writers since 1930.

Rewriting romance as satire and as social realism, or seeing the short story as social commentary, is characteristic of stories from the 1930s, 1940s and 1950s, especially in the context of the war. Robin Hyde's story/sketch was originally published in *Tomorrow*, an independent weekly which appeared in New Zealand in the 1930s, thick with news of the Spanish Civil War. Hyde's point about cultural change is affirmed in the succession of American servicemen who walk up Millie

Gladson's front path, and leave Walt Disney ornaments on her window sills, in Lyndahl Chapple Gee's story 'Double Unit'. It is more generally documented by the large numbers of stories which locate the problematic of female identity, especially within the primal political arena, the family.

A great many of the stories in this collection focus on the family as a place of constraint and repression; 'home' is a continuous re-invention of place and condition; marriage is the adoption of 'mother not father', imaged by Gwen Kelly in her story 'Country Show' as a cultural myth familiar throughout Australia and New Zealand:

> Good old eternal school exhibits, unchanging beneath the ever-changing waves of education theory – compositions 'My Home', drawings of trees and faces, so freely conventionally expressed; convoluted shapes of creativity, circles and cells and cells and circles. My home but not a home; mother not father, mother convoluted in the shapes of pregnancy, pressing the daily bread into our mouths while father slept with God knows who on sunny slopes, remote from never to be visited home

Genealogies and origins, culturally defining locations (weddings, meals, Christmas, holidays), and, especially in the later stories, mother, grandmothers and great-grandmothers as the expression of origins, are notably points around which stories in the collection cluster. The power of the mother, various and polyvocal, is reiterated from Christina Stead's mother who competes for (and wins) her daughter's lover, to Keri Hulme's bedridden bloodsmelling imprisoning mother in 'The Knife and the Stone', to Anne Kennedy's great-grandmother's unauthorised desires, to Olga Masters' young mother terrifying her children on the train or Yvonne du Fresne's unmarried schoolteacher, locked in at Christmas with elderly parents and her failure to achieve collective identity. It is as if the short story has borne witness to a displacement of female identity from wife to mothered and mothering daughter.

The gaze of the male lover upon his beloved, which constructed the nineteenth-century short story as romance, is deconstructed and rewritten in the twentieth-century short story. In reiterated associations of work and bondage, family and deformity, emotion and destruction, it suggests itself instead as the place in which the female self dismantles, or fails to dismantle, its frames:

> But she wanted to erupt, wanted her skin crawling breaking the images of pale cool masks, plaster hands, lips: she wanted to drink the milk, break the glass, carve up the painting, this masterpiece of perfection, get out of the frame. (Vicki Viidikas, 'The Snowman in the Dutch Masterpiece'.)

It is not just a question of bursting out of the frame, rewriting the self in opposition to the past, that is at work in the stories of women writers, but a more general destabilising of the boundaries which construct the gendered subject, calling into question all the terms which might presuppose identity: wife, mother, daughter, lover, woman, narrative, story.

A number of writers in this collection locate themselves as storytelling, writing women: Elizabeth Jolley, Janet Frame, Anna Couani are some of those who focus on what is more generally the self-representation of all the writers here, the text as signifier of a process called fiction writing. In Janet Frame's story 'Jan Godfrey', the narrator slides from 'wanting to write a story, today' to an assertion of fictional identity, the existence of the text, at the end: 'my name is Alison Hendry'. Claiming a new name, rewriting the world, affirming the text, breaking down divisions, rerouting the track that leads to the church door: the work of women writers has burst out of its romance frame and announces itself as polyvocal, polyglot, exploratory, different.

The predecessor to this collection, *Happy Endings*, represented the nineteenth-century woman writer as a homogeneous creature: white, Anglo-Celtic, her business was human emotion. *Goodbye to Romance* begins to deconstruct the univocality of the past. There are fifty-eight writers in this book. They vary in race, ethnic background, age, sexual preference, and in textual and narrative structures.

Together, however, their stories give some indication of the range of writing produced by Australian and New Zealand women during the past sixty years, and of their contribution to the literatures of both countries. And they add up, we hope, to a book which will be enjoyed by all its readers, whatever their ages, backgrounds or fictional preferences.

Lydia Wevers, Wellington
Elizabeth Webby, Sydney

Christina Stead
The Triskelion
1934

Arnold, the blind youth, waited patiently in the Matron's office. From time to time both hands played over the table as if he were reading Braille. The Matron's pen went scratch, scratch, writing in a register. Through the open window came sounds of voices and steps on the gravel drive, but neither moved. Then the sounds were heard in the paved hall, and in a moment the hall attendant opened the door and said: 'Matron, Mrs Jeffries, and Mr and Mrs Skelton, come for Arnold.' Arnold went directly to the visitors, saying: 'Good morning, grandmother; good morning, Aunt Sylvia and Mr Skelton.'

He sniffed and said with his thick articulation: 'You have got a nice scent today, Aunt Sylvia.'

'It is only lavender,' said the young woman indifferently.

'Smell mine,' said the grandmother, drawing a coquettish handkerchief from her bag and flicking its heavy perfume under the youth's nose.

'I can smell,' said Arnold, and sat down in his chair, fingering absently the pattern of the tablecloth, waiting till these creatures, supercilious because of their supernatural gift of sight, should think of him again and take him away.

He had been born blind. He had been five years a pupil in the Royal Institute for the Blind and now, at nineteen, having slowly and painfully learned a trade, he hoped to free himself from the bonds natural to his condition. His family was rich, but he wanted to be a workman: in the rare moments when he spoke of himself, he said: 'When I am a workman, I will do – so-and-so . . .' imagining a workman to be free, richly paid and respected.

He listened. His grandmother was giving the Matron the address of the bootmaker to whom he was to be apprenticed, and with whom he would board. Mr Skelton said to his wife: 'But I think the poor fellow should have a home: an orphan must feel lonely, and then to be always blind, alone in the dark... and never to have known his father and mother!' Arnold felt acutely, as the Matron saw dully, the singular look of animosity interchanged between the two women.

'He doesn't feel happy with us, you know that,' said Sylvia to her husband. 'Besides, how would he get to work?'

'Then with your mother, dear,' said the man submissively.

Mrs Jeffries hastened to say: 'I'm too old to be bothered with young men at my age.'

'At your age? What are you talking about, mother?' said the son-in-law mildly. The boy wondered why these people thought he was deaf because blind, instead of realising that he was all ear.

They had gone down the long drive to the car waiting at the gate, when Arnold came hurrying back, holding out his arms on both sides, to feel the bushes along the drive. He arrived at the stone verandah where we stood, and queried: 'Doctor?'

'Here, Arnold!'

He pressed into my hand something which I thought was a shilling, and started back towards his family. I called: 'Arnold, what is this? You have given me your "three-legs!"'

He hesitated: 'Take it, take it, Doctor!' and went on.

I smiled, and showed the Matron the round gold medal which Arnold had found one day, long ago, making sand castles on the beach: it bore as device, three legs radiating from a small circle. It had been his pride. After feeling it carefully for days, he had been able to reproduce the design. I said to the Matron: 'Poor little "workman"; he is putting away childish things!' The Matron, shading her eyes with her hand, looked at the car moving away and said: 'Well, that's the closest family that ever I met: I never got a word out of them about Arnold's parents, or anything else, not even the certificate. I suppose there was something wrong with the old lady's son, that the grandson's so queer.'

'Your medical report is birth certificate enough,' I said sadly.

The Matron said: 'I'd give a fair price to know who he is, all the same: there's a skeleton in the cupboard.'

'Matron,' I said laughing, 'your imagination runs riot.'

'All right, all right, I've got a long nose,' she said, ruffled.

Two years after, the Matron, who had an insatiable curiosity about the seamy side of life, from natural leaning as well as professional habit, showed me a copy of one of the two blackmail sheets the rich lively city can afford to support. *The Public Guardian* had printed the following paragraph: 'Mrs Sylvia Charteris Skelton, *née* Jeffries, or Jenkins, heiress to the Jenkins jam fortune, has left home, hubby and mother and gone to spend an indefinite holiday in New Zealand. What's the fly in the jampot?' Nothing more appeared on this subject, and the Matron, inconsolable, said: 'I'll bet those Jenkinses, or Jeffries, paid up.'

I went to see the grandmother to find out what Arnold was doing and found him in her house. Mrs Jeffries, a middle-aged woman of young appearance, formerly pretty and fresh, now showed marks of dissipation: she was clumsily rouged, a little flabby, talkative and had a number of tics which like little animals seemed to ravage her against her will. Arnold recognised my voice but did not move from his seat to greet me. I asked the grandmother about his health, and, softening over tea, she told me in a whisper that Arnold had been married almost eighteen months; that his wife, a young immigrant servant girl 'who married him for his money', had turned him out of the house; and that this event had sufficed to transform the boy completely. He sat about the place in a depressed, dull way, never answered his grandmother, and scarcely spoke to me. His fingers, not now thinking in Braille, wandered about his person and I saw that he felt the restraints of polite company no more than a dog or bird.

They asked me to see Arnold's wife. I wrote to her with the hope of getting information which would help me to a treatment for him. She told me, cannily, that I might go to see *her*. I entered a small grocer's shop bearing the name Arnold Jeffries, and saw her, a good-humoured, sanguine, hefty little woman of about twenty. 'Are you the doctor?' she said when she saw me. She showed me into her parlour, down two steps from the shop, curtained with coarse machine lace, red-clothed, with a canary, and old stuffed chairs, a perfect replica of parlours she must have admired as a little girl in the old country.

She came in without her apron and said cheerfully: 'I know you came to ask me about Arnold. Well; I put him out and I ain't goin' to take him back. It would suit me in the business to have a husband with me, but he ain't a husband, he's a – he's sick. I suppose his mother told you he put up the money for the stock here? Well, so he did, and every month, too, I send him what's fair, if there's any profits. Only, I can't take him back.'

'Why?' said I.

'Aw,' she said, hesitating for the first time, 'I just can't, he isn't natural.'

'Why do you say that?'

'I really can't explain, doctor,' she said, 'even to a doctor.'

I said: 'You mean, he has a certain malady, or is not very strong?'

She opened her eyes, 'Oh, no, with me he's very lively, that is, when it comes to kissing and that.'

I was astonished now. 'What then? Arnold is my old patient: I have known him since he was a child. Perhaps I can improve him, although he can't be cured. And now I am distressed to see him sitting there, half-dead, plucking his clothes . . .'

She looked upset. Deciding, she said: 'Arnold, he – well, I s'pose because he's blind, and can't see like other men, and he's so used to using his hands for eyes (but hands are like eyes that can see in the dark, and no matter where and go into the smallest corners like a match) – and, why, he can sleep all day if he wants to, but I can't, I've got to run the shop, and if you can imagine what it's like when you never get any sleep. Besides, my family was always very religious and very decent.'

I stared at the girl, and suddenly began to smile.

'It's no laughing matter,' said the girl, with spirit. 'It's a disease – cure it if you say you can. And all day and night his hands would be running, running, like a pyannist doing his scales.'

I did not tell this last adventure of Arnold to the Matron. Arnold was now, besides, irretrievably degenerate, and I expected him to die when he reached the difficult age of thirty.

I saw his wife again and told her this. She said: 'Do *they* treat him well?'

'Passably.'

'I'm making some profits now,' she concluded. 'I'll give him a fine funeral: there's a funeral parlour down the road does it on time-payment. You let me know: they never would.' She wiped her eye, and said: 'I mean him no harm.'

One day, not long after this, my friend, Kate de Lens Ormonde, the barrister, noticed Arnold's trinket on my bracelet and said: 'The triskelion!' There were tears in her eyes.

She continued: 'Pardon my crying over it! I've had the habit since childhood of crying in the presence of the supernatural.'

To my blank look she responded, 'You shall hear something curious!

'When I was six, we went to Terrigal, and since that time, three things have haunted me in imagination: a wild bull, for there was one loose in the district that could be heard bellowing at all times of the day; a wild boar, for there was one which had eaten a baby in its cradle and escaped and was somewhere in the woods; and third, the Skillion. The Skillion or Penthouse, is the headland which rises from the dark, tarnished lagoon at Terrigal. No one in my family knew what the name meant, and it haunted me and was ranged in my mind alongside the Sphinx, the Chimera, the Beast 666 and the Roc. We lived a month in what seemed to me the gloomy and marshy country of the Skillion.

'When I was twelve my mother took me with my five young brothers to "Ascalon", a fashionable boarding-house at the Lakes Entrance, at Tuggerah, which is not far from Terrigal. I saw, in anticipation, the familiar landscape drenched with romance.

'Now my mother and her maid were occupied with the little boys, so I had all the day to myself: and in the early morning I left the house, going through the thickets of she-oaks, banksias and ficuses, dwarfed by the sea-winds, and climbing the grass-cobbled dunes which overlooked the mangrove swamps of the upper lakes, and the seven-mile ocean beach. There I often sat all day in a hollow of the sand, returning only at lunchtime and in the evening, half deaf with the everlasting crash of the waves on the sand, the bellowing of cows, the thudding of horses exercised on the flats of the beach, and the perpetual conversation of the winds. The curlews cried by the lake, at dawn and dusk, and nothing was more appropriate to the dreary wastes of sand-rooted underbrush, the overgrown shrubbery full of tarantulas, the dreary wastes of the turbulent ocean, always peaked and foamy, and the bleak and ravaged headlands. O, that distant time, happy, morbid, cud-chewing dawn of adolescence!

'The sun set one evening yellow and red over the woods and lakes, purple over the sea and in the eastern sky, bands of purple and red. The wind hurried along the deserted beaches in spirals and eddies, and the rising tide hummed along the shelving dunes. The sun went down with a last pale gleam on clouds torn to ribbons. The light was lit in the Norah Head lighthouse and blinked out to sea. I had at that time marvellously long sight, not blunted and blinded as I am now, reading for examinations. Something moved in the obscurity under the distant head, at first I thought a buggy, and next it was like a giant turning hand-springs by the sea; then I saw a wheel with three spokes; it approached rapidly, and last I saw there were three legs sprouting from a hub, bound together at the ankles to form a wheel, by a twisted cord, grey as spindrift, blanched as stranded seaweed, trundling along at an unnatural rate towards the Entrance. The circumference of the wheel was about twelve feet: the legs were whitish-brown, thick and muscular, and all were from the right side. The appearance passed me with the speed of a racing chariot or faster, leaped over the Entrance and sped into the darkness of the cliffs beyond.

'I sat for perhaps a quarter of an hour, while the swart sea assaulted the beaches and rammed the dunes. I looked towards the thickness now enveloping the cliffs of Norah Head to see if another phenomenon would pursue the first, but there was nothing, only the long billows still visible rearing far out, and along the masked beach, waves drawn by the undertows, retreating from the sand. The white line of foam, invariable warning of dirty weather, leaped insatiably round the bombora, a mile from the Entrance, and the yellow lake water still striped the sea. The stars began to appear faintly in the dishevelled heavens, to light some grey-headed drop of spume or some belated leaf for a moment on its unfated way.

'At last I picked up my legs and went home slowly through the quiet undergrowth. When I reached the house, the gong was ringing for dinner and I went in preoccupied, but without a word: who would believe me?

'It happened that that night, as the wind made it a little cold, I went into the great kitchen, which was about fifty feet long, and was allowed to make toast in front of the ovens. The cover was removed, and I looked down into the fire, where wood, charcoal and twigs burned. "Look, look," I cried, laughing, "here is a Turk with long beard, fierce, with purple eyes: here is a stuck pig bleeding, here is a judge in ermine and red, and here is a barrister with his hand lifted, in charcoal."

'They came to see, the household servants, dinner being finished, the last dishes put in their places, and lassitude filling each one. "Yes, yes, so it is," they said agreeably.

'"You're seeing things," said my mother's cousin, Rhoda, the proprietor of the boarding-house.

'"Imagine what I saw this evening on the beach, Rhoda!"

'"What?" she said languidly.

'"On the beach at dusk I saw a wheel of three legs rolling fast as the wind."

'"Get along with you," said my cousin laughing heartily. "That's an old story: someone told it to you."

'"No, I saw it plain as day," I said, and though my eyes were wet with superstitious tears, as now, I made it clear what I had seen. I looked at the flushed faces of the kitchen men and maids on the other side of the great mantelpiece.

'"Something is going to happen," said Rhoda nervously, and went out of the kitchen. I heard her giving orders in the dining-rooms: "No one is to promenade along the beach to-night, do you hear? No walks, no fishing, no going on the lake: put up a notice in the hall. Shut up the cows: perhaps they will break loose: there is going to be a storm." There was a repressed bustle in the company for the rest of the evening, and the young folks, dancing and gossiping, would go off into explosions of laughter about "General Rhoda", and Carlo, a young fellow tutoring for the University, who had enormous success with the company, told an absurd tale of a "ghost train with ten bogies". In the midst of this the loving couples stole out to consult the amiable stars.

'Rhoda was annoyed. She said to my mother: "It is a sort of phantom: it is called a triskelion, and appears here just before a crime or other grisly accident occurs in the district. I shudder at the mere thought. For example, three brothers and a sister lived in a small house on the other side of the lake, and all were abnormally fat, horribly fat, so that they could scarcely walk. They sent for a quantity of that patent medicine, Antibese, supposed to be a sure cure for obesity: they took it and it made them fatter still, so that people could not bear to go near them, even the tradespeople, to give them food, or the postman with letters – monsters they seemed. The news spread and was authenticated that a young man had appeared to court the sister. He was thin, overdressed and spoke "plausibly", as the people say hereabout: by that they mean something disagreeable. The brothers refused his demand in marriage and chased him from the door. The woman eloped with him and they were married. It turned out that he was a showman attached to a travelling circus, and intended to earn his living by her. He whipped her (she had a nature as soft as jelly), forced her to appear, and lived meanwhile with the tight-rope dancer. The showman was found murdered in his caravan one morning, and the girl missing. The brothers were convicted, one was hung, and the other two are doing time. The girl has to earn her living now, and under another name she travels with the same troupe. The night the couple eloped, the triskelion appeared on the mud bank in the middle of the lake and was seen by all the passengers in the ferry.

'"Very commendable of it," said the mother, "but why didn't it alight on the chimney of the fat people?"

'"Another time," said Rhoda, "a man and woman were found hanging from a fig-tree back there in the brushwood. It was supposed that they committed suicide, because they had been vagabonding over the country for months, until every door was sick of them and the dogs were set on them. The night they hung themselves, the triskelion appeared rolling quickly over the sea, and rested for a time like a tired sea-bird on the tops of the wood: darkness fell and it could no longer be seen.

'"A third time was last year, when the bar at the Entrance was thrown up so high that the flood-waters could not escape and the lake was seething here outside the house. In the night I looked out to see the level of the flood-waters, and saw the sky flickering with lightning, although there was no thunder. In one of the flashes I saw the triskelion, on the submerged lawn there, by the she-oaks. I went round the whole house, into all the bedrooms, with a lamp to see if anything had happened in the house. The next morning people, and some of mine, were out boating on the rough waters, shooting the races and eddies, when suddenly the bar was broken through by the pressure of waters within, and the flood poured out through the Entrance in a fierce torrent. The boats were whirled over a mile in two or three minutes: they shot through the churning overfall at the mouth and were seen no more: wreckage was found along the beach and on the bombora. Eight persons were drowned that morning.

'"So you see I am anxious," said Rhoda. "Perhaps something will happen to the Jenkinses, who are coming late this evening. You know them, Thomas Jenkins, the jam man from Haviland Street. They have taken the large front room with the bow-window. Some of their luggage has come on already. They are staying for a month: and imagine that they have sent on already two cases of whiskey, one of liqueurs, one of champagne, and conserves, biscuits and fruits galore! They think they get nothing to eat here: or else, they expect us to be quarantined when they arrive! Provided they hand it round a little, and are sociable . . . ."

'At this moment we heard the distant siren of the ferry, and saw the lights across the water, now roughened by the rising wind. The young guests gathered on the verandah under the tossing Chinese lanterns and shouted encouragingly. The Jenkins family disembarked with a quantity of boxes, valises and handbags. They were scruitinised in the lamplight in the usual comic spirit by the established guests.

'Mr Thomas Jenkins, known to everyone present by his jams, was at least fifty years old, prematurely decrepit it seemed, with a small, creased, bearded face, on which a lascivious little smile played. He inclined frequently in conversation towards the person talking and in all ways displayed obsequious manners. Mrs Thomas Jenkins seemed a little over thirty, thickening towards the forty-year, pleasant, partly the conserved coquette, partly the made-over country girl. Sylvia, a self-possessed girl perhaps fifteen years old, sprung up unseasonably, thin like a sapling, and yet large-breasted, moved in advance of her parents and looked to left and right, sizing up the company and her surroundings with composure. She passed before them into the room reserved for them.

'Sylvia had not been in the drawing-room more than a few minutes before the young men had all gathered round her, questioning her and laughing at her sage or cunning replies. They angled with delicacy to know her age, but she replied directly, "I will be twelve next month: I am always taken for fourteen, at least!" She coughed a little and said she had a delicate chest. The boys, abashed by her youth, looked at that admirably moulded part and said, "What a shame!" Her father came into the room after a few minutes, and softly, with numerous polite little smiles, called her to bed.

'"Only eleven – what bad luck," said one: "such a jolly kid."

'"I don't believe it," said Carlo, a puppy Don Juan, chief buck of the troupe: but in a moment to controvert him, the mother appeared, soft, young and pretty, to explain that Sylvia was "only a baby", and had to rest, and that her father had gone out for a smoke.

'After the first day or two the Jenkins family spent little time with the other guests, walking alone, and even taking meals in its own room. The servants complained first, because they could never make the full tale of dessert knives and plates. There were always several in Mr Jenkins' room. Later, the ladies found Sylvia too pert for her age, too indifferent to the dignity of married ladies, and too assured with the boys. And she was dressed far, far too well for a child.

'The mother of a dark-haired, dark-eyed, timid and confiding little girl called Jean, said with despite "Imagine that yesterday that child changed her dress three times, I counted: I can't see myself dressing Jean so. That girl Sylvia's a ball of fluff: a nice coquette!" The boys were far from being so severe.

'The Vandenbrighs, family of social distinction, without whom the social columns of the city newspapers could hardly have survived, "cut" the Jenkinses entirely. My mother, a mild person, said shaking her head, to her maid, as they went over the boys' linen: "I don't cotton on to Mrs Jenkins at all." The report spread that "the whole family drank": the boys said that old Jenkins' jokes, off colour from the first, were now "too much of a good thing": solemn, excited little girls, guests in the house, brought to their mothers shillings and cakes given them by the old fellow, and were sent flying back to return these gifts. Rhoda said, "I shan't have them again."

'One day I lay under the boughs of a little hollow by the sandhills, listening to the pleasant distant cries of the Vandenbrigh boys, who had a separate pavilion higher up towards the ocean beach, on the border of the swimming channel, on this side of the lake. The breeze rustled intermittently. I heard a prolonged rustling, and looking over my feet, saw Mr Jenkins peering like a satyr through the branches. I sat up and said nothing: I disliked him as if he were a piece of dirty rag. He smiled ingratiatingly and approached. He sat down facing me, cross-legged, and began scraping in the sand between us, in a curious manner. Presently, he took a shilling out of his pocket and offered it to me, without a word. I pushed it away, while my heart thumped hard. His two small eyes were reddish and ichorous, as if they were two little wounds looking on an interior ulcer. I jumped to my feet, murmured some excuse about seeing my mother, and left him sitting there in the little hollow. I did not know why I was scared.

'One night I slept very uneasily, and waking, found myself, although conscious, paralysed. The darkness sat over me like an incubus. I strained from side to side, as I imagined, and beat on the bed, doing all I could to utter a cry that would waken my mother. Suddenly, I heard that cry, a dreadful cry, ringing in my ears. I found myself at the same moment awake, and my mother sitting up in bed.

'"Did you hear that?"

'"Perhaps it was I," I said. "I tried to call out."

'"I thought it came from outside, though."

'"It was a dog, or a curlew in the swamps," said my mother's maid, holding her knees, as she sat up in bed, with her curl-papers swarming round her head.

'"It seemed different from a curlew's cry, horrid as that is," said my mother, discontentedly, "but it may have been. How I hate those birds. And how I hate this everlasting gush and hiss of the sea, and those swishing trees. What, in heaven's name, possessed me to come to "Ascalon"? I hate nature: it is full of cries and tears like a female madhouse." She settled herself back in bed, and I heard her sigh and mutter several times before her regular breathing began again.

'In the morning, Rhoda came knocking on our door, to get us out in a hurry: little Jean, the dark-haired girl, had been found in the channel at five o'clock in the morning, by the Vandenbrigh boys and the others, going swimming. She had been murdered, and then thrown in. There was something secret about the business that we could not know. The police had been telephoned, but had to come seven miles by the regular launch, and would take some time to get there. Rhoda was getting the guests up, to be dressed and have an informal breakfast. No one could leave the house. The children spoke in whispers, if they dared speak at all.

'The Jenkins family was also still asleep. Their curtains were drawn and they did not answer repeated knockings. Rhoda said, "Pigs! They probably drank too much last night: I heard them talking late in their room: well, they've got to get up and look respectable before the police come." She thought with despair of her lover, who went there for two or three weeks, every six months, getting away from his family to live quietly there with her, in the off-season, on the pretext of a rest-cure. He was a brilliant lawyer, a labour turncoat, and was expected to be Prime Minister at the next change of Government. He could not afford to be involved in any scandal of any kind, nor to visit a house whose reputation was not high. They beat on the door, with irons brought from the stove, and when they had no response, the kitchen-man and the scullion forced the lock, and stood timid in the warm sleeping-chamber.

'Listening, gratified, we heard exclamations and the voice of Rhoda, trying to rouse Mrs Jenkins. They came out leading her, dazed, in her nightgown. Rhoda wrapped her in a rug, saying meanwhile, in a rage: "Pig, pig!"

'"Get yourself in hand," said my mother: "are the others like that too?"

'"The old fellow's lying in there weltering in his blood," said Rhoda, in a businesslike voice. "The little girl's nowhere to be seen. Provided she hasn't been murdered too. . . ." My mother began to moan. "Why should you cry?" said Rhoda brutally. "I'm ruined by this affair. Who will come here now?"

'Two days later Sylvia was discovered living in an hotel in a large market town seven or eight miles away. She had given a false name, but her appearance and clothes betrayed her. The mother, confronted with the daughter, accused her of the murder of her father, out of *jealousy*. The daughter, cold and assured, accused the mother! Terrified, the wretched mother immediately confessed that the father and daughter had cohabited for three years, and that the father, growing more depraved with advancing age, had for some time given the masterful Sylvia cause for jealousy. Sylvia at last, breaking down, like the child she was, admitted that she had killed her father in his sleep, "because he had betrayed her". She had suspected from his furtive manner that night that it was so; she questioned him adroitly, a past-master in the horrid art, and had proved her suspicions when he fell asleep: she did not know of course that Jean was dead. She had intended to make her way to the capital, and with the money she had taken with her, take a boat "somewhere".

'Poor Carlo, tender Don Juan, attended the trial, hardly able to keep calm when Sylvia was attacked and questioned, and when she was proved guilty, saying miserably, "How she must have suffered, how she must have suffered, to reach that point." He was perhaps the only person in the whole country that pitied her. She was sentenced to a reformatory for ten years, to be released after that if her family gave proper guarantees. The father of Carlo, a judge, moved by his son's desperate pleas, arranged for her to be allowed to enter a private asylum. She was rich by her father's will, and would inherit the whole fortune when her mother died.

'She had a boy child some months after she went into this house of correction, and the boy was brought up by the widow of the murdered man.'

'That boy,' said the Doctress, 'was unquestionably Arnold, the boy of the triskelion.' She looked at the coin which dangled on her bracelet.

'You can bear to wear that dreadful thing?' said a young lady.

'Poor Arnold!' sighed the Doctress. 'It is in memory of him.'

'I liked to hear your story, both your stories,' said the Balkan Lawyer. 'There is a sequel to all that, too, which I know by chance. Last year, an oldish woman with her daughter, both widows, it was said, and both rich, came to Vienna and made rather a sensation in the fast set of the foreign colony. There they met Count Winkel, a penniless young man of good family, good looks, and scruples: when I say scruples, I mean he had scruples about the people he took money from; he would not take it from a bankrupt or a beggar, for example! Count Winkel danced attendance on both ladies, determined to catch one and either. They did all the lidos, casinos, and fashionable resorts. They lived *en famille* for a month on a certain islet in the Adriatic, where it is said, no woman can go without losing her virtue.

'The daughter, quite a pretty woman, but delicate, believed that he and she were engaged, wore a ring and referred to him as "my fiancé, Cornelius Count Winkel, you know". They returned to Vienna. She waited for him one afternoon in the public gardens and presently saw him coming towards her, with her mother leaning on his arm. The mother radiant and triumphant, in pink organdie, rushed up and presented, with a little confusion, "the new stepfather". The marriage had just been celebrated.

'The daughter said nothing: the next morning the young man received by post the daughter's supposed engagement ring: the girl died forty-eight hours later from an "overdose of sleeping draught", as they say.

'The inquiry, which brought out these details, forced the newly-married pair to leave the city, and revealed among other things, that the young lady was Mrs Sylvia Skelton, divorced for serious misdemeanours, and the mother, Mrs Thomas Jeffries, a widow. The vice certainly flowered in that family in all its forms!'

'What a three-legged history!' said the Doctress. 'I begin to think it will never stop.'

'And you can still bear to wear that ornament?' said the young lady, irritably.

'If I throw it away, I am afraid it will start rolling again, making more business for clerks, registrars and judges,' said the Doctress seriously.

Helen Simpson

A Posteriori

1935

At about one o'clock on the last night of her stay in Pontdidier-les-Dames Miss Charters was awakened by indeterminate noises sounding almost in her room, and a medley of feet and voices in the street. It was not the first time this had happened. Pontdidier had belied the promise, made by an archdeacon, that she would find it an harbour of calm. The fact was, the town was too near a frontier, and too unsophisticated. When politicians in Paris, to distract attention from their own misdeeds, began to roar of treason, Pontdidier believed them, and the Town Council – 'nos édiles' – set up a hue and cry for spies. Miss Charters had not failed to observe this nervousness, and to despise it a little, without ill-humour; but to be roused by other people's unfounded terrors at one in the morning was a little too much, and she said so, in her firm French, to the landlady as she paid her bill next day.

'Je ne suis pas sure que je puis vous recommander à mes amis. Votre ville n'est pas tranquille du tout.'

The landlady sank her head between her shoulders, then raised and swung it deplorably to and fro.

'Las' naight,' said the landlady, practising English, which reckoned as a commercial asset, 'it is a man escape from the police. A spy that makes photographies. They attrape him, but the photographies – gone! Nobody know.'

'Un espion!' repeated Miss Charters coldly, as one who had heard that tale before. 'Esperons qu'il n'échappera pas.'

With that she walked upstairs to her room for a final inspection. Her hot-water bottle, as usual, had been forgotten in the deeps of the bed, and this she rescued thankfully. Going to the washstand to empty it, she set her foot on some round object, and came to the floor with no inconsiderable bump. The object, obeying the impetus she had given, rolled to rest against a chair-leg, and Miss Charters, turning to eye it with the natural resentment of one tricked by the inanimate, instantly recognised it as a spool of film.

Her mind, with a gibbon-like agility which unhappily never comes at call, leapt from the spool to the noises in the night; linked these with her own wide-open window, probably the only one in the entire façade of the hotel; and came to the conclusion that this spool had reached her floor by the hand of the suspected spy now in custody; flung as he fled. But there had been, her subconscious seemed to think, two noises in the room. She looked for another possible missile, and perceived, under the bed, a flat wallet of some kind. It was quite inaccessible, the bed's frame hung low, she had no umbrella to rake for it, and some vague memory of criminal procedure insisted that the police must always have first cut at a clue. It was her duty to go downstairs, display to the landlady the spool, which she had picked up instinctively, and ask that the authorities should be informed.

She set foot on the stairs, and even as she did so, halted. It became apparent that she would have to give her evidence in person, swear to the noise in the night, to the morning's discovery. This would involve missing her train, and its subsequent connection, with the expense of warning domestics and relatives by telegram. More sinister considerations succeeded these. The French were hysterical. They were spy-conscious. They would refuse to believe that she and the fleeing man were strangers. As an excuse for open windows a plea of fresh air would not satisfy.

Halting on the stairs, she rehearsed these reasons for holding her tongue, and came to the conclusion that silence, with a subsequent letter from England, would meet the case. To roll the spool under the bed till it lay by the wallet, and so depart, would be the dignified and comparatively honest course of action. But the turmoil of the morning had let loose in Miss Charters' mind hordes of revolutionary desires, which now found a rallying ground in the fact that she had not, in her forty-odd years, had one single unusual experience. She had never held unquestioned sway as chief talker at any party; she had never come within hail of being the heroine of any incident more lively than the spoiling of a Guide picnic by rain. The spool of film, now safe in her bag, tempted her; to take it home as proof of the adventure, to hand it over in the end, perhaps, to somebody from the Foreign Office or Scotland Yard! She hesitated, and the revolutionaries in that instant had her conscience down. No word of any discovery found its way into her farewells.

At the station she became aware of two things. First, that she had twenty minutes to wait for her train; second, that amid the excitements of the morning she had omitted a visit to that retreat which old-fashioned foreign hotels leave innominate, indicating it only by two zeros on the door. She cast a prudish but searching eye about her. The word 'Dames' beckoned; Miss Charters bought a newspaper and, apparently purposeless, drifted towards it.

The usual uncleanness greeted her, and to protect herself from unspeakable contacts Miss Charters sacrificed a whole sheet of her newspaper. It was newly printed, the ink had a bloom to it. Miss Charters, accustomed at home to entrust to newspaper the defence of musquash against moth, vaguely supposed that it might prove, on this analogy, deterrent to germs. She emerged without delay, glanced to see that her baggage was safe, and paced up and down reading what remained of *Le Petit Journal*. There were fifteen minutes still to wait.

Seven or eight of these had passed in the atmosphere of unhurried makeshift that pervades all minor French stations, when a commotion was heard outside, chattering of motor cycles and shouting. Through the door marked 'Sortie' three policemen in khaki and kepis made a spectacular entrance, followed by a miraculous crowd apparently started up from the paving-stones. The three advanced upon Miss Charters, innocently staring, and required her, none too civilly, to accompany them.

'Pourquoi?' she inquired without heat. 'Je vais manquer mon train.'

They insisted, not politely; and their explanations, half inarticulate, contained a repetition of the word 'portefeuille'. At once Miss Charters understood; the wallet had been found. (Who would have thought the French swept so promptly under beds?) She must give her account of the whole matter, miss her connection, telegraph her relations. Bells and signals announced the train to be nearly due; with a brief click of the tongue she summoned resolution for a last attempt at escape.

'Je suis anglaise,' she announced. 'Mon passeport est en ordre. Voulez vous voir?'

She opened her bag, and immediately, with a swift fatal motion, made to shut it. On top, surmounting the handkerchief, the eau-de-Cologne, the passport, lay the damning red spool, so hurriedly, so madly crammed in. The foremost policeman saw it as soon as she did. He gave a 'Ha!' of triumph, and caught the bag away from her. His two companions fell in at her side, the crowd murmured and eddied like a stream swollen by flood. As she was marched from the station, out of the corner of an eye she saw the train come in; and as they entered the Grande Rue she heard the chuff and chug of its departure. Hope gone, she could give undivided attention to her plight.

It became evident, from the manner of the policemen, and from the fact that she was taken to the Hôtel de Ville, that matters were serious. She made one attempt to get her bag; certain necessary words lacked in the formula of defence she was composing, and the bag contained a pocket dictionary. Her request was denied. A cynical-looking man at a large desk – mayor? magistrate? – fanned away her protests with both hands and listened to the policeman. So did Miss Charters, and was able to gather from his evidence that the wallet found in her room contained papers and calculations to do with the aerodrome near by. Could anything be more unlucky? The one genuine spy that had ever frequented Pontdidier-les-Dames must needs throw his ill-gotten information into her bedroom!

The functionary asked at last what she had to say. She replied with the truth; and despite a vocabulary eked out with 'vous savez' told her story well. The functionary noted her explanation without comment, and having done so asked the inevitable, the unanswerable questions.

'You found these objects at 10.45 this morning. Why did you not immediately inform the police? You insist that they have nothing to do with you. Yet you were actually attempting to carry out of this country one of the objects. How do you account for these facts?'

Miss Charters accounted for them by a recital, perfectly true, of her desire to shine at tea-parties. It sounded odd as she told it; but she had some notion that the French were a nation of psychologists, also that, being foreign, they were gullible, and sympathetic to women in distress. The cynical man listened, and when her last appeal went down in a welter of failing syntax, considered a while, then spoke:

'I regret, mademoiselle. All this is not quite satisfactory. You must be searched.'

The French she had learned at her governess's knee had not included the word he employed, and it was without any real understanding of his intention that she accompanied a woman in black, who suddenly appeared at her side, looking scimitars. They progressed together, a policeman at the other elbow, to a small room smelling of mice. The policeman shut the door on them; the woman in black ejaculated a brief command; and Miss Charters, horrified, found that she was expected to strip.

In her early youth Miss Charters' most favoured daydream had included a full-dress martyrdom, painful but effective, with subsequent conversions. She now learned that it is easier to endure pain than indignity, and amid all the throbbing which apprehension and shame had set up in her temples, one thought lorded it: the recollection that she had not, in view of the dirty train journey, put on clean underclothes that morning.

The woman in black lifted her hands from her hips as if to help with the disrobing; there was a shuffle outside the door as though the policeman might be turning to come in. With a slight scream, at speed, Miss Charters began to unbutton, unhook, unlace her various garments; as they dropped, the woman in black explored them knowingly, with fingers active as those of a tricoteuse. At last Miss Charters stood revealed, conscious of innocence, but finding it a poor defence, and ready to exchange the lightest of consciences for the lightest of summer vests.

The woman in black was thorough. She held stockings up to the light, pinched corsets; at last, satisfied, she cast an eye over the shrinking person of Miss Charters, twirling her slowly about. Now the words of dismissal should have come. Instead, at her back Miss Charters heard a gasp. There was an instant's silence; then the one word, ominous: 'Enfin!'

The woman in black ran to the door and shouted through it.

Miss Charters heard excitement in the policeman's answering voice, and his boots clattered off down the corridor, running. Her imagination strove, and was bested. Why? What? The woman in black, with a grin lineally descended from '93, informed her.

'And now, my beauty, we'll see what the pretty message is that's written on mademoiselle's sit-upon!'

The next few moments were nightmare at its height, when the sleeper knows his dream for what it is, knows he must escape from it, and still must abide the capricious hour of waking. An assistant in blue was vouchsafed to the woman in black. One deciphered such letters as were visible, the other took them down, pesting against the artfulness of spies who printed their messages backwards. In deference to Miss Charters' age and passport some decency was observed. Policemen waited outside the half-open door; there was much noise, but no threatening. The women heard her explanation (conjectural) of their discovery without conviction and did not even trouble to write it down.

At last the message was transcribed. The woman in blue compassionately gave Miss Charters back her clothes, a gesture countered by the woman in black, who refused to allow her to sit down lest the precious impression be blurred. With a policeman at her elbow and the two searchers at her back, her cheek-bones pink, and beset by a feeling that this pinkness ran through to her skeleton, Miss Charters once more faced the functionary across his table. The transcription was handed to him. He considered it, first through a magnifying-glass, then with the aid of a mirror. The policeman, the two searchers, craned forward to know the fate of France, thus by a freak of Fortune thrust into their hands:

'Et maintenant,' they read in capital letters, 'j'ai du cœur au travail, grâce aux PILULES PINK.'

The functionary's eyes appeared to project. He stared at Miss Charters, at the searchers; with a start, at his own daily paper lying folded, with his gloves upon it. He tore it open, seeking. Page 7 rewarded him. 'Maladies de Femmes.' said the headline; underneath, the very words that had been deciphered with such pains, accompanying an illustration of a cheerful young woman, whose outline appeared in transfer not unlike the map of a town. Silently he compared; his glass was busy. At last he looked up, and Miss Charters, meeting his eye, perceived something like comprehension in his glance, a kind of gloating, a difficult withholding of laughter – 'Rabelaisian' was the word which shot across her mind like a falling star. It was a hard glance to face, but all Englishness and spunk had not been slain in Miss Charters by the indignities chance had obliged her to suffer. She had one magnificent last word:

'Je rapporterai le W.C. de la gare aux autorités sanitaires!'

It was the best she could do. The larger threat which at first inflamed her mind, of complaints to the Ambassador in Paris, of redress and public apologies, would not do; both she and the Rabelaisian eye knew why. She could never, to any person, at any time, confide the truth of an experience so appalling. So far as vicarage conversation went, the thing was out of the question. Hateful irony! Something, after forty-odd years, had happened to her, and it had happened in such a manner that mere decency must strike her mute. In the words of a ceremony she had often in younger days read over fondly, she must hereafter for ever hold her peace.

Miss Charters held it. The relations who welcomed her a day later were of opinion that her holiday in France had not done her much good. They found her quiet, and discovered that what she wanted was to be taken out of herself. So they arranged little gaieties, at which Miss Charters listened silently, now and then pinching in her lips, to travellers' tales of those who had been seeing life in London and by the sea.

'But then,' as a relative remarked, 'poor Aggie never did have much to say for herself.'

Robin Hyde

America Won the War

1937

So there was the newest yellow building, right opposite. It was Spanish mission, of course, imitated by us from the Californians, who also imitated it from what they were not; and when they had finished about its having no shape and no sense, somebody had climbed up on top and poured cheese omelette all over it, the sort that drips in thick scallops. And there it stood. It looked so fat and helpless that somehow you couldn't hate the big boob, you could only wish the angel Gabriel, if he had a moment, would come along quick with a cheese-slice and scrape it away. That's the way with us sentimentalists. We get a name for lacking fastidiousness because we are sorry for so many things that disgust us. But if you were intolerant and wanted to hate the yellow building, humanity still got in your way. Every three seconds the nerve of Neon lighting twitched in its cheek, it twitched green, yellow, and scarlet, and when it twitched scarlet, gee, it was fierce. Gee, you could tell that tooth was simply redhot. My poor mother! Before the last was born, she had tic doloureux like that for three solid days, and what she didn't say about having babies! But a building can't roll on the ground and cry, 'I can't bear this; I can't bear it; God, I just can't stand this for another second.' Or can it? Is New Zealand architecture the good and sufficient reason for New Zealand earthquakes?

And there wasn't much rain, not enough to blur or soften the edges of things, only a few fine little slivers that made hasty scars and glanced off, not really wetting faces or stone.

What wild Artemis, arrowy in the night,
Half hound, half woman,
Drives her steel scorn against the flesh of men?

And so forth. Now to get map and perspective right, you should understand there was the pawnbroker's just here opposite the twitch, and a little farther along on the same side a crossing, and on the other side of that, more shops and houses. The street between was a dark street and quiet, like a winding bolt-hole that an animal might make for quick if it were frightened. Not far from its opening, there loitered an old standard gas-lamp, a left-over from the ebb of Time, and in its faint lustre, faces still looked harassed, but not so hard. But the trouble with this dark street was that it served as a short-cut between one main thoroughfare and another; and it had a very wide mouth, so that cars coming and going could pass one another easily without pulling up, and if there were two down-coming cars at the same instant, one could swerve outwards and make the gorgeous, gleaming sweep, screeching past the other. If you were a pedestrian, you had to look out, crossing that street. You had to take every precaution, and then, knowing still that you weren't fast enough for them, put your head down and scuttle across like some little ashamed animal, not good enough either for day or for electric light. But if you got across and walked down the bolt-hole as far as the gas-lamp, you could get your breath back and put your hands in your pockets, pretending you were somebody. And the lamp never knew the difference, for it had gone into a pearly blindness years ago, and was quite dotty, and thought we all went about smoking churchwarden pipes and arguing whether somebody shouldn't horsewhip Darwin.

There was more of Victorianism, if you like to apply that name to things in the process of being reduced to skeleton leaves, in the pawnbroker's shop, where the window held a stag's head, a china biscuit barrel, some greenstone, a skull, and several trays of medals and badges, labelled, 'Great War', 'South African War', and 'Miscellaneous'. On the Miscellaneous tray were neat little rows marked 'Crimean War', 'Maori War', 'Zulu War', and 'Indian Mutiny', with a tail-end row for unconsidered trifles. There were other things in the pawn-broker's window, but for one reason and another, they had lost their identity, and it was only if you stared at them for a long time that you could decide what they were. The pawnbroker's name was Alec, but mostly they called him Have-a-Heart-Alec. And Alec smiled with his little teeth, one gold-stopped right in the front, but he wouldn't have a heart; what he wanted was £ s.d.

Now into this shop I saw go, and out of it I saw come, an old, tall, imitation-ivory man in a suit of assam silk. He hadn't a hat on, as for some reason it had occurred even to him that a solar topee would be out of place on this slightly wet evening; so he swung past, bare-headed, only partly bald, and with white moustaches to match the white cockatoo poll of hair that sat up on his crown. As his face was divided by these moustaches into segments – firm if bristly chin, mouth thin as a rat-trap, enormous beaky nose, pale blue eyes that stared hard at some invisible regiment wanting to cry over the poor dead dummies – so his walk was divided between swing and shamble; and you saw the reason, in the gold-topped malacca cane he carried in one hand. That was a good stick; I like a good malacca. Every time it tapped the pavement, it recalled him curtly to a knowledge of that state of life into which it had pleased God and Her Majesty, Queen Vicky, to call him. He was an officer, and going to make somebody smart, just on principle. When he remembered this he swung and glared. But sometimes he took three or four paces without tipping the pavement with his malacca, and then he was merely shambling and old.

Into this shop he carried his malacca cane, and a moment later the short fat hand of Have-a-Heart-Alec shot forth and clawed at the medal trays. It took two medals from the South African tray, one, a Military Medal, from the Great War, and one from the Crimean row in Miscellaneous. I thought, 'It's not possible Father Time should have been in the Crimean and in 1914–18 as well.' But it occurred to me that perhaps his father had fought in the Crimean war, or his son in our later effort. Be that as it may, the old man came out of the shop looking both fiercer and more fragile, and without his malacca cane. I wondered, 'Does Have-a-Heart-Alec allow him more on the malacca than on the medals? Or does he just swap round, and be the well-groomed civilian when he carries the cane, and the Colonel when he has the medals?' But the old man seemed somehow pleased about it, and he was muttering a little to himself; and as I thought I would like to hear what he was muttering – mumble, mumble, mumble, put that in your pipe and smoke it, Sir – I followed him. But he was slow and shaky without the malacca cane, so I thought it would seem less suspicious to him, as he was probably a very important and suspicious personage in Time's army, if I walked a little in front.

Thus we reached the crossing, and hearing nothing but mumble, I was suddenly blinded and frightened half way over, and ran. The two cars swooped at the same instant, and the little one squealed like a rabbit, but the smooth-running black one, stoat or ferret, pounced almost noiselessly into the burrow of the quiet street, and tore the right-of-way out of the little one's screaming intestines. I was on the pavement then, and frightened; but I looked back to see how the old man was faring, and there he was, unharmed, standing in the middle of the road, tapping violently at the bitumen with the malacca cane that wasn't there. Mumble-mumble-mumble... He was dead centre where he could hold up the traffic, but in such bright light, in such a palsy of indignation and terror, that nobody dared to kill him. A motor-cycle with a girl riding pillion ripped its brakes within three yards of him, and the boy called, 'Scram, there, scram!' And the girl laughed, her hands clinging around the boy's waist. I saw her from a back view, so that it was plain how the pillion seat dragged her frock and knickers tight on her firm thighs and her hips; and several inches of her in a flowery frock stuck out all round, like a paper frill on a ham. She laughed high, and the boy, who had stopped his bike, yelled 'Scram! Beat it, you, beat it!'

Now I had been warned about these people and knew they were there, and that you've got to watch out for them if you don't want their laughter and their voices to tear you into shreds and tatters. Their radios turned on at the loudest bellowed over their back fences and out of their front windows, and spilled into their long flat streets, over which the moonlight floated unsurprised. And reliable people like W. B. Keats had more or less put them down on the map:

> That new commonness,
> That laughs, and hangs its paper garlands in the streets,
> For it alone is happy.

And they get in your hair in various places, but there are things you can do about that, such as leaving them to enjoy the mess they seem to enjoy, or cutting your hair off, or pinning it up very skilfully.

But the old man at that moment didn't know about them. He couldn't have been more surprised if he had been shot from a rocket and landed on Mars, to find himself surrounded by a crowd completely unintelligible, acting according to no rule or rote ever laid down in his childhood. 'Scram,' they yelled, 'Beat it.' And the horn said, 'Hornk, hornk, hornk,' and you could see him, awakened from Sebastopol, making a tremendous effort to pull himself together and deal with this situation, as he would have done in the South African war had a party of Boers arranged themselves with bayonets pointing at that chest where his beautiful silver medals were destined to shine. 'Say Pop,' they yelled, 'we gotta go t' the Speedway.' The old man made the bony hollow of his chest and shoulders quite immense, and cleared his throat. 'So now,' I thought, 'We're going to hear what Vicky's young men would have said about it, if Vicky's young men had lived to see the day, etc.' But out of his chest and mouth, gone suddenly slack, came only coughing; the sick way a baby coughs when it is going to have croup. Stumbling forward abjectly before them, he reached the pavement, coughing, 'An-herp-herp-herp-herp,' as if that furnished a sad excuse for his existence. Then the motor-cycle began to stutter and roar, ready to slide down the black safe street, and I thought perhaps I should step out into the middle of the road and curse them in the name of chivalry. But cursing what has never lived, in the name of what has died, would be too odd. I couldn't see the boy's face, but only the girl's back view, and thought, 'She's not a great whore, like Jezebel. She's only such a little one, you couldn't do anything with her but smack her, and she's sitting on that, all except a frill round the edges. So I'll not.' And the old man went off down into the safe street and got as far as the gas-lamp's pearly blindness, maybe; though not much further.

Still feeling that something ought to be done about it, I went down the road till I met a policeman, and said, 'Can't you do anything about the traffic at that bad corner? I was frightened just now by a motor-cycle, and so was an old man.' He said, gently shifting from one foot to another, with the tired incessant movement of an elephant, 'Diddja get the number Sister?' I hadn't done that; and when I thought back, it was plain the old gentleman had been quite wrong, standing in Sebastopol dreaming long after America had won the wars, and holding everything up. Also I hadn't been frightened by the motor-bike people, except in a way not actionable. The policeman repeated, 'Diddja get the number?' So I became angry and, talking in the best American I could, said, 'They were doing sixty, see? And on their wrong side, and that old man's a witness, and it's a pity you cops can't move as fast after real crime as you can after little guys selling a bunch of lettuce on Sundays. And this is a motorist's town which is the same thing as a murderer's town. If you don't believe me, go take a look at the broken pavement we walk on outside the hospital and in a hundred places more; and then look at the bitumen a foot away.'

'Diddja get their number, Sister?'

Then, in a car's passing light, I happened to see who the policeman was. I dropped my head and said lamely, 'I guess it doesn't matter. Maybe they're only fresh kids. Anyhow, I didn't get their number.' I felt relieved, now I knew who he was, that I hadn't seen the number. But he shifted his bulk from foot to foot like a tired elephant, and said gently, 'Well, I guess I'll go along out and take a look at the Speedway.' And he said, 'People like that can't be left shooting around, or they might kill somebody, see?'

I hadn't told him anything about the Speedway; and by that time I'd have given a lot to put him off their track, but I knew it was no use. Not when I saw how the shadows under his helmet made up his face, and how he shifted gently from foot to foot, as if he'd been trying through all these centuries to get people to have a bit of common, and was tired of it. I said, 'That was all a pack of lies I told you. The old man was holding up the traffic. But I didn't think they should do what they did to him, because he was so old; though I'm a pacifist myself and don't set much store by medals. But I suppose it's their world, and he should have kept to the bolt-holes, or looked better where he was going.'

'Well,' he said, 'I guess I'll go along and take a look at that Speedway. That can't do any harm, Sister.' And swinging his body forward from the hips, he moved off into the shadows, not shambling like the old man, or running, like the pedestrians, but sure – sure – as he has been, from Senlac to Sebastopol, and a million years before and after. He was dark and solid, and as he went the buildings melted away before him, and the twitch in the yellow one's cheek missed a beat, as it might have been one whole eternity set free from pain. I didn't think any more then of the old man, or of the two on the motor-bike, though I knew he had their number. And sure enough, it was all in the paper next morning. 'Shocking Crash on Morne Road...' 'Old Man Found...'

Isobel Andrews

Every Saturday Night

1940

Saturday afternoon – and there was nothing to do but sit at the worn window seat and wait for the time to pass. Soon there would be tea and then just another sitting waiting for the time to pass because she wouldn't be going to the dance tonight. Not tonight she wouldn't be. Not if Glory came and asked her to on her bended knees. Not after the way she had treated her last Saturday night. The mean cat, going off with Allan Briggans and leaving her to go on home on her own. And Glory needn't have been so proud of herself for going off with Allan like that after all, because after all what was Allan Briggans anyway but a motor mechanic even if he was in the Air Force? What sort of pay did a motor mechanic get anyway? And coming home at night with dirty hands and his face all greasy. Allan Briggans was no catch, even if he did laugh down at you the few times he remembered to ask you to dance. Well, anyway, she wasn't going to the dance and she hadn't spoken to Glory the whole week, and if Glory did come round and ask her she knew what she'd say.

And here was Glory coming along the street. Glory, by some strange chance entirely suited to her name in a crude, bright, flaunting way. Glory was tall and she had red hair that stood out from her face like a flame. She had a creamy skin and eyes of bluey-green-grey which were like nobody else's eyes.

Here she was coming to Mary at the window seat, saying, 'Come to the dance tonight? There's to be two Monte Carlos and a spot waltz and Joe Piper's going to do a tap dance.'

Mary said, sarcastically, 'Why don't you ask Allan Briggans?'

But Glory, not seeing the sarcasm, or for her own purposes ignoring it, said 'Oh him! He's gonna be late. What dress'll you wear?'

And instead of saying all the clever cutting things she meant to say she answered 'Oh, the blue one, I suppose.'

Glory said, 'O.K. I'll be round about half past seven,' and she swaggered away with her hair like Joan Crawford in that last picture at the Supreme Picture Palace and her black frock with the white buttons and collar and belt like the leading lady in 'Heart's Delight', only Glory's dress was home-made and the leading lady's wasn't.

Suddenly it didn't matter if Glory had let her down last Saturday. Here was another and she was going to the dance after all. The blue dress had to be ironed, the slightly tarnished silver shoes laid out, and the best pair of stockings washed. Then there was tea to be eaten with Dad reading the sports section of the paper in between bites, and Mum telling them all about yesterday's bargain hunt in town when she just missed a two-guinea bedspread for twenty-seven and six.

'It'd a done Mary's room real well,' she said, pouring out the tea. 'Just the right shade of blue to go with the new curtains. Aw well, we can't have everything,' and, not too disconsolate, she reached for the cooked ham.

After tea an anxious time was spent in the bedroom wondering if straight hair looked better straight or if it looked better curled at the ends like Garbo, or if it wouldn't be best of all done in tight little curls all over her head. The bedroom gradually became a pile of clothes and powder and cheap scent and the acrid smell of too hot curling irons on hair too fine to stand much of it, and all the while she was wondering if Allan Briggans would be there and if he would dance with her. She used to dream of him coming up to her in front of them all and saying, with his hand upon her elbow,

'This is my dance, isn't it?'

And taking her home in front of Glory and the rest of them.

Glory came for her at a quarter to eight. She had a new green dress made very tight over her hips and very scarce over her chest. Glory's hair didn't need curling tongs and it was a challenge to all who saw it.

Mum, a little grim about the mouth because she didn't think much of Glory and couldn't see what Mary saw in her, came to the front door with them.

'Don't you be too late,' she said, and closed the door behind them with a noise that was almost a bang and that held a note that was almost vicious.

Poor Mum. Not to be young. Not to be dressed in blue georgette. Not to be going to a dance on this cold clear moonlit night. Instead, to be going back to the dishes and then with the darning bag, settling down to the wireless. It was hard to think of Mum as ever young. Mary couldn't remember her mother except as she was now. Faded, a trifle grim, with a sense of humour which had gone a bit sour and had an acid bite to it. It was hard, too, to think of Dad ever making love, taking girls home from dances. Once he had come back from ten weeks' scrub-cutting when the depression was so bad and Mary had come home and found Mum in his arms. She had gone away because of the way they had looked, the two of them. She felt uncomfortable, as though here was something that she didn't know about. The thought came that perhaps Mum and Dad weren't just Mum and Dad, but that these had been the masks they wore, and that underneath the masks were the faces of people she had known all her life and who yet were strangers to her. The idea that her father and mother had perhaps a strange secret life of their own which she could never share was a disturbing one. Faintly disturbing and vaguely terrifying as though she had suddenly found herself alien in a land she had looked upon as home.

Their heels rang upon the bitumen of the roadway and the double row of houses all encased in their little gardens behind their little wooden fences looked watchful under the coldness of the moon. It wasn't summer yet, but spring was telling her approach with clear cold, windless nights.

The dance hall wasn't far away and soon they were in sight of it and the light of it spilled out across the road and drowned the moon. A board above the door announced that this was the Revellers' Hall, and that there was a select dance here Every Saturday Night. Subs: Ladies 1/6, Gents 2/6, Men in uniform Free.

The time was getting on and the orchestra under the direction of the tap-dancing Joe Piper was tuning up. A group of young men on the steps greeted them as they arrived. 'Glory be! Here's Glory!' 'Hullo, Mary. Howaya?' 'Gee, Glory, that's another new dress. How dya do it an' go straight?' Glory tossed her hair back and said, 'Maybe I don't.' Everybody laughed at Glory and the daring of her, except Jean Smith, who was jealous of Glory but who wouldn't admit it and just said she was fast. Jean was saying, 'It's a nice dress, dear, but a bit *obvious* don't you think?' Jean hadn't been to the movies for nothing. But Glory just laughed at her and said 'Poor old Jean,' which made Jean go up the stairs as if she was in a hurry, while only Glory knew the rage that was in her heart.

Mary said 'I don't know how you can say things like that,' and Glory said nothing.

Mary said 'People might think you meant it,' and Glory laughed and looked sideways and said 'Well, perhaps I do.' And she followed Jean up the stairs to the dressing room singing all the time under her breath.

The dressing room was a bit like the bedroom. Piles of clothes, but this time coats and scarves and sometimes hats, and still the smell of cheap powder and perfume all mingled with that other smell, indefinable, unmistakable, human.

There was a good deal of manoeuvring and milling round the one full-length mirror, but when at last Mary got a place she wished she hadn't bothered. At home the blue georgette had seemed all right and the fell work with the curling irons had been all right too, but now the georgette was crumpled and, anyway, all the other girls were out of georgettes and into satins and lace. The night air had done something to the hard won curls and most of her hair lay pale and straight against her throat. Nearly all the other girls had perms, but she hadn't been able to afford one this time, because she was still paying off her new coat. The glow left her. Even if Allan did come he wouldn't want to dance with her. All the other girls were so much more beautiful or at least were better at making themselves look that way, and now it was Glory at her elbow saying 'Come on, dreamy, the first dance's started.'

They went down the stairs again and out into the dance hall. The high roof had been made low with paper streamers twisted and pulled and all converging on to the big centre light. Wooden forms lined the walls and a little platform at the end of the room supported Joe Piper and his Melody Musketeers. A rhythm which had once echoed through the depths of a dark African forest beat against the walls, distorted, weakened but still with a thump and a quality that swayed bodies in the dance, quickened pulses and brought a new light into the eyes of those who heard it.

They went to a corner and sat down. He wasn't there. He hadn't come. As soon as she knew that she could look at the rest of the dancers with a fairly undisturbed gaze.

There was Jim Ritchie. He was slight and dark. He was wearing a bright blue suit, a pair of bright brown shoes, while the fold of a green handkerchief peeped coyly from his breast pocket. A lot of the male dancers were in uniform, but Jim was Essential Industry and had been kept on at his job at the Railway Workshops. His features were sharp and narrow. His hair was straight and heavily brilliantined and he wore it combed back from a bony forehead. His eyes roaming the room caught Mary's for a second and then passed on to Glory. She saw the look come into them. The look that men always had for Glory whether they were tall, disturbing giants like Allan Briggans, or little and peaked like Jim Ritchie.

When the dance ended those who had been dancing went to the benches round the walls. All at once the room seemed to have filled up and now there were no spare seats and most of the men had to stand in front of the girls or join the group by the door. Then the music started up again and Glory was the first girl up. And Mary was left alone again. It was always like that. The other girls would be taken and then perhaps she would be asked. Sometimes she had to sit the whole night through with only a few dances to relieve the times when she sat on the wooden form against the wall. That was the hardest part of all. Just to sit and see everybody else dancing. You had to look up and smile at the dancers and pass a few wisecracks with them, and pretend that that was what you came to a dance for and that the greatest fun in the world was to come to a dance and be left on the wooden form against the wall. Sometimes she would see Glory arguing with Allan and then he would come over and ask Mary, but when he did that she almost hated him.

But this time she wasn't going to be left. Here was Jim Ritchie. So she tossed her head back and said she didn't mind, laid her hand on his arm and they were off. He wasn't such a bad dancer and he knew all the right things to say. All the dull uninteresting things to say, like how good the floor was and how fine the decorations were and what was the name of your friend, the girl in green. Then, suddenly, there was Allan standing in the doorway and she smiled and waved to him as though she were having the time of her life and dancing with Jim Ritchie was the only thing she wanted to do.

When the next dance started Jim asked Glory. Glory, after a quick look at Allan who didn't look back and talked to Jean Smith instead, got up and danced with Jim. After that it was just like all the other dances except that whenever Allan asked her Glory was always engaged to someone else until at last he didn't ask her any more and danced with Jean Smith, and everybody knew that Glory and Allan had had a row.

Half-way through the evening Jim asked Mary if he could take her home, and she said yes. She said yes not because she wanted Jim Ritchie to take her home but because having a boy, any boy, to take you home was better than having none at all. Because later on in the dressing room when they said to her, 'Goin' home on your own?' she'd be able to say 'No. I got somebody waiting for me,' and she would be able to put on her coat, powder her nose and go out with the rest of them. Independent. Free. Not like it had happened so many times before when she had to make an unwelcome and uncomfortable third.

Not having a boy to take you home was as bad as not having a boy to go round with. If you never have a boy to go round with you never get the chance of getting engaged. So you don't start collecting for your Box, or choosing your wedding veil or making up your mind if you'll wear silk or satin. Not having a boy means that after a while you get to be a girl a bit apart from the rest. Shut out from that mysterious tie that binds engaged girls together and forms them into an exclusive kind of secret society.

So, because of all this, and because Allan Briggans would never ask her anyway, she said Yes when Jim Ritchie asked if he could see her home.

And it would happen that the very next dance Allan came up and she thought that perhaps he was tired of having a row with Glory and was going to make it up. But he asked her instead, and she found herself in his arms. Once there Jim Ritchie became the merest shadow of a man. Allan looked down at her and smiled, the way she had always wanted him to.

'Enjoying yourself?'

She nodded yes, unspeaking.

'How about letting me take you home?'

He had said it. After all those Saturday nights of waiting and wishing he asked her. She thought for a moment of Jim Ritchie, but she knew it didn't matter what happened to Jim Ritchie . . .

Soon it was Auld Lang Syne and God Save the King and the girls were hurrying up the stairs to collect coats and scarves.

'Goin' home on your own?'

It was Glory with a red spot on both cheeks and a hard glitter in her eye.

'No. I got someone waiting for me.'

'Who?'

'Wouldn't you like to know?'

'Not particularly,' said Glory, and she swept out.

She's mad because she's had a row with Allan – the thought comforted. Hurrying into her coat she gave a last anxious glance in the mirror and followed Glory. The hall door was curtained, and before she lifted the curtain she heard Allan's voice and Glory's. Allan was saying 'Then it's all right?' and Glory was saying 'S'pose so.' Allan said 'Let's go,' and added something in a lower tone. Glory laughed.

'Thought she was looking pleased with herself. Like a pussy-cat that's swallowed cream. We'd better wait for her.'

But Allan said 'God, no. It's you I want. Let's skip before she comes.' Glory giggled and said he was awful, but she went with him.

There it was then. You dream of Allan Briggans laughing down at you, taking you home, and when it seems your dream is coming true you wake up and see what a fool you've been. He had just wanted to spite Glory and pay her out for being mean all evening. It doesn't matter. Who's Allan Briggans anyway? A motor mechanic's no catch.

Now she would have to gather her courage and take herself down the front steps, alone, in front of them all.

There was a touch on her elbow.

'Thought you were never coming,' said Jim Ritchie.

'Well, for goodness' sake,' she said, tossing her head back the way Glory did, 'Well, for goodness' sake, can't a girl put a bit of powder on her nose without you men getting all impatient?'

She laughed the way Glory did and took his arm. They went down the steps together.

A motor mechanic's no catch.

Marjorie Barnard

The Party

1943

The footpath rang under her feet as if the hill were hollow. She had not been there before, and was convinced that she would not find her way. She stared incredulously at the street numbers and sought out, with a kind of fumbling desperation, like one learning braille, the landmarks that Rhonda had given her. She was late, and would probably be the last to arrive even at that sort of party. She had dawdled and dawdled, still thinking that perhaps she might not go, only in the end not going had proved worse than going. Not going would be a chasm of disappointment. It was enough to be late, she thought now, like the frightened man who believes his yawns will convince the world of his indifference.

This was the block of flats. An imitation stone staircase, mock baronial, mock grandeur, and behind the closed doors with their heavy antique knockers the same ordinary little flats, the same inescapable amenities. To the third floor. It wasn't only the stairs that made her heart beat so fast and high. It is shattering to go up to a smug, unknown door and ring the bell, knowing that a party lurks behind it. A close knit, if temporary, whole, a world whipped up out of conversation and sherry, to which she, the late comer, would be a stranger and an outcast, no matter how well she might know people. In the tight fitting, black frock that revealed so delicately the slender lines of her body, she felt that her heart was indecently exposed.

Well, she'd taken the plunge. A room full of people, all standing up, all holding wine glasses, talking as if they knew one another much better than they did, eating sausage rolls and gherkins. She knew at once. *John wasn't there.* There wasn't a hopeful corner of the room you couldn't see at the first glance.

Rhonda was beside her, in her eyes the look that said 'My poor darling, how are you?' The terrible tender solicitude of a friend who knows and understands everything. But she only said, 'I'll find Agnes for you.' Old fashioned to be embarrassed because you did not know your hostess. But if I am I am, so what can I do about it? This was Agnes, wearing a snood. What incredible affectation to wear a snood at your own party as if you had just arrived out of the blue, and hadn't been cutting sandwiches and impaling little what-nots on toothpicks all the afternoon. 'So very kind . . .' she said, and yes, she knew nearly everyone. Agnes you could see was the soul of kindness. Now she had gone to fetch someone. 'You must meet . . . so much in common.' It was just as if she had said kindly, confidentially, 'Now I'll go and get you a nice strong cup of tea and you will be all right.' What she was likely to have in common with anyone, she couldn't imagine. She felt rather as she might have done if she had wandered into the party, wearing a diving bell . . .

There was a solid wall of conversation, unscalable, impenetrable. 'Mallarmé,' someone said. So they still talked about Mallarmé at parties. 'In Spain . . .' someone said. You always counted four points if you had been in Spain. Russia counted double, and London in the blitz came somewhere in between. You could be nostalgic over Paris, but not over London, for after all, London had taken it and Paris hadn't.

'My dear,' said a strange young man solicitously. 'You have nothing to drink.'

With a wine glass in her hand, she felt herself immeasurably better equipped. Someone touched her arm. She thought for a blind second that it might be John, but it was Agnes with the soul mate. A dark young man with a scar. She looked at him with an enquiring smile, and took a slow sip. That was better. She was getting the hang of it now. She would be able, after all, to give a very good imitation of herself this afternoon.

'You sculpt, don't you?' he said.

'No,' and then idiotically because it was like the snapping of a very thin life line. 'I'm sorry. I would like to.'

'You mean,' he asserted, 'that you do but you think you're only at the beginning. There isn't any beginning, only a circle.'

'No,' she said, fighting desperately now against the clay. 'I mean no. I never thought of it . . .'

'You have a sculptor's hands,' he asserted.

In a moment it had become a nightmare conversation. She felt herself entangled in a net of meaningless words. She drifted into a group for protection, and when she drifted out she left him behind her.

'Darling, where have you been hiding? I haven't see you for ages.'

'My dear, you are actually thinner, some people have all the luck.'

'Don't slip away before I've told you what I'm doing. I've given up the violin and I'm working in a factory. It's more satisfactory. The pattern is so much thicker . . .'

No one even mentioned John. He might have been dead or forgotten, like a stone at the bottom of a well.

There was a picture on the wall, a red mouth with a Mona Lisa smile, set crookedly on a grey background. Just that and nothing more. A shutter flipped up in her mind and she saw it, really saw it. It was improbable but quite real. The solicitous young man stood before her, a plate in each hand. 'Oyster patties or sausage rolls?' It was one of those cryptic, irretrievable choices – heaven or hell and nothing to guide you. The casket scene. She wouldn't have either and he was disappointed to the point of despair. He had a beautiful maternal lust to feed people.

She moved on. She hadn't noticed the door behind the curtain. It came to softly behind her, leaving her in sudden quiet and enlargement. It was as easy to escape as that. The balcony, hanging like a bird cage on the clifflike facade of the flats, was as far from the party as Cape York. It was early dusk with its false evanescent clarity beginning to melt at the edges, a light that blent the noonday incompatibles into a scena. In the foreground, blocks of flats set at all angles, each flat a little box too small for the life it housed, so that it bulged out of the windows, hung over the balconies, burgeoned up through the roofs. Strings of coloured washing were as natural as vines. In William Street, narrow and living as an artery, coloured taxis moved like corpuscles. Over to the left, Woolloomooloo, pouring down the hill, houses, terraces, narrow streets fused into a solid mass, a grape bloom on its slates, a veil of light on the mediocrity of its stones and bricks. Beneath the swept stretch of the waterfront, the wharves running neatly out into the bay. Beyond the lovely, unreal drop scene of the harbour, blue water, timbered headlands, even the bridge etherealised, a grey bow drawn across the blue.

Her constricted heart dilated as if to the sweep of music. She could stand and look for a minute, her palms pressed to the roughness of brick, forgetting everything. Then her mind began to tear at its knot again. 'Why had John not come? Was it because he thought she might be there? Or for no reason so definite, because he had forgotten the occasion, the time or the place . . . the indifference of his freedom in which everything eventually was lost!'

The dark young man with the scar had found the door too.

'I lost you,' he said.

That didn't need an answer, but she picked up her wine glass from the parapet.

'Tell me,' he said, 'what do you do?'

'Nothing,' she said. 'That's killed it,' she thought, and then, because that sudden sweep of music had left her defenceless, she began to tell him what she saw. 'If I lived here I'd throw a line out of the window every night, and every morning I'd haul in a short story.'

'Writing.' He drove the metal of his contempt into the word. 'That's no good. You can imagine anything at all and write it down. No limits and no discipline, it's only a hide-out for people who haven't anything to say.'

That didn't fetch her because he couldn't possibly say anything that touched her now. She felt indifference like a dead weight.

'You're the sort,' he said with the insolence of a man who succeeds with women. 'You're the sort who promises everything and gives nothing.'

In a small cold voice she said, 'I would like another glass of wine and something to eat.'

'Certainly.' He held the door for her to enter.

In the crowded room conversation was already in a more advanced state. One cannot afford to drop out. Talking is, like drinking, progressive. When you are a few drinks behind everyone else, you are in a different world.

Rhonda caught her fingers in a quick, affectionate squeeze. 'It's a nice party, isn't it?' she said encouragingly.

It was a nice party.

'I'm so glad you clicked with Simon. He is doing something and going somewhere even if he is the world's greatest egoist.'

The something in common.

She told Agnes that she had a dinner engagement, that she'd have to tear herself away.

One of the boys, Agnes said, would see her down...

Please, please... everyone was so happy. Let her just slip away. It was so easy to break up a party...

She went into the bedroom. A stout woman had taken her shoes off because they hurt her, and was sitting on a low chair, smoking. Another was re-making her face very earnestly in a small mirror. Two more lounged on the bed. There was the intimate ease of women off parade, a freshet of laughter, a fragment of story like a tit-bit among gulls. Politely they suspended their conversation, politely made way for her. In the mirror she saw with surprise that the delicate mask of her make-up was still intact. She said good-bye, not remembering ever to have seen these women before.

She pulled the front door to after her. The air was suddenly cool, thin and flavoured with plaster. Three flights of imitation stone stairs, mock baronial, mock grandeur. In the street it was almost dark. She looked up and saw the lighted windows of the flat, golden in the blue dusk. She had left a world that, if it wasn't safe, was at least warm. It was being alone that was so terrible.

Ruth Park

Regatta Day

1944

Katia cast a quick glance over her shoulder to see whether Arthur was looking and as he wasn't she gave his plate a swift wipe with the hem of her skirt. And that showed how much closer to civilisation she was than her mother, who had been known to give a pot a quick once-over with the tail of a dog that happened to be handy.

But it was no good. Arthur had seen. There he was, with his reddish nose pinched up in disgust, his eyes yellow with bad temper, and his hair sticking up like the feathers of a ruffled bird.

'I ought to clout you, you filthy cow' he shouted, his rage obscuring his eyes so that he could hardly see her as she stood there, her lower lip stuck out sulkily, and her black eyes glazy with guilt. He wanted to kick her fat brown calf showing beneath the draggled skirt. He wanted to punch her in the stomach, or pull her unkempt hair. He wanted to do anything that would, however futilely, express his regret at having married a Maori woman.

'Here's your porridge. I pour it out, eh?' said Katia timidly, proffering the sooty saucepan.

'No!' he yelled, hitting it out of her hand.

The porridge trickled down her skirt in sluggish rivulets. Her lip trembled, and her eyes flashed fire.

'You're a dirty no-good pakeha!' she screamed. 'I get you out of jail. I sell my mother's land so I can pay your fine. I marry you, me, Katia Manawaiti, who could marry ten different nice fat Maori men and have lots of children. And what do you do? You never take me to the pictures. You never buy me fish and chips or a new shawl. And now you throw porridge all over my beautiful skirt that my mother wore when she was a little hine. And on Regatta Day, too. Ahe! Ahe!'

She ran out of the house and, sitting down on her heels, she rocked to and fro and wept aloud and luxuriantly. Arthur glared after her, his face pulled into long grooves of impotent hate. He scratched viciously at his scrubby chin. It was no use shaving. No one would give him work. Here, up and down the river, in all this bright farmland and rich pasturage, no one wanted a man who had been in prison for thievery. Katia's wails mounted, then suddenly stopped. Through her tears she had spied the steely brightness of the river, and a brilliant flicker of bunting in the bend.

'Ata!' She jumped to her feet and flip-flapped back into the house. She looked at him eagerly, with the unselfconscious glance of a child that has forgotten its recent chastisement. 'Ata! We better hurry!'

'I won't go,' he said sullenly.

She came a bit closer.

'There'll be girls dancing the poi,' she wheedled. 'And a band. And fine young men doing war-dances.'

His dull eye brightened a little. 'And the chops,' he said. 'I'd like to see Whaka Green make the chips fly.'

'And there'll be lots of people, eh? And a merry-go-round; you'll come with me on the merry-go-round, Ata? Maybe we'll hire a canoe, only a tikipeni for the hour, and we'll go out on the river?'

She stood behind him and pressed his head into her breast, and he remembered, briefly, the plump softness of her when they had first been married, and how she had laughed all day, and her dirtiness and untidiness and fecklessness had mattered not at all.

'Yes! Sure we will,' he said with a rising excitement. 'Put the kettle on, Kati, and I'll have a shave. And for God's sake wash your face.'

As he shaved, he thought with increasing anticipation and pleasure: Regatta Day, eh? Regatta Day, when the old Waikato reared up in its bed with fright. Crack rowing teams from all over the country, and the crowd full of strapping Maori wenches with rolling black eyes, sidling around for a kiss and a nip of sly grog. Yeah, and the old women with their lips tucked in where their teeth used to be, and the kids feeding their faces with watermelon and spitting the seeds at the passers-by. And what about the inevitable old guy who won't wear pants and goes about wrapped up in a sheet? He laughed out loud, and Katia laughed too, like an echo, happy to the depths of her childlike soul that he was happy.

She came out of the bedroom. She had oiled her hair, and it hung over her shoulders in two plaits as thick as his wrist. Her lips were heavy and red, lascivious-looking. She had scraped her skirt clean, and put on a salmon-pink blouse of thin cotton. She still had bare feet.

'My God!' he said. 'Haven't you anything that fits? That blouse was made for a woman three sizes smaller than you.'

Her face fell. 'I can't help getting fat, can I?'

'Ah, hell,' he said, as he struggled into his collar. 'forget it. And go and put your shoes on.'

Katia crammed her immense flat feet into white women's shoes, so that the leather bulged out into a row of little mounds over the toes. Proudly she waddled down the hill with Ata. He was little and skinny, and his hair was mean and sandy, and he had about him nothing of the bounding exuberance and generosity of Maori men, but he was her husband, and most of the time she loved him.

Down by the river there was a glorious riot of noise. Red-faced farmhands with painstakingly shined boots were taking pot shots at the coconut shy; countrywomen, already sunburnt, fed oranges and sticky lollies to their gawking children; here and there a sideshow barker laid a trap of verbal honey for the unwary. Arthur dragged the reluctant Katia past slanting boards where all sorts of trinkets winked in the sunlight. She heard a brief and alluring description of silver watches, genuine, as he pulled her onwards to a platform ringed about by gaping pink faces.

A gramophone blared tinnily through a loud-speaker system one of the dulcet melodies of old time Maoridom, and in rows upon the platform knelt twenty girls, each in a white blouse and flax skirt, whose parted edge displayed to the guffawing and delighted crowd a glimpse of pink locknit panties. Arthur watched from the outskirts of the crowd, then wriggled closer. He liked the swish of the flax skirts, and the neat tap-tapping of the poi ball as it swung and clicked. He liked the shine of the sun on the ebony heads of the girls, and the way they grinned, boldly and yet embarrassed, at their admirers in the crowd.

'Ahe!' sighed Katia. 'Only four years ago, before you and me got married, I did the poi dance, too, and the boys made eyes at me. Ata, don't you mind at all that the boys made eyes at me?'

There was a girl on the closer side of the platform, slimmer and lither than the others, with long silky straight hair, like an Arab. Here and there amongst her jetty locks shone a streak like a new penny, a throwback to the ancient aborigines of New Zealand, the red-haired Moriori. She looked from under her heavy lids with a sly, shy, sidelong glance. Arthur wanted to look at her closer. Impelled by something secret and furtive and urgent in his nature, he pushed closer, still dragging Katia by the hand, then suddenly realising how ridiculous he must look pulling a fat Maori woman about like a child, he let her go and tried to look as though they didn't belong together.

'Ata!' said Katia insistently.

She pressed her shoulder against him, and he felt her oily skin slip under the blouse and smelt sweat, and the buttery odour of her hair. Suddenly he hated her again, remembering how fast she had lost her youth and gaiety.

'Stop slinging your weight around, will you?' he hissed.

Katia's lip bulged with disappointed fury. 'What's the matter with you, Ata?' she yelled. 'First you bring me here to the Regatta for a good time, and now look! You won't buy me one of those fine brooches back there, only one shilling. You won't go for a ride on the merry-go-round. Only you stay here and make eyes at that girl up there, that Mary Hehe –'

She struggled to free her arm so that she could hit him between his staring, hating eyes, but the good-humoured press of the crowd was too great, and she turned and shoved her way out of it, swinging her hips like a cow in a herd. She heard above the laughter and the murmurs the light clicking of the poi balls rise once more.

The moment she was out of the crowd, her rage subsided and tears rushed into her eyes. She looked about her at the milling Maoris, barefoot, carefree, laughing, calling to each other like a battalion of Paul Robesons; at the white people, gingerly sucking peppermint sticks, their faces already streaked with perspiration. She didn't belong to either of them. She was the Maori wife of a pakeha. But being married to a white man counted for something. Even a white man who'd been in jail. Poor Ata! She felt a rush of sentimental softness for him. She'd buy him something – that's what she'd do, eh? Something to make him happy. A fine yellow tie to hold his trousers up with – No! Those watches! Ahe! Katia's eyes glistened. Those very fine silver watches, guaranteed to go! Her lip drooped. But she didn't have a shilling. Not a plurry bob. Not since she had sold her land had she had a plurry bob to call her own.

She wandered about, sulkily, till she came to the chopping enclosure, where a gigantic half-naked Maori was whacking the top off a twelve-inch block, spitting like a shower-bath through his teeth as he did so. A crowd of men pressed forward to watch, oblivious of the spray, their keen, serious, grey New Zealand eyes fixed with professional intentness on the axe strokes.

'Ahe!' said Katia in disdain. Then her eyes started. There between the feet of a plump-trousered man in front of her lay a silver watch, with a chain and all.

Breathing heavily, she stooped and withdrew it, her heart beating like a drum. It was shiny and round, exactly like the ones on the sideshow man's board. Finders keepers, but what if the fat-trousered man should –? She thrust it down the front of her blouse, where it made a conspicuous round lump. Guiltily she glanced about, but all eyes were fixed on the contestants.

Laughing to herself, Katia waddled off towards the poi platform. Her face was flushed to a deep carnation under her brown skin. She giggled with happiness at the surprise and joy of Arthur when he saw what she had brought him. The crowd was dispersing now, and Katia quickly reached her husband's side. She hardly noticed the slim, doe-like form of Mary Hehe slipping away from him, the hot look in his eyes, or the pois he twirled between his fingers.

'Look, Ata!' she cried. 'I found two bob, and I bought this very good watch for you.'

He looked at it, held it to his ear. 'It goes,' he said in a tone of wonder. Then, his face changed. 'By cripes, Katia. You're a sport, you are. Thanks, old girl.'

Katia hung on to his arm, breathing lovingly into his ear. 'Give us a kiss, Ata?'

He flushed. Out of the corner of his eye he could see Mary Hehe hanging about the ginger-beer stand. 'Not here, Kati. Everyone'll see us.'

'That's what I want,' she said in her simplicity.

'Oh, O.K.' He pecked hastily at her cheek. She looked about her triumphantly. Everything was all right now. He reached in his pocket and pulled out half a crown. 'Here you are, Kati.' He was impatient, trying to hide it. 'You buzz down to the river and hire us a canoe.'

She was incredulously joyful.

'For two, three hours?'

'Yes.' He smiled down at her, hardly seeing her, with Mary Hehe in the corner of his eye like a coffee-coloured moth.

Katia waddled off, so happy she did not notice her tortured feet. She had almost reached the river when she saw a man with a tray of sticky toffee-apples on skewers. She bought one, and, sucking its tart sweetness, she thought that perhaps Ata might like one, too, while he waited for the canoe. So she purchased another, and hurried back to the river flat.

There was something going on around the ginger-beer stand. She saw Mary Hehe slip out of the crowd and stand poised, ready for flight. Anxiously, her heart palpitating, Katia went closer. She heard a voice, 'When pockets are picked around here, Martin, you're the first man we think to search.'

There was a mumble, and then the voice was raised clearly again. 'Aw, come clean, me boy. You're got the goods on you. Come along now.'

The crowd fell back, and she caught a brief glimpse of the fat-trousered man, mouthing indignantly some unheard words, Arthur, viciously scarlet, and a placid policeman.

'Ata!' she squeaked.

Arthur looked at her with hate.

'You!' he said between his teeth. 'So now you plant stolen goods on me! I wish to God I'd never laid eyes on your flat face.'

Katia fell back, watched the melancholy procession disappear. She gave a long poignant wail, and the crowd jostled closer to listen and enjoy.

'Ahe! Ahe! My sorrow and my grief!' she cried, tears welling over and splashing out of her dark eyes. 'Now he is gone forever from me. What shall I do?'

She took off her shoes and spread out her skirt, preparatory to squatting down and making a proper wailing session out of it; then suddenly hesitated.

'No, by keriki!' she said. 'First I go and give that Mary Hehe a couple of black eyes!'

She sprang up, already feeling happier, and hurried off amongst the crowd.

Lyndahl Chapple Gee

Double Unit

1945

It was the only double unit in the street and it was occupied by two young marrieds, both in their attractive twenties, Mrs. Gladson, a blonde bleached to dazzling point, and dark Mrs. Dunbar. From their make-up to their morals they were opposites, yet they were sincere friends. The war which had sucked their husbands into its vortex overseas had floated them together to share a double unit and a multiple of confidences. Both women were mothers of sons six years old, but even this biological fact only emphasised their differences. To Millie Gladson, Jackie was an embarrassment she put to bed as early as she could; to Louise Dunbar, Sunny-Jim was a perpetual miracle and a constant companion.

Mrs. Dunbar's unit had a tidy garden in which she spent much time; her front windows had cream muslin curtains; they contrasted prettily with the potted scarlet geranium she kept on her sill. Mrs. Gladson's garden was still in the state of being dug for the first time; a 'corn-fed', homesick American soldier had started the digging, but had been moved on to the Pacific Islands before being able to plant anything; another American, a big 'blue' sailor, had continued the digging, but judging from the trough and crest upheavals of earth he left, he was more at home ploughing the waves. The windows of Mrs. Gladson's unit had frilled, pink curtains tied back with pinker bows; sunning themselves on her window sills were ornamental clay animals with Walt Disney exaggerations and imbecile eyes.

Mrs. Dunbar and Mrs. Gladson had one mood in common; they were both often lonely; Louise Dunbar was lonely for the company of one man; Millie Gladson was lonely for the company of men in general. They reacted to this loneliness according to type, Louise romantically, Millie remedially. Of course, from the start the neighbours talked. Grass widows and gossip go together. The double unit was at the end of the street, and the Army, the Navy and the Air Force had to pass every other house to get to it.

Sighting a uniformed male coming her way, Millie would say to Louise, 'Look at 'em all watching at their windows!' And, indeed, a little curtain-disturbing breeze did seem to accompany Millie's male visitors as they came along the street. Louise enjoyed talking to Millie's men friends, they could tell her many of the things she wanted to know about the war and army life; she questioned eagerly those returned men who had been in Egypt or in Italy, where Joel was now. Millie Gladson's husband, Rodney, was in Italy too, but Millie asked no questions; Millie's main interest was in the man of the moment. Usually their overseas letters arrived regularly. When there was any irregularity Louise would worry and Millie would chaff her philosophically. They often read each other extracts from their husbands' letters.

'Listen to this bit,' Millie said one day to Louise, whose dark head was bent over her own mail with concentration. Louise looked up obligingly. 'The further north we get in Italy the more beautiful the women become – even though half-starved, they are lovely to look at – they will do all your washing for a crust of bread, poor devils.' Louise only half-listening, nodded; Joel never mentioned women in his letters.

'H'm, I'm going to ask Rodney what they'll do for a piece of cake!' Millie decided. 'What does Joel say this time?'

'It's mostly about how he's missing me and Sunny-Jim', Louise said with the faintest of blushes.

'Still old Faithful, eh?' Millie probed.

'Of course he is.'

'Do you honestly believe that after nearly four years away he's –'

'Yes I do, I KNOW he keeps true.'

'Well,' Millie declared fatalistically, 'I'm darned if I think Rodney will be all he was before he went away; I wouldn't expect him to be after four years' separation.'

'Wouldn't you really mind a bit?' Louise asked curiously.

'Not so that it would worry me. Would it worry you that much?'

'Horrors! Yes,' Louise admitted emphatically. 'I've been faithful to Joel!'

'I guess I was faithful to Rodney, too, once – before conscription and the 'Yanks' came! I guess you just can't be faithful and patriotic too!'

Big Ben chimed on the radio indoors; to Louise it was always a sombre sound like the hollow quavering voice of old Father Time himself. She got up from sitting on the porch steps to go in and listen to the war news, a session she seldom missed. Millie skipped off to her own half of the house, there to turn on full volume the 'swing' station recently introduced on the air for homesick servicemen.

Sunny-Jim Dunbar and Jackie Gladson had few memories of their fathers; both had been three years and a month old when conscription had settled like an unshifting cloud upon the land. Both knew their fathers only as photographs upon the mantelpiece. There were other children at school who had photograph fathers too.

Jackie Gladson, endowed with his mother's appetite for adventure, played 'soldiers' constantly. Sunny-Jim, his lively imagination at work, would watch Jackie realistically bayonetting and bombing Japs and Germans until he had 'gooseflesh' at the thought of so much blood. Then he would seek his mother and the magic circle of security she represented. He would ask for his paints or a book to read, or some seeds to plant. Jackie considered Sunny-Jim a 'sissy.' Sunny-Jim considered Jackie a 'bully.'

Louise had grown to hate the coming of night. Unless Millie was having friends in or a party, evening accentuated the quiet that would possess her half of the house and stalk her from room to room.

Sometimes Millie would be going out and then Louise would promise to look in to see if Jackie was asleep and covered; it was odd going into Millie's unit; the rooms, replicas of her own, seemed the wrong-way round. Millie was fond of saying that the Government architects, when planning double units, simply drew half a plan in ink and doubled it over while still wet.

With Millie out at night Louise always suffered from nervousness; she never found a way to combat it; if she turned the radio on she was afraid she wouldn't hear if anyone was prowling about the place; if she turned it off she was afraid she would hear someone prowling! Her indecision in itself was a strain upon the nerves.

Louise and Millie had several false alarms concerning the return of their husbands. Someone or other who had someone or other in a Government job had told someone or other that a troopship was three miles off the coast. Any time now Louise and Millie would receive notification that their husbands were due to walk in.

'Gosh!' said Millie to the final rumourist, 'I hope the bottle man gets here first!'

When Sunny-Jim and Jackie were told that their daddies might soon be home there was a backyard fight.

'I bet my father has killed more Germans than yours,' said Jackie vain-gloriously.

'Anyway, my mother said my father doesn't like shooting Germans,' Sunny-Jim declared.

'He must be a spy then,' Jackie accused.

'He's not a spy!'

'He must be if he likes Germans. I'm going to tell on him when he comes home, and they will shoot him at dawn!'

'He's not a spy!' Sunny-Jim yelled, suddenly scared that he had betrayed his father.

'He's a spy and I'm going to tell!' Jackie out-yelled.

Sunny-Jim, in a blaze of fear, struck at Jackie's wide-open, noisy mouth.

Jackie, in true 'Flash Gordon' style, butted with his head and laid Sunny-Jim low; then, with his hands holding imaginary 'gats', he stood over his sobbing Victim and drawled in imitation of his favourite comic-paper character, 'Waal, you've had it, son.'

Coming up behind him, soft-footed, with a green willow stick in her hand, Millie caught Jackie unawares; not until Jackie was out-howling Sunny-Jim did she cease punishing; then, looking down at her sobbing victim, she drawled in imitation of her favourite radio serial heroine, 'Now you've had it, boy!'

Louise and Millie at last received the Government's word on it that their husbands had landed in Wellington. In her bedroom Louise, overwhelmed with relief and excitement, went down on her knees and thanked God for her dear man's safe return. Millie found the news unbelievable in another way; she had a party brewing for the week-end; it would have to be put off. 'Hell!' Millie muttered. Both wives went to the station to meet the troop train – and both couples returned together in an Army car loaned by the Government for the occasion. Every front curtain in the street hid a watcher as the 'honour and glory' car drove up and came to a standstill.

Mrs. Smith-Smithson, public watcher No. 1, seething with patriotism and repression, began preparing a speech the minute the front doors of the double unit opposite closed upon the re-united couples. 'I trust you will understand my motive in telling you,' she began, but something about that uneasy word motive didn't suit her. 'I think it my duty to tell you –' she began again; yes – that was more patriotic; that was how she would word her revelation when opportunity offered. She decided to begin cooking up a cake and the opportunity at once; those poor dear soldier boys would appreciate some home-cooking – especially Private Gladson!

Having Joel home again was not as heavenly as Louise had anticipated; she tried loyally and patiently to regain her pre-war paradise, but Joel's appearance, manners, speech and love-making had coarsened, and he drank. Within a month she told herself with her first cynicism that one evidently didn't taste heaven twice in a lifetime. Still loyal, she reminded herself after another month of it that at least he had remained faithful – which counted for a lot.

Sunny-Jim, too, was finding his father's presence more often a pain than a pleasure. Sunny-Jim couldn't get used to this parent who expected him to obey the first time told, and who ordered sharply, 'Get cracking, you!' if he didn't obey. He wished his father, who talked continuously about the 'bloody Eyeties', would go back to the war.

Millie was also finding readjustment difficult. Rodney was changed; he had no fun left in him and he wouldn't drink. He looked and behaved like a middle-aged man, and his love-making had no warmth in it; she supposed he had worn himself out. Well, that was the least of it. She could take anything except too much of his silence.

Jackie was disappointed in his father, too; he had hoped for souvenirs and war stories, and all his father had said upon his request was, 'It's all better forgotten, son.'

Discussing fathers with Sunny-Jim, Jackie said laconically, 'Mine won't talk!'

It was better for Louise and Millie when their husbands were rehabilitated and back at work. It was more like old times having the house to themselves. Before very long Millie suggested she should go to a Saturday night show while Rodney minded Jackie. 'It'll be a treat to get out at night again,' she said, unblinkingly. 'Go by all means, the change will do you good,' her husband agreed.

During her elaborate dressing for the 'show' Millie hummed bars of 'The Blonde Sailor'; her humming faded out every now and then when she remembered that Rodney was home. She caught the seven o'clock bus. Mrs. Smith-Smithson saw her go and went to the cake tin.

This same Saturday evening Joel spent with the 'boys'; spending Saturday night talking over old times with the boys was a regular habit now; Louise accepted the innovation with concealed relief. Joel's instability was beginning to wear on her nerves.

Sitting thinking about it, Louise wondered what was going to happen, if Joel never overcame it; with sudden clear insight she saw her own love of peace and quiet being eaten away by Joel's corroding habit of restlessness. Her thoughts were too much for her; she reached for the snapshot album and the past, to take her mind off the present and the future. She began sorting Joel's soldier snapshots; she was holding undeveloped films up to the light, when Mrs. Smith-Smithson padded across the road with her cake for poor Mr. Gladson.

Mrs. Smith-Smithson could certainly cook! Rodney thanked her sincerely for the cake and waited for the woman to go.

'I'm only sorry I couldn't ice it,' Mrs. Smith-Smithson said, with one foot in the doorway.

'It looks very tempting as it is,' Rodney assured her.

'Icing sugar is rationed,' Mrs. Smith-Smithson insisted on explaining. 'These war years are very hard – these war years are hard on women in more ways than one – especially on young wives.' Mrs. Smith-Smithson was circling her prey.

'Yes,' Rodney agreed. He was half-lowered into his chair to read his paper again. Mrs. Smith-Smithson gathered herself for the spring; her face twitched.

'Mr. Gladson, I think it my duty to tell you that your wife –

I have every reason to believe – was unfaithful while you were away. She had men here –'

Rodney Gladson stood upright again. His face showed no emotion.

'Thank you, Mrs. Smith,' he said, 'there's the door – and here's your cake – raffle it for some worthy cause – the Mother of Man Movement – is about the worthiest I believe – good night.'

Mrs. Smith-Smithson, still twitching, backed out of the light into the night again. 'He acted as if he knew – he didn't blink an eye! Who could have told him? That sly Mrs. Binn, perhaps –' Mrs. Smith-Smithson, on a new scent, sniffed her way over to Mrs. Binn's.

There were six of them, undeveloped films of Joel and a girl, evidently a 'Wog' as Joel called Egyptians – Joel kissing the girl; Joel in pyjamas, with the girl in neglige sitting on his knee; Joel in swimming, with the girl in her birthday suit bobbing alongside of him! Louise sat very still in her chair remembering things: a soldier boy she had met at Millie's who had told her about 'evidence day' on the boat coming home, when bunches of soldiers had turned out their kits and pocket books for letters and snaps and cabaret programmes to destroy – E day they called it. Apparently Joel had forgotten to toss all his evidence into the sea. Dispassionately Louise recalled other things; jokes Joel had told; he had quite forgotten her distaste for them. Then, with the past despoiled and the future soiled, Louise made two vows – to live her life for Sunny-Jim and never to have another child to Joel. She made these vows on her knees at Sunny-Jim's bedside; her promises to God were not lightly made.

When Rodney Gladson sat down after his visitor's exit – it wasn't to read, it was to think. All the time overseas he had been trying to sort things out – the war and politics mostly. Now there was this home problem to worry him; he had half-anticipated it; it was a common enough problem. His wife's unfaithfulness accepted as just another of life's low jokes, he thought back to his own faithfulness – and wiped it out as now worthless. Well, and what other left-overs did life have to offer him? A man had to have some spar to cling to or sink. What had he? His gardening – and his hobby of writing; he had roughed in his war experiences and was on to his political beliefs (both subjects tended to turn red under his pen) and, of course, there was Jackie. Well he'd see it through if only for the boy's sake. In a mood of deep disillusion he walked into his son's room.

'It's a bloody world and no fit place to bring children into,' he decided bitterly.

Sunny-Jim was only too glad to swop the Commando knife his father had given him for Jackie's collection of Egyptian coins. 'Hot diggety!' Jackie said, unsheathing the knife. 'I wish we could swop fathers too!'

Margaret Trist

The Bridesmaids

1951–52

Under the high white dome of the sky, against the rolling miles of flat, dark earth, with its yellow grass tussocks, straggling trees and drunken fences, the children looked small and lonely. The windmill, its legs planted four-square and defiantly apart in the way windmills have, shook its head slowly and crooned clank, clank to itself, as if afraid to break the after sunset hush that had fallen. Then a sudden, sharp little wind rose and the windmill shouted clank, clank, savagely and joyously. A flock of parrots drinking at the trough beneath it rose chattering into the air, wheeled about to display their scarlet and emerald and turquoise plumage, and settled, squawking, on the rim of the trough again.

The children, two girls, one eleven and one twelve, went towards the big gate. They staggered from the weight of the two large black Orpington hens each held in her arms. The hens were angry, and puffed feathers and outraged wings into their faces.

'My, Cunnamulla's a weight,' puffed Gertrude, the elder of the pair. 'I guess she just gets heavier and heavier every day.'

'She's not as fat as Jondowie,' gasped Sookey. 'You'll have to open the gate. Bakingboard'll break loose if I take even one finger off her.'

'Maryborough's restless, too. Maybe I can open it with my teeth.'

At the gate they paused, squeezed their struggling captives tighter, and glanced back towards the house. Even from this distance it looked clean, as if the activity of cleaning that had been going on in it all day had seeped through the outer walls and given them a quality of shining foreign to the weathered grey wood. The windows were awash with flame reflected from the sunset. Mother and Miss Elmer had been cleaning at it all day, because of the wedding on Saturday and because

Uncle Albert and Auntie Clare and their daughter Alison, who was to be the bride, were expected later on that evening. Mother was in a dither because she wanted everything to be just so. Miss Elmer was the governess, but in times of emergency there were never any lessons. Anyhow there was no need for Sookey or Gertrude to learn anything. Gertrude was going to marry when she was sixteen and have nine children; Sookey had been born a fully fledged author and felt no need to acquire knowledge. For a prospective mother and someone famous there was no need for Miss Elmer with her tiresome sums, her tattered copy of Florence Wickens, and her censored *Merchant of Venice*.

Gertrude and Sookey having looked at the house long enough to be sure that they were undetected, began struggling with the gate. Sookey inserted her knee under one of the wooden bars, while Gertrude applied her teeth to the block which wedged it shut.

'Push,' mumbled Gertrude.

Sookey pushed. The heavy gate gave a bare inch. They then turned sideways and battered at it with their hips. It yielded grudgingly enough space for two skinny girls to worm their way through. The hens bunched in their arms squawked protestingly.

'Shut up, you silly things,' ordered Gertrude. 'I think I'm about tired of this game.'

'But they love it so,' said Sookey pointing her chin towards the chooks. 'They wouldn't like it if we didn't bring them out any more.'

'I don't think they like coming. I'm not going to do it again. It's silly. It's just carrying two big chooks and giving them a swing when they don't want it.'

'But they're our little brothers and sisters,' protested Sookey. 'You know we swore it.'

'Well,' said Gertrude firmly, 'I don't feel like that, now.'

Sookey paused and regarded Gertrude steadily, 'I must say I've noticed a change in you lately,' she said.

'Yes, there has been,' Gertrude acknowledged softly. 'I guess it's been since I fell in love with Ronnie.'

Sookey shrieked and nearly dropped Jondowie in her astonishment. 'Ronnie. Not Ronnie. Oh, Gertrude, how could you fall in love with Ronnie. You know he's to be married to Alison on Saturday.'

'I know. It's terrible. But I couldn't help it. It was the night he came from town, bringing the ornament for mother to put on top of the wedding-cake. He looked so tall and rugged standing in the lit doorway. Grand, somehow, yet humble and slender, and oh, everything a man should look. My heart went out to him. That story you wrote about unrequited passion. I know what you meant now that it's happened to me.'

'But unrequited passion is for always,' said Sookey. 'After all, you were in love with Mr Smitherson last week. Perhaps –'

'No,' Gertrude shook her head. 'This is the real thing.'

'But the children –' murmured Sookey.

'They will have to be another man's children.'

'Oh dear!' wailed Sookey. 'You really mean you're going to marry a man you don't love for the sake of the children. I don't know what mother's going to say. We're only to marry for love, she says.'

'But you're not going to marry at all,' said Gertrude cruelly.

It was Sookey's turn to sigh. Sookey was harrowingly plain and so had relinquished the hope of marriage. She had a narrow face covered with large brown freckles, pale-green eyes, a mouth which reminded her uncomfortably of a frog's when she looked at it in the mirror, and lank dark hair, the fringe of which fell in her eyes. On the other hand, Gertrude had a round face, mostly flushed pink and powdered with agreeable pale freckles, a soft red mouth, grey eyes, and a fuzz of red-brown hair which never grew very long but made two fat, short plaits to her shoulders with tiny curls and tendrils of hair escaping from them.

They walked on, Gertrude slowly as befitted one weighed down with sorrow, Sookey jigging despite the weight of the chooks, excited by Gertrude's outrageous, noble, but hopeless love. She was always weaving fantasies about it, and Jondowie feeling the arm about her slacken took immediate advantage, wriggled herself upward, clawed at Sookey's shoulder, spread her wings, flew a brief foot or so, flopped heavily to the ground, and, wings still outspread, made back towards the gate.

'Oh blast!' exclaimed Sookey.

Jondowie, every ruffled-up feather proclaiming that she was a furious fowl, made another gigantic effort, managed to get herself into the air and took the fence, not gracefully, but with unmistakable determination. Her indignant cackling filled the air.

Sookey, clasping Bakingboard, firmly ran towards the swing, which was a piece of rope looped from the bough of a tree, plumped her on it and started to push rapidly. Bakingboard, however, fell off dizzily, staggered drunkenly, then followed Jondowie.

'You see,' said Gertrude, 'they don't like it any more.'

'Well, I'm blest,' muttered Sookey. 'I wonder why they've turned against it?'

'Everything ends, that's all,' sighed Gertrude. 'When you're older you'll understand about it.'

'I don't see why it's got to,' Sookey countered mutinously. Gertrude was only one year older than she was. And since Gertrude had been a baby during that extra year, there didn't seem any reason why she should know anything more than Sookey.

Mother and Miss Elmer were worn out. There was a scratch meal set out anyhow on the kitchen table. Father eyed it resentfully.

'Where's my tea?' he demanded.

'It's to be later when Albert and Clare get here. I've worked it out that they'll be in round about nine o'clock'.

Father went stamping into the pantry and returned a moment later bearing a fowl on a brown plate. He set it on the table, went to the dresser drawer for the carving knife, came back and started hacking at a leg.

'Oh Edward!' moaned mother.

'Damn it, woman, there're half a dozen chooks lined up there!'

'Yes,' said Sookey sadly. 'Bundaberg, Oakey, Jondaryan, Kaimkillenbun, Toowoomba, and Helidon. That one looks like Jondaryan to me.'

Father put down the knife and looked at mother. 'Ettie, do you mean to tell me you killed the kids' chooks?'

'Why, the dirty old things!' retorted mother. 'It's time they were killed.'

Father shook his head. 'A downright mean trick, I call it. Never mind, girls, but seeing it's your fowl, you'd better have a leg apiece.'

'It might choke me,' murmured Gertrude. 'But I guess I'm pretty hungry.'

'Me, too,' admitted Sookey. Gertrude had been right. Things ended.

Father hacked off the legs and handed them across. '*Vale*, Jondaryan,' he said solemnly. Then, as Gertrude and Sookey started to chew industriously, he cried, 'Cannibals!' He sliced the breast for himself, helped himself to seasoning and pushed the remains towards mother and Miss Elmer.

Quietness fell in the kitchen. Mother was so disgusted with father she wouldn't bother to talk to him. They were all startled to hear footsteps coming round the side of the house, stumbling footsteps that didn't seem to know the way properly.

Mother jumped up. 'Oh my heavens, not already!' she exclaimed. 'I figured out – Edward, do up your collar. Gertrude, there're grass-seeds in your hair. Oh, my goodness! – I don't believe it.'

But it was too late not to believe it. In no time Uncle Albert and Auntie Clare stood in the doorway, Alison hovering behind them.

'Oh my goodness me,' stuttered mother, trying to push a jam-tin out of sight and hold her wrapper round her, and smooth loose hair into place. 'Oh my heavens! We didn't expect – do come in and sit down – no, not in here. In the sitting-room. Oh my –'

'Now, now, Ettie,' boomed Uncle Albert. 'Don't get het-up. We're ahead of ourselves and that's a fact, but here we are and here we stop. Left the car at the big gate because we weren't too sure of the place. Fifteen years, you know –'

'How are you, Ethel?' said Auntie Clare, and advanced on mother and kissed her soundly. 'Nice of you to have us for the wedding and let our girl be married from here. It's the old family home, I said to Albert –'

'Well, I thought,' interposed mother, 'that as I asked you to have Ronnie when he was going to town and his mother having been a school friend of mine and seeing they'd be living in the district –'

'Fifteen years,' roared Uncle Albert. 'How goes it, Ted? I'm going to take a hand with milking the cows in the morning. I said to Clare on the way up we're not going up there and sitting on our backsides eating them out of house and home and having them give our daughter a wedding without earning our keep. I know how it is in the country. Always need a hand. I'll be up bright and early for the milking. How many do you put through?'

'One,' said father. 'Have a wing?'

'Oh Edward, how can you?' moaned mother. 'Now, everyone get out of the way and I'll set up the meal properly. No, it's to be in the dining-room. Miss Elmer –'

'Just a cup of tea, I beg of you, Ethel,' said Auntie Clare.

'Oh, but we've plenty –'

'And to spare,' said father. He got up deliberately and went to the pantry, coming back with a fowl in one hand and a ham in the other. Miss Elmer darted in and brought out a bowl of potato salad. Father unhooked kitchen cups from the dresser, rattled them into saucers and set them on the table. 'Help yourselves,' he offered, and sat down to his own meal.

'Oh no, not here! In the dining-room!' wailed mother.

'This'll do us,' yelled Uncle Albert, who appeared incapable of talking in a normal-sized voice. 'It'll do us all right. We're rough and ready. No frills about us. We'll take you as we find you.'

'Oh dear! Oh dear!' muttered mother.

'If you women would only stop prancing,' said father, glaring at mother and Miss Elmer.

'Well, my goodness me,' said mother, 'This must be Alison. She was a little girl when I saw her last, Clare.'

'Fifteen years,' began Uncle Albert, but Gertrude and Sookey didn't hear any more because they suddenly saw Alison. She happened to be the most beautiful girl in the world. She had stepped right out of the radio serials, the romances they smuggled out of mother's room, the stories Sookey herself wrote. She was the princess Sookey dreamt and talked about, the one she dressed in flowing red and blue robes and set in motion against a background of burnt earth, swaying wheatfields, clustered sheep, and all the things she knew and loved.

Alison kissed her aunt, gave her lovely little white hand to

Miss Elmer, then came up behind Gertrude and Sookey and put a hand on each of their shoulders.

'Are these my bridesmaids?' she asked.

Gertrude's eyes popped and she stared straight ahead, but Sookey twisted her head and looked up at Alison, her green eyes light and shining under the tangled fringe. She looked the way that had earned her name. Alison was so beautiful it hurt. Sookey found herself sniffling, then sobbing. Tears began to fall out of her eyes.

Alison looked surprised and took her hands away. Sookey wriggled out of her chair, pulled at Gertrude's sleeve, then fled through the door, howling unmusically.

'Good gracious!' said Auntie Clare. 'Is she highly strung, Ethel?'

'She's something,' answered mother distractedly. 'Fetch a clean cloth, Miss Elmer, do. Oh, if you will have it here – please, Edward –'

'The other one's gone too,' said Auntie Clare.

'You're an awful nut,' Gertrude told Sookey as she took a seat behind her on the front veranda steps. 'What the devil made you do that?'

'I guess I was overcome,' answered Sookey. 'First the children, I mean the chooks, and then seeing a beautiful woman. It's the first time I've clapped my eyes on a really beautiful woman.'

'She's Ronnie's woman,' murmured Gertrude sentimentally.

'Yes. It's pretty awful for you. Do you feel bad?'

'He – he deserves her,' acknowledged Gertrude hollowly.

'Gertrude, you're magnificent,' cried Sookey enthusiastically.

They sat soberly gnawing gristle from Jondaryan's legs.

Across the paddock the windmill loomed, a silver blur in the darkness. It crooned tenderly to itself. Clank, clank, it went, clank, clank.

Greville Texidor

An Annual Affair

1952

It almost seemed to be blowing up for rain. Every minute or two the wind came across the paddocks, like a lorry changing gears, and round the lonely store corner. The store looked lonely because it was closed for Boxing Day. The orange drinks and weeties in the window and the country scene with stout letters, KEEP FIT, cutting across made you feel sad, as if you had eaten too much. The wallops from the wind made you feel tired. Joy sat on the step of the store.

Come on, get up now, her Mum said. You don't want to dirty your dress before we start.

Joy got up. The wind passed again blowing up dust and rain. It was late. It was nearly nine. Mum reckoned Auntie Laurel was holding them up.

Before the lorry came round the corner they could hear the kids screeching. It was like a cage of cockatoos on wheels. Uncle Nick was in front with Dad. Behind, besides the kids, there was Auntie Laurel and a flash lady from town. She had brought something for the children for Boxing Day. It was some crackers, but they couldn't pull them because Mum said it wasn't the proper time. Mum didn't think much of crackers.

The Domain in front of the hotel was packed out with cars and lorries. Dad growled because the place near the fence where they always parked, was taken. Mum only said, I thought we were going to be late. The cars looked funny all packed round the hotel because there was plenty of room along the beach. The hotel stood by itself away from the baches. It was tall and a dark red colour like the one in Joy's Granny's picture, *The Broad Way*. They didn't have pictures like that in Joy's home. They had one of a bunch of pansies and one of a cathedral. In Granny's picture the hotel had a Union Jack on top and through the windows you could see the people inside, playing cards and dancing. But the real hotel windows were always closed. It looked as if nobody lived there, but round at the side there was a small door and men going in and out.

The old jetty was standing over the mud with only its last two legs in the water. Brian and the boys made a dash for the trolley, that was used for loading timber in the old days, and started to push each other up and down, but Mum yelled to them that they'd fall in the water, and Auntie Laurel said the jetty was dangerous and ought to be seen to.

Mum and Dad and Miss Jenkins, the flash lady, sat down on the step of the lorry. Miss Jenkins had several rows of rolls on top of her head, and slacks which were tight behind, and dark red finger-nails. She said how pretty everything looked after the rain.

Dad kept looking hard at Miss Jenkins's finger-nails, then looking away.

Everyone seems to think it's nice down here in the summer, Mum said, of course we're used to it.

I suppose you always come here, Miss Jenkins said.

We always manage to get down for the picnic, Dad said. It's an annual affair.

Mum said, It looks as if we've been unlucky with the weather though.

Dad said, It's generally like this round about Christmas.

But anyway, Mum said, it does make a change and the kiddies do enjoy it.

Dad took out his cigarette case and offered Miss Jenkins one but she said, No thanks. She did occasionally, but not just now.

Dad said, Excuse me, he had to meet a chap, and went over towards the hotel.

It began to rain a bit and the wind was chilly. Mum said they might as well go for a walk as it wasn't lunch time yet, and Miss Jenkins could see the view from further up. Everyone always said it was rather nice, only of course the tide was wrong now.

Joy had to fetch Terry and Mavis. Mum was nervous about them falling into the mud. They were right at the end of the jetty pretending to fish. Jim was there too, he had rigged up the lines for them.

Jim didn't come round to Joy's place any more. Dad reckoned that scholarship he won hadn't done him much good. He had just picked up a lot of weird ideas and was always slinging off at everything. Dad would say, Where's the Red Flag? And Jim couldn't be bothered with Dad, so he didn't come round any more.

But the first Christmas Joy could remember he was there, and gave her a bell that was meant to be put on a tree and soon got broken. What she remembered about that Christmas was the colour of the bell. Auntie Laurel said that it was a nile green, but it wasn't at all like a nile green dress Joy had. She never could get it with her paints either, so after the bell was broken she never saw that particular colour again.

They had the socials at the station hall then, and Mum and Dad still went out together sometimes, and the imaginary man came at night to keep away danger. He wore historical clothes and was called Mr Charles but he looked very like Jim.

And after that nothing much except the picnics. Jim went away to the town and didn't come home very often. He was saving up for a trip to Europe, he said.

The kids didn't want to stop fishing, and Joy had to promise they could come back later on. I'll be seeing you later on, she said to Jim.

With Terry and Mavis dragging behind they walked along past the baches. The baches were mostly empty, and as they hadn't been painted for years, were grayish-white like the sky.

The Dacres were coming. They talked away to each other looking along the ground, not seeing Mum and her friend till they got quite close. Then they stopped and smiled and were introduced to Miss Jenkins. They said the glass had gone up quite a bit this morning.

When the Dacres were out of sight Miss Jenkins said she *would* like a smoke now, so Mum suggested they climb up the bank and sit under the pines where they would be sheltered from the drizzle and not be seen. Mavis slipped down the bank and dirtied herself but Mum was quite calm about it. She had brought another dress and panties for Mavis to change to for afternoon tea.

You keep them so nice, Miss Jenkins said with a smile.

When they got back to the lorry it was lunchtime. Auntie Laurel was there with the rest of the kids, waiting. She said she hadn't seen Uncle Nick all morning. He's always Hail fellow well met, she explained to Miss Jenkins.

They sat on the grass on coats and macs. Mum took off her hat with the felt feather. Whew, isn't it hot, she said. The sun had come out and it was stifling hot between the cars. Mum unpacked the peanut-butter sandwiches, and the date scones she had baked on the Happywork stove Dad gave her for Christmas. Well we might as well start, she said, as Dad hasn't come. She sent Brian off for the hot water from Mrs. Withers. Then she passed the scones to Miss Jenkins. I baked them before we started this morning, she said.

Miss Jenkins took one. Oh aren't you clever, she said. I must confess I often pop round to the Cosy Cake Shop for scones and things, you know how it is in the city. She didn't look at all ashamed of it though.

They say our baker bakes a fair fruit cake, Mum said, but I prefer my own. You know what's in it.

I suppose you do, Miss Jenkins said.

Dad came and sat down and started fooling with Terry, turning him over and pretending to smack him. Terry didn't know what to make of it but he laughed till he turned red and hiccoughed. Dad had red patches on his cheeks and his eyes were swimmy.

Brian came back with the teapot. In his other hand he carried the broken off spout wrapped in a handkerchief. Mum couldn't let fly at him with Miss Jenkins there. Dad took it as a joke.

The tea was terribly strong and Miss Jenkins said, Couldn't we borrow some hot water from the hotel? But Mum said, I don't care about asking favours when we don't know them.

You needn't trouble for me, Dad said. He wouldn't have a scone either. He ate one sandwich quickly, then started telling one of his funny stories to Miss Jenkins. He said he knew some better ones than that, but he didn't think he could tell them. This made Miss Jenkins laugh but Mum was rather quiet. She was handing round some of the Christmas cake. This year it had white water-icing and desiccated coconut, but as Mum said herself it had turned out rather plain. No one took any. Terry was being a bad boy because Dad had been taking notice of him, he was wanting his banana now, but Mum said, No, you know they're for later on. But he howled so loud she had to give him one and then the other kids grabbed bananas too out of Mum's bag, which was bulging with bathing togs and things to change and knitting and Miss Jenkins's *Gone with the Wind*, and other things for later on, and ran off to the shore. Mum called after them not to play in the mud and not to go on the jetty.

Miss Jenkins said she'd had such a lovely lunch and she thought she'd retire to the lorry and have a smoke. Dad offered to go along with her. Only in fun of course.

Pull your skirt down a bit Joy, Mum said. The Reverend Allum was walking over their way. He sat down on the grass beside Joy and smiled all round. He always smiled in a special way as if he were much happier than everyone else. Joy looked away so as not to be hooked with his smile and be asked something. She'd been in his bad books since she let out that she was reading the Bible verses at night. The verses to be read were marked on the card and if you were regular you could get right through the Bible in five years. Only the morning wasn't really a good time, Mum was tired after having done so much before breakfast, and the kids had to be got off to school. But the verses are your armour for the day, the Reverend Allum had said. You wouldn't put on your armour when you lie down to sleep would you now? Whoever heard of such a thing as that?

Do have some tea, Mum said, it's rather thick I'm afraid.

Thanks but I've had a cup with Mrs. Withers, people are so hospitable. I only wanted to enquire about your little laddie. The one who wasn't at Sunday School last week.

It was only a cold, Mum said, but they hate to miss. It's nice for the kiddies having the Sunday School so near.

Yes and for Mum and Dad too, Joy was thinking, they can have a lie down on Sunday afternoons.

Miss Jenkins came out of the lorry and was introduced. Dad stretched out his legs on the grass till his foot was touching hers, then said, Oh, beg pardon.

Quite a good crowd down here today, Mum said. But the Reverend Allum's smile was for Miss Jenkins.

I expect you must find it pretty quiet, he said.

Oh no, she said, I love a day in the country.

You're right too, the Reverend Allum said. When she was

younger Joy had used to think that when the Reverend Allum said You're right too, she'd hit upon something clever. It always turned out though, when he'd enlarged on it, that it wasn't what she had said after all.

The Reverend Allum took a deep breath in and a long look all round him. Yes, he said, on the outgoing breath, when all's said and done nature takes a lot of beating. Jim was walking past, carrying a bottle with a straw stuck in it. They all looked away and pretended they hadn't noticed but Auntie Laurel said quietly to Mum, Fancy bringing it out here, where everyone's having their lunch.

But the Reverend Allum went on as though nothing had happened. We country-dwellers now, I sometimes think we're apt to forget perhaps. He looked all round him again. His all-embracing glance skipped the hotel and threaded its way through the cars to the strip of shore. The tide was nearly out. There was only a gray snake of water in the channel, and the steep mud-slopes were steaming off in the sun.

Yes, it's a pity Muriel and Winnie couldn't get down, Mum said. They've been in hospital with their appendixes, she explained to Miss Jenkins. Doctor thought they might as well have them done together and get it over.

Yes. We only see the sunny side of life over here, the Reverend Allum said. It's difficult to imagine what it must be like over there.

Dad had his eyes closed and a dribble of spit on his chin. Joy gave him a quiet agonised poke and he opened his eyes and smiled, looking like Terry. Mum was getting on with her fancy work. Yes. Quite a good crowd here today, she said, but a lot of them have to leave early for the milking.

I don't know what other's opinions may be, said the Reverend Allum, but personally Miss Jenkins, I like to think of this little affair as a sort of commemoration. The settlers in these parts landed here. Quite near where we are sitting now I believe.

There wasn't anything here then, Mum said, her eyes on the hotel.

The settlers had faith, said the Reverend.

Too right, said Miss Jenkins, putting her hand to a yawn.

Dad had found a pair of pink art silk panties that Mavis had

had for Christmas. They had been in Mum's bag for Mavis to change to. Dad kept holding them up and squinting between the legs in a comical way. The Reverend Allum went right on about the settler who had stuck in the mud and they never found the body, but Joy felt hot all over. As if something awful might happen. She got up quietly and walked away to be out of sight of Dad and the lot of them.

She said hello to the Dodds, the Band of Hope Dodds, they always came early and got the best place nearest to the hotel, and went round to the yard. The hotel backed on to the shore and the yard was quiet and secluded, with empty cases to sit on and a nice view over the inlet. Jim was there smoking a cigarette with the cider bottle and the straw beside him.

Hello, she said, what are you doing here?

Oh, nothing, he said.

I thought maybe you had a date.

Who with? he said.

Joy pulled little bits off the straw, wanting to cry. Mum had stuck to it that the navy was just as smart and safer for washing, and the perm she could have next year when she worked at the store. Next year it would be all too late. The other girls had florals, the kind with elastic round the waist that fits almost anyone, and their hair nicely set with steel clips and invisible hairnets. Merle had blossomed out with lipstick too, but really it didn't look so hot with her pimples.

Cheer up, Jim said. How's old stick in the mud?

As usual, Joy said, he's on the settlers again.

And your Dad and the others?

As usual, she said. Dad's had a few of course. You know what he always says, It's a free country.

The curfew shall not ring, but Dad shall turn the wringer tomorrow. He'll have to take his headache to church as well.

Jim was always making fun of Dad and Mum. It wasn't true either, Dad didn't go to church any more. There was only the wringer. It was always like that with Jim. Just as you were settling for a nice yarn he would start slinging off at Dad, or his Dad, or the capitalist system, so that it never came to anything. Still, of course, there would never be anyone else.

It was sunny and quiet in the yard. The people walking up and down, up and down, between the hotel and jetty, stopped and turned back where the metalled path ended. Joy moved along closer to Jim on the box. The people seemed far away. It had to happen then that Murrey popped his head over the fence, grinning at them, showing his black stumps. A horrible boy Murrey, with filthy tricks.

It's only Murrey, Joy said. He'll be having his new teeth when he leaves school, his mother says.

The big thrill that only comes once in a lifetime. Well, my big thrill will be getting out of this. I might get my trip to Europe after all.

More likely land up in the desert though, Joy said. Why couldn't you help your Dad milking and get exempted? You don't want to go and get killed do you?

Get killed for these stick in the muds? But you have to think of the future. A lot of chaps are relieved to get into camp. It's a change from mowing the lawn and all that. It's going to be more of a change than they think though. A change is going on all over the world. Before the war governments had to make camps because the prisons couldn't hold the political prisoners. It's never happened like that before. The bosses are hoping it will blow over, the war will give people something else to do. It was only the old red spectre walking again, they think. But the change that is coming is rising like the tide. It will reach even this little place one day. But I'm going to be on the spot when the big things happen. You have to think of the future.

Joy was looking at the hills across the inlet, not thinking of the future, thinking the hills looked empty and strange today. She had always meant to go over there some time. It looked lonely, but pretty and peaceful, the grass a soft green, not the metal green of the properly fertilised paddocks, the hills split softly into creeks full of scrub and shadows. There were Maori lands over there. Better than on our side, Dad said, they are dirty and carry diseases. There wouldn't be much to see over there, he said, but Joy had always wanted to go some time.

The sun was bright and a cool wind blew from the coast. It was a lovely day now. Cheer up, Jim said. Joy sat still, for fear of disturbing his hand settled on hers, feeling his cool fingers and the heat inside her hand where the straw was crushed.

A man came out of the hotel back door. He was little and sandy, and walked slowly and sadly. He must have lost his way.

He crossed to a box and sat carefully down. Then he remembered something and got up again with a nervous look round the yard. He saw them but it was just too late by then. He took out his false teeth and was sick on the ground.

Joy got up. Jim said he'd have to be getting along too. Outside the yard they ran into the Young Men's Bible Class and the Reverend Allum in bathing togs. They were larking and making funny remarks like a boys' school story. Come along in and have a good swim, they shouted to Jim as they passed, it would do you good.

I'm afraid I haven't been introduced, Miss Jenkins said to Jim when she overtook them, but I've heard such a lot about you. Joy introduced them and she got confidential at once. Rather a queer idea for all the men to go in swimming together, Bible Class or no Bible Class, she said. And it was pretty hard to keep up a conversation with some people, and she asked him, had he read, *Gone with the Wind*?

Jim said, Well, yes, but he had to be going himself now. He started up his motor bike with a bang and rode off up the hill, the bike making scornful explosions.

After that there was nothing much to do. It began to rain again, and Mum sat on a box in the bathing shed with her fancy work, pegging away at the big rose in the middle she had promised herself she was going to finish today. Joy could see there was something wrong but Mum said it was only her legs.

They swelled up, generally in the evenings, about the time Dad came home, and she would say to him, Just look at my legs again, it's from being on them all day.

You must have got up too early, Miss Jenkins said.

Oh no, I always get up at five, Mum said. I like to get things done before breakfast.

It's a puzzle what you find to do all the rest of the day, Miss Jenkins said.

I find plenty to do thank you, Mum said, as if she'd been offered something she didn't like.

You must have a gift for it, Miss Jenkins said. And she laughed.

Like some people have a gift for fooling round with men, Mum said. Joy felt as if something horrid was going to happen. But Mum couldn't have meant Miss Jenkins.

The Bible Class was swimming still in the rain, and the other unmarried men must have been in the pub.

When it cleared up it was time to get Mavis changed and line up for the ice cream. Mrs Dodds, Murrey's mother, and Mrs Chapman were doing the refreshments this year. Mrs Dodds always got first prize at the show with her sponge surprise, or else with her ginger kisses. But when Mum tasted the ice cream she said there was nothing in it but those powders, and Auntie Laurel said, Mrs Dodds and Mrs Chapman might have put in a bit more sugar and a drop of cream for the kiddies. And only those cheap soft drinks.

The soft drinks were mixed in two kerosene tins. One of the drinks was red and the other green. There was plenty of it and some of the boys got as many as ten drinks. To end off with there was an orange, but Mum said that was extravagant at the price they were now.

Then Brian was sent to fetch the hot water again, and Mum and Miss Jenkins and Auntie Laurel had afternoon tea again with the rest of the Christmas cake. The kids hung round, pestering to go in swimming and Mum kept saying, No you might get in the current. You know you can't go without Dad.

Mrs Chapman passed with her husband. We're off home, she said.

You've got him well trained, Mum said. That was one of her jokes.

Terry getting sleepy, worrying to be taken notice of, was saying over and over again, Where's Dad?

Now what did you promise me this morning? Mum said. What am I going to tell Dad when he asks if Terry has been a good boy all day?

Daddy's having his tea somewhere, Miss Jenkins said.

But Terry said, I know where he might be. Drinking beer in the hotel.

Mum suddenly gave him such a crack on the side of the head that he couldn't even yell for a minute or two.

The tide's about right in, Joy said. It made noises like smacking kisses under the banks where the kids were sitting looking down at the water. After a while Mum came over and said as the sun was going and Dad hadn't come yet, they could put on their togs. But they mustn't stay in for long, it was getting chilly. The boys rushed off to the shed to change. Joy and Mavis undressed in the lorry.

Terry stood on the bank and cried while the others were in. He hadn't been allowed to paddle because of his cold. The sun was off the water now but he cried so long that Mum undressed him and put on his bathing pants, but when he got down to the water he wouldn't go in.

Joy rubbed down Mavis and dressed herself quickly and walked away along the shore as if she were meeting someone. Passing the Withers she saw the dinghy tied to a post by the beach, and got in and let it drift into the mangroves. The wind had died down. It felt like a warm damp hand across her hair. The ugly old twisted mangrove trunks were all covered up and only the branches with dark green leaves were showing. The water made roads between the tops of the trees. Joy moved along the roads and little lanes till a branch scraped the bottom of the boat. Then it was not a road but only all that water underneath, enough to cover a tree.

She began to row out across the inlet. The sun had set and the valleys and creeks on the other side were smoothed out. The hills were black and flat, like the advertisement letters across the picture, painted across the sky for some reason.

When the boat swung in the current she turned. The kids had stopped shouting on the jetty and everything was quiet, and over towards the sea a crack in the sky opened into a still shiny lake, exactly the colour of the Christmas bell.

When Joy got back Brian and Mavis were sitting in the lorry because it was getting chilly, playing I Spy. Terry was asleep on the floor. He had a blue mark down the side of his face. Mum was walking up and down outside. She said Auntie Laurel and Miss Jenkins had gone home hours ago with somebody else.

It was quite dark when Dad came out at last. He said he had had to stay for Uncle Nick who was not feeling too good. Mum wanted to have it out with him but he only smiled. Might as well be the wind blowing, she said. But perhaps you'll be feeling differently tomorrow.

Mr Chapman, who hadn't gone home after all, sat in front with Dad. Uncle Nick was inside. He was carrying on about his kidneys, how bad they were, they didn't seem to get any better, he was sure he wouldn't pass the medical test, and everyone ought to do their bit, and the loved ones at home. He got so worked up about it he started to cry.

The kids feeling a bit awkward, piped up, *Roll out the Barrel, We'll have a Jolly Good Time*, just to change the subject. I wish it was next year, Brian said, for the picnic.

Joy said nothing. Brian was such a kid. He never stopped to think that everything might be different next year.

Sarah Campion

Amble

1953

We of the Servants' Hall are not so much superior to the great ones beyond the green baize door as a race apart. We eat different food, off different crocks, with different tools, and at different hours of the day: when the great ones have finished nourishing themselves in the dining-room we do not, as is popularly supposed, fall-to like wolves upon their broken meats, but eat in our own good time our own specially cooked dishes, taking care to be as leisurely as we wish. Underline the leisure: it is our prerogative. The Big Chief, or Old Jellybags as Amble calls our employer, may be at the mercy of any caller with an axe to grind, a plaint to make, or a bee in the bonnet needing release: but we are not. When such a caller calls at mealtimes and is ushered into the study by Amble, Old Jellybags must rise from his seat, wipe his mouth, and leave his dinner to cool while he listens to the reason for the visit. His is a public ear, he's paid for the use of it: and the public see to it that the cash is earned. But we of the Servants' Hall – we live as best we can on the meagre wage which dribbles from Jellybags' pocket, and are by no means too proud to make sure that we have leisure for our meals. When, at these mealtimes, Jellybags' piping organ-note of need comes wistfully down the hall towards the green baize door – when Amble hears our employer bleating 'Ambo-ool!' – he does not immediately rise from his food. Not he. With a shrug and a good-natured obscenity or two he stays just where he is: and after ten years or so of this (since the English mind is slower than the Australian to accept inevitables) Old Jellybags will realise the futility of calling for his butler at that butler's mealtimes.

This Amble is my solace, he is so steadily himself. Most of us are undecided, either uneasily English or furtively 'continental'; but Amble has no scruples whatever about being a dinkum Aussie. Lean, stringy, with tufted sandy hair and a roving sardonical blue eye, he has also a pleasingly irreverent tongue. His humour spares no one, neither our employers, Jellybags and Momma: nor our difficult and forever-on-the-point-of-giving-notice house-parlourmaid, Gertrud: nor even me, the precious Cooky. I may be conscious, as I sweat my way through a seventy-two hour week for a two-pound wage, that I am the thirteenth cook this household has had in five years, and that I shall do nothing to prevent its having a fourteenth, so soon as I have found myself somewhere better to go: while everyone else in the Servants' Hall knows how precious I am and treats me with careful tenderness lest I up and leave them in a huff. But Amble is held in by none of these considerations. He subjects me to that easy flow of blistering comment and affectionate contempt which he pours on everyone but his little English wife: and if I don't like it I can do the other thing.

Amble will do no placating. Mrs Amble treats me delicately and calls me 'Miss' Campion, a courtesy which has only so far been extended to the fourth cook of the line, a Lady Chef who was in the habit of leaving her dentures grinning overnight on the kitchen table: but Amble knows it is not he who will have to go out and comb the agencies of Melbourne if Cooky goes, and, even if it were he, he still would not forgo for one moment the sharp pleasure of his tongue.

So, I get the weight of it: a Pommy is always fair game for an Aussie. It is Amble who incites the butcher's lad to march straight into the kitchen, slap a bleeding, naked sirloin on the kitchen table, and go through the motions of a smacking kiss while crying 'It's all for you, Sweetheart!' This is a bracer for my watery Old World democracy: Amble will have me a true democrat before I leave. It is Amble who comments at least once a day on my freckles, thus disciplining vanity: Amble is a noted taker-down of females. It is Amble, finally, who adds pithy comments to my little daily list for Momma headed 'Kitchen Wants', thus:

SR flour
B. powder
grd. ginger
LOVE,

the last in Amble's hand, embellished with a few pierced

hearts, arrows of affliction, and other symbols of erotic yearning.

It's true, our kitchen and our Cooky both lack love – but only Amble would be cheerfully cruel enough to point this out.

He spares none, least of all those distinguished guests for whom our state dinners are given. The whole establishment east of the green baize door will be in an uproar for days, humming with preparations for feeding a Governor-General, a Lord, or an Archbishop's widow: the frigidaire will bulge unseemly with chickens, oysters, Norwegian creams made by me in despair and blind-eyed sleepiness the night before; the whole floor will bloom with enamel bowls containing water and French beans, it being Mrs Amble's vain but pious hope that the vegetables will thus remain crisp: the smell of scorching linen will blue the air while Gertrud irons her seen and unseen smalls: but still, in this female bedlam, Amble keeps far crisper, cooler than the beans. The women can fret themselves to a frazzle if they will, he contains himself in easy contempt till the night itself, there and then to use all his powers to garner everything he can for our lewd entertainment. Which is the only reward we shall ever get for hours of overtime, lost nightly sleep, and a general feeling, on the day after, of having been put through the mangle.

See Amble, then, on one such gala night. It is the night upon which we jointly lay our fancy for the Melbourne Cup, and I can see it all as clearly now, and smell it, almost, as if I were back there on an antipodean evening, with the drizzle plopping from the Moreton Bay fig-trees outside the window, the smell of drenched lemons wafting in from the kitchen-garden through the door we have opened to let out steamy kitchen heat and let in steamy winter air – I can see it all so clearly, and Amble at the head of the table pluming himself in full rig.

We are discussing the dinner-party he has just successfully brought to the coffee-and-brandy stage beyond the green baize door. Amble, as always on these occasions, strikes the eye as remarkably fine: his bosom glinting like a skating rink, his sandy hair stunned into smoothness by Vicar's Violet Pomatum, his blacks extravagantly black.

It is his night. The ladies hang upon his lightest quip – Bessy the little outback parlourmaid, flushed from handing round vegetables and sweets while holding her unworthy breath (an exercise, this, demanded from all her parlourmaids by Momma) – Gertrud the housemaid with her dark Swiss countenance and her bristling Swiss moustache – Cooky smouldering as warmly as her own oven – and an anonymous lady, all ears, known to us as 'The Occasional'. To these, and with relish, Amble is describing the person of the chief guest, a Brigadier's relict.

'Looks too young to be the Ma of that great gawpy galoot she brought along – musta had her face lifted. Dress wanted lifting, too – when I handed her the entrée I hardly knew where to put me eyes. Old Jellybags did, though; his was poppin' like organ stops. He'd have ordered her outa the house if she'd bin a Nobody – comin' here dressed like that, gapin' all the way down to Glory. Cripes, you shoulda seen Aggie, too: skipped her bath again, the young weasel, and only washed half of her neck, and that in a hurry.'

Gales of giggles from the ladies. Amble, very much the gentleman, leans back, lights one of Jellybags' cigars, lounges there puffing it and carelessly ignoring the eye of Mrs A. She, suddenly intimidated by his shirt front, changes the intended glare for a smirk of wifely pride; and basks awhile, with a hazy expression, in the reflected glory of her man.

'However,' continues the hero, 'let joy be unconfined, let giddy merriment be you-know-what, for the Honourable Mrs has expressed herself in a Honorarium. Order what you like, ladies, order what you like: it's on the house.'

And he holds up a coin. It is a florin.

Being somewhat new to the strict Trades Union rules of the Servants' Hall, and altogether new to Australia, I am about to say that I think this is rather nice of the Honorable Mrs, when the slow flush on Mrs Amble's cheek checks me. Mrs Amble has a face like a bee's, all proboscis and brooding darkness: if you can imagine a bee blushing, you have Mrs A to perfection during this awkward moment. She not only reddens in spite of herself, but she must also allow tears of outrage to soften the serpent steadiness of her eyes.

'The Jezebel gave you that – for all of us?' says Mrs Amble at last.

'Don't take it so hard, ole girl, she meant well. I've spent a considerable time working it out,' adds her spouse with heavy haste, 'and it comes to fourpence apiece.'

'We can put it on a norse,' cries Gertrud suddenly, her face aglow. But for the fatal lure of Tattersall's, poor Gertrud would have got home to Zürich many years before.

Mrs Amble plunges from the table and stumps about in the butler's pantry, slapping all the wineglasses and tumblers on to the wrong shelves. She always does this in a crisis, and lovely is the calm with which Amble puts them all back again, next day.

Our heads arc hung together over the evening paper, while Amble jabs a black-nailed forefinger down the column.

'Sum bust!' he crows, 'Sum Bust! That's it! What a name eh, what a name! And, though I'm not allowed to talk about it (Mrs A being fussy as you know) I wish you'd all of seen it for yourselves, acres and acres of it, with the Mongdayseer powder lying on it in drifts like the snows on Mt Kosciusko! Sum Bust, I'll say it was! That's the horse for us.'

Unfortunately, no; for Sum Bust proved its name too nearly, suffering at the beginning of the race a form of lackadaisical stupor which just allowed it to bring its head as far as the starting tapes, no more. Amble explained this disaster in great technical detail and a wealth of horsey anecdote; but most of us agreed with Mrs Amble that it served us right. We shouldn't have soiled ourselves by taking the money, in the first place.

J. C. Sturm

Where to, Lady?

1950s

It was my day off, or strictly speaking, my afternoon off. Not given, you understand, just taken. The best kind, I told myself defiantly, walking firmly down the path, walking out on the house, the family, a long long week of 'life's responsibilities', and turning a cold shoulder to the ones ahead. How many of them between now and then I wondered glumly on the road. Never mind. It's high time I made a gesture and I stood beside the Russian Embassy perched on the brink of the city and gathered myself together for the plunge. I should be Joyce Cary, I thought, looking down at the harbour, then I might be able to translate all this into words. Maybe a huge earthenware bowl with a chipped rim and a puddle of pale blue milk in the bottom, would do. Maybe. Anyway, no matter how you looked at it, it was a perfect day, one right out of the box, all clean and fresh and carefully ironed hanging up ready for somebody to step into. That's me, I said right out loud, and I ran down the steps and picked up a tram.

But it's never as simple as that. I mean, you just can't move out of one world and into another simply by boarding a tram. For one thing it's usually a help if you know where you want to get off. And I didn't. Sitting in a tram not knowing where you are going and waiting for the conductor to come, is nearly as exciting, and much more pleasant, than sitting in a tram knowing where you want to go, and knowing too that it doesn't make much odds because you haven't got enough money in your purse anyway. So you just sit quietly waiting for the conductor to notice you while the tram covers miles and miles of line, and you pass the time away wondering what you'll say to him and what he'll say to you, and whether he'll take your word and your address, or whether he'll tip you out at the next stop, both of you red in the face with indignation, and leave you stranded and acutely ashamed about being ashamed.

'Where to, Lady?' asked the man himself, bringing my reflection on trams and conductors to an abrupt end.

'Where to?' I echoed, searching his face hopefully for the answer.

'Yes, lady, that's what I said,' and he looked patiently out of the window over my head.

'Oh, the cenotaph,' I suggested, 'that's if you go that way.'

Well, I thought, as the tram cast me high and dry on the small island of grass and concrete, of all places in the world, why did I have to choose this? And I walked round the monument examining it carefully for the first time in my life. Maybe the day could do with a memorial, but not this one. I might just as well have settled on the sphinx. I turned my back on the pile of stone and bronze and made for my nearest friends.

The wife wasn't wearing lipstick because a mosquito had bitten her on the lip, and the heat of their upstairs flat had made her a little vague, but there was nothing the matter with her welcome. She just stood in the doorway and smiled.

'What a pretty dress,' said the man as I walked into the living-room, and he did some deft juggling with a baby, a book, and a teddy-bear. 'How clever of you to wear a girdle instead of a belt, much more becoming with that, and your sandals – my dear, where *did* you get those sandals?'

'Yes, isn't it, aren't I?' I smiled, and sat down because that's what he really had said. The room steadied itself around me. Books, books everywhere. And pictures. Every conceivable size, shape, and colour, of book and picture. But it was the pile of cushions that held me fast. There seemed to be dozens of them, every one a different colour, all clustered gaily on a dark navy couch like so many miraculous flowers in winter, while behind them hung a long, graceful, gently moving yellow curtain.

'Oh, beautiful,' I murmured, forgetting the cenotaph.

'Well, not quite,' said the wife, smiling tenderly at the baby, 'but she's beginning to look almost human. The poor wee thing hasn't been sleeping very well lately. She doesn't know how to cope with mosquitoes yet, and this heat makes her so cross.'

'Me too,' I said ruefully, flapping the front of my dress for coolness.

'Like some tea? We drink it all day.'

'I'd love some,' and I tried to think back over the years to my last meal.

'Take a look at this,' said the man offering me his open book, and there it was, all spread out before me at last, another world. Tiny blue figures that could have been human, dwarfed by immense black symbols and gold animals, and between them, immeasurable space, space everywhere.

'Their cosmology is amazing, absolutely amazing,' he told me, 'and you wouldn't believe it but it works. I mean it draws all the strands together, shuts all the doors, answers all the questions, tells them everything they need to know in this world or any other, and finally directs the whole. Can you imagine it?'

'No,' I replied, shivering slightly. 'No, I'm afraid that kind of living is quite beyond me, not my cup of tea at all.' The wife appeared carrying a tea-tray and began to conjure innumerable cups out of a doll-sized teapot. 'Now this,' I said, picking up a book of short stories I knew better than any friends, 'this is different, this is what I can imagine.' And all the pain and passion, discoveries and loss, waiting and disappointments, the unending unanswerable questions, and the unwanted final statement, crept from between the covers and nestled in my hand. 'Some book' I said 'and what a woman. I wish I knew how she does it,' and I watched the baby grasp handfuls of nothing from the air above her head, examine them intently then kick and coo with delight at the wonder of it all.

'Oh that,' he said, rearranging baby and bear, 'why can't people in this country write about what they know *now*, instead of something somebody knew fifty years ago, or something they hope we might understand when we've grown up. Honestly, you'd think life was a sequence from a Kafka novel. Wouldn't you?' and he looked across at me suddenly with suspicion.

'Nice cake,' I said to the woman. 'Did you make it?'

'Of course she did, she makes all our cake. Wonderful cook. Wonderful woman.' And he grinned up at his smiling wife, jigging the baby between them.

'Well, I really think I'd better go,' I said slowly.

'Must you?' asked the woman, breaking the tableau, 'I

thought you meant to stay to tea,' and the three of us roared with laughter. 'We've got pumpkin pie. Lots of it.'

'Good heavens pumpkin pie. I've not even heard the name for years and years.' And the book I was still holding dissolved into an American magazine open at a double page of incredibly coloured foods with a huge pumpkin pie sitting triumphantly in the middle, and my mother was telling me –

'No, no,' I said, getting up hastily, 'I've imposed my appetite upon you too many times. I really must go home. After all it's getting rather stupid.'

'What did you say?'

'I mean it's rather stupid to stay when it's obviously going to rain and I'm wearing only this,' I explained, shaking my light dress. There was no doubt about the rain. The room was still warm, but had darkened with the sky, and the three of us seemed slowly drifting apart on a sea of shadows, our faces growing paler and indistinct, and our words too ineffectual to measure the distance. Only the yellow curtain billowing above the cushions remained.

The rain was coming down steadily at the first tram stop, and no tram in sight, so I walked slowly up town, taking shelter under the shop verandahs. The street was scattered with people like me, sauntering along with nowhere in particular to go, window shopping, talking and laughing, filling in their Sunday afternoon, or making the most of it. I could have been any one of them. A group of young bloods came towards me speaking to each other quickly in a language I didn't understand. Immigrants, I guessed, looking at their solid rubber-soled shoes, their long slicked-back hair, their long dazzling ties, their long straight jackets, their – that's enough of that, I ended grimly, bringing myself up with a jerk, and I turned my attention to a menu outside a crowded milk bar. Eggs, mince, sausages, pies, spaghetti, no fish, and I moved on. 'Oh you'll *never* get away, you'll never *get* away, you'll never get *away, you'll never get away*,' gloated the juke-box after me. Is that so, I thought, watching my tram approach, pause, gather speed again, and disappear slowly, slowly round the far corner.

The library was closed 5.30 pm–6.30 pm. The milkbars were over-crowded or had their juke-boxes going full blast. Even the bus timetable read no bus. I was almost in despair when I found myself outside a grill-room, not one of those brassy, glassy, we-can-offer-you-anything-you-want-with-fluorescent-lighting restaurants, but a poky, cheap-looking, open-twenty-four-hours-a-day kind of joint, just one degree better than a pie cart, and definitely grubby. Oh no, I panicked, not here, of all places, please not here. And my mind reeled back to a different age, and a different me standing on the same spot with another all lost forever a lifetime ago. When I came to I was staring wide-eyed at a man sitting at one of the tables just inside the door. One cheek was bulging with food, but he had stopped chewing and was regarding me with growing interest and a certain amount of expectation. I knew what he was seeing. An odd young woman, who looked as though she had just been touched by a ghost, standing in the rain without a coat, taking hours to read a menu written on the window in large white letters and plain English. There was only one thing to do. I walked in.

The small room seemed full of men all shovelling food into themselves as fast as they possibly could, but at one of the side tables sat a half-caste Maori woman by herself, and as I hesitated in the doorway she pulled out the chair beside her and nodded to me.

'Takes you a while to make up your mind,' she smiled as I sat down, 'you looked kind of funny standing out there in the rain.'

'I bet I did,' I said, feeling my face go red, 'I don't often do this, I mean, I'm not used to having meals in town. I usually cook them myself.' A waiter slid through the back curtain like a ferret and sidled over to me.

'Yes, lady,' he smiled into my lap, 'and what do you fancy?'

'Oysters, please.'

'Sorry, lady, no oysters.'

'Whitebait, then,' I said, forgetting the time of the year.

'Sorry, lady, no whitebait swimming around these days.'

'Well,' I said, leaning back in my chair, 'what can you offer me?'

'Eggs, mince, sausages, pies, spaghetti.'

'No thanks,' I shook my head desperately, as the room began to spin.

'How about a little sole with salad?' he whispered, his smile sliding to ankle level.

'Oh, that will do fine,' I sighed with relief, and he brought me the largest, flattest flat-fish I had ever seen lying on a plate.

'Nearly all bones, honey,' chuckled the woman, as she caught my expression, 'and I ought to know. I cook hundreds of 'em a week. I'm third cook at the City Club Hotel,' she finished with dignity.

'Good job?' I prompted through my fish.

'Not bad, at least the work's all right. I like to cook. But the people these low-class pakehas who think they know everything – ugh! The lady-boss, she's okay. She's hard as nails but she's fair. She says to me, do what you're paid to do, that's all I want, the rest is over to you, so when the kitchen-hands start any dirty nigger business I get my slap in first. I'm not going to be pushed out of a good job by any silly so-and-sos. Would you?' She picked up her plate and walked out the back before I could say anything. Dirty nigger, I wondered, as I watched her go. Not by any possible manipulation of the words or their meaning could I make the description fit. She was a large woman, a little stout, but well-corseted and with a good posture. She was wearing a black and white gold-printed ever-glaze frock, with a fitting bodice and a very full skirt, the kind of dress I had admired hundreds of times in shop windows. Her court shoes, like the handbag she had left lying on the table in front of me, were good plain black. Well-dressed by anybody's standards, if you cared to apply them. Not that clothes or posture or even dignity are any protection, I thought wearily, if somebody wants to call you a nigger. She looked a little flustered and embarrassed when she came back from the kitchen.

'Going any place tonight?' she finally asked me.

'Not really. I had thought of going to the library, but it's not important,' I replied, wondering what was coming next. There was a long pause.

'Well, look, things are in an awful mess out there. There's a rush on as you can see, and they're short-handed. They want me to help out with the dishes, and they thought you might keep me company.' I turned my sole over carefully.

'I don't know,' I said slowly, 'I really should be getting home, but I suppose, for a little while –'

'Good,' she said, not waiting for me to finish, 'I thought you would.' The ferret was hiding behind the curtain when we went through.

'Pleased to see you, lady,' he grinned, offering my lips a cigarette. 'Come and meet the boys and make yourself at home.' You could hardly move for bodies and food and dirty dishes, and the steamy heat and smell of burning fat was almost overpowering. One side of the room was taken up by a huge sink and bench, while along the other side were gas rings, a steel grill, and a wooden table where the cook, sweat running down his face, was working like a madman. We tied dirty aprons round our waists, took a deep breath, and started. For nearly an hour we went flat out, shovelling dishes in and out of the sink, stacking them in drying racks, washing and shredding lettuce and slicing tomatoes. Home, I thought ruefully, was never like this. When things had slackened off a bit, the woman and I went out to the nearly empty dining-room to cool off.

'On the house, ladies,' sang the ferret, banging down glasses and two bottles of raspberry fizz, 'just call for more when you run dry.'

'Gawd, my feet,' sighed the woman, drinking her fizz steadily. 'Some night out you're having, honey,' and she smiled uncertainly at me.

'I'll say,' I said, feeling sticky and smelly and dirty. 'I've just about had it. Anyway, I'd better get back to the family.'

'Family?' she said, putting down her glass. 'You got kids?'

'Only two.'

'What you done with them?' she asked me sternly.

'My husband's at home. He's minding.'

'What?' and she burst out laughing.

'Where's the joke?' I asked, on the defensive.

'Oh nothing,' she said, wiping her eyes, 'but they won't all come at that game, you know, honey. You're a lucky one. What happened? Walk out on him?'

'Sort of. But only for the afternoon.' She burst out laughing again.

'Well, you've got the right idea, anyway. Break 'em in young. Show him you can still stick up for yourself.'

'I suppose so,' I said, collecting the empty bottles and glasses, 'but I hadn't thought of it that way.'

Back in the kitchen the woman and the cook started ragging each other.

'You must be crazy crawling into a hole like this with that dress on,' and he eyed her bosom critically.

'Want me to take it off?' she threw back at him. 'Anyway, you can't be too bright yourself, taking a job here. What you doing it for?'

'Money,' he said, patting his pocket, 'they don't give you anything else these days. You wouldn't believe it, but I used to run a show like this myself once. Made a little pile of eight thousand. Then I settled down quietly in a pub and blew it all in three years. So here I am, starting all over again. Got two jobs to hurry things along, this all night and another all day. Keeps me healthy. But money never worries me. Now women,' and he smacked his lips together like a goldfish, 'I like 'em.' And God help 'em, I thought, taking in the short wiry hair, sharp blue eyes, rat-trap of a mouth, the whole stocky strength of the man.

'What, back again, kiddo?' he asked, catching my stare. 'I thought you'd turned it in.'

'Oh, it's early yet,' I said, running the tap.

'Sure. But you don't want to strain yourself. What do they call you, kiddo?'

'Sally, when I'm good.'

'And when you're bad?'

'They don't call me anything. They don't even know me.'

'Too bad,' and he looked at me thoughtfully. 'Say, that's a pretty dress you've got on. I like that kind of tie thing round the middle.' His hands were busy feeling for lumps of fish in a big enamel bowl of batter. 'Want to know something, Sally? You ought to come to town more often. Drop in anytime.' The ferret slipped between us, curled himself around me, and dropped a clean plate in the sink.

'Sure,' I said, turning away. 'I might do just that.' Kafka, I thought savagely. Kafka nothing.

'I've changed my mind. I'm going now,' I told the ferret.

'Hold your horses, there's no hurry.'

'There's plenty of hurry. I can hear the kids howling.'

'Okay, okay.' He shrugged his shoulders and reached for the phone. 'Calling you,' he crooned, 'there's a little lady here wants to go home. What are the chances?' There was a pause while his grin slowly widened. 'Could I?' he smirked all down the front of himself 'or could I?' He ushered me through the door, winking broadly at the others.

'See you next Sunday?' he asked when we got outside. 'Say yes, and I'll get off early. How about it?'

'Can't make it,' I said, wishing the taxi would come.

'Aw come on, break it down. You can't treat a guy like that.'

'Oh can't I?' I said, facing him squarely as the taxi drew up. 'Look. I'll let you know what my husband says.' And I climbed into the back seat.

A pity, I thought, as he slammed the door without a smile. After all, five bob, raspberry fizz, cigarette, sole with salad. Maybe he lives alone in one room without a hot-point. Maybe he's got six kids and a sick wife. Maybe I look like a girl-friend who let him down. Maybe. I tapped the driver on the shoulder.

'Where to, lady?' he asked through his Sports Post.

'Where to?' I echoed. 'Home.' And I sat back, shutting my eyes against the city lights.

Ethel Anderson

The Rector's Wife Tempts the Bishop with a Brew of Nyppe

1956

Several brown birds, mere specks in an infinitely blue sky, were telling an inattentive heaven what a lark it is to be a lark, while, below them, the tide of Parramatta High street bustled and flowed, as lively as a Scottish burn in autumn.

Everyone for miles around had come to town. The same people were exchanging greetings with diminishing ardour as they met in shop after shop, every lamp-post was decorated with a nag's head held to it by looped hide, the medley of vehicles quite blocked the road, clarences, barouches, phaetons, landeaux, drays, carts, and Dr Phantom's Hyde Park, neatly drawn up beside the kerb outside the chemist's, his groom (whom he designated Second Murderer) sitting in it bolt upright with folded arms and eyes fixed on space and a spine like a ramrod, and, next to him, the coachman (designated First Murderer) whose deportment was equally correct.

The cockades on their hats were new. They had something to live up to; for one thing, they felt the power of Miss Juliet McCree's sparkling eyes; she was a critic on style whose opinion they valued, and the Vicarage buckboard was drawn into the sidewalk contingent to the Doctor's piebald Waler. For another thing, Miss Aminta Wirraway, in a stunning pelisse, had stopped – a mere instant – to curtsey to Dr Phantom and to thank him (in a reproachful voice) for the return of a pink lawn Irish handkerchief 'taken in mistake for his own'.

The lane beside the chemist's had, besides a row of pepper-trees, a spreading camphor-laurel round which scores of Green Fanny and Blue Fanny butterflies were vanning the air, and these did nothing to detract from the charming picture Miss Aminta made as, quite bewitching in olive-green and burgundy, colours that went so perfectly with the curtains of the Hyde Park that they might have been designed for riding in it, she lingered on – a mere fraction of time – to say her few shy words.

'Have you ever known anyone who owned a butterfly?' Juliet McCree asked Dr Phantom as, together, they watched Miss Aminta's elegance, still pursued by butterflies, being as it were, 'rubbed out' by scores of rustic figures.

Dr Phantom's level and deliberate gaze met hers, as long, perhaps, as a lacewing settles on a daisy.

'No.'

'When you blush,' Juliet noted, in an interested aside, 'the red starts just above your stock, and when I blush it begins on my cheek-bones and then goes right through.'

The observation did not disturb the flow of her main discourse which she resumed immediately, while Dr Phantom's roving eye followed a flight of starlings bent on keeping a *rendezvous* on the King's School lawn. He did not care for children, but, finding Juliet waiting there, he had, on coming out of the chemist's, stopped to enquire after her 'grandfather's lumbago'. In asking after the Vicar one picked on any complaint that came handy; he had them all.

'The story about the ravens feeding Elisha and that other one about the widow's curse should never have been written; they have done a lot of harm. They give people such wrong ideas.'

Juliet, who was standing in the gutter, holding her horse's head, took a fresh twist in the reins.

'Look at poor Grandpapa,' she continued, her eyes very bright under her 'reed' straw hat (from China), 'if people did not believe in miracles no-one would expect him to live on £90 a year and keep his son's widow and her children – Donalblain and me. Everyone seems to think – and I am certain those stories are to blame for it – that the holier a man is the less he should have to eat, and the shabbier his clothes ought to be, and the more hungry children he ought to feed, and the harder he and his wife ought to work, however old they may be, and give pennies to beggars, and have no other pleasures because being holy is enough reward for anyone, as of course it ought to be.'

Dr Phantom made no answer, still, he lingered, his glance tracing the course of a pigeon very high up and as white as snow. It looked like something straight out of Paradise. He felt extremely happy, and he thought. 'The earth must be like a pear that has one perfect moment, and this is that moment; the sky has never been so blue, the sun has never been so beneficent, the air has never been so soft, or the trees so golden.'

'And you know perfectly well that in any rich household a loaf of bread cuts into eight slices – eight thick slices, for what use are thin ones? – but at the Vicarage it has to be cut into twelve at least.'

Dr Phantom looked directly into Juliet's orange-tawny eyes and then withdrew his glance; he made no comment.

'Then – hasty pudding! Have you ever had hasty pudding for breakfast, week in, week out?'

'No.'

'I thought not. I suppose you don't even know what it's made of?'

'No.'

'Flour and water – just that. Of course sometimes you have a spoonful of milk with it, or a taste of brown sugar, and of course there is simply no one cleverer than Grandmama in making helpings go round! A casket of molasses is very good for growing children – no one denies it – and there is enough nourishment in it to last a month at least, and it is very good for children. Don't you think molasses is very good for growing children?'

'Yes.'

'And have you ever eaten 'choke dog'?'

'No.'

'Oh, well, that is quite good really, it is made of beef suet and currants and it has a thick sauce made of flour, and when the lemons happen to be ripe it has a lemon flavouring. And a 'Lady Belmore' is quite appetising too, and it is made of rice and currants boiled in a pudding cloth, and it has some thin sauce with it, and when it is nicest it is made of arrowroot, and the pattern of the china comes through on your plate, which is interesting really. Only Donalblain, who is four, does not care for it much.'

Juliet, with a caressing pat, restrained her horse from biting the nose of the piebald Waler.

'Grandmama thinks the way clothes wear out is a perfect pest, and even the ravens did not bring Elisha a new suit.'

She gave Dr Phantom the full benefit of her lively regard.

'Of course, you understand I am not criticising God in any way?'

'Oh, no, of course not.'

'Here comes Grandpapa. He will give you a tract. You could let me have it back, sometime, if the pages are not dog-eared.'

The Reverend Phineas McCree (B.A. of Trinity College, Cambridge) at eighty-four was getting a little past his work. So benevolent a countenance as his made many of his parishioners feel reassured about heaven and earth merely by looking at his white woolly hair, his bright blue eyes, his nobly hooked Roman – or Wellington – nose, his red, tremulous mouth; but he supplemented this unconscious influence by an eleemosynary distribution of texts, for he had some difficulty nowadays in speaking; the words did not come easily off his tongue.

Some people thought that he should retire, but, they asked themselves, if he gave up his parish who would feed him and his dependants? It was wiser and more comfortable to beg the question.

Dr Phantom, therefore, was not surprised when Mr McCree, making his way towards him by very slow degrees, simply handed him a text without speaking, and then turned away to tackle the difficult ascent of three steps that looked like flattened soup ladles, which made entry into the buckboard easy on a *Lucus a non lucendo* principle.

Handing his groom the leaflet, which bore the title 'Is Your Soul A Social Success?' Dr Phantom set himself the task of hoisting the Vicar up, wondering, meanwhile, who would assist him down again.

Juliet had already seated herself in the driver's seat, her whip set at the correct angle, the reins smartly assembled. She looked quite enchanting.

Indeed, she caught the eye of the Governor himself. He was, at that moment, trotting past, helter-skelter, with a great clattering of hooves, as he was driving tandem in his London curricle.

His Excellency was a descendant of King Charles the Second – as indeed who is not? – and whenever he appeared in Parramatta all women between the ages of sixteen and sixty would inviolably withdraw into hiding until he had passed.

With predatory smiles creasing his distinctly 'Caroline', rubicund, yet swarthy, face, he was about to pull up beside Juliet when the A.D.C.-in-Waiting leant across to say urgently. 'That is Miss Juliet McCree, the granddaughter of the Vicar of Mallow's Marsh, and she is twelve years old' – and clucked twice (to the horses).

'She is a personable girl for her age,' commented Sir Charles, as he acknowledged salutes from Dr Phantom and the Vicar and the small crowd that had quickly gathered, and he moved off reluctantly with a spectacular display of horsemanship.

Dr Phantom stood a moment looking into the crown of his beaver hat, then he said, briskly, 'Good-morning, Vicar, good-bye, Miss Juliet! I have to return two baskets in the direction of Dural and Hornsby Junction.'

Getting nimbly into his Hyde Park he was bowled gallantly away, with four curtains fluttering in the wind of his passage.

Meanwhile, running across the road from the grocer's, Miss Loveday Boisragon detained Juliet to ask after her Grand-mother's liqueur.

'Indeed, Aunt Loveday, it is brewing nicely, thank you. Dear Grandmama manages to keep the lid on with three flat-irons. The Churchwardens are taking a great interest in it, and Mr McWhistle has donated – very kindly – two gallons of French brandy and a hogshead of Jamaica rum. The recipe is written in a faint hand in faded ink and it has been difficult to decipher it, but we think the ingredients and quantities are correct.'

'And what, dear child, are they?'

'Oh, walnut rinds, oat-malt, beans, fir and birch tree tops, and three handfuls each of *Rosa solia* and *Carduus benedictus*. There are two handfuls each of burnet, betony, marjoram, avens, elderflowers and bruised cardamom seeds. Then there is a handful of wild thyme. And ten new-laid eggs. Grandmama has yet to add watercress and a generous rasping of horse-radish. Of course the chief things are the milk of two dozen coconuts, three gallons of French brandy and double that quantity of rum. My great-grandpapa, as you know, was a nabob in Calcutta, and we found the recipe in a box of his. There is a note in his hand-writing saying "This brew is bettered by the addition of a pound of ginger, some sassafras, madder, red sanders and *Enula campana*." We shall put those in. Another postscript says, "This Nyppe is strong enough to make a cat speak."'

'Do you call it Nyppe?'

'The name for it, Grandmama thinks, is 'Nyppa Wine' or wine made from a tree. But she is adding various other things, such as brook-lime and wild parsley, and she thinks it will be more of a liqueur, really.'

'I ho-pe,' Mr McCree began, in his slow articulation, to which his hearers listened with reverent looks, 'that the concoction with bib-beady bub-bubbles winking to the b-brim, will ch-cheer the d-dear Bishop! He c-comes on a p-pastoral visit next month.'

Mr McCree looked triumphant.

'Good-bye, dear Aunt Loveday!'

With great judgment Juliet achieved the feat of turning the buckboard in its own length, and, feeling very grand, she whipped the young draught-horse in the shafts to a majestic trot, and the Vicar, bowing this way and that, like Royalty, and sometimes stopping to hand out a text (he had given Miss Loveday Boisragon a pamphlet on 'Lessons to be Learnt from the Construction of the Ark'), was borne westwards along the dusty road on which, five miles away, the Vicarage and village of Mallow's Marsh was situated.

In a community where news is so scarce it is not to be thought that information about Mrs McCree's liqueur would not leak out; the Vicarage during the subsequent weeks was besieged by callers; one almost expected straw to be laid down on the road.

Even the Governor, with his dashing A.D.C., rode over one Monday morning, when Tabitha the housemaid, Cook Teresa, Mrs Cog the laundress, and Abigail the Orphan, who, while learning the laver's art, assisted Mrs Cog with the washing, were pegging clothes on a line.

When, therefore, he visited the laundry, where a large earthen cauldron reposed itself beside the copper, His Excellency was flapped in the face by wet sheets and caressed by other garments, about the ownership and uses of which it would be profane to guess.

Mrs McCree, who at once locked Tabitha, Abigail the Orphan, Cook Teresa and even Mrs Cog securely in the linen cupboard, and was herself closely attended by the Vicar, on affording Sir Charles the privilege of a sight of the cauldron which contained the now golden-tinted liqueur, produced, from a box kept on the copper, a wine-glass and a toddy-spoon, and ladled him out a sup or two of the so-famous 'Nyppe'.

'It is not yet mature, Sir, of course,' Mrs McCree was complacent, 'but it will give you an idea of the flavour. Though red sanders, *Enula campana*, ginger and sassafras have still to be added – and a third quart, I think, of French brandy – its bouquet, I flatter myself, is unique.'

Sir Charles bent his head and sipped.

A look of extreme and ineffable joy ran like sunlight over his face.

'My dear lady!' he ejaculated.

He sipped, he savoured.

Ecstasy succeeded astonishment.

His eyes shut, with the look of a man in a trance, he tasted, he rolled the Nyppe round his tongue.

He finished the glass.

He stood, vibrating, almost locking his gaze in that of Mrs McCree, his expression one of utter unbelief.

He was then understood to say something like 'Shend mesheveral bottlesh' – 'Gimme onemorsh' – and the two outdoor menservants and the A.D.C. having assisted His Excellency into the saddle, and handed the horse's bridle first to His Excellency, then to the A.D.C., he was led home by back ways, ecstatically, deliriously happy.

But he was as helpless as a new-born babe.

Mrs McCree with a quiet smile went indoors to let the four maids out of the linen cupboard, and having done so, she put her feet up on the drawing-room sofa and engaged herself, with a somewhat mystic air, in the perusal of a book (perhaps *Crockford's*) which gave lists of Deans, archdeacons, canons and prebends of cathedrals, their pay, emoluments, residences, perquisites and privileges, their precedence at banquets and royal levees, and their titles.

The Bishop was expected in about three weeks time.

As a girl Mrs McCree had lived on the Picton Hills not far from the Razorbacks, and this morning, in the intervals of her reading, her eyes looked through her drawing-room windows and lingered on those blue, authoritative ranges. She remembered them in her childhood to have been thatched with trees, now they were denuded; the buff grasses clothing them were intersected with many red channels in which the rains of autumn were accustomed to pelt downwards.

'As a girl,' she mused, 'I used to look across to Mallow's Marsh and watch the thick mists rising at sunrise from the green fields, and the roads that led, I fancied, to the sea, to cities, to a wider life than I had known.'

She dropped *Crockford* on to the threadbare carpet.

'It is true that I adored my home, that there was no-one in it that I did not love, no simple everyday happening that I did not value and enjoy. The first apple-blossom! Never shall I forget seeing that! The stunted violets that come before the big ones – never shall I forget how sweet their scent used to be! Ike, the gardener, sitting in the moonlight practising 'Cherry Ripe' on a penny whistle! How mysterious and beautiful it seemed, how clear the faltering notes were! Never, never shall I cease to value those memories! But I imagined that elsewhere I should know a more wonderful life! And here I am at fifty-five looking at two minute, bare churches, one with cows feeding in the churchyard, one with two old horses grappling with the tough yellow grass – the wife of a poor parson trying to live on £90 a year!'

Mrs McCree looked searchingly round the room.

She critically regarded the two owls mounted as fire-screens that stood on either end of the mantelpiece, the silhouettes of her great-grandparents, grandparents, parents, uncles and aunts – so many soldiers, so many sailors, all idealists, no money-makers; the two teasets in her china cupboard, one patterned with raised strawberries and their leaves, in a china like pumice-stone, the other sprawled with marsh-mallows and having blue bird-bolts on the back of each cup and saucer. She carefully examined the dessert service, imitating fig-leaves, the glass paper-weight enclosing a cottage on which snow fell if one shook it. Her treasures! Oh, well! They were very sweet, really.

The tapestry covering the Empire chairs was, however, 'shrill'; the worn carpet had belonged to her Aunt Martha.

Heaving herself up, Mrs McCree walked to the window, the better to see the hills of her youth.

'Lovely still! Lovely, always!'

'Other people,' she told herself, 'get more out of life than I seem to have done. What defect in my character has landed me here? What was my weakness? What was my mistake? My apparent freedom has been an illusion! I have had no real, no personal choice in any important crisis. My parents refused my first offer of marriage without even telling me of it – what gay adventures might not that young husband have given me?

'And why on earth did I marry Phineas?

'A poor parson nearly thirty years older than myself?

'Why? Why? Because he looked so woebegone! Because I felt sorry for him! Yes! That was why – I just gave myself away, body and soul, out of charity!'

Another thought struck her. 'But was even this marriage entered into of my own free will? At home, as money grew short, I was an extra mouth to feed, I was a burden from an economic standpoint, it was necessary to lighten the family of such a drag! It was a question of having to get rid of me! Oh, I see that! It was taken for granted that I must say 'Yes'. I realised that at the time. Daughters must marry. So I did.'

Mrs McCree turned away from the dazzling light.

'My fault has been – generosity! I gave all I had to give – and it has never been enough!

'Thirty years spent in this cramped house. Well, I shall end all this! The consequences? The consequences! I just don't care! I shall make the Bishop tipsy with my wonderful Nyppa wine, my miraculous liqueur! Yes! I shall! Even if I can't make him give Phineas a deanery! Even if he won't make him an Archdeacon! Or a Canon! (There are several Canons over eighty in the Sydney diocese.) He might at least add twenty pounds a year to his stipend.'

Mrs McCree picked up *Crockford.*

With a careful regard for syntax, learnt from Little Mary's *Grammar*, dimly remembering the calamity brought on the man in the mill-pool by a lax use of will and shall ('I will drown and nobody shall save me') Mrs. McCree lifted *Crockford* high in the air and declaimed in a ringing voice (which she hoped her Guardian Angel would hear): 'I *will* make the Bishop tipsy, and nobody *shall* stop me!' In case of error she varied this formula by a second declaration of her intentions: 'I *shall* make the Bishop tipsy and nobody *will* stop me.'

Having done this, throwing her book on the carpet, Mrs

McCree to her own complete astonishment burst into tears, sobbing into the silence of the threadbare room. 'Oh, Phineas! Darling! Wonderful, wonderful man! A gentleman! A scholar! A Saint! Oh, never, never was there such a kind, loving husband! Oh, Phineas! To see you so neglected! So ignored, so underpaid, so overworked! It's a scandal, a perfect scandal! I can't bear it any longer!'

Drying her red eyes Mrs McCree then marched in a resolute way to the laundry, where she poured a third gallon of Jamaica rum into her witch's brew and gave Mrs Cog orders to keep a gentle fire burning in the copper for the next three weeks.

With a relentless and determined face – indeed, she looked more like Lady Macbeth than any actress ever has, before or since – the Vicar's wife re-read her great-grandfather's directions, to make quite certain that no vital, no necessary, ingredient was omitted; tipped yet a fourth bottle of brandy into the cauldron and dropped in a pound of ground ginger and a handful of quick-lime (in mistake for brook-lime), after which activities, and recollecting the effect of one wineglass on His Excellency (a four-bottle man as everyone knew), she buried her face in a damp sheet and laughed till she got a stitch in her side.

The day set apart for the Episcopal Visitation was one of the most perfect Mallow's Marsh had ever known. The sun had very easily dispersed the thick mists, called locally 'the pride of the morning'. Though cool, the air was not cold. Though warm, the sun was not hot. With the most discerning tact a zephyr sometimes stirred the wands of the pepper-tree, the swathes of the willows, the grey plumes of the wattles, already tasselled with buds. As if merely to display their delicate gradations of colour, ranging through buff and amber to bronze and dun, this subtle wind rustled, sometimes, the long grasses that veiled the Vicarage garden, the unending by-ways; even the main road meandering from Sydney to Picton was fringed with blue grass and red fescue, which swayed this way and that.

Was the sky blue?

It was.

The Vicarage was early astir.

The menu at launcheon was to be –

Roast Pork with apple sauce.
Beans, baked potatoes.
Summer Pudding.
Whipped Cream.
Coffee.

An oratorio of the most heartrending sounds had, two days previously, accompanied the slaughter of the best of the Vicarage pigs. A roomy flagon of Nyppa wine (or 'Mrs McCree's Liqueur') had been lowered sixty feet down into the eighty-foot well, to cool off; the most exact calculations having been made to ensure that, though close to it, the bucket in which it reposed should not touch the water.

In the Vicarage every duty allotted to Cook Teresa, Abigail the Orphan and Mrs Cog had been faithfully performed. The garden (the bit, that is, between the front gate and the porch, over which a Maréchal Niel rose was in full flower) was actually neat. A clump of polyanthus (very late) was in bloom by the front steps; there were six clove carnations out.

The service in Church had been most inspiring.

Sixteen sulkies, gigs, buggies and buckboards had brought a congregation of thirty, the Offertory (12/6) had been a record, the organ had produced sounds distinctly resembling music, neither of the choir boys had sneezed during the sermon, which, in its measured cadences, its august prose, its exact, almost poignant scholarship, in the richness of its classical allusions, in the masterly ease with which the Bishop had ironed out a crease in Deuteronomy (or was it the Pentateuch?) and in its dramatic opening sentence, 'WHERE ARE THE YOUNG MEN OF MALLOW'S MARSH?', would greatly have impressed anyone able to take it all in. The good Bishop never gave less than his best, even to the most sparse, the most rustic congregations.

Much in the spirit that Art students are sent to Italy, Abigail the Orphan had been 'spared' by Mrs Cog in order that she might see the goffered frills on His Lordship's lawn sleeves. She sat in the Vicarage pew beside Juliet and Donalblain. It was hardly to be expected that the ladies from the household where the Bishop was to lunch should appear, but there they were! Mrs McCree in puce surah with a rose in her 'pork-pie hat'; her lovely daughter-in-law, who seldom appeared, looked quite ravishing in a Garibaldi – black, of course.

The Bishop seemed to be such a true 'Prince of the Church', and his eloquent words so moved Mrs McCree, that almost she relented; but her Guardian Angel, a good creature, not very bright, was no match for the old firm, Apollyon, Beelzebub, Mephistopheles and Co.; she refused to weaken; she *would* make that lordly being tipsy!

In her dining-room with its rows of Regency chairs upholstered in red rep faded to magenta, the table positively sparkled with crystal (it really was crystal, three engraved goblets were dated 1683) and glittered with mirror-like silver (it really was silver, mostly of George the First's time).

The green fig-leaves from the dessert service, filled with grapes and hazel-nuts, the immense silver epergne garlanded with yellow roses, and a silver tazza, given to some ancestor who had been chaplain to Her (late) Majesty Queen Anne, made the table look magnificent.

Mrs McCree was proud of it.

'After all,' she thought, 'only Lady Mary's plate can rival ours,' and with infinite care she gently levered the huge glass flagon full of Nyppa wine on to the sideboard. The liqueur was chilled to that clammy yet inviting coldness that only the deep-delved earth can give. Its colour was not bright but treacherous-looking; it had the unsafe look of a bog, strangely unluminous, yet deep-toned. It did not seem to be inanimate! Continually, a kind of subterranean glow radiated from it, its surface would be sucked in, in a thousand dimples, and then, with a sort of sucking sound, released, to flow to the rim of the jug. A volcano that was not in eruption but which was brewing lava would perhaps be a simile that faintly hinted at its mysterious and peculiar qualities; it appeared to be as thick as treacle, but it wasn't! As for its bouquet!

Juliet and Donalblain were having a meal in the Nursery with their mother, for the lovely young widow of the Vicar's son seldom appeared, it was only the Vicar and his wife who bowed their heads when the Bishop said Grace – in Greek.

The Vicar, who was greatly enjoying the company of an old friend of his undergraduate days, had twice already capped a line from Horace with a quotation from Sallust and (let it be whispered) Catullus.

The two outdoor menservants, wearing white cotton gloves, waited at table, Cook Teresa having elected to carve. She could not bear, she said, 'to see my lovely leg mucked up'. She deftly laid four pinkish, whitish, creamish, fragrant slices of pork on each Crown Derby plate, with its crispish, tannish, delectable-looking strips of crackling flanking them, each with a mound of apple-sauce to add lustre to a perfect mouthful. The beans were strips of chalcedony and chrysoberyl. The potatoes! And the gravy! Oh, my dears!

'Ah, yes,' the Bishop murmured in his exquisitely cultivated voice, while he waited for the Vicar to be served, 'I very well recall, during the early thirties, questions arising in my thoughts as to whether we could really be so cocksure in taking the absolute truth of the evangelical formula for granted. One of the great watchwords was the right of private judgment. We used, on Sundays, to have to find texts to sanction it.'

Here a slightly mystic air attested to the excellence of his first mouthful of pork.

'Side by side with our classical work we were obliged to find sanction in defence of Justification by Faith, Sanctification, Total Depravity, Election and Final Perseverance.'

'We were taught to look on anyone who did not ag-ag-gree with us with a kind of awful dismay,' the Vicar recollected, smiling.

He, too, found the pork very good.

'Of what use were all those glib quotations from the minutes of the Council of Trent?' the Bishop wanted to know.

'There was always a doubt as to whether K-K-Keeble was really sound on the more vital aspects of the Christian Faith,' the Vicar hinted.

He was quite holding his own.

As the meal proceeded Lucretius Carus wrestled with St. Jerome, Epicurus attempted St. Augustine, Apuleius supported by Aemilia Pudentilla, confronted even St. Paul himself.

It was a merry repast.

Directly the pork was in play Mrs McCree, rising from her place, the flagon held in hands that did not falter, said in gentle, confiding tones to the Bishop 'You will taste my little elixir, Bishop? It is made from a recipe left me among the papers of my great-grandfather, Major-General Willing-Toper, of the East India Company's service.'

'But, my dear Lady! It is not for you to wait on me!'

Jumping up, and gallantly possessing himself of the jug, the Bishop poured himself out a full glass, using, not the goblet dated 1683, but the hearty Georgian tumbler, with a capacity of one pint.

Returning the flagon to the sideboard, and smiling a faint, almost terrified smile, Mrs McCree went back to her chair.

'My memory is as good as ever,' the Bishop remarked, in parentheses as it were, 'and for years, if I am not mistaken, I have addressed you as Jessie – yet, if my ears do not deceive me, I have today twice heard Phineas address you as Lucretia?'

'That is my middle name,' Mrs McCree answered, throwing a warning glance at her husband.

Here the Bishop tossed off half a glass of Nyppe.

'Of course, in those days, after the appearance of Tract No. 90, the chief points held out for our consideration were Scripture, the Church, General Council, Justification by Faith, Purgatory, the Invocation of Saints, Masses, Homilies, the Celibacy of the Clergy and – er – er – other matters of importance.'

The Bishop finished his glass and in an absent-minded way got up and refilled it at the sideboard.

Mrs McCree became anxious.

Neither of the menservants had reappeared to take away the plates and dishes. Cook Teresa, ably assisted by Tabitha, was, in rather a flurried way, performing these offices.

'Where are the men?' Mrs McCree whispered, as Cook Teresa removed her empty platter.

'Lorst to the worrld, Mum,' Cook Teresa whispered back. 'They must have sumpled the Nyppe. We managed to drag theer buddies into the scullery. I've covered thim with a blankut, and they look very, very happy theer. Very happy indade! Abigail is after climbing into a clane gown, and she will be here immejit.'

When the second course made its appearance, Abigail proving herself a treasure, the Bishop poured himself out a third tumbler of Nyppe.

'Your elixir, dear lady,' he said, turning with a smile (the smile known to the ladies of his Diocese as *his* smile) to Mrs McCree, 'has the three qualities necessary to a good drink. It is cool, it is subtle, it is stimulating.' And he resumed his interesting discussion with the Vicar. 'It was Tait of Balliol who entrenched himself so ably behind the Thirty-Nine Articles. Did you ever meet Tait?'

'No. No.'

'Nor Pugin? Bloxham's "umbra"?'

'No, no.'

'The Master was not pleased with Pugin. He considered he had humbugged Bloxham.'

'Ah, yes, so Gooch told me. Did you ever run across Gooch?'

'No, no. But in the May Term of 1836 I ran across Bowyer in Athens, and he told me about Gooch. That is, he mentioned him.'

Because in their day Englishmen went to Greece much in the same spirit that the crusaders went to the Holy Land, Athens led to Delphi, Thebes to Helicon; there for the next ten minutes they rambled.

'I found the Boëotian plains very striking.'

'Ah, yes! As I came down from Cithaeron on the way from Eleusus, they lay before me, rising beyond Asopus into reddish, gentle heights!'

'*Helicon, the grey, distant summit, not unattainable!*'

'*The dim, huge, majestic mass of Parnassus!*'

From Mallow's Marsh they looked back on their Heaven.

Mrs McCree, who had been waiting in vain for the return of Cook Teresa, noticed with a failing heart Tabitha's agonised face appearing round the door, and obeyed her beckoning finger.

She was hardly at all astonished, on being led to the kitchen, to find Cook Teresa sitting stiffly on a deal chair, and gazing into space with extraordinary concentration.

'There were a drop or two left in the cauldron,' Tabitha explained.

'I brought this on myself,' Mrs McCree told herself, beginning to get a little alarmed. Should anything (as she put it) *happen* to the Bishop how could she deal with him? Dear Phineas certainly could not lift him. She peeped into the scullery at the recumbent forms of the two menservants, and remembering a maxim of her great-grandmother's, went across to unfasten their collars; neither stirred, yet they looked happy! She was reassured by reminding herself that a note in her great-grandmother's hand, written in the margin of the recipe had stated: 'This Nyppe is good for diseases of the head and for cold stomachs, and nobody can pine away when embalmed in so powerful a preservative.'

Not a little comforted she returned to the dining-room.

She circulated dessert.

Tabitha and Abigail brought in coffee.

The flagon was half empty and she noticed with awe that the Bishop was not in the least the worse for liqueur. His noble countenance was decorous, not flushed, his articulation was meticulously exact; indeed, as she entered, he was, with perfect *sangfroid*, asking Phineas if he had 'caught this new craze for the cultivation of rhododendrons'?

The word presented no difficulties. His long legs, too, in their elegant gaiters, stepped with their usual graceful precision as he went across to the sideboard and poured himself out an eighth glass of Nyppe.

Sipping at her Mocha coffee, bolstered up with cream, the Vicar's wife, however, felt the first faint stirrings of a real alarm when (Phineas having dropped into a gentle doze) the Bishop drew his chair near to hers, and, with a kind smile, a very kind smile, laid a white hand, wonderfully kept, and given a look of sanctity by the Amethystine Episcopal ring, over hers, and said, lowering his mellifluous voice almost to a whisper, 'For some months past I have been hoping to find an opportunity of mentioning to you a subject very near my heart.'

'Great Heavens!' thought Mrs McCree, 'Is he growing amorous?'

It was a contingency that had never occurred to her.

The Bishop's grey eye certainly looked beneficent.

Was his cheek, perhaps, a little flushed?

'I have not been unmindful of your devoted labours, dear Jessie,' he continued. 'I have greatly admired the wonderful way you have managed the feminine, the economic, side of my dear old friend's responsibilities in so remote a parish. You are almost, I have noticed, self-supporting! I feel that your gifts should have wider scope. Will you not, dear Jessie, accept the office of President of our Ladies' Auxiliary?'

Mrs McCree had been very well brought up, but she gave a little gasp – was it of relief? Was it of horror? Of disappointment?

It woke up the Vicar, who, looking at his watch, said in his usual direct way. 'Th-th-three o'clock! Your man will be at the door by this, I th-th-think.'

Rising, he went to look.

Yes! There was the Bishop's Brougham.

And, after the customary ritual common to the departure from a seldom-visited friend's house in the country; the search for the lent book; the borrowed coat; the bestowal of packets of sandwiches, of three pumpkins, two dressed chickens, a sucking pig, a dozen eggs; the assembly of the family: 'And – I have added a few bottles of Nyppa wine,' Mrs. McCree murmured, giving them to the groom to stow away in a carriage already packed with gifts. 'I have already sent some flagons to the Governor, and to Mr McWhistle and other friends.'

The early afternoon had not belied the morning's promise.

The sky was just as blue, the sun was just as temperate, the zephyr as discreet; all nature was keyed to the perfection of an autumnal, a mellow, beauty, as the Vicar, his wife, his daughter-in-law (who so seldom appeared), his two grandchildren, Juliet and Donalblain (who was four), accompanied the good Bishop to his waiting Brougham.

His shovel hat was like a mirror, his gaiters exemplary in cut and fit, his apron quietly orthodox, his handsome face urbane, as with precise, undeviating steps he walked down the narrow path – so sweet with cloves and thyme – and seated himself with his customary aplomb, and a gracious expression of gratitude, in his smart carriage, and was whirled away to his Palace.

'I blame myself, Jessie, I b-b-blame myself.' Mr McCree fully realised how disappointed his wife was. 'One rather g-g-glosses such things over! Where an Oxford man is concerned, that is! I q-q-quite forgot that Pussy' (for so he called the friend of his youth) 'had been at Wadham College. Yes! My dear girl!' the Vicar shook his venerable head, 'I should have remembered that the Bishop was a Wadham man. In his day they were all six-bottle men at Wadham.'

Helen Shaw

Singeing the Cockerel

1957

More than a few years ago, one Saturday afternoon, old Mrs Brockieburn stormed her henhouse and hushed the life out of a protesting cockerel, using her husband George Brockieburn's axe. Then after plunging the bird into scalding water she knelt down on newspapers spread over the yard and began to pluck. While Mrs Brockieburn plucked she sniffed and sneezed, and rubbed her itching nose with the back of her hand, but, just when she was ready to singe the cockerel with a taper the front doorbell rang.

'Drat it! Mrs Pringle, and half an hour early as usual. Say I've been resting, Andrew,' Mrs Brockieburn said to her young grandson as she sneaked inside, taking the cockerel to the pantry. Glad of something to do, Andrew, a boy with curls as long as a girl's, opened the door and ushered the visitor into his grandmother's draped and dresden, cuckoo-clocked drawing room.

'A dreadful storm's brewing, Andrew,' said Mrs Pringle, sing-songing through a thin, woebegone nose, and she folded the child in her best black silk arms, pecked his cheeks, and popped a sweetie into his mouth. The skin of her neck was loose and yellow, soft, and mottled with moles like the breast of a thrush. Three hairpins were about to fall from her bag-pudding of hair. 'It's high time they cut off your curls, Andrew,' she said. And the bird in the clock jumped out and cried 'Cuckoo! cuckoo! cuckoo!'

Soon, completely transformed, old Mrs Brockieburn made her entry. Gone the dustcap and bloodstained sacking apron, edged with ticking, she had worn to kill the cockerel. Now she glittered with black sequins. A lorgnette on a purple ribbon, beads, and a golden chain festooned her plump neck, but as if she were in mortal agony she came tottering into the drawing room, shaking her white head and clinging to the arms of chairs for support. I've not set foot outside the house for days, Euphemia,' she lamented.

Tall, tallow-faced Euphemia, wife of Deacon Pringle the draper, bestowed a kiss on her friend's forehead, assisted her to the best chair in the room, the chair nearest the fire, and arranged cushions at her back. 'Such is life, Annie,' she remarked. 'But you look the picture of health, ducky dear,' she added. 'Have you heard what happened to poor Miss Gilkison?' she asked. At the prospect of the post-mortem Euphemia's gooseberry eyes lit up and watered, and her hands trembled with excitement as she loosened the feather boa wreathing her shoulders. Then shedding a tear she peeled off her gloves, finger by long grey silk finger. 'They say . . .' she began, but old Mrs Brockieburn knitted her brows and turned to her grandson.

'Run to your room, Andrew, and shut the window please. It looks very much like rain,' she said, and she gave the sailor-suited child a little push. After that for a long time Andrew stood at his window watching the clouds boiling up into fabulous beasts, until at last he heard his grandmother slowly leading Mrs Pringle along the hall to the front door, saying 'If only you knew the pain I'm having in this arm, Euphemia!'

'Old age, ducky dear. Take care of yourself. What a filthy sky,' Euphemia replied. The front door opened letting in a gust of cold wind, and then was shut and locked, and in his starched, waxed room the child peered out and saw Euphemia Pringle's skinny, befeathered ghost being blown across the lawn like a moulting bird as she disappeared into the stormy night.

But now that the visitor had departed Mrs Brockieburn bustled around and brought Andrew a bowl of bread and milk from the kitchen, white bread cut into cubes like Holy Communion bread, soaked in hot milk and then sprinkled with sugar. 'I don't like the look of the sky either,' Mrs Brockieburn declared, rattling down the blind and pulling a cream web of lace over its inky surface. 'When you've eaten that up, Andrew, off with your clothes. Your bath's drawn,' she said, and she left the child with his supper. No sooner had he emptied the bowl and struggled out of his clothes, out of every blessed stitch he had on except his socks, than he heard a tremendous hammering on the wall of the house.

'Thunder,' shrieked Mrs Brockieburn. Something fell and smashed to smithereens in the kitchen. The next second old Annie Brockieburn came careering up the passage pulling light cords and, heralded by a violet flash of lightning brighter than day, burst nearly swooning into Andrew's room, her face white as chalk. 'Heaven help us. George, George!' she shrieked, clutching her chain and beads. 'Woe, woe!' she moaned, the poor wretched creature, and then she whirled her naked grandson along to the bathroom and dumped him into the bath with the socks still on his feet. But before he managed to lisp his indignant protest, thunder again hammered on the walls of the wooden house.

'Save us and preserve us, why doesn't George come home?' wailed Mrs Brockieburn. Beside herself with fear unholy or holy she lifted Andrew out of the bath, ran with him to the dining room and hid on the crimson carpet under a great round claw-footed mahogany table, then found refuge for a while from the thunder among the folds of plushy curtains hanging in the hall, and finally came to rest in the pantry. 'Woe, woe! God is angry,' groaned old Annie, going down on her knees on the cold stone floor beside a tin of eggs embalmed in slimy looking snow. And loudly she blew her nose, basting it with tears so that it shone like an end of melting candle. 'Woe to the wicked! Woe to the wicked on earth,' groaned old Annie. But at last the thunder sent to try the spirit of Annie Brockieburn rolled away into the distant hills. When she got up off her aching knees she saw something she had clean forgotten – the pink and shadowy form of the cockerel lying on a cracked plate in the safe, where she had put it when Euphemia rang the bell. 'Andrew, bless my heart and soul, Andrew!'

Not only the sight of the cockerel, but the sound of her shivering grandson sneezing his head off brought Mrs Brockieburn back to earth. 'Your figs and senna, Andrew,' she said, reaching out for the jar, and when the child had eaten figs and senna for the good of his body, and for the good of his soul, Mrs Brockieburn tucked him into bed and put out the light. 'Sweet dreams,' she whispered. Then leaving him alone in the dreadful dark she returned to her pantry to singe the pin-feathers of the cockerel.

'Upon my word, woman, what a smell of burning in this house,' said George Brockieburn when he came home after the storm.

Eleanor Dark

Serpents

1959

It would be pleasant to believe that Science, when it grouped snakes under the name of Squamata, was indulging in a spot of imaginative whimsy, for the most conspicuous thing about these creatures is their manner of locomotion, and for this no more aptly descriptive term than squamatous could possibly be invented. But imaginative whimsy would, of course, be a very improper thing for Science to indulge in, so we must regretfully accept the fact that the word refers to their scales, and not to their movements.

All the same, it is the erroneous interpretation which will probably linger in our minds, for the attitude of most people to snakes is less scientific than emotional – an attitude which, we suggest, dates from the very earliest recorded association of man and reptile. We do not wish to harp unduly upon the Garden of Eden, but it naturally keeps on popping up, for the events which took place there set the pattern for much that goes on in the Lane, including the uneasy relationship between ourselves and representatives of the order Squamata.

It will be remembered that when sentence was passed upon Adam and Eve, the Serpent also did not escape uncursed. Indeed, grim as were the words which condemned our first parents to swink for ever among thorns and thistles, they seem almost mild when compared with those which so terrifyingly pronounced doom upon the Serpent. UPON THY BELLY SHALT THOU GO, AND DUST SHALT THOU EAT. Appalling! The mere sound of it is enough to chill the blood – and that, apparently, is exactly what it did. When there is added the further decree of perpetual enmity between men and snakes – the former neglecting no opportunity of bruising the latter's head, and the latter making a dead set at the former's heel – no mystery remains in the fact that the generally prevailing good-neighbour policy in the Lane here comes up against a formidable psychological obstacle.

It is true that the sons of Adam are inclined to be tolerant of carpet snakes, and when they see one basking in the sun, spread out along the tops of the pineapple plants, they will usually allow it to slide away with its head unbruised. But the daughters of Eve, on their own ground, are less forbearing. 'I know it's harmless,' they will say, gazing with distaste at eight feet of richly patterned reptile squaming indolently across the verandah, 'but I just don't *like* snakes, and I *will not* have them in the house, so you just get a stick while I watch it.'

What makes the gentle sex so savage is precisely this habit snakes have of entering houses. The women allow them to be a fair enough hazard out of doors, but resent finding them in the bath, or lying along the kitchen mantelpiece behind the tea and sugar. And who can blame them? It was surely not unreasonable of Myra to be riled when a copper snake fell out of Aub's shirt as she picked it up? And when Marge, having found a four-foot Black crawling into the top drawer of her dressing-table, seized a broom and violently pushed the drawer shut upon it, can we fairly censure her for gazing in sombre triumph at the corpse which Bruce presently extracted, and flung out the window? As she said indignantly: 'I was just going to get a pair of socks, and I might have put my *hand* on it!'

Note the form of this protest. She does not complain that it might have bitten her; she merely has the horrors because she might have touched it. Had it been a carpet snake, Bruce would undoubtedly have made the asinine, and typically masculine reply that it wouldn't have hurt her if she had; but this point of view is totally irrelevant, for what women feel towards snakes is far less fear than aversion.

Consider, too, the illuminating lament of Heather Arnold when she perceived a sinuous shape stealing across her bedroom window-sill, which is at least ten feet from the ground. 'I can never,' she cried passionately, 'get used to the way they *climb*!' This is the very voice of evicted Eve. In the time of innocence before the Fall, she must often have watched, with admiration and pleasure, the Serpent elegantly weaving its way through the top-most branches of the Tree of Knowledge – but now her deepest instincts are outraged by the sight of a snake climbing anything. They clamour that the wretched thing should stay down on its belly in the dust, for thanks to its machinations she was landed with domesticity, and if she must work out her sentence, should it not do likewise? Insult, she feels, is added to injury when it assumes the perpendicular for the purpose of invading her own exclusive domain.

So snakes of any kind are for it once they cross the threshold or the window-sill, and the poisoners are for it anywhere, unless they can make a fast getaway. Not that they don't have a good run for their money indoors, where there are so many things for them to retreat behind, or beneath, and one cannot swipe at them so freely. The one that go under Amy's wardrobe stood siege for nearly an hour, defying the united efforts of the family to eject it. But Biddy effected what is unanimously allowed to be the neatest capture in the history of our community, and she did it all by herself, too, for Tim had gone to Rothwell, and she was alone in the house, except for the children. Admittedly, the snake played right into her hands by entering the fridge when she had it open for defrosting; but she slammed it shut like lightning, and turned on the current, so presently hibernation set in, and when Tim came home the creature was too drowsy to know what hit it. This execution – so clean and simple – was in marked contrast to the bloody massacre which took place under the Dawsons' bed. That invader was a really big Black, and when Aub and Myra came in and switched on the light, it decided to make itself inconspicuous by stretching out under the bed, close up against the skirting-board. This was not a bad idea at all, and would have been successful if it had not passed between the wall and one leg of the bed, leaving its tail protruding. The tail was not noticed however, though Myra must have almost trodden on it when she arranged her pillow; the discovery was made only because Aub stood on one foot while he removed his shoe from the other (a thing which Myra is always telling him he is no longer young enough, or slim enough to do), lost his balance, and bumped the foot of the bed, thus pushing its head hard against the wall. In such circumstances even the most stoical snake must have betrayed its presence by a convulsive movement.

For once there was no question of you-watch-it-while-I-get-a-stick. The thing was caught, and the only problem was how to hit it. If you have ever tried to hit a snake which is pressing itself closely into the angle of floor and wall underneath a low double bed, you will understand why Aub's efforts merely made him very hot, breathless and profane. At one stage he even advocated pulling the bed away, and letting the ruddy so-and-so escape, because at this rate it would be time to rise before they got to sleep. But Myra vehemently opposed this suggestion, and in the end they both crawled under the bed, and Myra pinned its head against the wall while Aub cut its throat with the bread-knife.

The harmless snakes are pretty safe out of doors, though. (Of course the word 'harmless' is rather ambiguous, and the affair in the Griffiths' fowlyard shows that there are limits to the indulgence of the menfolk.) Packing-sheds are, by tradition, sanctuary for carpet snakes, and Biddy just has to put up with the one that lives in theirs. She tries to find consolation in Tim's assurance that it saves him pounds a year by eating the rats which would otherwise eat his wheat and laying-mash; but all the same, when she is packing pines she keeps a wary and hostile eye on the squamiferous coils looped round the rafter above her head.

Sue Griffith used to be the weak spot in the women's united front, for she is by temperament disposed to love all creatures – even snakes. This may have been all right, perhaps, for St. Francis of Assisi, but it is an extremely difficult stance for farmers to maintain. We are surrounded by so many creatures, nearly all of which seem to exist for the purpose of impeding or frustrating our efforts to make a living. We may manage, with a good deal of determination, to subdue our feeling of malevolence towards Brother Leech, for he merely sucks our blood, and we can spare a little of that without actual damage to our bank accounts. We can forgive the Brother Tick who confines his attentions to ourselves, but we are implacably hostile to the one who attacks our cattle. And it calls for a greater degree of Christian forbearance than even Sue can command, to love Brother Borer, Brother Fruit-fly, and a host of other brethren whose activities contribute so largely to our financially depressed condition. It is also discouraging to observe that while we strive conscientiously to love as many creatures as possible, they make no attempt to love each other. Sue frequently finds herself troubled and embarrassed by

Brother Snake's penchant for devouring Brother Frog, and by the rapacious appetite of Brother Hawk for little Sister Chicken.

Nevertheless, she used to insist – before the episode in the fowlyard – that she quite liked snakes. There is reason to suspect that she has deliberately taken her eyes off some which Henry has bidden her watch while he fetched a weapon, thus conniving at their escape; and she always used to speak heatedly about the wickedness of slaying poor, inoffensive carpet snakes. She declared indignantly that no snake had any real wish to intrude, and, when it accidentally did so, was only too anxious to withdraw without causing any trouble. No one argued about this, but the other women said it was not the point; when she ganged up with the men about carpet snakes, and even sabotaged operations against more dangerous Squamata, they took the view that she was letting the side down.

But all that is changed now, and we shall tell you why.

One evening, when Tony and Aunt Isabelle, escorted by Jake, had gone to a birthday party at the Bells', Sue and Henry settled down for a nice, peaceful evening. Henry went to sleep in his chair with an open book on his knee, and Sue went to sleep in hers with some knitting on her lap, and the nine o'clock voice of the A.B.C. composedly reporting the sensations and disasters of the past twelve hours, fell upon two pairs of happily deaf ears. But although tidings of floods, tornadoes, revolutions, murders, juvenile delinquencies and exploding H-bombs failed to disturb their little nap, an ominous outburst of noise from their own backyard brought them both to their feet in a split second.

Seizing a torch, Henry dived out the kitchen door, with Sue close upon his heels. In happened to be one of those quite abnormal occasions when neither moon nor stars glorified our sky, and the night was inky black. From the henhouse came the kind of hysterical clamour which only panic-stricken poultry can emit. The ray of the torch, sweeping to and fro, came dramatically to rest upon a long, dark, shining, gliding shape. 'Holy smoke!' exclaimed Henry. 'What a whopper!'

At the same moment, the whopper (which was next morning found to be, by Bruce Kennedy's precise measurement, twelve feet two and a half inches long), realised that escape rather than banqueting must now be its aim, and, doubling swiftly back upon itself, sought egress from the fowlyard by the same hole in the wire netting which had allowed its entry. Perhaps it takes some time for the rear end of so long a snake to grasp what its front end is up to; at all events, there was a brief, but fatal hitch in its execution of this manœuvre, owing to the fact that it found the hole still plugged by about three feet of its own tail. This seemed to confuse it a little, and Henry, summing up the situation in a trice, called out to Sue: 'Grab it while I get a stick!'

Much may happen in the human mind during a second or two of crisis; indeed, almost the only thing which does not seem to have occurred to Sue was the advisability of retorting: '*You* grab it while *I* get a stick.' Instead, she apparently condensed into one tick of the clock enough anguished spiritual indecision to have kept Hamlet going for a year. To grab, or not to grab? That was the question. On the one hand were her Franciscan principles – for not only was this a poor, inoffensive carpet snake, but it was doing everything in its power to demonstrate the truth of her contention that Squamata in general only want to get away. To grab, therefore, would be shocking. On the other hand, she was, as custodian of the chooks, aware that her egg-money would be gravely jeopardised if poor, inoffensive carpet snakes were to consume her hens whenever they felt so disposed. Not to grab, therefore, would be silly.

And yet – quite apart from Franciscan benevolence – she hesitated. For although she is always handling such things as frogs, mice, spiders, crickets, worms and lizards, the only snakes she had so far handled had been dead ones, and she was now astonished to discover in herself a strong, emotional disinclination to obey Henry's command.

Meanwhile, Brother Snake had got his problem worked out, and his head was posted beside his tail, superintending its withdrawal from the hole; a bare two feet now remained outside the wire. Henry, rummaging about on the wood-heap for a suitable weapon, was holding the torch in such a manner that its light played only dimly and fitfully over these proceedings, and the smoothly flowing movement, half-seen, of dark and shining coils filled Sue with a sudden abhorrence which brought her vacillations to an end. She perceived that if she did not stop the tail from going in, the head would speedily come out, and for more reasons than one, this was clearly undesirable. So she took a deep breath, jumped forward, and grabbed. It was comforting to know that Henry was just behind her, and, presumably, now armed.

'Oh, blast,' said his voice in a tone of mild annoyance, 'this stick's rotten. I'd better go and get the brush-hook.'

And with these words he departed, taking the torch with him.

Darkness closed about Sue and the Thing which she was grasping. Perhaps, since it wrapped itself so fiercely about her wrists, we might say with equal exactitude, that it was grasping her. At all events, they were joined together in a struggle as fearful and implacable as man's struggle with sin. There was a terrible sound of thudding and threshing; the earth vibrated, the fence-posts creaked; something splintered. The wire netting strained outward under the writhing weight hurled desperately upon it; then it strained inward as Sue, dragged forward, lost her footing and fell against it on her knees. Awful thoughts jostled each other in her mind. It was very old netting. It probably had other holes in it. There might be one quite near. It could give way anywhere. She might suddenly feel great, cold, powerful coils encircling her. She scrambled to her feet, dug her heels into the ground, and pulled with the strength of terror. The Thing in her hands – the hard, chilly, muscular, squamiferous Thing – leapt and wrenched and dragged against her. She could hear its other extremity banging against the bit of corrugated iron on the gate. Perhaps it could get under the gate . . .?

She screamed.

'What's wrong?' called Henry from the packing-shed.

'What's *wrong*?' shrieked Sue between gasps of panic and exertion. 'Have I got to stand here all night hanging on to a bloody snake's tail?'

'Calm down, old girl,' said Henry rebukingly. 'It's only a carpet – it's harmless. Tony must have left the brush-hook out somewhere, damn it. Don't let go, will you?'

'I *can't* let go!' yelled Sue furiously. 'I *daren't* let go! It might be coming out under the gate! How do I know where its other end is? Oh! Oh, Heavens! *Hurry up . . .!*'

The last words were a squeal of despair, for the Poor Inoffensive had changed its tactics. It had now anchored itself firmly to a post of the fowlhouse, and was settling down to a really serious tug-of-war. Sue lifted her voice in frantic appeal.

'Quick! Oh, Henry – *quick*! It's pulling!'

'Good grief,' cried Henry disgustedly, 'what do you expect? I'll be there as soon as I find this ruddy brush-hook. All you've got to do is hold it.'

Sue's plight was now dire indeed. She gave ground inch by inch. Her hands, dragged down and down, touched the earth, scraped along it, and came up against the wire. In darkness atavistic memories stir, and ancient evils breed. Never, since the first day of the Creation had there been a darker darkness than this. She was no longer grappling with a mere marauding reptile, but with a monstrous and malevolent force out of the time when time itself was young, and innocence was first imperilled . . .

Well, it is remarkable what powers of exorcism may reside in a four-and-ninepenny Woolworth torch. 'Hullo,' said Henry, approaching behind a blessed beam of golden light, 'got you down, has it? Never mind, just hang on a few minutes more – I've got the brush-hook.'

When the execution had been accomplished, and the still writhing remains flung upon the wood-heap, Sue stumbled up to the house on legs which wobbled slightly.

'What's the matter?' enquired Henry when he saw her in a good light. 'I thought you liked snakes?'

Sue has not told us what she replied to this, nor have we asked. There are moments in every marriage when husbands must expect to hear, in precise and forceful terms, just what their wives think of them.

Sue is still kind to spiders, and goofy about frogs. She still pleads for mice, and declines to tread on scorpions. But she no longer rushes to intervene when there is a scurry out of doors, and someone calls for a stick. To her, nowadays, as to all true daughters of Eve, every snake is The Serpent.

Janet Frame

Jan Godfrey

1961

I am wanting to write a story today. I am wanting more than anything to write a story. I am sitting on my bed with my typewriter, typing words that are not a story. I have my new slippers on, the ones my landlady gave me for a present, red and blue with butterflies on the toes, and I am wearing my new watch which says ten past two. Perhaps I will be here for years and years and there will be no story.

Last night I lay in bed, and thinking kept me awake so that I could see the moon through the window lighting up the scribbles on the wall beside me. A little girl made the scribbles with an H.B. pencil that I lent her, round and round with her fat dirty hands, and afterwards the landlady said My best wall-paper, O my best wall-paper.

I should have got up in the middle of the night and written my story. I am like a dead person typing now.

I am looking at my room. It is small, but not as small as the other room where I felt like Juliet lying covered with a bell jar, and put in the tomb with of artificial flowers that are made into wreaths and the dead people.

I can see some of my books from here, the poetical works of Robert Browning. I am up on the second storey where I can look out of the windows and know the stars coming and going and the meteors shooting and the clouds forming. I have always liked the poem about the Grammarian. I can see my book of Giotto that was given for an art prize. Here is the age of Innocence by Sir Joshua Reynolds, Study it carefully and then write an appreciation. And here on this board is Don Byrne's Hangman's House. Write a critical survey of this picture forty minutes girls, and remember this is an exam. They gave me Giotto for a prize, poor Giotto with the sad thin mountain sheep and St. Francis blessing the birds, and the crucifixion with the people beating their heads and crying.

There is nothing so real as the funny twisted people out of Giotto.

I have no pictures on my wall yet. There are only the bunches of blue and pink flowers on the wall-paper. In the old bedroom where I slept as a child there were asters round the top of the wall and we played I spy with my little eye something beginning with . . . you can never guess, it's high up. It was the asters, dark blue and red, like flowers on Grandma's coat, all round the top of the wall-paper.

But I have wandered from my story. I knew I would wander. I will write about the girl who sleeps in the room with me.

This story came last night. Everything is always a story, but the loveliest ones are those that get written and are not torn up and are taken to a friend as payment for listening, for putting a wise ear to the keyhole of my mind.

hell
me
me
me

I am writing a story about a girl who is not me. I cannot prove she is not me. I can only tell you that her name is Alison Hendry.

Alison Hendry. Margaret Burt. Nancy Smith. We cling to our names because we think they emphasise our separateness and completeness and importance, but deep down we know that we are neither separate nor complete nor very important, nor are we terribly happy (Alison Hendry, Margaret Burt, Nancy Smith, children) playing mud-pies by ourselves in a tiny backyard when other kids are out in the big playground over the fence, Look what I've made, Race you Charlie, Tell tale tit your tongue shall be split and all the little puppy dogs shall come and have a bit.

You can tell that the kids in the playground haven't got names. Charlie? It's a poem of himself and everybody else, an awful poem certainly but a sincere one because its unconscious and a beautiful one because What the heck you've got my football, Garn you're meant to be the enemy, Die go on die. It's a terrible thing to be commanded to die by Charlie or anyone else.

You see I have wandered again. I was a teacher once. I taught at a school here in the city, prepared lessons, heard tables and reading and people of other lands, talked in a casual way about Robert Bruce and the Spider and King Alfred and the Cakes, and smiled at the kids when the inspector came, and spent all dinner-hour putting stars on neat work, it was an orderly life really.

But I got tired of it and I went to the hospital in Dunedin. It was warm the night I was admitted. I was frightened to go to sleep in case I would miss something, so I lay there watching a night nurse roll swabs of cotton wool and swot anatomy and read Philip Gibbs, and then somebody gave me two brown pills with medanol in them, sleep sleep and then wake up fresh in the morning.

But I got tired of that hospital and they took me to another one. It was like being a shipment of something and going from port to port, and it was all the more exciting because I had never been to sea before. I could look through the porthole (being a shipment I was down in the hold) and all I could see was green and blue wave and some of the whales out of the Forsaken Merman, sailing 'with unshut eye round the world for ever and aye'.

I got tired of that hospital too, but they didn't send me away at once. They gave me porridge and toast for breakfast every morning, and bread and butter for tea every night except Sundays, when it was bread and butter and gingerbread, and for dinner I had semolina and silver beet.

I didn't stay in bed in that hospital. I walked all over the building, but not outside because there were locks and wired windows. I walked into the bathroom where the taps were locked because you never know, and there was soap with N.Z. Gov. written on it, and a list of directions for bathing printed on the wall, A patient must be... An important rule of this institution is... Nurses should pay strict attention to the fact that... It is understood that on no account must...

And I walked into the linen room with its labelled shelves, drawers, chemises, smocks, canvas jackets, I tried on a canvas jacket just to see, and Ivy who was another patient said Bugger bugger hurry up. Ivy swore, every time she spoke she swore, it was like having pickles with every meal.

But I have wandered again. I am really writing my story of Alison Hendry. I have written two pages of it now, but I cannot prove it is Alison, nor can I prove it is me, though I would like to, for a long time ago my mother and the rest of the family sat round the table at home, and my mother put on her fairy-tale voice and, running her finger under the words in her red-letter Bible, said slowly and softly Prove all things, but now I can prove nothing. I cannot even prove me nor Alison Hendry who shares my room nor the rest of the world that is named and labelled and parcelled.

Alison Hendry, Margaret Burt, Nancy Smith, children.

Alison, I have told you, shares my room. She is sitting on the bed over there, tall and dark and quiet like a big mouse and mouse-like, dressed in grey. I am too tall what shall I do I am too tall my head pokes forward my shoulders hunch I knit here in secret with my yellow needles going tap-tap tap-tap. I do not read the books you read, I have came to the city to be a tailoress, I have never been away from home before. I wake up in the morning and say to you It'll be sunny it's warm and you say Yes it'll be sunny and it really is warm, and that is how we are, two people touching in the dark and then moving away.

I live in the country where the gorse is in bloom now and the new lambs wag their tails as they suck and the calves have knobbly knees like in a cartoon, but that is not what you know. Some of the lambs are dead in the frost and the ewes make a forlorn bleating in the clean sun and the orchard is white.

I am learning to be a tailoress. I sit and sew and do not speak. I have never slept in a room with another girl before. When I undress I turn my back so she cannot see me, and I slip quickly into bed drawing the sheets over my body to hide myself, and in the morning I wait till you have gone into the bathroom before I get out of bed, and when you come back into the room smelling of Protex and Kolynos I blush because I am timid.

I speak all the time though there are not many words to my speaking. I am in the city. At five o'clock a traffic inspector holds up his white gloved hand at the Exchange, people go into shops and buy and get parcels wrapped for them and say thank you, and people get on trams and sit silent because they are frightened, and their smiles are chilly but only because they are frightened.

I tell you I speak all the time, I say Why are they afraid, but what will I do I am too tall when I went to school the teacher said Shoulders back don't poke your head.

I am afraid. I am neither separate nor complete nor important. I have never been away from home before. My mother has a picture of the stag at bay over the mantelpiece, and a photo of Baden Powell and Lieutenant Colonel Robin V. C. There is a new tractor on the farm. In autumn the stooks stand arm in arm in the paddocks. Magpies settle in the gum-trees and cry 'quardle oodle ardle wardle doodle', at night you can smell the milky smell of the sheds.

I have lived in the country all my life our school caught fire once and we cheered and we had to go to the hall for lessons my mother is on the institute giving talks and bringing mottoes for afternoon tea and having her name in the paper, Mrs Hendry presided, my mother is on the Institute, buying little frilly cake-papers cake-papers, cake-papers.

My name is Alison Hendry.

A. E. Batistich

A Place called Sarajevo

1963

The launch chugged up the river. Mrs Zelich sat on a coil of rope in the prow, but Ketty stayed in the cabin with Mr Zelich. He kept his eyes on the river and said little, but once he let her take hold of the steering-wheel and showed her how to guide it. The river was still, except for the swish-swash of the launch's wake. The shore seemed far away – already it was becoming shadowy with evening.

They came to Paroa. The launch slowed down and Mr Zelich jumped out and called to his wife to throw down the rope. She tossed it over and he caught it expertly and tied it to the jetty with a loose knot. He called to Ketty to jump and he would catch her. Mrs Zelich gathered up the parcels she had bought and told her not to be frightened. It would be all right. She climbed on to the rails, shut her eyes and jumped. Mrs Zelich did the same, only when Mr Zelich held out his hand to her she didn't take it.

They made their way down a track through rushes and toi-toi, and when they came to a clearing, there was the house. It wasn't much of a house. It wanted paint and bright curtains and the grass around it cut. Then it might have been all right. But it had a kind of mystery, sitting there in a hump with the cabbage trees ringing it round and a huge lump of flax at the door.

They went inside. Mr Zelich put down the sack he was carrying and lit the lamp. The wick flickered palely in the half dark, throwing out huge shadows that made the walls seem alive and menacing. Ketty found herself wishing for the comfort and security of the gas mantle glowing in the rooms at home. Mrs Zelich had taken off her coat and hat and hung them on a nail. 'Take yours off, too,' she said to Ketty, 'and I will show you where you are to sleep.' She came close to her and smiled and stroked her face. 'It is nice to have someone here to talk to,' she said slowly. 'It is so lonely on the farm.' She spoke in the old-country language. Ketty followed her to a room that led off the kitchen. It was small and dark and the paper hung dankly from the walls. There was a bed in one corner and a dressing-table. Mrs Zelich brought in some sheets and made up the bed. They were fine linen and embroidered with red initials.

They went back to the kitchen. Mr Zelich had lit the fire. It burned brightly, and Ketty felt more cheerful when she saw it. A kettle was boiling on the stove and there was some soup heating in a big iron pot. It smelt good. She was hungry and hoped they'd have tea soon.

Mrs Zelich spread out a newspaper on the table, took some knives and forks and spoons from a box and put them down with a plate for each place and a loaf of bread on a board. She lifted the lid of the pot and looked at the soup. It must have been ready, for she then took out three deep plates with green leaves on the rims, and ladled the soup into them. 'You sit there,' she told Ketty and gave her the one chair in the place. She and Mr Zelich sat on boxes.

The soup was good. It was cabbage with a flavour of bacon. Mr Zelich drank his noisily and held out his plate for more. Mrs Zelich took sips at hers, but she couldn't have liked it, because she soon pushed it away. Ketty finished all hers. Then they had some boiled meat with tomato sauce.

When the meal was finished, Mr Zelich stretched out his legs and lit a pipe He asked Ketty if she had had enough. She nodded. Mrs Zelich gathered up the plates and washed them with a clatter in the tin bowl. Ketty found a tea-towel made from a flour bag. She dried the dishes and stacked them up on the bench. Mrs Zelich smiled at her all the time to let her know she was glad she was there. But Mr Zelich said nothing to anyone.

Outside the quiet had taken hold of the farm. Once a morepork called, 'More pork', and another answered. The quietness outside and the quietness inside made Ketty feel frightened again. Why had her mother let her come? This was a funny place. At home the house would be blazing with lights and full of people talking and laughing but it didn't seem as if anyone ever talked or laughed here. She tried to say something herself, just so it wouldn't be so quiet, but no words came. So the stillness stayed broken only by the un-human clatter of the dishes on the tin bowl.

When they had finished the dishes, Mrs Zelich sat down on a box by the stove. She moved the chair over for Ketty and told her to sit down. She smiled gently and took some needlework from a carved box by the fireplace. The box was finely made. When it was opened, Ketty saw that it was filled with linen and bright silks. Mrs Zelich took out a cloth – a beautiful cloth, the work on it half-finished, bright reds and blues and greens in a symmetrical design. Mr Zelich had fallen asleep. The pipe lay smoking in a tin beside him. He began to snore and Ketty felt that even the snoring was some company. It was better than the silence.

Mrs Zelich looked disdainful, but she didn't say anything. She threaded the needle and began to sew, her long fingers drawing the red thread and the green thread into the pattern; her face had a calm beauty bent over the sewing. Her eyes were very dark and her hair was black as the night outside. It was wonderful hair, thick plaits wound round and round the head.

She must have seen Ketty looking at it for she smiled and put up her hand and stroked the hair from her face. Little tendrils had escaped, and they made her look young, and somehow tender. Then she spoke. 'You like my hair?' And from the way she said it, you could see that it was a vanity of hers.

'It *is* lovely,' Ketty answered. 'It must be very long.' And Mrs Zelich took out the pins that held it up, and the plaits fell down and they came almost to the hem of her dress. She twined one hand through a plait, and the black hair and the white arm were beautiful.

Mrs Zelich bent towards her as if she had something to tell that she did not want her husband to hear. 'In Sarajevo they called me *Kossara Dyevoyka*, the girl with the long hair. I would sit at my window, at the full moon, and passers-by would look up and call to me from the street. "*Kossara Dyevoyka*, come down!"'

She put down the fancy-work and her eyes were far away. 'Now I dream about it at night; in the daytime, it is lost in here' – she put her hand to her head, vaguely – 'but in my dreams, my house of white stone with the oleanders growing at the door . . . and the nights smelling of musk . . . and the minarets picked out by the white moon!' Only she didn't say 'minarets' but '*djamiye*', but Ketty knew what they were because her mother often said the word in the songs about the Turkish *Begs* (noblemen).

'Sometimes I wonder if there is such a place at all.' Then she began to cry softly and unhappily. She looked around the room, hating everything that was in it. 'The muezzins call in Sarajevo, but the pukeko and the morepork, they are my muezzins here!' And her eyes became wild and her hands tore at the fancy-work and the tears fell down till it looked as if it had been left outside in the rain.

Ketty remembered all she had heard her mother and the other women saying about Mrs Zelich being strange. Their voices died to whispers there. She remembered the story of the quick courtship and the hasty marriage, the disapproval of the women when they heard that Steve Zelich had come back from his visit home with a Bosnian wife. 'He should have married one of his own.' That was what her mother had said. 'A Bosnian is half a Turk!' It could have come from the pages of a book, not something that happened really. Steve Zelich walking through a street in Sarajevo and the girl, seeing him from the window and knowing him for a stranger by his dress, and called to him: 'Young man, where are you from?' And when he answered, 'New Zealand,' calling back, 'Marry me and take me there!' And Steve finding himself quickly married to the beautiful girl before he knew what had happened to him.

'Poor Steve,' her mother said when she spoke of Mr Zelich. 'A big, plain, clumsy man, but good.' Those were her mother's judgements. It was too much for a child to understand, but she looked at Mrs Zelich crying and wished she had words to comfort her.

But the tears passed and the woman took up the fancy-work as if nothing had happened, and she laughed a little and said would Ketty help her set the dough for the morning's baking. And when they went into the kitchen Mr Zelich woke up and said it was time for bed. 'You go,' Mrs Zelich said. 'I have company for tonight.'

They heard his clumsy movements about the bedroom and the creak of the bed when he got into it. Mrs Zelich took out the flour and the yeast and mixed them in a big pan. She stirred the dough, mixing it gently with her hand, as if she loved it. When it was ready she broke off two pieces. One she twisted into a *kolach* (ring-shaped roll). 'For you,' she said, smiling, 'and this is for me.' Her long fingers shaped the dough, and Ketty saw that it was a manikin she was making – legs, arms, head and all of a man. She set him beside the bread and covered it all with a blanket, the *kolach* too. 'Now we will go to bed,' she said briskly and gave Ketty a candle and told her to be careful and put it out before she went to sleep.

In the middle of the night Ketty wakened. She heard voices from the kitchen. Quarrelling voices. She lay listening for a while, then she got up and peeped through the door. It was the littlest bit open. She saw Mrs Zelich standing in her nightdress with her arms held out to something. Mr Zelich was telling her to come to bed. 'You will catch cold – you will catch cold,' he kept saying to her, but Mrs Zelich took no notice. She kept saying the angry things and started to laugh and laugh and her husband told her to be quiet, she would wake the child, but she wouldn't stop. He hit her on the face and her nose began to bleed. The blood ran down her chin and on to her nightgown.

The fancy-work was lying where she left it and he picked it up and wiped off the blood and threw it on the floor, and there was the beautiful work, with the bright red stains jagging across the red and the green already there, crumpled as if it were a rag. But Mrs Zelich didn't see or care about it. She just stood there, crying in great gulps, her arms held out to the darkened room.

Ketty climbed back into bed and pulled the blankets over her head. There was a world she knew nothing of and this was it. She fell asleep thinking, and when she got up Mrs Zelich was standing by the stove getting the breakfast. Mr Zelich came in from the shed and sat down at the table that still had last night's newspaper on it. Everything looked so ordinary she began to think it had been a dream last night, but when she looked, there was the fancy-work lying on the floor with the blood on it. She tried not to see it, but it stayed there accusing the room.

During the meal she said she was sick and wanted to go home. Mr Zelich looked up quickly. 'Are you unhappy here?'

he asked, but she shook her head quickly.

'No . . . no . . . .'

'Mrs Zelich is so lonely,' he said. 'It would be nice for her if you stayed.' But Mrs Zelich broke in quickly.

'It is lonely here for a child, there is not much for anyone . . . sometimes I think God himself does not know this place.' She said it thoughtfully, not wildly at all. It was just something that she knew.

When Mr Zelich had gone back to the sheds they went to look at the dough to see if it was ready. The bread was a soft, humped roundness, and the *kolach* had risen too. The manikin lay in bloated caricature beside him. It was all put to bake. When it was done Mrs Zelich opened the oven and took out the tray. There were the loaves all golden with baking, the *kolach* and the manikin beside them. 'You have your *kolach*,' said Mrs Zelich. She laid the loaves on a cloth. The manikin she put by himself. He lay spread out on the cloth, grotesque and sad.

Ketty wondered who would eat him, but she wasn't left wondering long. Mrs Zelich picked him up in her long fingers and stroked him, then she began to eat him, legs, arms, head and all – each part separately and slowly. Ketty shuddered. It was like eating somebody she knew.

There was none of last night's strangeness about the woman now. She was gay and even laughed once. 'I will come to see your mother soon,' she said.

But when the cream launch drew up at the jetty and Mr Zelich called out that there would be a passenger she took hold of Ketty, hard, and looked closely into her face and said,

'There *is* a place called Sarajevo, isn't there? Look in your books and tell me when I come.'

Judith Wright

The Nature of Love

1964

Villers-Bret (call it that) was a decayed soldier-settlement from the First World War; by 1938 few of the farms still existed. Some had been taken up into others more prosperous, some had gone back to bush, their tottering gates propped back, seedling eucalypts growing over their entrances. On one of the last remaining apple-orchards, tucked away under the shadow of Mount Jameson, I had discovered the Schwarzkopfs.

They had not been there long; less than a year. We seldom went out towards Mount Jameson; it was at the back of our place, and Villers-Bret was at the end of a dying road. But one hot day in November, someone had dropped a match on the other side of the mountain ('those careless idiots over on Spencer's Creek'). It was dry, and windy from the north-west, and the grass and low scrub on the flanks of the mountain were sapless as kindling. When the fire appeared over the spur, the wind was already blowing blackened leaves and ash in our direction.

The fact that the Schwarzkopfs' farm also lay in its path was, for us, incidental. Their cleared flats were the best place to fight it, since the creek was accessible and a break could be burned back there, in the windless shelter of the mountain. My father, my sister Helen and I galloped there over the short-cut through our back paddocks, that had once led to Villers-Bret's store, when that was still in existence.

When we reached the farm, a man was standing on the verandah of the four-roomed house, coughing and gripping the rail with one hand, a hand with what seemed, for a farmer, curiously long white fingers. My father shouted at him, gave him one glance as he replied, and went on along the creek. 'New here,' he explained to us tolerantly; 'these blasted migrants don't know enough to keep themselves alive.'

At the fence, however, we found Lisa. She was standing

beside three old kerosene-tins of water that she had carried from the creek, and a pile of wet bags, and she was waiting for the fire to reach her. It was perhaps a quarter of a mile off and burning well, and she would not have had a chance against it.

At first she refused to let my father light the grass to burn a break, thinking that he was merely abetting the intentions of the fire. I had to explain things to her while Helen and my father did the work.

She listened carefully and nodded. 'I see now. It is very good of you to come to save us.' As I knew that our corn-cultivation two miles down the creek was in fact our first consideration, and our stock and fences the second, I was then ashamed. She set to work and helped with the break, and by the end of the afternoon we had turned the fire into the swamp country where it could burn itself out without doing more damage.

However, incidentally to saving our corn and fences, we had saved the hundred old apple-trees on the Schwarzkopfs' farm, the six cows that Lisa milked, the old horse that she guided in front of the single-furrow plough, and the little cultivation where she grew potatoes and pumpkins. These things had kept the Schwarzkopfs in food and supplied mending-cotton and skeins of wool, with which Lisa criss-crossed their clothes until they had become little more than web-work of the neatest convent darning.

Accordingly she took us back to the house and fed us with apple-strudel from the earliest windfalls, chokingly sour, and thick cream and coffee, while Eric talked to my father and played host. I saw her large eyes shadowed by her cheekbones, as she moved about above the kerosene-lamp on the table, and her capable hands from which she had scrubbed the charcoal with a worn old floor-scrubbing brush on the tankstand outside, and fell in love on the spot.

Not with Eric, though he was the beauty of the pair; but with Lisa. It is necessary, at seventeen, to be in love, but there was no one my own age to be in love with. I was filling in time at home, waiting to be allowed to take a job somewhere in the city (seventeen was considered too young for a girl to leave home), and meanwhile teaching my young sister while the boys were away at boarding-school. Helen, of course, fell in love with Eric; I could see her across the table, watching his pale wax-clear profile, presented with a slight upward tilt of the jawbone and sidelong glance. He had a tumble of hair and moustache as glossy as a horse-chestnut, and a way of playing a few bars of something on the old propped-up piano they had brought with them (a scrap of *Träumerei*, a snatch of Wagner), that was obviously meant to ensnare.

My instinct, however, I see as I look back, was right. There was no profit in Eric; but to love Lisa was to receive. And I was hungry; at seventeen one is always hungry, to be taught, to be admired, to be loved.

Lisa's broad cheeks, her tilted anxiously-smiling eyes, her wide hard hands and the dragged-back hair in a madonna-bun on her nape, all proclaimed that she had no time to waste on herself. Unlike Eric, all she did was thorough and complete; she left no corners unswept, her cows were thoroughly stripped, her cowshed cleaned, her pumpkins and potatoes weeded. And when, on my Sunday afternoon visits, after the dishes had been washed and put away and the coffee drunk, she finally sat down to her piano, she would square her elbows, draw a breath, and without pausing or looking up would plunge into, through, right to the end of a Bach fugue, a Franck prelude – something, anything, earnest, methodical and somehow noble.

If that had been all, perhaps I would not have sat so long to listen; but Lisa always had something more than one expected of her, still to be given, and before long the piano would change its song and the lightest and most delicate notes would come pouring from it as smoothly as though Mozart himself had been playing.

Eric, who never finished anything, would lie round for a while listening, ordering 'Play the E minor rondo, Lisa,' but would get up after a while and stroll off somewhere, to eat apples or whittle wood. As for me, I had not enough of Lisa to waste it, and would sit on the cane chair that had lost all but two canes in the back, and watch her and her hands.

Those hands could do anything: milk a cow, scrub a room, sew that exquisite convent-sewing (she had darned my shirt so that my mother exclaimed at it), pour out Mozart or cut noodles with perfect accuracy from the big sheet of paste they had just rolled into mathematical evenness. I received so much at those hands, during the time I knew them, that it was no wonder I poured my unspeaking love towards them whenever I watched.

'Well, Alice,' Eric would say wickedly, tossing his shimmering hair, 'I hope we'll see you next Sunday. Poor Lisa, she never sees anyone, you know, except you – I don't mean to say that you aren't anyone – and of course me. But I don't count. Do I, Lisa?' And without looking at her (they seldom seemed to look at each other), he would pick up her hand and kiss it, lingeringly, directing the gesture at my jealousy, not at Lisa's smile.

Eric was well aware of me, and naturally did not like my imperviousness to his beauty. Every foolishness I let slip was picked up, whittled to sharpness and at last, perhaps weeks later, lodged exactly in some sensitive part. Unpractised in the rivalry of love, I could not return these pricks, and looking back I think it served me right.

As to how the Schwarzkopfs had come to Villers-Bret, why they had bought the little dying farm from old John Perkins (who always referred to them as 'the Huns', having been one of the original soldier-settlers there), I never asked. Simply, they were there, and in being there served the purpose of my seventeen-year-old heart, which in its pursuit of experience and relationship was in reality as cold as a frog's though I did not know it. I watched Lisa with the devotion of a dog watching a bone, and listened to her playing, and saw and heard nothing at all.

My mother and father, however, were much more interested in these questions than they were in Eric and Lisa themselves. It was said the Schwarzkopfs had come from South Australia – lots of Germans down there – and had brought with them enough money to buy the farm, tied in a spotted handkerchief in the bottom of a suitcase. This was so scandalous that my mother refused to believe it. Money belonged in banks or in cheques, and to carry it round naked, as it were, was like parading the street in one's underwear.

'Some people will say anything. It's just because they *look* a bit out of the common. But it's certainly a queer place to come to – those Continentals generally stick together. Don't they ever tell you anything, Alice? Goodness knows you've been over there enough lately to have their whole life-histories.'

'I don't ask,' I said, immediately making a virtue of this. 'I don't ask because it's their business. I hate all this country-town inquisitiveness.'

'Hm; more likely you never thought of it for yourself. Well, they can't have been here long, good as their English is. I notice it's her job to do the work outside, ploughing and milking and all, and that's regular peasant-style German for you.'

'She only does it because she's stronger than Eric. He's been ill.' Secretly I criticised her for doing so much for Eric, and putting up with his shiftiness over work; but I did not want anyone else intruding into that secret world which contained Lisa, and thus worked by its own laws. In fact, I wanted Lisa to myself.

By this time, Lisa was teaching me music, as well as giving me her friendship and kindness, and her Sundays – the only day, I now believe, she had for anything except hard work. When I reached the farmhouse it was always clean, the dinner cooked ready, even if it was only potato-cakes and cheese and noodles. Eric would loll at the table, eat half-complainingly, sneer sweetly at the presents I had brought for Lisa. Certainly they must have seemed to him, and perhaps to her, almost mockingly useless – a home-made lavender-bag, a hand-embroidered handkerchief, a pot of jam – and the Schwarzkopfs were not getting richer.

Winter set in hard and cold, and the westerlies began early. Dry cold air poured over the landscape and searched through the thickest clothes like snow-water; the cows cropping dry scraps of grass grew as bony as clothes-racks under their staring coats. My mother began to worry about the Schwarzkopfs, and sent joints of meat from the Friday killing over with me most Sundays. As far as I could see, it was all the meat they ever ate.

Once, Lisa was out when I came; she had gone far up the mountainside, and came home staggering under a sheaf of grass she had cut herself with an old scythe. It was mostly blady-grass, and very dry, and when she put it in front of her favourite cow Gretel, Gretel took no notice. She was lying near the bails, not far from her calving, and very weak.

'She will not eat,' Lisa said. She bent over the cow for a moment, then stood up and folded her arms. 'Eric wants to kill her, for meat.'

'I've brought you over some mutton,' I said. 'That'll be better than killing poor old Gretel. You may be able to save the calf.'

'There is no milk. The other cows are almost dry. It is better for the calf not to live at all – I suppose.'

'But you can't kill a cow near calving,' I said. 'She may have a heifer – and then if the weather changes, and it rains, you might keep them both.'

'The weather will not change,' Lisa said. 'I feel there is much worse to come. But no, I am not dreaming of letting Eric kill her. If she dies, she must die in her own way, not in his. I will not have her killed.'

It was not the first time I had suspected a note of hostility, almost of spitefulness, in her tone when she spoke of Eric; but this time it was unmistakable. There was also another note, of woe almost, that must have slipped in unawares because of her physical tiredness. She might perhaps have been asking for an ear into which to tell a story; appealing for a friend.

I am ashamed to remember how quickly I withdrew. Behind the high-cheekboned Madonna into whom I had turned her, a real Lisa suddenly looked out, a face grimacing in pain, a wry mouth that might suddenly call for help, or demand some acknowledgment in me of a common humanity. I had nothing to give such a woman, though from her hands I had taken a great deal. Instead, I pulled from my saddle-bag the parcel of meat my mother had sent over, and gave it to her with a few light self-protective phrases. Lisa looked at it for a moment in silence before she thanked me.

Inside the house Eric had lighted a big fire; the stove was hot and the kettle singing. We had mutton chops and baked pumpkin and coffee. Eric was very gay, flushed with the heat of the fire and the dry air, his eyes sparkling. The warmth melted me towards both of them; we seemed to sit in fellowship heightened by the angry sound of the wind outside.

'Just for once, Lisa,' Eric said suddenly, 'a bottle of the white wine, do you think? This is good food, and good meat requires wine. We have been cold all day, and now we are nearly warm again; let us celebrate Alice's kind present and our good fortune.'

Lisa nodded and opened the cupboard. I could not help

noticing how little was in it – the other half of the pumpkin, a few potatoes, a pound or two of flour, a tin of treacle. There were two bottles lying on their sides on the bottom shelf, and she brought out one and opened it.

Though I was seventeen, I had never tasted wine, which my mother regarded as faintly sinful, my father, probably, as cissy, since he came from Scotland and drank whisky when he drank at all. I thought of refusing, but in the end took the thick glass that Eric filled for me.

'This is the first meat we have had for days,' said Lisa cheerfully, confirming what I had suspected. 'It is a pity Eric is such a bad shot. He missed a rabbit on Wednesday – and we were very anxious for that rabbit.'

Eric threw another big log on the fire. 'Lisa is only rude; she cannot shoot at all. And my hands were frozen to the rifle. I thought Australia was always warm and sunny, Alice; the world is always destroying my illusions.'

He laughed and talked, Lisa answered more cheerfully than usual, and I took sip after sip of wine and felt the heat of the fire making my face burn and my eyes sting. I began to feel myself truly out in the world at last, in Eric's sophisticated company, for he was talking of things I had no more than heard of: of the ski-runs of Tirol, of the Rhine running under ice, of vineyards and vintages, of the famous wine-makers of the hills near Bonn, of castles and islands. Leaning intimately on the table, we began to sing, first in English, then Lisa began a German song and went to the piano, and Eric joined in. The bottle was empty and I was half-asleep. I put my head on my arms and listened to their voices which mingled lightly and sweetly, and tears came into my eyes at the beauty and worth of life and Lisa, and the beauty and worthlessness of Eric. I fell asleep, warm and melancholy, to the sound of their singing.

When I woke, however, I felt I had been awakened by something unpleasant, though I did not know what. They had stopped singing. Eric stood at the window, hands in his pockets, staring out at the bare flats and the trees struggling with the wind. Lisa was playing, stubbornly and rather heavily, a Bach fugue.

'I must go,' I said, 'the pony will be getting cold and it's dark so early now. I'm sorry I went to sleep and missed the singing.'

Lisa closed the piano and got up. 'Please thank your mother for us, Alice, for the good meat.'

'Yes,' Eric said, 'please thank your father too. It is lucky for us we have such kind rich neighbours.'

'We're not rich,' I began, but thinking of how much less rich the Schwarzkopfs were, I was silent. I determined to come over as soon as I could and bring them something more – a cake, some preserves, whatever I could beg from mother.

Lisa looked at Eric with her head bent forward dangerously, but said nothing. She came with me to the yard, where the pony was tied, and together we examined Gretel the cow. She lay there as before. I knew that a really weak cow will lie sometimes for days, unable to give birth, but I did not say so. I helped Lisa to tie an old rug made of sacks around her as well as we could, and rode home in the half-dark.

Next day, Helen had a bad cold, and was made to stay in bed and miss her lessons. I was free, and went with my father riding round the paddocks, looking for weak cattle to be moved into the nearer paddocks, where they could be given a little extra hay.

After two days, Helen's cold was no better, and we had still one paddock to go through. It was the far paddock, bordering the short-cut to Villers-Bret.

'I'll look through them tomorrow,' I told my father; 'it won't take long.' I would go to the Schwarzkopfs afterwards and take Lisa a plum-cake.

I had asked my mother about this, and she had promised it rather reluctantly. 'You're getting too involved with those people, Alice.'

'Pooh,' I said, 'involved! It's just that they're having a hard time of it. I can't take music-lessons without paying something for it.'

There was a gate from the paddock on to the old road, so I packed the cake in a sugar-bag on the saddle, and rode straight out there in the morning. There was a lot of timber left in the paddock, which made it hard to muster, but left the cattle plenty of shelter from the wind. I quartered it systematically, but found few cattle; evidently they were huddled in the little hollow near the road gate, above which a curving ridge ran, hiding the valley except from its crest. When I reached the top of this ridge, I could see into the hollow as if it were an amphitheatre. In this amphitheatre a very strange scene was taking place.

The cattle I was looking for were there all right, and a small mob of sheep as well – my father's best weaners. The cattle were staring, heads all one way, as cattle will at anyone unexpected. The direction of their gaze led me to the unlikely figure of Eric, dressed in a tweed knickerbocker shooting outfit, and hidden from the road by a clump of trees. He had dropped to one knee, and was just steadying his gun on his mark, which was one of our fattest wethers, feeding a little way from the mob.

It was like a sudden gush of cold water, making me gasp, yet react very fast. I could not possibly let him shoot; nor could I withdraw, for in a moment or two he would look up and see me clearly on the ridgetop, not a hundred yards from him. In any case, I was righteously enraged, remembering the cake in the sugar-bag balanced on the pommel of my saddle; and I felt a strong sense of property in those wethers, which I had known since they were lambs.

I tried to shout something, choked, and cleared my throat. However, Eric heard me, and with a violent start looked up. I had no way out but to ride over.

'Out shooting?' I decided to say carelessly. But the words refused to come. Eric must have known from my expression that I had clearly understood the scene. To my complete stupefaction he now raised the rifle again, but this time pointed it at me.

This was absurd. It was reasonable enough for people to steal a sheep occasionally; I had never found anyone doing it before, but I knew it often happened. But nobody threatened other people with rifles – that was behaviour quite outside reality. I had been strictly brought up, and I knew that you did not allow the business end of your gun to point at anyone, even if you knew perfectly well it wasn't loaded. Accordingly, I did not believe it was happening, which must have made me appear brave and in charge of myself, when in fact I was not so at all.

'Put that thing down, Eric,' I shouted; 'you'll get into trouble handling a gun in that silly way.'

Eric, however, had clearly lost his head. Pale and sweating, he in turn shouted at me. 'You will tell no one of this, Alice. Nobody at all. Promise, or I will shoot. Swear you will tell nobody.'

I saw with purely practical alarm that his hands were shaking violently. 'You point that thing at the ground,' I ordered.

Slowly Eric lowered the gun. 'I know you will be sensible, Alice. I was going to shoot a sheep – I admit it. It was for Lisa. She is hungry and she needs good food. We have no money, and Lisa is going to have a baby. You understand?'

'A baby – Lisa?' I quite forgot about the gun.

'You understand? A man must kill for his wife and child.' Eric sounded so pompous that I began to laugh. He looked at me with real dislike.

I found all sorts of considerations balancing themselves in my mind. 'All right,' I said at last, 'I won't say anything – that is, if you leave our sheep alone. And other people's too,' I added, thinking of the Simmondses nearby, and their ewes in lamb. 'I'll bring Lisa what I can, and you can practise shooting rabbits – there are more than enough of those to keep you going. As a matter of fact, there's a cake in this bag for her now. You can take it home with you. I won't say anything.'

'Particularly not to Lisa? She wished nobody to know . . .?'

I was wondering if Lisa had any idea where Eric was. It was the first treacherous thought I had had about her, and before I could stop it another came, which was that we had not counted those sheep for some time. 'I'm mustering these sheep,' I said falsely, 'and my father will be wondering where they are if I don't hurry. You'd better get on home.'

I went round the sheep and took them up the ridge, while Eric walked back, dragging the gun and holding the cake-tin, and looking, in his knickerbockers, extremely foolish and out of place. This pleased me. However, when I had counted the sheep and found that none were missing, I began to remember the round black hole in the rifle-barrel, and how decidedly it had been directed at me. I thought my mother had been right in saying that I was becoming too involved with 'those people'.

So on Sunday, instead of going over for my music-lesson, I cut out a dress, and pretended I was too interested in getting it tacked and fitted, to want to go out anywhere. That would have lasted all the afternoon, except that by three o'clock I heard voices in the garden, and looking out saw Lisa talking to my mother.

When I went out, rather reluctantly, I thought she seemed shy with me. No, she would not stay for a cup of tea; she was late in getting home and the cows must be milked; she had only come out for a walk and to thank us for the cake; Eric would come home and wonder where she was. I had never heard her talk like this, with a shrill edge and uneasily, and my mother too looked at her thoughtfully.

'Did you really walk all the way?' I said. It was a good six miles across country.

'I had a lift, with Mrs Carter; she was to town going. But I wanted to walk, it is good exercise.' It was not like Lisa to invert her sentences, either; and I thought this was no time for her to need more exercise, when she worked all day in any case.

'Of course you mustn't walk home,' my mother said. My father had taken the old utility truck, our only vehicle, over to the bottom paddock dam, where the cattle were beginning to bog as they came in to drink, and corduroy had to be laid. It would be a long dirty job, and he would not be back before dark.

'I'll catch Helen's pony and my own,' I said, 'and we'll ride home, and I'll lead the pony back.' She protested earnestly, but I was already on my way to the horse-paddock. Besides, I was curious to know why she had come.

She was not at all a good rider, but once in the saddle she stayed there like a sack of flour.

'But you should not have done it. I would have enjoyed the walk, and the cows have so little milk now that the milking is soon over.'

'What happened to Gretel?' I said.

'She died a few days ago. The calf was born dead, too.' Lisa looked at me sideways. 'Eric was angry. He said I should not have kept him from killing her; she would have made good meat, but it was spoiled.'

'Oh?' I said, but the subject seemed rather dangerous. I changed it. 'I'm glad the cake arrived safely.'

'It was for that I came to thank your mother – and for all the other things, of course. I did not expect to see you.'

'Why not? I was coming over today, but I had a dress to make...'

'We cannot expect you to come every week. Eric was lucky, meeting you on the road that day. He tells me it was quite an accident.'

'Well, yes.' I felt my face going hot and a giggle coming, at the word, but I choked it down into a cough. 'I thought he had better take the cake. I was – out mustering sheep.'

Lisa had turned half round and was watching me, and her face too was burning. 'And – did you have much to say to each other?'

I examined this for a moment, since the way it was spoken seemed to hint a trap. How much did she know?

'No, we just said hello. He was out shooting, but he – hadn't shot anything when I saw him.'

'You are sure you did not intend to meet him?' She was jerking nervously at the pony's mouth, and he began to prop and sweat.

'Don't do that, Lisa, it's bad for his mouth.' This was awful. I was now certain that she knew or guessed what he had been doing. 'No, indeed, I didn't know he was there. If I had, I mightn't have – well, you know I never can find much to say to Eric.'

'Oh, no, you never say much. But you look at him. I have seen you.'

I was struck as if by lightning; turning round to look at her, I found myself breathing through a wide-open mouth. My image of Lisa and of the world cracked across and rearranged itself drastically. Was that why she had come over that afternoon? Had she wanted to see if I was out – with Eric?

'Lisa,' I cried, 'you're completely wrong. If I've come to see you, it's only been for – for you.' She laughed sharply. I began again. 'Look, Eric did tell me one thing, and – and it pleased me a lot. About – about the child.'

She let out a small cry; her eyes turned black and her face white. I had evidently not helped the situation.

'I'm sorry, I forgot – he told me not to tell you I knew.' I stammered on, for she was crying now, large incredulous tears. 'But why don't you want people to know? I think it's lovely – I'm so glad you're having a baby.'

Lisa dropped her head and began to plait her fingers in Robin's mane, but she had stopped crying, with a gasp. She rode on in silence.

'He told you that I was to have a baby,' she said at last. 'You are sure of that?' I nodded, deep in distress.

'It was a lie. Now you must tell me. He would not have told you a lie unless he had some purpose. What had you – what had he done?'

My throat swelled with panic and I said nothing. She pulled up the pony and dropped the reins altogether, crying out, 'Alice! What had he done?'

I could see no way out, and I got off my pony. While we sat together on a log, and the ponies cropped dry grass in the cold wind, I told her how we had met.

She thought it over for a while, and then she began to laugh. I laughed too, since there wasn't anything else to do.

'You have told me,' she said at last, when she had stopped laughing and so had I. 'Now I can tell you. I owe you that, since all the while I had suspected you and you were only being kind.'

'I wasn't!' I exclaimed. 'I came – I come because I want to. I come for you, because you're so – good to me.'

'Now you are being kind again. You won't have to bother any more, because we're going away.'

Wind stung in my eyes and my lips were cold.

'When? It will take a long time to sell that farm.'

'We won't trouble. We can borrow enough money to go back where we came, and there's the piano. But first I must tell you.' She took a long lock of her hair, that had come out of her bun, in both hands, and quite calmly began to pull it. Some of it came out. I watched in horror.

'Eric is German; I am Swiss. Eric is married, but not to me – I think not to me. No, wait. He married his cousin, a Jewess. He too is Jewish, partly Jewish.' She pronounced it Yewish, so that for a moment I did not understand what she was saying. 'They had a baby.'

I winced at this.

'We had known Eric for years, for my father keeps a hotel in Geneva and Eric was a traveller, you know, a commercial traveller, in German wines. One day he knocked at the door;

he asked could he stay for a little, there was trouble. We knew what it must be.'

'Hitler,' I mumbled.

'He stayed awhile; then we told him, if he could get his wife and the baby out, we would take care of them, because the news from Germany was bad. He went. When he came back, he was crying and weeping; we could get nothing from him. I was sorry for him. Eric is good at crying . . .'

'But surely . . .'

'No, wait. Then he told me his wife was dead, the baby dead. He was afraid for himself. Would I marry him and we would go away together? I was very sorry for him; I married him in Geneva. My father had cousins out here; he gave us a little money, and we came out to Australia. We got work in the vineyards, with my people.' She paused for a while.

'Then came out another man, a man who knew Eric. When he saw Eric in the vineyard, he said to my people, what are you doing with this man? He has betrayed his wife into a concentration camp, and his own child, and to save his own life, and he ran away and left them.'

My breath stopped as at the climax of a horror-picture.

'We went away from there next day, with our money, and found this farm because it was cheap. Eric says none of that is true, all is lies. But Eric too tells lies. Who am I to believe? Eric is a coward, I have found that out too. Perhaps he would even have killed you – I don't know. But the child? No, no!' she exclaimed, forgetting me altogether and twisting her hand in her hair with an extraordinary gesture. 'He could never have done that to the child!'

We sat there for a long time, not moving.

'Now we are going back,' she said. 'I have known for a long time that we must go back. We will try to find them. Perhaps they are not dead.' She untied Robin's reins from the fence and gave them to me. 'I can accept no more of anybody's kindness. I shall walk home and tell Eric we are going. You must take the horses back; look, almost is the sunset.'

'Please ride him the rest of the way, Lisa,' I begged, 'it's another three miles and it's so cold. I should never have told you. I can't forgive myself.'

'Goodbye, Alice. I am sorry I did not trust your kindness,

and I have told you such things. You must forget them.' She slipped under the fence to take the short way home.

I followed her beseechingly, stammering about the pony. The tears on my cheeks were cold as snails.

She took my hand through the barbed wire, and turned away. I watched her set off, then turn back again.

'Do you know what is the worst of all, Alice? It is my wickedness. I hope they are dead – both dead.'

She walked away through the thin trees, the tress of hair blowing and her bun coming out of its pins.

After a while I rode home again. I felt as though I had climbed some very steep cliff, following painfully after Lisa, but from the top I could now perceive something of the nature of love. It was the last thing she gave me, and I did not see her again. That was in July, 1939.

Thelma Forshaw

The Grand Passion

1966

'Come in, dear – we are all ready and waiting for you,' Mrs Nesbitt carolled, meaning, of course, Zelda supposed, the afternoon tea and general air of expectation – the way people graciously clear a space in their lives for a visitor and his tidings.

Zelda had not seen her aunt since she was fifteen; now she was twenty-two and going the rounds of her relatives like a town-crier, telling of her recent betrothal. She had considered the matter with her mother, and they had decided that the clan was too ill-assorted and the feuds too subtle and complex to bring all together at an engagement party. It was not wholly because they were of Irish extraction and might fight. It was just – well, it was better to see them separately, that's all, Zelda's mother pointed out rather sombrely. She did not want a donnybrook in *her* home.

Zelda held up her left hand and, smiling, wiggled a flashing ring-finger before her aunt's eyes like a ticket of admission. Mrs Nesbitt's mouth opened and her eyebrows lifted in the impressed way expected of her. She admitted Zelda and led her into the sitting-room where infra-red strips were glowing on two walls, warming the air, and Mr Nesbitt sat in a crouching position on the divan, his elbows on his knees like a statue of The Thinker. He stood up and shook her by the hand after she had flashed the ring at him, too.

'Hooked someone, eh?' he said, then: 'What does he do?'

Zelda said that he was a mining engineer and was away at present mining – or engineering – whatever it is such people do. Neil had never really explained it to her and she did not know. One day she would ask him about it, she believed it was essential for a wife to understand a man's work to a certain extent . . . she trailed off vaguely. She was not sure why.

'How delightful you are,' Mrs Nesbitt said bitterly, as she wheeled up the tea-trolley laden with cups and scones and cakes. 'I'm pretty certain that's how men prefer one – not *quite* understanding what they are up to. *Not* knowing what makes them tick.'

Zelda's eyes widened at this sudden swath of analysis her aunt had cut through the pleasant, sleepy Sunday afternoon where she was ready to tell, with a pardonable touch of triumph, all about her prize and his capture. She took her cup with a murmur and glanced at her uncle. He had the look of a mandarin. Bland and inscrutable. She thought of a burglar with a stocking pulled over his face, blurring the features. She could not remember if he always looked like that, or if he had just pulled the stocking over his face when his wife spoke. He had grinned peculiarly on her arrival. Crookedly, as if trying to convey ruefulness through the welcome.

'Is he mean?' asked Mrs Nesbitt, squatting down on a pouffe and balancing her cup and saucer on the points of her knees.

'Mean?'

But it had not been a question – Mrs Nesbitt wanted to pronounce: 'Romance cannot live with meanness. It dies the death.'

Mr Nesbitt stuck his little finger into one ear and shook it rapidly as if *vibrato* speech affected his eardrums.

'No, he's not – he's, in fact, very –'

'*He* used to send me to his sister's clothing factory when I needed a dress or coat and there I had to choose 'seconds' or remnants at a lower price than if I went to a store like other women. We hadn't been married a month. The honeymoon barely over and I mad with love of him!'

Zelda was aghast. 'Mad with love' was an expression she had never heard spoken before. Still, it was true that 'mad with love' and 'remnants' did not sound right together. She imagined that 'seconds' ought to come later, a year, two years . . . perhaps after the children.

'It's not as if he was poor,' said Mrs Nesbitt. 'That one could understand. No, he was never *poor.*'

Mr Nesbitt smoothed his balding head and tried not to seem like a robber-baron. However, the idea did not repel him and he could not avoid a somewhat sleek look. Zelda felt he had secretly received as a compliment what was intended quite otherwise.

Her aunt said: 'We are now living in opposition to his old regime. Now that he 'has it', as he calls it, he would like me to dress up and show off. I refuse. It's too late. And I will not be bought. Furthermore, I will not advertise his success for him.'

And, indeed, Zelda noticed that her aunt was wearing a pair of baggy old slacks ('seconds' she wondered) and a scruffy sweater, her hair pulled back into a queue with a rubber-band. She did, in fact, have a what-the-hell look. It was a shame, as she had heard that her aunt had been rather stylish once.

She drifted off a little, gazing at the white blaze of her ring, then said, because she wanted to talk about Neil – that was what she had come for, after all: '*We're* very much in love. I know it's true love because I've never felt the same with anyone else.'

This seemed to act as a detonator, for her aunt burst out: '*No one* could have had more than we had. I fell for that man hook, line and sinker.' Her voice trembled and deepened. 'I gave him everything. Everything. Ah, God, I thought it was going to be so wonderful.'

Mr Nesbitt hunched over his spread thighs and sipped his tea with eyes squeezed shut as if unnerved even by the memory.

'But what happened?' demanded Mrs Nesbitt, as if Zelda might know. 'Mammon! Mammon! Mammon! That was *his* god – not Eros. The pursuit of hard cash. Business. Business. Business. And I on fire for him.'

Zelda had never heard the words 'on fire for him' spoken either. She had read an old book of her mother's called *The Sheik* at one time, and her aunt seemed to be emanating rather sheik-like feeling.

'He was always deep and secretive,' Mrs Nesbitt went on. 'I think that is what got me in. Attracted me – you know. He *seemed* very passionate –' she paused significantly – 'a bit of the actor in it, I often think now. But I'm not taken in any longer. I prefer celibacy. But there was a time – we would lie with our lips glued together each striving to drink the other in. Oh, don't tell *me* about sex.'

Mr Nesbitt looked up alertly, ears pricked , like a dog hearing the rattle of the biscuit-tin. Then subsided.

Zelda flushed, and her aunt went on fierily: 'That's what he's lost. That's what he traded for his miserable business. Don't get the idea we're past it. The heart has its reasons,' she said cryptically, despite having let the cat out of the bag.

Zelda said with great calm and an air of commonsense – she was always good at critical moments – 'Neil and I are very compatible.'

She had not intended to challenge, but her aunt pounced: 'Compatible!' She laughed. 'Oh, ho!' Then said, 'There is compatible – *and* compatible. Those who get on and those who *prefer not to get on.*'

Zelda digested this profundity with a quick glance at Mr Nesbitt who, ever so slightly, lowered his eyelids at her, perhaps inscrutably as he once did to her aunt, enthralling her with his mystery. She had the feeling that he specialised in silence and inscrutability, preferring to communicate by mime. She did not find this particularly attractive herself – she liked a man to 'come straight out with things'. She wondered if he had teased Mrs Nesbitt into her grand passion with his mystery. If so, her aunt had fought back, all guns blazing, to breach the wall. It had apparently come as a great blow to her that an inscrutable man could in the end be so *mundane* as to choose business instead of spending his life romantically mystifying her. Her aunt had yearned while Mr Nesbitt totted up figures with absorbed satisfaction.

Zelda said peaceably, 'We believe, Neil and I, that tolerance counts a great deal. Fortunately, we both like the same things. We share the same feelings, so –'

'*No one* could have had more than we had,' Mrs Nesbitt retorted. 'We were complementary – I, the outgoing one, he reserved and introverted – not to say *sneaky*,' she qualified, replacing with scorn her old enchantment.

'That's often a good combination,' Zelda said tactfully. 'The attraction of opposites. Only, Neil and I are very much alike.' She found herself sounding apologetic.

'Alike, eh?' Mrs Nesbitt seemed to consider this with grim tolerance, then she waved a finger, Zelda was not sure at whom. 'Better a dinner of herbs where love is than a stalled ox without', and before Zelda could think of a polite response to this: 'Make no mistake, I love that man!' Mrs Nesbitt said, pointing.

Her husband cringed.

'But he has had to realise that spiritual values come before the material. I have had to teach him. He is learning it slowly and – mark my words – *painfully*.'

Zelda, by now acclimatised, said tranquilly: 'Of course love conquers all, and Neil and I find our little differences just melt away when we –' she dropped her eyes and smiled warmly. 'Well, we are very much in love – romantically in love,' she added, perhaps to correct a false impression, or with a touch of reproof.

Mr Nesbitt, condemned to spirituality for the materialism which had spoilt his wife's grand passion, looked wistfully at this gentle girl who would never, it seemed, offer a man more than he could tackle.

'A dinner of herbs,' repeated Mrs Nesbitt, 'than a stalled ox without. I've said it to him down the years. Now he offers me a stalled ox.'

Mr Nesbitt looked surprised.

'But *I* say I don't want your bounty – I have had to pay too dearly for it.'

Zelda looked at her admiringly and would have liked to commend her principles, but just then noticed Mr Nesbitt peeking hungrily at her bare knees, and she drew her skirt down as far as she could and said quickly, with faint defensiveness, 'We are being married in November. You're both invited. It's at St Adrian's. An all-white wedding.'

'I was married in a miserable registry office,' her aunt flung at her. Zelda felt like a capitalist reproved by a communist. She said, 'It's just a simple wedding. Only two bridesmaids.'

'I had no bridesmaids,' Mrs Nesbitt went on communistically. 'And a so-called honeymoon locked up in a flat for which he had paid key-money – locked up because he thought if we went away someone might come and squat in it. I was not a honeymooner but a *caretaker*.'

'We've bought a block of land at Seaforth,' Zelda said very gently, 'but it will be some time before we can afford to build on it.'

'But the whole point is this –' Mrs Nesbitt stood up, her slacks bulging below the knees where they had stretched. She collected their empty tea-cups. 'The thing holds together like steel. No one could part us. No one on earth.'

Mr Nesbitt looked doubtful.

'I shall love him till I die in spite of everything. *That* will show you the power of *mature* love.' She nodded one upmanship at Zelda. 'When you have no illusions left, when it has all been stripped down to the bare bones, and there it is still – shining like the Curie's minute speck of radium –' she lifted her face ceilingwards exalted, while Mr Nesbitt, miming wry puzzlement, scratched the back of his head.

'See my hand.' She extended her left hand. It was bare of rings. 'Lost in the surf years ago. Never replaced. Same with anniversaries. They mean nothing to me. What is the point when *you know*.'

Zelda did not think she would enjoy getting quite so far down to bedrock. She turned to Mr Nesbitt to ask why there were no rings. He said, 'I have offered her an engagement ring, wedding ring, eternity ring – the lot. All brand new.' He seemed haughty with affront.

Mrs Nesbitt gave them both a triumphant glare as if they had ranged themselves (albeit hopelessly) against her merely by exchanging a few words. Fiercely, Medea-like, she gazed at them. Mr Nesbitt looked upward with raised brows, his eyes bulging with wonder. Zelda thought of a bird and snake rapt in mutual fascination. Feeling extraneous, she considered if it might be time to go.

'Wait!' cried Mrs Nesbitt. 'There's something I want to give you.' She vanished into some other room, while Zelda was left to gaze uncertainly at her uncle, who lowered his eyelids at her again inscrutably, without effect. It seemed to devastate only Mrs Nesbitt.

Mrs Nesbitt returned and said, 'Stand up.'

Zelda and Mr Nesbitt both leapt to their feet.

'Not you,' she said, waving him down. '*Never* you,' she added significantly, thrusting him back into his cell. She held out to Zelda a silver disc suspended from links on either side by a thin silver chain – a disc the size of a cent on which were inscribed curious characters which for some reason Zelda took to be Arabic. She nervously asked her aunt what they meant. She herself felt they might well mean 'Abandon hope all ye who enter here'. Mrs Nesbitt pursed her lips and, holding the disc between two fingertips, suddenly spun it before Zelda's eyes. The rapidly spinning disc clearly spelled out I LOVE YOU and, as it ceased to spin, once more resumed its indecipherable markings.

'Take it for luck,' urged Mrs Nesbitt cynically. 'I forget where I got it – I've had it so many years. It's of no value to *me*.'

Mr Nesbitt looked chastened, even crushed. He had given it to her as a courtship gift twenty years ago, in the days of the grand passion. Pure silver, too.

Zelda allowed her aunt to fasten the silver chain around her neck and deftly drop the disc behind the collar of her frock. She felt uneasy . . . even itchy.

'Thank you very much,' she said, 'but are you sure you don't want it?'

'Why should I want it? What is the need for signs and symbols when you *know*? It is no use to me. It means nothing when you have extracted the essence.' As if love had been a marrow-bone she had gnawed through.

Zelda took up her handbag and murmured good-bye to her uncle, who got to his feet and scraped them at her in farewell, a man condemned to spirituality.

Mrs Nesbitt drove the girl before her through the hall with brilliant smiles: 'Good-bye and good luck – and I *mean* good luck.' Zelda wondered at the fury of her farewell. She had come to display her ring and to recount the lore of young love, but her aunt had, instead, showed her the lean and stoic gleanings of what people tend to call 'an unhappy marriage'. 'Look! We have come through!' she might have shouted, flashing the badge of a wounded veteran, finer than any engagement ring.

Zelda turned, as well as she could with Mrs Nesbitt close on her heels, and waved towards Mr Nesbitt's robber-baron face hovering in the background. She went away feeling thoroughly trumped, not to say routed.

Lyndall Hadow

Act of God

1967

It was two o'clock, the night alive with moonlight and a warmth that breathed up from the gentle hill country of their part of the Great Southern, when Jenny's mother stopped the car at the gate that led from the road to the first paddock of the farm. Jenny opened the gate, her mother drove through, Jenny closed the gate, adjusted the heavy chain. All her father's gates, solid and trustworthy, had chain fastenings; over the years they wore grooves in the jarrah but they held. Only an act of God would demolish a gate that Marmion had built and chained. As a child she had not been able to handle the heavy chains and her father had made a small gate here for her own use. Even then, it would have been easier for her to slip through the five-wire fence, but a sense of loyalty to her father forbade this. The school bus would be waiting, classmates at the windows calling for her to hurry, the driver lighting an impatient cigarette. She would come panting to the small gate, open it, close it, fasten it carefully. Her father had said that a fence was to keep stock in, a gate for people to go through. Neither schoolmates nor bus drivers would prevail on her to question his wisdom.

Now, so many years later, at the Marmion farm, no one came to or from the road on foot; the small gate was no longer in use though kept, like all gates on the property, in good order and repair. 'Who knows,' her mother sometimes remarked, 'but you'll have children of your own going to school from here and they'll need a small gate.' But as she drove through tonight and Jenny followed, neither gave it a thought.

When you are young, to wake in the quietness of the dawn, to know you are under the same roof as your father, means you wake with a warm comfort wrapping you around. Your happiness is such, as you lie in your small white bed looking out through softly blowing curtains, past the firm, solid trunk of the she-oak to the open door of the shed where Father's car, expensive and important, is garaged, that you lie still, very still, while the feeling of comfort and warmth, a soft, pink feeling, creeps up from your toes and laps you around. Your eyes are fixed on the polished sleekness of his car and you know that he loves you more than he loves it, large and important as it may be. You know that Father thinks you are the most intelligent, most lovely person in the world, he knows you can drive the car even if you are only nine years old, and this will be the first time you have ever been allowed to and when his life is threatened by great danger it will be you who will sit up behind the wheel and turn the key and put your sandalled foot on the pedal and drive him away from it, drive him (just you and he will be together) away, away to the end of the world and over the edge, into the valley of soft gold light. You dream on and then you sleep again and when you wake, this time you throw off the bedclothes, grope for your slippers under the mat where Lassie had rounded them up last night; you drag on your gown and run to the kitchen. You must not miss one moment of this wonderful day. You are home from school, long holidays stretch before you, days of delight, every lovely hour of them, with Father. First, you will go riding with him.

Father it was who sat you up on your first horse. Mother had said a pony, but Father knew you could handle a real horse so Sultan had come into your life. You rode with Father when you were home, but during school term Sultan had no exercise. Mother did not ride, too old she said, but you knew she did not ride well enough, anyway. It was because of Sultan you met Gareth. Lucky for him, he did not have to leave home to board, there was a boys' public school in the town; being a day boy gave him time to exercise Sultan after school each day, his people were glad to stable such a fine horse and at the week-ends Gareth rode him to the farm and took your place, company in the paddock for your father. Holidays came and you would be home to ride again; that meant Father passed over his mount to Gareth. 'Getting too old for hacking around, the ute'll do me.' You overheard him and Mother. 'Anyway, gives Jinny a chance to have a mate of her own age. He's a good cut of a youngster, that Gareth.'

So! Father approved of Gareth. You would be nice to the lad for Father's sake.

That was years ago and you and Gareth had been mates, mostly, when you were not fighting like brother and sister. Until you both left school. You saw less of each other, now you worked in the city.

As Jenny and her mother drove up from the road gate through the soft-breathing night, lambs snuggled with their mothers; nestlings disturbed by the brightness of the moon-drenched landscape added their twittering plaint to the magic of the hour. Faintly the throb of the homestead plant came over the last hill and as they topped the rise and their headlights beamed on the house gate, there was Lassie-Two grinning her hardly contained welcome; there was the firm handshake, the hearty greeting of her father. 'Here you are Jinny,' and as he took her case from the car, his expected comment, 'So you came down on the train?'

You came down on the train.

When you were young, at most school holidays Father would drive Mother up to the city and you would all come home to Marmion Farm together, except at harvest time in the days when Father grew all wheat. Then Mother would come alone for you or you would travel down the two hundred miles by train and Mother would pick you up at the station in the middle of the night, and ten more miles out you would be home in time to see Father's searchlight shafting across the paddocks, the tractor moving slowly, taking the crop off. When it came about, in the course of years, that you spent your days in the city, that you saw Marmion Farm and Father and Mother and Lassie-Two but rarely, you came down, driving your own car, impatience eating up the miles, you came swiftly over the dark-winding highway that rib-boned over the ranges and unwound into the open plains of the Great Southern, until triumphantly you topped the last hill at home and in the ray of your headlights Lassie-Two's eyes shone, unblinking.

But tonight you came by train. Otherwise you'd not have reached here, you'd have turned back at the causeway. There could have been no going on. Indecision, your constant companion in the last few months, now no longer with you, indecision turned now to a firm resolve upheld by the recognition of your adulthood and the right of every adult to self-determination, your indecision would have returned. Instead of going ahead from the city, out over the causeway, easing your car into the flow that slides smoothly down the first few miles of the highway, imperceptibly fanning out into the quiet streets of garden suburbs, the semi-rural conscience of newly-developed areas, you would have pulled out of the line of homing five o'clock traffic, turned out of the company of those who had reason to be here. Instead of leaving them behind, forging ahead steadily down the highway, heading through the night for home, for Father and Mother, past the first gate, for the heart-moving drive through the paddock, up the rise and triumphantly over the hill to the house gate and Lassie-Two and Father and Mother and Gareth, instead of going ahead with your decision to make your own life, you would have turned off the highway at the causeway, skulked in a side street, watching playing children with unseeing eyes, remaking your decision; you would have turned tail and fled back to Andy, back to Andy the strong, Andy who had taught *you* to be strong.

So you came by train, knowing there was no turning back when you came that way. You came by train, thinking as the miles went by in a wind-carried pandemonium of iron wheels on iron way, not of what you were to say to Mother, not of how you would tell Father you did not agree with him in his choice of a husband for you, not of how you would, in so few short unequivocal words make it known to Gareth himself. You thought as the wheels bore you away from Andy into the desert of the rich countryside that had always, until now, been your haven, your home, your solace, your retreat, you thought, as the wheels drew you away from the warmth, the comfort, the light of the city that now held all of life for you, you thought only of Andy.

It had been a long day.

The sun woke you, fingering calmly through the venetians you had closed against the flashing of neon signs that otherwise lit your flat alternately with red and blue, the sun not to be denied woke you and, as you twitched open the blinds, reminded you, with the sight of your week-end bag packed in readiness, that today you must travel.

Your day went on in its usual well-ordered fashion, nothing hurried, detail on detail. The breakfast on the tray, looking over the city to the purple line of near hills, the note to the woman who need not call tomorrow or the next day or the next to empty ashtrays, wash breakfast dishes, make the bed, throw out wilted flowers. The thanks for the Shell man as, tank filled, he made his embarrassing gestures of servility masquerading as service, the traffic flow down the Terrace, following the white lines, sorting out at the lights, parking by the river, a thousand cars, two thousand, three, in ordered rows, the walk to the office.

Then the smiles, starting at the lifts, the smile as the crowd surged in, up and out, deploying into its boxes. Gilt on polished jarrah; enquiries, general accounting, public relations, staff liaison; through to editorial, past the chrome and glass; chief of staff, general reporters, subs, sporting, women's, agriculture, photographic, to the board-room, to the carpets of the managing editor's suite; and always the smile.

The day went on its ordinary way. You had few duties. Answer the telephone. No, I'm sorry the managing editor is not in, would you speak to Mrs Wallis? The smile for the chairman of directors, good morning, Sir Robert. He likes to surprise the hive before sunrise. The smile for the flower delivery. The managing editor prefers roses, but while he's campaigning to *save the wildflowers* Mrs Wallis would like smokebush and yellow morrison for the suite. The smile for Mrs Wallis herself, protein-waved, her suit Fifth-Avenue inspired. The smile for her newest typist, still smarting under the caustic of Mrs Wallis's self-purging comment on present-day inadequacies in commercial education. The smile for the managing editor himself, iron grey, tailored also from the pages of *Esquire*, last night's Scotch still warring, at eleven, with the morning's liver salts. The smile at cafeteria-time for the copy runners, advertising clerks, the comptometrists from accounts, the secretary to the manager, circulation. Always the smile.

On through the afternoon, yes, Mrs Wallis, no. Yes, the managing editor is out of town, the features editor will take your call, I'll put you through. The smile continuing with you on your ordered way to the last inter-office memo, the switching in of the alibiphone, the pleasantries, at last, with Mrs

Wallis. Going home for the week-end, it's months since I've seen them. The leaving, down from the arid, air-conditioned heights to the sunlit pavements of late summer afternoon. You carry your week-end case, you did not leave it locked in your car, you knew you must not go back to the parking area, you knew you must walk to the railway station and travel down by train.

Andy was waiting for you where he had come off the bus from Uni. Your hearts met even before you looked into each other's eyes, before your hands could touch. You did not smile now, a smile cheapened by today's tawdry use was not currency between you and Andy. You gave him the keys of your car. Use it for the week-end.

But you should let me drive you down. I should meet your people. Be with you when you tell them.

No! You were vehement. No! They'll spoil it. Everything.

You were walking down the Terrace in the lambency of late afternoon sunshine, homing crowds hurrying while you went slowly, week-ending streams eddying you out of their way as you drifted to your favourite tea-shop, Australian oasis of quietness and calm and light that owed nothing to fluorescence, in a desert of continental coffee-lounges, hissing and steaming in chromium and colour lavishly spread around cassatas and granitas, gelati and cappuccinos. You were settled at your table in the cool of the quiet tea-shop. He asked you, why?

They're not going to know about us until we're married.

Oh, magic words. Until we're married. Until the arms enfold, until the blood will sing, until you drown in the darkness stabbed with light, ringing with a myriad of bells, until the blood no longer surges, until you lie calmed and comforted, cherished. Until we're married.

Always, you said, hand shaking, eyes bright, ears throbbing at the exquisite knowledge and its exquisite expectation, always, you said, they've known everything about me. Always they've ordered my life, always known about my friends, always they've contrived and managed and organised my day, yes and my night. Here's your dolly, here's your Milly-Molly-Mandy book, we bought you a Mee's encyclopaedia and there's the stand to keep it on. There's your bicycle, see, we had it painted in your favourite colours. We've had your name down at Girls'

Grammar since you were born; oh joy to be with your friend Dulcie at Grammar, but later, no, no Dulcie, we've decided against Grammar, there's a place for you at Ladies' College. Go there, come here. Your kittens, your dogs, your piano, your ballet lessons, your riding hack, your guided tour through the capitals of the country, your friend Gareth, your personal portable, come here, go there, your friend Gareth and your transistor set a present from Father and Mother, your friend Gareth, a nice young man. We were going to Europe after the shearing but that can wait until you've finished your Leaving. Go, go, you cry inside you. And your friend Gareth, we approve of him, we should have had a brother for you, we left it too late, but there's Gareth, just like a brother, and who knows, some day you might marry him? And now your car, see, it's out there in the garage next to Father's Lagonda and Mother's Austin, we know you like the colour. You don't, you would have chosen grey. And your friend Gareth, we've bought a block of land for you, a view down the river and you can see the city lights at night, you might build there some day; but you want the sea, winds off the ocean and surf-crash through winter; and your friend Gareth, we chose him for you, he's not going on with his studies, he doesn't want to be a chemist and take over his father's business later; no, he's keen on farming, this'll all be yours when we pass on and by then he should be competent to manage it for you.

Always, you say to Andy, always they've ordered my life, my thoughts, they even arranged my job through a friend of Father's. Why did they let me come up here to work? They wanted me at home, Country Women and Junior Farmers. I told them I wanted to come to the city, I'd have to see something different from life on the farm. They never denied me anything, so here I am and they're waiting to know how long before I'll go back and settle down with them and Gareth. Even then they'll live my life. I'm not myself, I'm an extension of Father and Mother.

Andy says, as his hands and eyes farewell her, 'Send for me if you need me,' and the train takes her away.

Now her mother drives to a stop at the house gate. In the gentle warmth of soft-breathing night, the house itself is lit in welcome. Lassie-Two contains her impatience beside the implacable boots of the master at the gate.

'Well, here you are, Jinny, glad to see you, Gareth's just 'phoned, he's delayed in town, he'll be out in the morning.'

This, then, is decision-time, you should speak now but, all your indecision past, you can safely leave everything for the new day. 'I could do with a drink,' you say, 'and is there anything to eat?'

When Jenny marries Andy and goes to live with him in Abadan or maybe Pakistan, Marmion, who never questions his own motives or reviews his own actions, will call it an act of God. Jenny's mother, a very lonely woman who does not speak her thoughts much, will call it privately an act of Marmion.

Kylie Tennant

The Case of the Blond Beast

1967

My cousin George Peebles of the firm of Barnstaple & Peebles often asks me to do some confidential work for him. He is actually the senior partner; Barnstaple used to be, but it is a sad story and the wife never even found out what happened to her jewellery. The firm is still Barnstaple & Peebles long after everyone has forgotten the judge's remarks.

George was sitting in his private office looking self-satisfied. He is a man who values quiet and respectability – no solicitor is perfect – and he will do almost anything to keep a client's case out of court, for he claims barristers charge too much. Because he is divorced himself, George believes no woman should ever have alimony, and many a man has vowed that George has been his best friend when George was acting for the man's wife. He cannot help sympathising with all husbands and sees they are treated more than fairly. So many of his clients are women.

'Who was that went out?' I asked, flicking the dust off the desk with my glove.

'I have just had a run of libel cases,' George said, with a smirk. 'All of which I have succeeded in keeping out of court.'

'A run of them?' I asked, surprised.

'It's funny how you get a run of a certain kind of case, Leonie. Actually this wasn't much more than nuisance value, but I advised them to settle. Just the usual threat, but better to nip it in the bud. Someone writes to a publisher demanding that a book be withdrawn because the hero, whose name is Clive Dogswithers, seduces the heroine in chapter two in a ship's cabin, and the writer can prove that his name is Clive Dogswithers and that he was in a ship's cabin. Not that he ever seduced any beautiful girl there. So he wants all copies, even those translated into braille, withdrawn at once as they bring him into ridicule and contempt, and besides his wife doesn't believe him. So we offer him a hundred in full settlement of any claims and he settles for a hundred and fifty.'

'Think of an honourable man wounded by the laughter of his friends being forced to take a miserable sop like a hundred and fifty!'

'It happens all the time,' George said lightly. 'Of course, in one newspaper office they keep two spikes, one for writs over ten thousand and the other for those under ten thousand. They just stick them on a spike, and ninety-nine point five per cent are never heard of again. That's because newspaper-owners have the hide of zoo elephants. But book publishers always pay to keep it out of court. They are usually men who wear glasses and have indigestion, and they don't want their fellow publishers to know they got hooked. It's like some social disease for a book publisher to get into court.'

Now I know all about the laws of libel in this country. In the early days, when a newspaper was brought out by being nailed to a tree after dark, the editors never spoke of the local governor without using all their stock of asterisks, and the governors spent their time writing in new clauses to the laws of libel until you couldn't mention anyone alive or dead unless you said he was a fine fellow. Since then, of course, the laws have been brought up to date by saying that you can't mention his wife or relations either.

Our conversation would have passed from my mind had it not been that I was reminded of it by the loudly expressed grievance of a young neighbour, an author of promise whose new novel had been hastily withdrawn. We met outside the butcher's shop one Saturday morning and he poured out his whole story. His novel, he said, had no hero because it was a modern novel, but the villain, known as the Blond Beast, was so gruesome that his publisher at Witherspoon Press was for once optimistic about covering the costs of publication. Publishers never make a profit. If they say they will cover their costs, it means they are wildly enthusiastic. The novel was, naturally, set in a Melbourne slum, and the Blond Beast went under the alias of Serle Brodsok.

'I could have sworn I made up that name! Who on earth would want to call himself Serle Brodsok? Now it seems some oaf who claims he is tall and fair – and I suppose villainous –

has written to Witherspoon Press claiming that he lives only three streets away from the scene of the first crime. Can you beat it? My book is held up until they dicker. Months will go by, possibly years. If there's anything frightens a publisher it is the threat of libel. Anyway, Joe Hanks has a weak heart.'

'You say you made the name up?'

'I thought I did. It's just one of those nightmares.'

I moved on, pondering. When you see two white crows, one after another, it gives you a strange feeling. It naturally did not worry me that this young author, whose work I knew all too well, should be prevented from pressing on a shuddering and reluctant public yet one more work that would best be described as 'powerful and stark'.

I mentioned to Ma Jones, as a matter of interest, that I had been glancing through Cousin George's files and could see no reason for the sudden upsurge in letters threatening libel suits.

'After all, George is only one solicitor,' I speculated. 'Suppose there are others?'

Ma did not feel that there was anything which struck her instinct for investigation. 'Serle Brodsok, the Blond Beast,' she mused. 'I like a good read myself, but I can't say I'm rushing in to buy that if it ever comes on the market again.'

Ma Jones sticks to the old Australian fiction in which a drover moves along behind thirsty cattle until they come to water. 'Or something about a sheep station,' she added approvingly. 'Preferably going broke. Nice and peaceful. And maybe a little horse-breaking thrown in. Or building a dam.'

It is surprising how many people share Ma Jones's view of what constitutes literature. Give them a description of a horse and they don't care whether it is a blond beast or a chestnut.

It was a week or so later that Ma Jones rang me up. She had taken a job as matron of a hostel for Asian students and had been busy finding them jobs over the Christmas vacation. 'Wasn't the name of that imaginary villain – the one that sued your pal – Serle Brodsok?'

'Yes. Why?'

'A funny thing happened to one of my students. You see, Serle Brodsok has got to be a gag around the hostel. Anyone who does anything more than usually dumb is called Brodsok. Dropping cups when washing-up made you Serle Brodsok till someone else earned the title. So when Ching Wah saw the name on a cheque, he took notice. Excuse me a minute.'

She came back to the phone, explaining that they were good boys, but they would play their transistors full blast. 'Well,' she resumed, 'Ching Wah, who's a medical student, got himself a holiday job sweeping up in a motor-dealer's yard where they sell second-hand cars. A man came in – tall, fair chap – who handed over a cheque made out to Serle Brodsok.'

'So there really is a blond beast, after all!'

'Yes,' Ma said slowly. 'It interested me. Got me quite curious.'

Our suburb of Balm Point has quite a scattering of professional people. Coming home on the ferry that evening I sat next to a tall, pretty girl called Joyce Pater and asked her what she was doing these days. She was, she said, working for a publisher.

'Have you had any libel suits lately?' I asked.

'It's strange,' she replied, 'that you should ask. They've just called in a high-up legal expert, George Peebles. As a matter of fact we are all quite pleased that the heads are in such a stew. They're beastly to us, so we naturally love it when someone knifes them.' She lowered her voice. 'An author called Spender Esmond – she's actually a little old lady in a wheel chair – turned out this torrid sex story, and now a woman has written in saying it libels not only her but her whole family. It was only released last week. Someone must have seen a proof copy or got wind of it.'

This was the third white crow, and when I reached home I rang Ma Jones.

'Well, it's no skin off my nose if someone is working a racket,' Ma decided. 'I take it this publishing firm is rich?'

'Joyce says they are not only rich but beastly. They underpay their staff and speak nastily to the typists. Witherspoon Press is the name.'

Evidently Ma Jones must have had an interview with the rich but beastly Witherspoon Press, for she got in touch with me later that week. 'Now,' she told me, 'I haven't got a car, Leonie, so I thought you might care to come with me on a cold trail. First call on Saturday is the car-sales place where Ching Wah is working.' My feelings for Ma Jones are such that any time spent in her company is a pleasure. She makes even strangers want to do her a favour.

'Mind you,' she said gloomily, as she settled into my little car with the air of a hen who has found a nest she is not sure about, 'we haven't much to go on. Besides, I've been making some enquiries about Witherspoon Press. The head of it, Joe Hanks, had a flourishing chicken-noodle-soup business. He went to America and studied the latest schemes in merchandising and brought back an expert with him. Then he bought into the publishing game and, as he told me himself, he is completely revolutionising it. In the old days, before he came, Witherspoon Press just sold books here and there. The head of the sales office would stroll over to the pub with the directors, and they would have a pint before going home, talking to others in the book trade who dropped in.

'A good deal of business was done in that bar. Authors would drop in, too, and get signed up. It was all very casual. Then came the take-over bid from this man, Joe Hanks, and Witherspoon Press had a big fire that burnt up all their old stock and most of the building. Hanks put up a twenty-storey office-block on the site, and moved Witherspoon Press out to a six-storey warehouse at Yellow Wattle Bay. He put in a bar in the directors' office where the executives are all expected to drink with the other executives if they want a five o'clock reviver. Then they go right back and work until eight or nine o'clock at night. They never get out of the building.

'In the morning, before work begins, they are all marched in two by two to sing hymns in praise of Witherspoon Press. This Joe Hanks,' Ma said with distaste, 'gave me a song-sheet and asked whether I was interested in a package offer of *Simpkin's Etiquette, The Encyclopaedia of Modern Knowledge and World Affairs* in twenty-three volumes and *How to Raise Your Child to be a Success* in eight volumes.

'Each salesman learns off his patter by rote and is trained to stand perfectly still, resisting all attempts to remove him until he has finished the whole long speech. It would be a pleasure,' Ma added, 'to turn loose on Witherspoon Press the droving outfit for which I once did the cooking on a five-hundred-mile trip.' She read slowly:

Press forward – for-ward, for dear old Witherspoon;
Right will triumph, profits will rise.
Raise your voices to the skies.

Sell – sell – sell,
Fight – fight – fight.
We are ever loyal through strain and stress
To our own Witherspoon Press.

'This is incredible!' I exclaimed.

'What is more,' Ma said glumly, 'I'm supposed to make confidential enquiries, and this Joe Hanks is *paying* me to find out who is behind the libel suits. Of course, I'm supposed to go about it with the utmost discretion. Those were his very words. We both agreed that whoever was working this had some connection with the publishing game. Whoever he or she is, the pounce was made just after the books came on the market. This argued they knew when to strike.'

'I've been through George's files,' I said. 'One claim came from a country town in Victoria, one from the back of New South Wales, one from a Sydney suburb, and two from Melbourne.'

'The joker must get about a lot,' Ma commented.

She did not seem to have her heart in her work, and was letting me do much more than usual. I was naturally proud of this case, which I felt was something like a plant I had raised by careful tending in my own garden. Give Ma a murder and she will settle to it with gusto, but I myself do not care for violence of any kind.

'It certainly is right up your alley,' Ma agreed heavily, as she got out of the car and was greeted by a smiling boy with a somewhat pale skin who had been looking out for her from a yard full of cars behind a wire fence, all with big placards on them giving their price and announcing in big white letters, 'Good buy', 'One owner', 'As new'.

In the glass-fronted office was a large pot of orchids, many flaring posters and a man with a shrewd and wrinkled face and very sharp eye-teeth. His ash-tray was full of cigarette stubs, and the dust from the road blew in over account books and forms on his desk.

He shook hands with us, saying that Tommy – that was Ching Wah – was a good boy and any friend of his was welcome, what could he do for us, all in one breath. 'Tommy says you want to see me about some joker with a brum cheque.

Well, ladies, I am always made very anxious when I ever hear the words 'brum cheque'. I start like a nervous horse at those words, I do indeed.'

He had already decided that neither of us was the deserted wife of his client, Ma because she was in the wrong age-group, and I because, if I may hand myself a compliment, I do not look like anyone's deserted wife. These are either vindictive or bewildered. Had we looked like a deserted wife, he would naturally have defended his client.

'Not a brum cheque,' Ma explained. 'A very curious cheque. It was paid to a man who claimed his name is Serle Brodsok, and there is some doubt whether Serle Brodsok ever existed.'

'Now, lemme see,' the manager said rapidly. 'Big fair chap comes in here interested in the station-wagon, registered, two new tyres, nice job, as new. Bit of a knock which he mentioned, but it was nothing much and he seemed the sort who would know his way about.'

'What did he look like?'

'Big fair cove in sports clothes, probably fight welterweight, but going to flesh – not fat, I didn't say *fat*. Fair curly hair, blue eyes, smooth talker. A salesman, I'd say. He wanted to go for a run round the block and business was slack, so I took him out and left Tommy in charge. When he came back we argued a bit about the price, and he said he could give me cash if I'd take a cheque as part payment. Now, mind *you*, I wanted time for that cheque to clear. He said the cheque had just been given him as part of a sale he made – fair enough. In fact, there were two cheques – a smaller one to a Miss Someone-or-other – but they were both endorsed and I waited for the all-clear from the bank before going ahead with the sale. As far as I know that was that.'

'Credit good?'

The manager nodded. 'A reputable citizen. Now, you, no doubt, are going to ask his name, but, ladies, much as I would oblige you, I thought this over since Tommy mentioned it, and it would not do me any good to let on who this citizen is. For all I know, he might be very incensed and even, as a man who could once have fought in the welterweight division, he might resent it. You see my position? I should like to be able to swear that, if you are baying on his trail and he turns out to be some underworld boss, he is not in any case to raise a big stink about my part in this.'

'You are quite right,' Ma said approvingly. 'Never let it be said that a man was set up for a dong on the nose through me. We are grateful for your help, and if you ever care to drop in to the hostel and see how our Asian lads are treated, I hope you will come with Tommy, as you call him, and look me up.'

'I might do that.' The manager eyed Ma with the warmth that all shrewed judges of character bestowed on her. 'I should be interested to know what are the ins and outs of this.'

'And to show you,' Ma said, rising, 'I am not going to offer you tea and cake, but some sherry that came from a friend of mine who has a vineyard in the Barossa Valley.'

'It is a date,' the manager said warmly. 'What is more, I will tell you something else. This very reputable joker has a gold ring on his left little finger somewhat tight.'

'If we ever catch up with him,' Ma said, 'we will remember it and thank you.' He saw us to the car. Ma chuckled as I drove off.' 'He is still anxious,' she said, 'about that cheque.'

'Well, we didn't get very far.'

'Ching Wah noticed on the receipt that the man's name is Charles Truepenny, and he lives at Montgrief Mansions, 2 Surf Crescent, Chosen Vale. I just wanted a good description. Ching Wah – I wish he wouldn't tell people his name is Tommy – only said: "His eyes hide behind his cheekbones so that he can smile." I think that is a good description. Will we try and find him?'

So we drove across the city to the scallops of surfing beaches, and found Montgrief Mansions was a pile of purple brick with light blue roughcast, in a long row of such buildings some distance from the beach. They were baked by the sun and blown upon by the cold southerly wind, but in the ground-floor flat, overshadowed by the building next door, with its cement yard and garages, very little in the way of light and air would penetrate. A group of little fair-haired children were sitting on the doorstep.

'Daddy,' one of them called through a window with wire across it to keep out stray burglars, 'come out and get Kitty off the garage roof. She'll starf to death.'

'Kitty knows what she is about,' a patient, lazy voice said.

'She's sitting on the garage roof because she wants a little peace. So do I.'

'Daddy,' the little children called, 'there's two ladies here looking for you.'

A muffled explosion of a man hard tried suggested that a heavy body was climbing out of bed.

'Hold on!' a voice called. 'Who'd you want to see?'

'Mr Charles Truepenny,' I said firmly.

'Well, wait a minute.'

We held a conversation about kittens with the little blond children, who confided that Mummy was in hospital with the new baby, and Daddy was looking after them. 'We have fish and chips every night,' the eldest, who must have been five, said proudly, 'and ice-cream all the time.'

Indeed, when Charles Truepenny appeared on the doorstep, his first move was to distribute silver and send his young speeding for ice-cream. He explained, leading us to a living-room in which all the blinds were drawn and the lights on, that no one who had never had a wife in hospital and no relations to send the kids to had any idea of what it was like. He had dressed with great speed, and must have shaved earlier because he was as neat as a top sergeant, except for the gold ring on his rather fleshy little finger.

'I was just having a read in bed,' he said, his blue eyes retreating behind his high cheekbones as he smiled. The smile tucked in the corners of his mouth, giving him a square-jawed, honest expression.

'You are fond of reading?' I asked. He was waiting to find out the reason for our visit.

'Never look at anything except the newspapers,' he said quickly.

'But you work for Witherspoon Press, don't you?' Ma asked. 'I was talking to your Mr Hanks on Wednesday.'

His expression changed very slightly. 'Well, you may have heard from Joe Hanks – Withers, that's our name for him – a sort of affectionate moniker – that the gold star went up against me this week. They'll tell you I'm their top salesman. I have got rid of more of their Three-in-one Package Deal than any other salesman in Australia. And since you know my name already,' he went on pleasantly, 'maybe we better be introduced?'

We told him who we were and sat down.

'Now anything that affects Witherspoon Press,' Ma began, 'is naturally, your Mr Hanks suggested, the concern of the very loyal sales force.'

'For sure,' Mr Truepenny agreed doubtfully, cocking one ear against the return of his blond-headed young.

'Marching in two by two in the morning to give three cheers for Witherspoon Press before starting the day with song?'

'You wouldn't be having me on?' Mr Truepenny suggested. 'Maybe a lot of us don't go for all that guff, but I don't see it does any harm, and if it keeps Withers happy, what of it?'

'Loyalty to the firm?' Ma purred. 'Mr Hanks mightn't care a damn if other publishers are taken for a ride, but to have *Lust and Hunger*, out of which he intended to make a packet, withdrawn on top of *The Blond Beast* has made him just about as pleased as a starved jaguar.'

'The sales department has nothing to do with the publishing side,' Mr Truepenny riposted. 'I don't know what you're getting at.'

'Well, I'll tell you.' Ma outlined the evidence. 'And once the cheques are traced, it will not look good,' she finished.

'You haven't a thing on me,' Mr Truepenny said at last. 'Excuse me a minute.' He left the room to scatter the invading force of ice-cream eaters, which he did gently enough. 'Daddy is busy,' he told them. 'One minute, and I'll get little Kitty down from the garage roof.'

Amid shrieks of joy from the children, and presently their howls as the cat escaped from their clutches and they set off in pursuit, he returned to the room.

'Now I'll tell you how it is,' he said carefully. 'Even with bonuses for good selling Witherspoon Press doesn't overpay you. I have always been a good churchgoer and, frankly, there is a good deal of this modern stuff that I wouldn't care to leave lying around. When I come across something that doesn't appeal to me, I do the community a public service. But I naturally would deny everything and I have very good legal advice.'

'I would be interested,' I put in, 'in the name of your lawyer.'

'He's an old cove that lives up in a shack in the mountains.

He used to be senior partner in a high-up firm, but he struck a bit of trouble and retired. He's still a silent partner, just takes his cut but does nothing. Sharp! That man could take the eye out of a needle and you'd never know it was gone. You've maybe heard of Sigmund Barnstaple? Well, Sig has always said to me, "Deny everything", and that is what I am doing right now. I don't know what you want to make out of this. I'm perfectly honest about trying to put away enough to make a little home for the wife and kids. I admit that in the past I may have played the races and done my dough, but that is in the past, you understand. The firm won't let you use the car at the week-end to take your family out. You've seen my family. They've got to get out. I have a deposit on a chicken farm, and I was all set to buy it too.' He sighed. 'All I needed is a little capital. Oh, well, I guess my father-in-law will back me. We've got to get out of this flat because the landlady won't have children. Sig Barnstaple has this place up in the mountains next door to where I am getting together this chicken farm. He's a nice old guy. He likes the kids. If you met my wife you'd know that there is a woman who'll stand by you. Whatever you may say about me she has nothing to do with it.'

'Not even signing the letters claiming she had been libelled?' Ma suggested callously.

'I'm not admitting anything. I deny it. You can get in touch with my solicitor.' His mouth was drawn back in what would have been a salesman smile if there was anything to smile at. It was just that he was accustomed to smiling at everything.

'If you were in gaol for false pretences,' I put in, 'your wife would take the children home to your father-in-law.'

'Why, hell!' he said harshly. 'It was a profitable side-line. Just a hobby that needed brains and know-how. Naturally I'll deny it, and you needn't think you've got a witness. The baby was eight and a half pounds. It's a boy.'

'Well,' Ma said, heaving herself out of her chair, 'I'm not going to keep you worrying over the week-end. You can tell your wife she got you out of a nasty jam by having an eight-and-a-half-pound baby. You quit as from now.'

He did not even look relieved because his face was not trained for any expression but cheerful attention. 'It's a pity,' he said regretfully. 'You know how every killing is going to be the last. I can see now you've put the bullet through as neat a paying side-line as a man ever thought up.'

'Foo!' Ma said. 'Why don't you give some credit to your wife?'

'I've always hated books,' he said with quiet ferocity. 'Imagine selling *books*! Why, they're not even good to wrap things in. Hanks took me over from the chicken-noodle-soup business. Now, that *was* a line, but books! You no sooner get one going, and there's another, and the authors all complaining about their sales. Why do they keep writing them?'

The small rabble of fair-haired children had the cat up a tree in the street. 'Daddy,' they were calling, 'Kitty can't get down. Poor Kitty is miaowing because she can't get down.'

'Coming,' Daddy called. 'Now we'll all get cleaned up and go out in the car till it's time to see Mummy at the hospital.'

'Cheek!' I exploded, as we drove away. 'And what are you going to tell Witherspoon Press?'

'A firm that starts the day with three cheers for itself and a little hymn!' Ma said. 'I'll just tell them that I was out of luck. They wouldn't think that a woman would amount to much anyway.'

'I wonder if Sig Barnstaple put him up to it?'

'He's in it somewhere. I wouldn't mention this afternoon to George Peebles if I were you.'

I had been anticipating the pleasure of rubbing the account of the Blond Beast into George. He would have been most distressed. 'Why not?' I asked.

'You know how some solicitors always believe the law should take its course? He'd want to start things moving, and this might spoil his reputation for other libel cases. You know how publishers feel about cases coming to court?'

'Maybe you're right,' I said, then added sternly, 'but what you are doing is condoning if not aiding and abeting a felony.'

'What about the kids?' Ma contended. 'The only people who can afford to go to gaol are bachelors, and there's not enough of them to go around.'

I have told this case of Ma Jones' because it is one in which she did not show to advantage. Much as I admire her, this sentimental streak, which from time to time she shows, is something that can only be regarded with disapproval. Where would society be if every time a man said 'I have three little children and a wife and a baby in hospital,' he automatically got off?

'Cheer up, Leonie,' Ma Jones said carelessly. 'I know it was your case and you were pleased with it. Just remember that in each life some eggs don't hatch out.'

'You sound like Charles Truepenny's chicken farm.' We drove in silence for a while and then I said, 'Why is it that book salesmen should hate books? Dress salesmen don't hate dresses, cheese salesmen don't hate cheese . . .'

'And cheer, cheer, cheer for dear old Witherspoon Press?'

Gwen Kelly

Country Show

1970

Show time. Beside the oval in the mud of rain, pavilion with floors patterned in woven mud. Remember one flick and it's gone; risen to the plastic paint newness of the latest model sewing machine – a stitch in time – properly timed cakes, brownies, sponges. Funny how brown the sponge became that vacation – sponge tea brown with the stained water from the bathroom. And you, prickly sea-urchin wrapt in wind-swept hair, lifted sponges swept by sea into rock pools – anemone fringed – fringed-edged pyjamas above your spindly anemone legs – first prize Mrs Robinson best iced cake – Did I give you first prize? – freckled, hard cored, swept by love or non-love into beaten carved core of rock? But not rock that first night – clay smooth arms in my arms, little sister breasts – I had a sister but I never had a brother – I had a sister and I loved her but she died – and I smoothed your hair and said, 'Hush, we are living both of us.'

Brother Roberts dispensing healing beneath the canvas tent – 'Come into my tent and for a small coin the Lord will save, the laying on of hands' – but my hands lay on you sea-anenome swaying beneath the living hands; untutored in love except mother love and sister love; but they taught you the soft, gentle, gentle, gentle female love. What gaudy embroidered cushions tight-stitched with lighted harbour bridges! Was I your cushion sea girl, mother cushion of flesh, that night in my arms?

You never had a brother and what was your father, weak inadequate father; old Father Time, see the chronometer acrobats tick, tick, round and round they swing on impossible ropes. And the clock on the school wall said tick, tick, and I watched your face helpless, young, vulnerable to the children, milling, yelling, grabbing the pellets of paper circling round and round the room. And you placed your shell-pink hands on your shell-pink ears and screamed, 'Shut up, shut up.'

Good old eternal school exhibits, unchanging beneath the ever-changing waves of education theory – compositions 'My Home', drawings of trees and faces, so freely conventionally expressed; convoluted shapes of creativity, circles and cells and cells and circles. My home but not a home; mother not father, mother convoluted in the shapes of pregnancy, pressing the daily bread into our mouths while father slept with God knows who on sunny slopes, remote from never to be visited home, freely expressing, convoluting shapes of creativity in some new body.

Circles and cells, cells and circles, and I said kissing the stained water from your neck, 'There's no need to fear. There is nothing, harsh or rough or dirty here. Only the soft hands of childhood.'

You loved me. I know you loved me. Watching the sand trickle quick gold silver through your shell fingers you said, 'I never wanted a brother and I loved my sister and I love you.' But it was fairy floss, spun sugar, dolls on sticks. Poor doll on stick. I should have swung you freely by your elastic, not bound you with tinsel thread across your body. Shall I buy a new car – tempting shining new? Did the new car tempt you, little groping sea creature with pink webbed feet trapped on a mountain beneath the rough male body, the tweed, sweaty, tobacco coat?

Poor sea creature. Poor Miss Matron Anders, thwarted anxious would-be-mum Anders, tucking the near suckling children into dormitory cribs, tractor driven by anxiety, too dumb to find a man and too scared to love. Swinging her grey, long plait. 'Where is she?' I said. Wring your hands. Moan, moan. 'She hasn't come home. She went with the boy in the new car.'

Two p.m. says the show-ring clock. Two p.m. and the horses parade, and the cattle parade, and the riders jump the fences in their bold masculine coats, showing off their polished martial boots. It was 2 a.m. on the mountain and I came because I knew you were innocent and you ran click, click heels of sandals on broken twigs into my arms, not his, and you said 'he refused to drive me home' and you shivered inside my coat and I drove and said nothing and you said 'my father had no guts and I never loved him' and I said 'there's no need.'

Later I sat on your bed and held your cocoa warm between my hands and you took it and I smoothed your puff-ball floss of hair and kissed you for the first time as you fell asleep.

How dark the tent; the rough board tables and sloppy milky tea and the Salvation Army pie. Was it rough board you really wanted, swaying uncertainly in front of the children with the powder of chalk falling on your fingers and dusting your lungs? I said as you wept, 'You can handle the children. I can help you. Let's forget about them for a week-end. I have a house at the beach.' Turquoise tropical sky. I waved to you skimming gull-like the water behind the white boat, brown water. And you dropped your skis on the sand and when he tried to take your arm you shrugged it away – shrug, rug. My God, crocheted rugs – anachronistic eternally the same country shows. But I was your rug and your shell-tipped fingers gripped my arm and your body curved to my caress and you said, 'I hate men.'

Men. The square, squat building, the hole in the wall notice; but always ladies on the other notice, rarely women. Oh Brother Roberts, ask your God in your Evangelical tent, why can't we be women not some spurious social concept constructed out of gentility? Lesbia, let us love in the freedom of tent or house or sea. Women only. Woe men. My mother never had a husband.

Sea-urchin festooned with dried salt what did they say to you that night – with the hard core faces pressed around you beneath the light? – poor Matron-mum Anders dragged from early-to-bed routine and you with sleep in your eyes lit by the righteous fires of school council. Such counsels I gave to you, my darling – did you say love or did you say hate – face turned away from me – the negative side. Colour slide section. Best in show and also negative; frail dragon-fly pinned by a spear of grass to the waving blade – dragon-fly you, blue dressing-gown and your hair like gauzy wings. And they said to me 'you must resign', and I said, 'resign?'

Turning wheel pivot of show. If you had turned your face and I had seen love in your trapped eyes I might have resigned. 'You have a lover, you have a lover. Swing on the lighted wheel, swing to the clouds. I have a lover, I love.' I could have resigned, laughed in their faces, but you turned your head away hard core of rock and I said 'why should I resign?' and they said, shopkeeper fleshed family man lips rolling decently and in order back from ring of confidence teeth, 'we think you know, Miss Drayton.' And I said to sea-anemone dragon-fly you, 'must I resign?' and you rushed from the room, tears streaking down rock cheek and pushed my hand away and somebody said 'in that case there will have to be an inquiry.'

Inquiry; inquiries for lost children, come to the lost children's tent and let the police help you find your little one. We were lost then, too, lost before I stood before the tribunal of elders and you took the boy's hand and I thought of mountains and the night and crackling twigs and hot bodies. Buy a hot dog. No thanks, no thanks. You don't like tomato sauce, do you? – but you took his red rough hand and he patted it and he said 'don't be afraid. It wasn't your fault. You were young'; and you looked at the chairman and you said, 'she forced me to go with her. She's the senior mistress.'

Irony there. That week-end at the beach we kissed and kissed and I gave you confidence and the children in the chalky room began to like you. Come to Christ, oh Judas, bite the maternal breast, the soft breasts of childhood. Little girls want softness, too, just like their brothers. Coiled in the soft womb of conception, they drink the blood of their mothers and you do not cry shame.

Cry havoc, rock-faced one. Wrap your water-waving willowy tendrils around me, shut out from your shell eyes the screaming children and your own 'shut up, shut up'. 'Not fit to be in charge of children.' Recite it as you lift your children with the strength I gave you. 'Not to be employed in any school of our religious denomination.' And did you add 'amen' to the morning prayers?

I saw you this afternoon between the fairy floss and the creamy waffles and the tomato-sauce hot dogs; slipping with your hand in his around the corners, with your eyes sliding over my grey hair, trying not to see but unable not to see. Blue eye, brown eye; eye to eye, lip to lip, body to body. Your eye knew mine, sea snail wavering uncertainly with surf sound beating on the fringes of your hearing beneath the fringed quilt and the fringed pyjamas.

Jump on the wheel with your lover, swing away from me

with the music up into the sky. Turn on the endless Ferris wheel, turn and turn for ever until you become dizzy in time and space trying to escape the mud of rain time, the pavilion with floors patterned in woven mud.

Oodgeroo Noonuccal

Mumma's Pet

1972

Dad had built a billy-goat cart for us. Dad always built things to last, and this was a sturdy, heavy construction. It consisted of two large bicyle wheels and a wooden-box frame. It looked like a large box on wheels, and had two shafts protruding from it.

We used the cart for all sorts of carrying jobs. One of us – usually me – would back into the cart like a billy-goat, take hold of the shafts, and pull while the others pushed from behind. When the cart wasn't in use for some labouring job or other, we children often played with it. Our garden was covered with buffalo grass, which tends to creep over everything in its way. As we lived so near the swamp marshes, it grew quick, green and abundant. We became expert at racing the billy-goat cart over the grass, especially where small dirt mounds, grass-grown, stuck above the ground. It didn't matter how roughly we treated that cart, it took all our punishment; Dad's carpentering was so thorough that it didn't even lose a nail.

One day my sisters and I decided to play with the cart by ourselves. My elder sister often showed resentment of my younger sister; she used to call her 'Mumma's pet' – it was true that Mother was inclined to make more of a fuss of my younger sister, and as a result she was a bit spoilt. Today, however, we were playing happily together, good friends for once. My elder sister decided on a new game. She thought it would be fun to put our younger sister in the cart and for me – as usual – to be the billy-goat while she pushed from behind.

We were going great and my younger sister was yelling with excitement, while my elder sister ordered me to pull my weight and stop being lazy. I wasn't being lazy; I was putting all I could into pulling the cart, but it was a puny effort compared to my elder sister's unlimited strength. Carried away by the excitement of the game, my elder sister tried to get more effort out of me by pushing harder. We were going around and over the tops of the bumpy grass tussocks when suddenly my puny strength gave out, I lost my balance, and the cart tipped over.

My younger sister went sprawling over the side of the cart as I tried to regain my balance – but the cart was too heavy for me, and as she fell, one wheel came down on her outstretched arm, I fell on top of her and my elder sister fell on top of me. Our younger sister let out a yell of pain. She always did that whether she was hurt or not.

Finally we got ourselves sorted out, and righted the cart. Our younger sister was holding her arm and whimpering. My elder sister told her to stop play-acting. We knew how good she was at putting on an act – she never succeeded in impressing us the way she did Mother. Now, still holding her arm and whimpering, she said, 'I'm going to tell Mum! You hurt me!'

'Oh, why don't you grow up, Mumma's little pet?' my elder sister retorted furiously. 'Don't be such a cry-baby!'

'You did hurt me,' my younger sister whimpered.

'All right, so we hurt you. Well, that means you have the right to hurt us back. That's fair, isn't it? You can hit us as hard as you like, provided you don't tell Mum what happened.'

So my younger sister walloped into both of us with the arm that hadn't been hurt. 'Take that!' she kept yelling as she hit us again and again.

My elder sister winced in mock pain, and cried out for my younger sister to go easy and not hit so hard. She was a great ham actor herself.

We decided to put the cart back in the toolshed and go indoors. My younger sister dragged along behind us, not speaking to us.

During the evening meal my elder sister and I watched her out of the corners of our eyes, wondering whether she would squeal on us. We didn't really trust her in spite of the pact we'd made. But my mother noticed that her youngest daughter was eating very little, and was strangely silent. Her face had a strained expression, too. At last Mother called her to the head of the table, and looked across at Dad.

'Ted,' she said, 'this girl looks sick to me.'

Dad looked at his youngest daughter. 'Come here, girl,' he ordered.

He ran his hand gently down the arm she had half lifted; it looked stiff against her body. She suddenly gave a scream of pain. It sounded genuine all right. My other sister and I exchanged glances.

'Mum, this girl's arm is broken, I think,' Dad said.

'How did it happen?' Mum asked our sister, but she just looked towards us with pained eyes, while we stared back at her with vacant expressions.

Dad summed up the situation fast. 'All right,' he said, turning to my elder sister, 'what have you been up to? How did this girl get hurt?'

My elder sister blurted out the story of the billy-goat cart. 'We were only playing together,' she finished lamely.

'Well,' Dad said, 'she's got a broken arm as a result of your playing, and how are we to get her to a doctor? You know the doctor here only attends to white people – he doesn't treat Aborigines.' Dad was really angry.

Mother cuddled our younger sister and made soothing noises as Dad gave out orders to our brothers. 'Row out to the channel and see if there's a boat that will take her to a doctor on the mainland. Let's hope there's a decent white man out there.'

My brothers ran off to the dinghy, and they did find a white man who came to the rescue. He placed his auxiliary yacht, *Flockwing*, at Dad's disposal, and I acted as Dad's offsider on the boat. We set sail with a stiffening breeze blowing and a storm brewing in the west. During the trip the weather turned very rough, but luckily the engine kept going. My sister's condition worsened during the trip, and she was violently ill. When we reached the mainland, the doctor there put her in hospital for the night. She was suffering from shock and seasickness as well as her broken arm.

What happened to my elder sister and me? We got the hiding of a lifetime from Mum – and when she was angry, she could wallop good and hard.

When my younger sister returned from the mainland, she was treated as a V.I.P. – both Mum and Dad spoilt her rotten. She took full advantage of this situation. My elder sister and I kept out of her way as much as possible during her convalescence. After her arm healed, everything returned to normal. But we never asked her to join in any games with the billy-goat cart again.

Vicki Viidikas

The Snowman in the Dutch Masterpiece

1974

She stepped into the blue Jaguar, a piece of sky fell away almost as blue, as he closed the door swiftly behind her. They sped silently across the Harbour Bridge, lines of traffic poured multi-coloured streams into a waterfall of light which fell away to nothing. 'The menu is very good', he said, flicking on a cassette of Hendrix; two speakers in the back of the car pushed out perfect sound, perfect reception.

A million lights gleamed lavishly as Julia leant her arm on the window sill. She smoked a perfectly rolled joint as Hendrix wailed and fell through 'Foxy Lady,' 'Hey Joe what'cha tryin' to do?' Buses, legs and hats floated past the window. She was going outwards, going away from the city and this perfect stranger was driving.

At the top of the restaurant stairs he guided her to a shadowy corner, brass lanterns threw an orange glow over their faces. Delicious indefinable smells drifted by, waving. She felt anonymous under her shiny cap of hair, beautiful, it could have been anywhere.

'Oysters to start, then *coq au vin*, etc. etc.' The order could have been flaming yak's tooth, stuffed tortoises or sixteen Kiwi rissoles – she was being handled expertly, and he was smiling.

Dinner was superb and through it he talked of Bangkok, Afghanistan, Nepal, opium houses in Calcutta. 'They have tiled floors with hard mosaic headrests for pillows and a cistern of tea bubbling out the back. An old man sat with me to keep the pipe burning okay, and I just smoked and smoked, you have to lie down, and go into a dream baby, you just dream your day away. Sometimes I'd get a rickshaw back to the hotel and read a book or maybe play some dice or sleep. It's beautiful baby, it's a good life, a good trip.'

They lingered over coffee and she knew then he'd take her to his apartment. 'I've got some very fine dope there, I'll drive you back in the morning.'

Well he wasn't so handsome, he was sharp with dark eyes and his face sunken a little in just the right and enticing places. Faded jeans, sterling silver belt and black leather jacket, $200 on his back and a Moroccan leather wallet. He was distant and unbuyable, could afford anything that night. He had Chinese ivory cards, a ritual where the chosen mustn't move too close, even at the risk of coldness, rigidity, of not having anything to lose.

Steering her to his car he said his apartment was temporary till his current deal came off, then he'd fly again to London. 'The place is cool, that's why I chose the North side. It pays to appear like everyone else.' Obviously. 'I could be any other businessman, a young designer on the make or any well-heeled executive.'

The car flowed in through a pair of high white gates to a lawn with potted palms, blood-red rose bushes, a private beach with water lapping at the end of a slender pier. Safety devices, spy hole, the door so white in the darkness she felt she was entering a gilded cage, a shrouded and unwalked kingdom.

Not even the black leather lounge could unnerve her, its round openings like glistening fleshy stomachs. Not even the Thai silk lampshades, an enormous stereo, the television with its tinted blue screen, the perfumed toilet paper. She laughed at the perfectness of it and, 'What's amusing?' he asked, but she was thinking of flea-ridden terraces, peeling walls, junk-filled backyards, friends opening cans of soup. The rusted typewriter, sordid poems. They called that freedom, the price of wanting to know who you are. And here she was being treated like a decorative object, nice sometimes, like buying candy, something special. But think of poems in soup cans.

'Sit down babe, I've got some very fine whisky,' appearing with a decanter, ice cubes, glasses, ashtrays. 'I've just come into some very good cocaine, do you dig coke? you do? fine,' he materialised a silver box from Bali and took out a bag and tiny ornate mirror. Tipping a small white heap on the mirror he handed it to her. Like that.

Maybe $40 worth. She licked a little with one finger then

sniffed slowly. As her tongue, nose and throat went numb he smiled taking off his jacket, the belt flashed on his hips.

The whisky was so cold it ran down her throat like a hard steel stream, a glittering avenue in her body, she could feel her face melting. A record was playing softly as they nodded and dreamed in the arms of the black sofa.

'You have a very fine figure babe, ever put it into movies? You can get very good bread in Hong Kong for blue movies, you know, nothing too off, that's up to you, just have your boobs and cunt photographed, that sort of thing.'

'No,' she said. 'No I haven't,' trying to tell him how she'd chickened out on a job in a disco for the very reason she didn't like flaunting her body, leading them on knowing they'd remain empty-handed. 'Prick teasing,' she said. 'You know if they so much as lay one finger on you there's ten bouncers to throw them out. It's crazy! getting paid for giving them nothing,' and she felt she sounded so moral, so lame . . . 'Peep shows.'

'But they dig it babe.'

'Yeah but I guess it depends on how much you want the bread eh?'

'But babe, what are you going to do without bread? You can't make it without it. I mean, give the suckers what they want, why worry about what they're getting? They aren't going to feed you for having ideals. Sure I can dig what you're saying, those jobs are pretty degrading really, I guess it's different for a chick, but why be missing out on comforts because of their ignorance? They're only crass pigs.

'I tell you, what do you think I'm doing? A few more hauls and I'll be sitting sweet, I'll be able to say fuck off to all those gigs, let them rot in their nine-to-five lives, their peephole nights out, I ain't going to pay for their stupidity! Hell they don't even know how to have a fuck! If I'm prepared to take the risk of going in the can for ten years and put up with their moralising shit: You're selling your soul, You're corrupting our society, to make some loot to get away from them, then hell babe it's better, I'll be free to have ideals . . . I mean I'll have the bread to do it then, won't I?'

And she sat back silently feeling like a two bob watch slowly ticking the hard way. He leant over and touched her face. His hand felt cool and strangely unattached to anything, something distant out of snow, glossed over depths. 'Another whisky?' he filled her glass.

Standing by a huge bay window she looked out over the beach where yachts were moored just off the shore, like giant pale insects their bodies frozen, wings flickering gently. It was unreal, a reality so super real it was unbreakable, timeless. Everything fitted as perfectly as a Dutch masterpiece, the milk frozen in mid-air, the picture so pure, the girl's face a white mask.

He seemed to be asleep on the other side of the room, so she took her drink and a transistor into the bedroom and turned on the lamp. Soft yellow light seeped across an immaculately made bed. Turning back quilted satin covers she undressed, arms and legs pouring from the clothes, long hair streaming down her back, red feathers, red and white and yellow into the sheets.

It could have been hours later she felt him next to her, long arms around her waist, his face on her breasts, licking. He murmured and kissed her throat. It was snow everywhere falling and melting coolly inside and outside her, ruffling the feathers, red and yellow, he was a running snowman, dark and brown, hard and soft . . . distant. He didn't seem to like her touching him, pushing her hands away, he turned and placed her just how he wanted, remaining separate, in control.

But she wanted to erupt, wanted her skin crawling breaking the images of pale cool masks, plaster hands, lips: she wanted to drink the milk, break the glass, carve up the painting, this masterpiece of perfection, get out of the frame. But the snow remained, drifting them out to sea.

'Snowman snowman you'll get through . . .' that song . . .

His ritual was complete. 'Want some hot chocolate?' disappearing in a silk dressing gown to the kitchen, returning with cups, cigarettes, 'It's good coke isn't it,' and she nodded, dazed, unable to feel happiness, everything fitted in the cage.

Noon sunlight flooded into the room as they woke to the radio still playing. He said he'd had a fine sleep, 'fine' was always his word, everything was fine, fitting. 'You've got fine skin babe,' eyeing her with a critical expression in the daylight. And he got up and went to make breakfast, came back with a tray, percolated coffee, eggs, etc. two tightly rolled joints. 'I always like to have a smoke in the mornings, makes you relax into the day better I think.' Perfect. Perfect. Clearing away the tray, 'I'm sorry I don't have much for you to read,' tossing down a few *Time* magazines. 'I know you dig reading, I haven't any poetry, I'm not into reading much myself.'

So she lay around flicking through magazines, eating halva, smoking and painting her eyelids blue while he made a few mysterious phone calls in another room.

Mid afternoon he announced something had come up and he wasn't going to the city till late that night. She had nothing else planned so they drank some whisky and sat around playing records. He amused himself reading a travel book on the Far East, kept asking her if she was comfortable and apologising for not having any 'literature' for her to read.

While he was away buying some more dry for the whisky she curiously went through his drawers. Silk shirts, a snake-skin belt, gold bracelets, a diamond watch. He had very few possessions, one each of a few essentials. There were no books, trinkets, phone numbers, photos, no papers to show his identity, that he voted in Bengal or had a property in Texas, a wife or communist grandmother. It was weird. He had three suitcases and a mink coat because he dug, 'soft things against my skin.'

'It's a damn shame a chick like you doesn't make something out of your looks.' They were sitting on the lounge drinking whisky with the Stones.

'What's this writing jag going to do for you anyway, there's no bread in it, and those shits won't recognise you, assuming you've got something to say, till you're ninety-nine and dead in a crummy room by your typewriter, cockroaches crawling over your slippers. Then they'll lay a claim on your stuff, call it 'another great work of art' and make a lot of stash out of it. And I bet you'll say you don't want to write shit books for bread, so what's it going to do for you, keep your soul pure?' and he snorted into his drink. 'I think you deserve better than that babe. Why shouldn't you?' And hell it was really nice grass they'd been smoking and she couldn't think too straight, Julia was feeling nothing like Julia, and it seemed those things he was saying were kind of making sense, kind of getting to her. She couldn't very well define that 'pure soul' he'd scoffed at.

'I guess I just have to do it,' she offered.

'Perhaps it's a matter of life styles.' Poverty? Madness?

'I don't care about money.' Not true! She'd had dreams about bacon, huge strips of it walking towards her juicy and friendly – being able to afford bacon with eggs for breakfast.

'It makes me feel real, I know who I am then.' Rubbish! The million faces leering back at her. All her own.

'It seems natural,' dubiously, 'It's not a question of money or lack of it. It's trying to understand things, see things, you know, make something.'

'It's like quality, the quality of things, people, food.' Andersons bacon. Home on a pig's back. Ghastly generalisations.

'Yes!' she sucked at her drink like a fish at air.

'No, it's not that simple,' drifting off again.

'Ah honey, you're crazy! You don't have to do anything to prove yourself to those shits.' (Which shits exactly?) 'They're blind anyway. They won't satisfy you. Come here beautiful,' he pulled her close to him, playing with her breast, almost bit the nipple off. 'What about some more coke eh? Relax.'

Out came the little mirror and they swallowed some with water this time. The leather lounge squeaked and rustled as she felt all that snow descending, softening words, meanings, smoothing things out; the day was any day, any time.

The Stones rang through 'Satisfaction'. 'Paint it Black', 'Let it Bleed.' They oozed along the lounge together, Julia, the snowman, snowing in that room, under their skin, coming closer together, apart, distant though their bodies touched, catching sight of each other, falling, not knowing who the other was, forgetting, strange.

It must have been night, the phone rang and they both jumped like firemen. She could see him through a bright haze mumbling into the phone, then he wrote something down and rang off. 'It's okay babe, I don't have to go into the city tonight. So I can take you back anytime you want.'

'Oh thanks,' was all she could muster. Then, 'I'm feeling

really good, actually I'm feeling brilliant,' getting up and wandering round the room. He smiled, 'Fine.'

Neither of them felt like eating so Julia decided to take a bath. She put in bath salts and sandalwood oil and brought in the radio and a heater. 'Want to take a bath with me?' she called. But he seemed rather annoyed, becalmed. 'No babe, I prefer to bathe alone,' so she undressed feeling self-conscious that she'd asked. Funny. As if there were rules and she was moving in too close.

'Tralalala trala trala,' she sang and chuckled in the bath, splashed, soaped her breasts and blew on them, listened to the radio, ran in more hot water, generally made a racket, she was feeling so good. He stuck his head in the door, 'It's only a bath babe,' then he was gone. She threw some suds at the back of the door. Funny. She was of course breaking up the Dutch painting, the milk maid was pouring milk all over the floor, lifting her skirts, dancing nude in the kitchen. Dropping her mask. Out of the frame.

They made love under the quilted covers again and she bit his shoulder and he said, 'Ouch', and told her to stop it, and pushed her hands away. Silently. Controlling that intimate ballet. He told her to lie still and did she have to root around so much like a beaver, and she was mad and funny, and they were high and fine. Later he made them hot chocolate.

Next morning he brought in the breakfast tray with two joints, then drove away in his sky-blue Jag. 'Don't answer the phone, and don't answer the door,' was all he'd said, 'I'll be back in a couple of hours.' So she wandered round the flat looking at magazines, turned the TV on then off. There was just nothing in that gilded cage to involve her. No rubbish or disorder. It was perfection. So she mentally filled it with garbage.

Looking out through the blinds the sun was shining on the pier, the little beach was deserted. Boats were dead white, clean, moving ever so slightly, no one on board. Thinking of the Flying Dutchman, if she stared hard enough perhaps he'd appear on deck, the sails of his yacht be moved by invisible hands, unseen winds.

But there was no one. And he didn't want her to leave the

flat, didn't want anyone to see her, even know she was there. So she undressed and got back into bed, listened to the transistor, drew pictures with an eyebrow pencil on the back of a *Time*, tried to write a poem. But she felt anonymous, frozen, like a beautiful vase in a glass case. Back in the frame.

She must have fallen asleep because he was bending over her, 'Hello doll, I've got something for you,' throwing a package on the bed. Inside was a novel by Colette and some short stories by Somerset Maugham. He grinned almost sheepishly, 'I hope they're all right, that's all they had in the newsagents,' and she said, 'Gee thanks, how amazing.'

They had coffee and a joint and he'd bought steak to cook for dinner. No one mentioned when she was leaving. 'Don't you think we could go for a walk on the beach, it looks lovely out there,' just on dusk, she was feeling restless. But, 'No babe, it's not cool really. I don't want anyone to know you're here. It's better for both of us,' he waved an arm towards a block of apartments near by, 'Never know who's in there, it pays to be discreet, even paranoid sometimes.'

He cooked steaks served with mushrooms, broad beans, baked potatoes, red wine. He told her he'd lived with a chick once who'd had a kid. And he'd packed her off with a few thousand dollars to make sure she and the kid would be okay. 'That's a rather big thing to do isn't it, giving her all that money?' Julia asked.

'Well I reckon it's the only thing I could have done, till she got a job and organised herself. She was a good babe but I needed to be free, you know, if a deal suddenly comes up and I have to fly immediately, what do I do about her and the kid? She might not even want to go to Pakistan or somewhere, and she didn't. Chicks always want something you can't give them. They just don't dig the fact you might want something other than them and a nice little domestic scene.'

'Yeah I guess that's true, but women seem to need the illusion that something is total, that there's something to completely consume them, anyway something other than the fragments...' Julia was feeling very strange, stoned again and faceless. 'What do you mean, fragments? A chick can do what she wants, just as much as a guy. But they don't, that's all!

They do some piddling thing and expect everyone to notice, to praise them eternally. A guy just takes a trip, smashes his car, makes some loot, gets a fuck – he just does it! That's how things are! Fragments!' he snorted.

It was very dark outside and they were alone with the remnants of a meal. Julia didn't know what to say any more, and he seemed to be feeling the same. Turning on the TV he flopped in front of it smoking a cigar. The screen lit up cars, stallions, stretch bras, cigarettes with extra length, jeans, flyspray. She stared at the piece of fat on her plate. She seemed a long way removed from her lopsided terrace with its rancid backyard.

There were a ton of words she called 'art' lying in a front room there. Along with cockroaches, rejection slips, four letter words dotted out, losses. Complaints. That was poetry? Art? She had exactly $3.65 in her purse and ten cents in the bank. No job. A house full of people referred to as 'friends' who read books, smoked dope, patched each others' jeans, etc.

She knew she needed money, food, a regular income. Why didn't she bash someone over the head and steal his wallet? Settle down as a secretary? Marry a rich old bastard? 'Keeping your soul pure?' that's what he'd said. So what about the buyers who really needed that fix, their eyes hanging out, just to stay alive? Too bad eh? You take what you need. Uh huh. The sum total was confusion.

He spent the night watching television while Julia prowled around with her eyelids painted brown this time. Staring through the blinds at the never-changing harbour, the perfectly empty beach. Finally flopping into bed to read the Maugham stories. He came in later, deftly made love to her, followed by hot chocolate – eternally the perfect host.

Let me in, she dreamed, hammering on the door of a sealed room, a distant order.

In the morning over breakfast he announced he'd take her to the city that day. 'Take a shower, get yourself cleaned up, I'll drive you in about one.' She felt suddenly deflated and he'd gone off into another room.

On the way back the car glided like a porpoise through streams of traffic. They didn't talk much, he seemed preoccupied, aloof, just the Stones grinding and bumping out of the cassette. 'I'm going away soon babe, probably next week. I might see you when I'm back. I won't have time before I go. It's been fine,' touching her on the face, smiling into the Oriental future, the door suddenly closed, shut, the beautiful car melting away silently into the city.

Outside the frame, looking down at the dirty street, the twentieth century greeted her, offering its greasy mask.

Margaret Sutherland

A Servant of the People

1974

A black jersey seemed appropriate. I wore little lipstick. It was still not time when I parked. A few faces looked out from nearby cars. I did not want to intrude so I waited until the service was underway. Someone handed me a hymn-book as I went in. The usher beckoned me up to sit with the others, but I went into the back row of seats and sat close to the wall. It was a very small gathering.

I had found Edgar Adams in the Deaths column. I knew nothing about him, but I did not think he would mind me looking on at his funeral. The coffin was on a black marble slab raised like an altar. There was a bunch of home-picked flowers and one wreath. It was a Salvation Army service and several men and women in the customary uniform were there. The relatives of Edgar Adams were seated on four chairs in the front row. Three were elderly; there was one boy, perhaps fourteen.

They began with *I Am the Resurrection and the Life*. The boy cried a great deal. I cried too; not for Edgar Adams who certainly had no use for tears, but for the boy and the rain and the downcast proteas. It was not a real mourning. It would hardly have made any difference if there had been no Edgar Adams inside the closed coffin. The tears were something apart, born of nothing, like the organ music which bellowed out on cue when there was no organ there. The prayers offered were of hope, life, eternal reward.

Once, coming up from my snifflings, I saw the coffin had vanished and primitive fears sprang to life until I saw the relatives file up and drop, each of them, a white carnation into the void that had appeared, magically, in the centre of the catafalque. I went up last, and let the last carnation fall, and tried to believe in Edgar Adams. It was hard, though a woman sobbed, and the boy's face was terribly swollen and puffed. He looked, in his unhappines, epileptic. As I went out I saw one of the women in Army bonnet put her arm around him. 'He is not dead,' I heard her say. 'He is not *dead.*' I went away quickly.

Half a mile down the road I stopped at a milk bar and bought a chocolate milk shake and a sausage roll. As I ate I remembered I had not offered a single prayer for Edgar Adams who was dead and in a coffin scattered with white carnations. I sat in the dairy and said a guilt-prayer and brushed pastry crumbs from my lap. When I thought my eyes were less red I drove back to the crematorium. There was no one about now. The mourners had left. The place seemed deserted. I found another chapel, larger than the first. It was empty.

In the gardens were small apertures let into the wall like private boxes at a Post Office. In the halls and corridors I could not find anyone. I went back to the gardens. A man came down the path. He was dressed neatly, and walked purposefully, and I did not think he was a visitor. He was a Maori, with an old scar twisting his mouth into a curiously wry expression. He said he worked there. I explained that I needed to know about cremation for a book I was writing. He did not think that odd.

It only cost twelve dollars to be cremated, he told me. At the other place it would cost me double that amount. We're government, he said; for the people.

I said it sounded very cheap. It must cost at least that, surely, for the fuel.

Diesel, he said.

I mean, I said, it would have to be so hot.

Hot all right.

About how long, I wondered, did it take?

About an hour.

Coffins and all? Or did they . . .?

No, they didn't. People said they did, but they didn't. Coffins and all.

And what about the ashes, I asked; and wondered what I would do with the ashes of someone I had loved. Nothing came to mind. He pointed to the wall spaces I had already seen.

Seven dollars sixty, he said. For maintenance and so on.

A year, did he mean?

That was it, he said. The lot. He looked pleased that I was impressed.

All the time we were moving through the gardens as though the buildings were drawing us in. We went through the main door, and he led me into the empty chapel, and showed me the button which controlled the lowering of the centre part of the marble slab. The heat of your hand was enough to set it off, he said. It had to be unobtrusive. He pointed down into the space.

They pull it through there, he said.

There was a drape covering the end where the head of the coffin would lie.

In the side room he pointed out the tape-recorder.

For the music, he told me. People think I'm a funny guy; working here.

He'd gone off to the war at seventeen. His job had been to get rid of the dead. Sometimes they'd had to use bulldozers. He'd been sick in the nights.

But you get used to it after a while, he said.

I believed him.

So that, he said, this job seemed pretty clean, if I took his point.

He said they weren't really supposed to. But after all there was nothing to hide. He held the door open for me. The room was tidy and clean, and centred around the three black cylinders. It was a little like entering a ship's engine-room, except that the throb and the smell of oil and grease were missing. It had something of the same practical and cheerful atmosphere all the same. There wasn't any smell, apart from the Maori's hair oil.

The other man there, a closed-up fellow with small eyes, noticed me and came towards us. Was it all right if he went ahead and...? He glanced away to the two coffins set on biers at the end of the room. Yes, said my friend. It was all right. And he went on explaining about the gratings through which the parts that did not burn fell down, and were ground up afterwards. He indicated an object like an outsize mincer.

Did he mean bones?

Yes, he said. That's right. Bones, mainly. Screws, nails, they had to pick those out, naturally. You can see, he said, it's pretty hot in there.

The other man had wheeled a coffin across. He'd left the trolley and gone to open the furnace door. The light was golden and fiery. He had to stand back a little and take a run up, to give the coffin a push. It slid through the door perfectly. I had been half-afraid the momentum of his run might take him in after it. He fixed the door shut, and dusted off his hands.

People say we take the handles off, my friend said; but you can see for yourself.

I asked what happened to them.

They melt, he said.

We went behind the furnace so he could show me the ashwell. It was empty. A faint roaring sound came out of the ashwell and, now and then, smoke.

It's only the varnish, the other man said.

And after a few minutes the smoke did not billow out any more.

You can see, said my friend as we walked back outside, that we haven't anything to hide. I wouldn't mind going that way when the time comes.

I said I wouldn't mind either.

Of course, he said, Maoris were superstitious. They weren't supposed to go in for cremation. But times were changing. Like with the Catholics. They weren't supposed to either. But times changed. He was a Catholic, he said.

I said he must have problems. Being a Catholic Maori.

He grinned back and said not really. The only thing that bothered him about the job was the way people came and blamed him when vandals got into the nearby cemetery and broke the vases and moved the angels about and tipped out the flowers. They got upset, he said, so they blamed him. How could he tell them the truth, that vandals had been in and broken the vases and moved the angels about and tipped out the flowers. He didn't want to upset them more. So he was a sitting duck. They got angry, he said. He felt like saying, Well go on and look under the hedge and you'll find the pieces where I tidied them away. He'd gone after the vandals some nights, but he hadn't caught them.

It's like the flowers, he said; and pointed to them, banks of colour rising from a kind of platform at the front of the building. Might be a couple of hundred dollars' worth there after a big do. They had to lie there and rot. Otherwise people came along and accused him of selling them. Once they'd phoned from that place down the road . . . the nut-house . . . and asked for flowers to put in the wards, and he'd had to refuse because they weren't his flowers to give. He was only a public servant if I saw his point.

So they just lie there, he said; and we shovel them up when they die.

I was thanking him when the other man came outside. He walked over, treading round the puddles. He smiled and looked less closed-in. He said his lunch hour was at twelve if I liked to wait. He had a little room down the back. We could have a cup of tea together.

I told him thanks, but I'd really found all I needed. He winked and went back inside.

I caught up with the Maori.

Would he mind saying to his friend, I had to take the children to the doctor . . .

He grinned. Don't you worry about him, he said. He fancies himself as a bit of a Romeo, like.

I was sorry to say goodbye to him, but I felt all right, leaving the second time. Anyway, I thought, Edgar Adams was in good hands now. My friend stopped me as I was backing the car from the parking area.

By the way, he said. If you're writing that book. Tell them we don't sell the flowers, will you?

I said I would.

Finola Moorhead

Where are you, Ellen Spalding?

1976

The night brings you back into my mind, and I remember the word 'hate' embossed with the scabs of hairpin torture on both your arms. Your arms were a legend at the school, but your face has disappeared – disappeared among the crowds of girls who are dragged into custody for being 'exposed to moral danger'. Into those institutions I am afraid to even investigate as a sane conscientious journalist. I am afraid to see the colour of the paint on the walls, above and below the line at shoulder height. I envy your ability to spit and not be intimidated by them. I cry much more than you do for the punishment you get, for the bigness of the act and the smallness of your saliva. They tell me television is going into the Reformatory to make a serial. They will feed the living rooms hungry for sentimentality with happy endings. Spit, Ellen, spit, my girl. Let that saliva, no worse and no better than the Pope's, roll down the full gloss paint – catching the light. Cameramen pull out your focus, zoom in and make that little drip a drop of dew on a faded leaf; you dare!

Tonight is not the first time I've thought of Ellen Spalding. Of all the hundreds I've taught, of all the names I've ticked on a roll, I remember the name Ellen Spalding, but she was at the school maybe a month, maybe less – a disruption, of course. A class of the third year students – nubile girls, littler boys – in square desks along the long room. The rows disturbed by Ellen, a natural creator of chaos. And what did we have, that stern elderly nun and I, to control her with? She, her stick, her temper, her detentions; but against those you had your freedom, your fearless or imperative anarchy, your four-letter words, and you could deal as savage a hurt as she. A state of war with weapons. I don't suppose I wanted your love – that obsessive sado-masochistic infatuation with older women would have been too familiar to you. The round of orphanages providing you with a painful surfeit of aunties, you knew the cruel distance of their kindness. Many wounds, having no right to expect more. So what did I have, your young English teacher overwhelmed by the noise of third formers? 'Nothing!' reverberates and echoes in the deep chasm of your need, nothing. Not even the desire to enter the knotty web of your life, just respect for the pain and emotion of that word on your arms. Both. The guts of it, this product of an ungenerous society. Don't think for a moment, Ellen, that I was curious about you then. No questions were levelled by me as to your background to any more informed member in the gossip-warmed confidence of the staff room, not one. I overheard a little while I munched cold salty scones provided by a junior domestic science group. You see I was aware that society is a monster and people are its victims. You were my problem only forty minutes a school day; with the sigh and raised eyebrow of many a teacher I could suffer it through to the end. Ticking up a few more hours 'experience'.

When you ran away from the Home, and hence the school, you were talked about for a day, and then forgotten – information alone fuels interest. No one knew where you were... I had visions of you on the Hume lifting your thumb to passing trucks. Ellen on the road. Ellen cheeky and confident in her freedom. Ellen drinking the rain outside some roadhouse. Ellen ready to suffer and tackle anything. Through necessity. Necessity so absolute that it gave you jokes and philosophy. So I saw you popular, truckies and junkies providing you with a roof, food, piercing cans of beans with your eyetooth and obtaining all the skills of alley life. At first, I saw you riding FJ Holdens with skinheads through East Gippsland, inside the mysterious leopard-skin car seat privacy of that world. Your sneaky fears well covered with bravado. Once free, you were never a victim again. Not in my mind. The abuses to your person came under the heading of masochism and were your own. You remained superior. A woman with the indifference and infinite patience of mother earth. Plus the disinterest and cruelty to deal unplanned and sudden revenge – the secret to have nothing and be alone – ultimate distrust – pure righteous hate. Emblazoned on your forearms.

But you were only fourteen, and a fat unattractive girl, knocking about the classroom clumsily gathering bruises on your thighs and more for your store in insensitive insults, even from those whom you called your girlfriends. They, adventurous sophisticates from down the line, took you up as an oddity, as a source of stories and jargon on the volatile subjects, so fascinating and forbidden. That was obvious from the tone in the giggles you caused. Cats with a mouse. Their slight difference, Ellen, came from the fact that they or their parents were a cut above the average. Those brief friendships you had in that class were with the charmed, the lucky, and they delighted to use you. They delighted, also, after you left, in wearing expensive clothes, in following fashion . . . Do you know that one of them, the chief, actually is a model now? A slave to materialism, up to her neck in decadence and more of a whore than you could ever be, no matter how desperate your privation: believe me, Ellen. Yet I know with all your hate, you would feel more guilt than she. You have the dignity of woman, and feel the offences against mother earth. Indignity would make you angry. And it has nothing to do with how you seem on the streets in the eyes of the observers and keepers of the law. How you can laugh! How you can scream! How you can throw your insides to the wind from the top of the big dipper at Luna Park!

You think it's easy for me to write these things, Ellen, sitting in moderate comfort knowing that life will not knock on my door with rude demands. I have the luxury of a room and the choice of whom I wish to be with. I will not be disturbed, the mother nature in me will not be called to minister cures and comforts. There you are, still illiterate but bright and cunning, in the brown gloom of a flat behind the Cross, by-passing the joint as it goes round, waiting for the intrusion which will call upon your fundamental common sense. You would grow up, I think, to know people well, to understand and give advice – or perhaps your field is medicine. You know what to do for diarrhoea, hepititis, V.D. Can massage. Have a repertoire of herbal remedies.

It would gratify me as an old teacher to see you behind a microphone backed by a blues or rock band screaming out with full-lung passion. 'I'm an evil girl's daughter and you can't hurt me no matter what you do, oh no no no.' Insinuating a giggle through the power in your voice. And for what it's worth having fans trample each other to death for love of you. Mass love in place of the quiet oppressive security of Mum and Dad at breakfast time. That which you never had, and that which psychiatrists will say was all you really needed. 'Dear dear, the milk is spilt. All we can do now is find a mop and use it.' Any sort of a mop. With a certain type they could make you a model too, Ellen. Here is where I ask you to spit. With all the disgust of a have-not. Middle-class feminists will envy your parentlessness, having discovered the family is the root of sexist oppression. 'I'm an evil girl's daughter and I don't care what you say and do, oh no no no.' The real anarchy at the rear end of a corrupt society. 'I've been beat and I've been screwed, it don't make no difference to youse.'

I'm waiting to hear your name, Ellen Spalding.

It was a particularly bad day at school, for me. My engagement had just been broken. I did not have the emotional strength to direct the activity of thirty people for the next forty minutes. Especially as they would be enraged by the conduct of the stern elderly nun who preceded me in having the right to tell them what to do. Deaf to the rhythms of nature. Be late. Ruffle through the meagre teaching aids. A box of photographs. A cassette recorder. Laden with equipment, tools of distraction. 'Okay. Take a photograph. Listen to the music and write a poem. Respond to the audio-visual stimulus . . .' What? Erk. Oh. Do we have to? '*That* I had trouble getting. I'm trying to make your life more interesting. Just relax, go to town. Write whatever you like.' Do we get marks? Are you going to collect them? 'I don't know yet. Now get to work. I'll give you half an hour. Then I'll have a look. If they're good I'll mark them if they're bad I'll throw them in the rubbish tin.' Now to dream of my lost lover, and listen to the music. One photograph left and Ellen staring at me. Hate. Oh no. The picture left was by far the ugliest – a blank television set and a floating head of a baby. Repulsive. 'Ellen. Come here.' The walk expressed hate and reluctance, and I remember that I wished my life had not led me to cross the path of this girl. As she kicked the legs of others' desks and nudged their writing arms, I fantasised that I should take her outside, walk with my hand on her shoulder and ask her the meaning of the word on her forearms. If I could do that . . . she was beside me. Challenging. I silently picked up the ugly photograph and handed it to her, and motioned her back. The strength of indifference. Because I didn't care, the class was silent and the music played for thirty minutes. The machine clicked, snapping me out of daydream and the lethargy of melancholia. Besides, suddenly I was curious. 'Righto, either keep writing or read something else. I'll look at them now. If you talk I'll lose concentration. Then the only course of action will be to rip 'em up wholesale. And today's goody person can take them down to the incinerator and watch them burn.' You wouldn't dare. 'Wouldn't I?' Shshshs. They were pretty good and I lavished generous marks, rewarding them more for the half hour peace than literary quality. Ellen.

Yes, Ellen. I'll always remember your name. And that day. That repulsive photograph. The look of the page on which you had written: grade one lettering, quarter-inch high printing, uneven, abominable spelling . . . Yet my red pen was arrested mid-air as sharply as Abraham's dagger was above Isaac's body. I looked at you and you shrugged, distracted, wondering whether your girlfriends were about to make fun of you. I was embarrassed also. I couldn't whisper 'Beautiful!' breathlessly as I now feel my response was. 'May I keep it?' You were surprised, almost generous, for a second. But 'Nup,' perversely. 'May I copy it out?' So I sat at your desk and copied it out reverently, speaking to you, poet to poet, suggesting where a line might end, a new stanza. You had no such finery, just words arranged like cows in a paddock. The baby challenges the television set with his life, his innocence, his ignorance. The television is dead. The baby will never contain as much knowledge, but the television set is dead. The blank affirmation of life. You, woman, with 'hate' engraved on your arms! 'Do you write other poems?' Of course not, never. What has happened to that spring of poetry, Ellen Spalding? An invisible dimension you had not indulged, do you indulge it now? Are you riding a Janis Joplin course from pimples to power, throwing yourself in with all your might, but now you would only be eighteen or nineteen? Or have you married already and weighed yourself down with babies and a man you control and who controls you, an ingrown toenail of a life? There are no middle of the road happy endings for you, my girl, not with that disastrous dichotomy. You ran away almost immediately after that day because I did not have another chance to educate the poetry in you, and I was disappointed. For with that affirmed, you would have had at least one staff to take with you on the road – but one little time? You did not believe me, might not have known that I knew. I could have convinced you had I time. But you were gone. The answers to my enquiries were horrifying searches and awful words like 'No they haven't picked her up yet.'

Please, Fate, I hope you turned that poetry into native cunning and warm womanliness so she escaped authority and was loved by her friends. Is.

Ellen, I believe in your inner freedom, I saw it. Where are you, Ellen Spalding?

Today I sat in a restaurant cupping a mug of coffee in both my hands, nodding.

'Yes, a poet can be illiterate.'

'How come she couldn't write?'

'Oh I don't know, pillar to post, school to school, punishment to punishment . . .'

'You don't believe in schools?'

'No way, that's an old argument of mine, don't get me on to it.'

'Whatever the particular art, it is a matter of environment, conditioning.'

'Yes if I could dance what I wrote I'd dance it.'

'Of course.'

'Art is the only thing that teaches. You know, you snap your fingers and say, "aha"?'

'Mmm?'

'I don't mean skills . . .'

'But you'd think if they were doing a series on the Reformatory and girls put away because they're exposed to moral danger, you'd think they'd tell the truth.'

'But the truth is hardest of all. It's so complex, the real understanding is not in knowing the facts.'

'But washing cars is hardly a happy ending. Yellow uniform. Actress smiles. Credits. Ads.'

'But it'd take a great writer, director, etc. to really convey. Or a great society.'

'Let's create Mighty Woman.'

'One way or another.'

How many people have kept you in bondage under the name of love, Ellen? Or are you still young enough to believe in the great miracle of happily-ever-after? But I imagine you have a serenity by now, an eighty-year-old eighteen-year-old . . . that you have become reliable in the disillusionment of it all . . . that your poetry has turned into useful philosophy, a pragmatic thing. Something as simple as 'You give and you get.' The sadness of that word on your forearms five years ago is that whatever life has done to you, it will not have given you, unless you have worked at obtaining the skills of an art, the means to translate its significance into something which will change society. I wish you hadn't written that poem, rather that I had taken you outside and forced you to tell me what hate meant – the poem was too easy. Distant. Maybe your real poem was your escape. Ellen on the road, fourteen, fat and courageous. Destined, according to sociologists, for the Wayside Chapel dependent on mainlining heroin. Mainlining heroin you may well be doing, wasting yourself, turning in on your hate – festering in a spiritual, social and physical sickness. I don't believe it, that gentle affirmation of life you gave me, and your sleeves were rolled to the elbows, was too deeply ingrained – at that young hopeful age you expected nothing. The tension between possibility and reality was set up ready. Friction. Fire.

Perhaps I superimpose my optimism on your life, which had it been mine may have plunged me into suicidal despair. Somehow I am here, remembering you and your name. My soft sensitivity over-reacting to the accidental and external; you have every right to scorn me in much the same spirit as you forbade me to keep your copy of your poem. I watched you passing the rubbish tins but I didn't see you screw it up, probably you did throw it away somewhere out of my sight. I would have kept that copy more carefully than the one in my handwriting, and I guess you knew that. Now you may scorn me for avoiding the social realities which have made your life a trial, social realities I am too weak to even observe and record – scorn me for wanting the sentimentality of fiction – scorn me for making you into a small heroine. Capable of scorn. Absolute.

Yet I'm crying for your shame, the babyish handwriting. Your hesitation in going up for that photograph. The pride of it! Don't let them touch that. Keep it wherever you are, Ellen Spalding.

Glenda Adams

Wedding

1976

This is the story of a wedding and a wedding night.

I wanted to wear a lovely nightgown on my wedding night. I wanted to be the loveliest, most desirable woman my husband had ever seen. I wanted him not to recognise me on my wedding night. I wanted him to look up in surprise and delight when he saw me in my nightgown and ask: how can this wonderful woman be the plain, dull, everyday girl I thought I was marrying, who stayed in my room secretly after visiting hours and shared my bed, loving me silently and fearing all the time we would be discovered.

I searched for a gown to transform me and please him. I fingered the nightgowns of Fifth Avenue. Then I went to the bargain basements of West 34th. And there I found my nightgown. It was delicate cotton, striped blue and white. It lay entangled in a mass of mark-downs, among nylon tiger and leopard patterns, purple pyjamas with feathers, and soiled baby dolls.

The label on my nightgown read: designed for Intrigue, a division of Exquisite Industries. I held it against me and knew I had to have it. It was topless.

An old sales lady, a crone with a brown tooth, loped up to me. 'He'll love it,' she said and looked around at the other customers. I smiled and frowned at the same time. She fished in the lingerie on the table and found a little pink jacket.

'This goes with it,' she said. Then she winked and laughed. 'But you'll never use it. He'll never let you put it on because he'll be too busy taking the rest off.'

The customer next to me, a man who was holding a nightgown with brown and black leopard spots, turned to look at me, first at my face and then at my breasts. Then he turned back to the leopard gown, which had slits from the armpit to the ankle.

My nightgown cost eight dollars.

After the wedding ceremony and the cake and the champagne, we went to a friend's apartment, six of us: my husband and I, my husband's room-mate, the friend whose apartment it was, a girl my husband had gone to college with but who was never his girlfriend, or so he said, and her husband. She had come all the way from Washington with her husband especially for our wedding.

The room-mate had prepared a special spaghetti dinner for us. We sat with plates of spaghetti on our laps. I thought: you are married now and this is your first meal with your husband. I felt warm and benign, even radiant. Our suitcase with my nightgown in it stood by the door.

I sat with my plate of spaghetti on my knees, and I kept my head bowed, looking at the plate sitting on my white dress, a fancy tablecloth, and I wondered if I could get a knife and fork and a glass of wine on this tablecloth, beside the plate, and stay still enough not to disturb or upset anything.

My husband had difficulty eating because he had burnt his lip. He said 'ouch' and 'ow' every now and then. The night before he had gone to the Village with some friends to bid farewell to bachelorhood. He burnt his lip with a cigarette at Your Father's Mustache. By the next day his lip had swollen, and it hurt him to smile. The burn showed as a dark spot in the wedding photographs.

The room-mate said: 'Do you think China will get into the United Nations?'

And someone said: 'Well, I happen to be in a position to know for certain that...'

And someone else said: 'You're dead wrong because it...'

And my husband said: 'If this country would only...'

And the girl who was never a girlfriend said: 'Even if it did you'd still have the problem of...'

I remembered not to forget to call my mother.

I noticed I had spilled two drops of marinara sauce on my wedding dress. It was the prettiest dress I had ever owned. I bought it for forty dollars at Franklin and Simon. It was fine white netting with white woollen flowers embroidered all over. It had long sleeves and came to just above my knees. When I tried it on I felt tall and slim and lovely. I bought a new white bra and new white panties with a flower design to wear under my beautiful dress.

The morning of my wedding I got dressed very slowly. I was alone. I stood before the mirror that rested on the dresser and looked at my face and the top half of my dress. Then I stood on a chair before the mirror to see the lower half. I was worried about my knees. My brother called them potato knees. I said to my knees in the mirror: just pretend you're going to a costume party, and you're going as a pretty girl. It's only a costume party. It'll be fun. I met my husband at a costume party, after all. I wore a black mask and just an ordinary dress. But he fell in love with me. He said he liked the way I danced.

On the morning of my wedding I was ready too soon and they were late coming to get me. I sat and waited and watched the snow coming down.

They came for me and took me to a little room next to the room of the wedding. My husband stood in a corner and nodded when I came in. I saw the burn on his lip. He turned his head away. He's nervous, I thought, and I smiled at him. I looked around for someone to tell me how pretty I looked. But everyone was busy. Someone was writing the zip code after the return address on our wedding announcements. Someone adjusted the carnation in his coat. Someone offered my husband a cigarette. Which he declined.

The men went into the wedding room first, and I was left with the photographer. He photographed me close-up looking out the window at the snow. Then he backed away for a full-length. I smiled. The photographer lowered his camera and made a silent whistle, shaking his head.

'You're the first bride I've ever seen in a mini-skirt,' he said.

So that was why no one said anything. That was why my husband could not look at me. They are all ashamed of me. How can I go in there to be married in this dress, with my potato knees. Dear God, what can I do? The last time I wore a dress that was too short was at my father's funeral. It was the only black dress I owned. I had made it myself when I worked as a salesgirl one summer. They let me go right through the service and then, just before it was my turn to place the flowers on the grave, my aunt said: 'Don't you think your dress is a little too short for a funeral?' I wanted to die.

The photographer said: 'Aren't you going in?' Then someone came to get me. 'What are you waiting for?' this person said and led me into the room where the people waited. I held my breath and walked across the green carpet, before their eyes, and stood next to my husband. 'I thought you weren't coming,' he whispered, and I could not tell if he was joking or angry or hopeful.

And we were married.

I thought I would wear my wedding dress often afterwards and tell people this was the dress I wore to get married. But just a few weeks later, as we drove through France, the suitcase with my dress was stolen. I cried. I looked in flea markets and thrift shops for my dress in every town we came to. I still look for the girl who must be wearing my wedding dress with the red marinara spots. When I see her I shall go to her and ask her to give it back, for sentimental reasons.

I still have the panties with the flower design, however. The nylon has greyed and the elastic has gone. They are in an old laundry bag waiting to be used as a dust rag.

I ate my spaghetti and I ate my salad.

'You have only to compare the situation in South Africa . . . but the French in Algeria finally learned that . . . and the Russians of course are another matter altogether . . . well not altogether, look at it this way . . .'

I wondered what a good wife would do: sit smiling and show a lively interest in the topic under discussion; sit without smiling and eat; try to change the subject, or go and lie down in the next room. I did not know the answer. I had only been married for two hours.

So I told myself: how fortunate you are to be sitting here in this room where clever things are being stated. How fortunate you are to be a bride sitting here eating spaghetti and listening to clever people, one of whom is your husband.

Between salad and dessert I went to the bathroom. Between dessert and coffee I went to the kitchen for a glass of water. After coffee I checked the suitcase to make sure my nightgown was there. I reminded myself, again, not to forget the phone call.

'You and I met at the wrong time,' said the girl, who was never a girlfriend, to my husband.

The room-mate looked across to where I was bent over the suitcase, to see if I had heard. The girl's husband from Washington was in the bathroom.

I went and stood by my husband and put my hand on his shoulder. It felt firm and comforting.

'If I were the government of South Viet Nam,' he said.

I squeezed his shoulder, meaning shouldn't we be going now.

'But you're not the government,' the girl said, 'and if you were you'd find that...'

I smiled and squeezed my husband's shoulder again and said into his ear: 'Don't you think...?'

'I would tell the Americans,' he said.

'But that would run directly against your interests,' said the girl.

I thought I would go and lie down on the bed in the next room. But the room-mate was looking at me and his eyes said: how are you going to be able to satisfy the brain of such a brilliant man in the years to come?

So I sat down again, and listened, leaning forward and nodding, and I said every now and then: 'That's a good point,' or 'There's more to it than that, don't you think?'

My husband looked at his watch and said: 'Good God, why didn't you tell me?' and we stood up to go.

'But the phone call,' I said. And we called my mother long distance to tell her that all had gone well. We also told her the cake was delicious, and we passed the receiver to the others so that they, too, could tell her.

Three women had prepared the cake. My mother and her neighbours, Mrs Hamilton and Mrs Wilson. It was a rich, dark fruit cake. My mother bought the ingredients and mixed them together. The cake was baked in Mrs Hamilton's oven, for it could be relied upon to maintain an even temperature. When the cake was baked it was taken across the road to Mrs Wilson, who had a special recipe for marzipan icing. Her marzipan looked like fine alabaster. She spent the whole afternoon icing the cake for she always had time on her hands.

They packed the cake in a cake tin and tied it in a closely fitting cotton bag and mailed it to me. Inside the tin was a note: We wish you a wonderful journey through the future. Love is a wonderful thing. Mother, Mrs Hamilton, Mrs Wilson.

On the morning of my wedding they came to take the cake to the room where I would be married. The cake was a square slab. It weighed five pounds. They carried it on a plywood board covered with aluminium foil. They had to transport it only a few blocks, but on the way the car skidded and the cake fell to the floor of the car. The icing was cracked. To cover this fault line they took small white chrysanthemum blooms from the flower vase in the corner and laid them across the top of the cake.

When I walked into the room in my white dress and saw the cake with flowers I wondered why it looked like a little square grave.

We kept a piece of the cake. We took it home to our apartment and wrapped it in foil and put it in the freezer compartment. Our friends said we should keep it until the birth of our first child. After two years I took the cake from the freezer and unwrapped it and held it for a moment. Then I threw it away. My husband asked me why I had thrown it out without even tasting it. I told him it had defrosted and refrozen so many times in the course of the years that it would be dangerous to eat it. He nodded.

We still have a photograph of the cake, with the flowers, and whenever anyone gets out the wedding photographs we tell them how it was made and what happened to it. It makes a good story, especially the part about patching up the crack.

'Can we drop you off?' said the girl who was never a girlfriend.

My husband said: 'Are you sure it won't be out of your way?' He whispered into her ear where we were going, for I was not to know. It was to be my surprise. The girl and her husband drove us across the park and down Park Avenue to the Waldorf.

We got out and thanked them and they said: 'Have a good night, but don't be too good.'

We were led to the honeymoon suite, which had an enormous bed and long mirrors along one wall.

'This is a lovely surprise,' I said. I went into the bathroom to put on my blue nightgown with the pink jacket.

'Look', I said. And he looked and smiled and said: 'That's very nice.' He had turned on the television set and was changing channels with one hand.

'It's your surprise,' I said. I went and sat next to him on the bed and began to unbutton my pink jacket to show him what a special nightgown it was.

'*Wuthering Heights* with Laurence Olivier,' he said.

'I've seen it,' I said. 'Years ago, when I was still in high school. I fell in love with Heathcliff.'

'Would you mind terribly if we watched it now, I've never seen it?' he said.

'Of course I don't mind,' I said.

We sat together in bed and watched the movie. It was the first time I had ever had a television set in my bedroom and watched a movie in bed. During a commercial I went to stand by the mirror to see if my nightgown really looked lovely, or if I had made a mistake. I wished I had bought the leopard pattern with the slits instead.

When the movie was over we phoned our breakfast order to the desk. Then we turned out the light and lay back in bed.

My husband stretched and groaned. 'I'm really tired,' he said. Then he looked at me and saw that I wanted to make love. We did.

The next morning a steward in a white jacket brought breakfast on a serving cart. The bacon and eggs and toast lay on silver serving platters under silver domes. The breakfast cost eight dollars. The same as my nightgown. I still have the nightgown. But the sales lady was wrong. I always wear it with the pink jacket.

Marion Campbell

Peepshow

1977

The front door is pressed back into the shadows away from the garden. Dull white of animal fat, the fibro-cement exterior. Moulded into it, the great meat slab of the painted verandah. The wide overhang of roof bends its shadows around this, darkening the complicated play of passing cloud and reflected leaf venetian blindfolded at the windows. The red cement tongue of path suddenly arrested at the letterbox. The roof heaps up its tile upon tile, variegated green to the big blue. The lawn is luxury. There is a name for it. Superfine. It subtly rashes legs afterwards like the lingering irritation of riverwater. The banksia's roughness against the superfine skin between the legs. Gnarled but strongrooted, it balances again and again away from its history of disequilibrium. The four legs lowered from the tree tilt the feet horizonwards. Knees blind nudge the suburban street unfurling apron lawn upon apron lawn. Drop to a soft thud on the lawn. Something must have provoked the: I'll show you his picture if you like, but that's gone now.

They used to say: the carpet is mushroom wall-to-wall. The carpet is mushroom coloured superfine and even now, mushrooms are the carpet colour digestible as oysters the sea as they slip away, the deepsea smell, the big wet organism contained in the neat membrane. The Chiffonier is pruned back by the frame of the door, but as you advance, turrets arise in all sorts of inextricably complex postscripts to the first impression.

Pillars wind around their own axes, mirrors snatch glimpses of tree ramifications, syncopated butterfly flights, other accidents. Her pale pale unblinking eyes and the paler stubble, wheaten, of the lashes. Pushing, recoiling, gesturing, recesses and bulges. The key is in one of the recesses, on the cool marble part, below the tier of mini-drawers. It jerks into the teeth of the lock. The door on right pulls away. Sheer sonic veil behind: the crackling static of summer insects. The carpet is uniform wall-to-wall, but it has embossed mounds. They imprint textured welts on your knees and shins. The shoebox is split on the side. Spills its slippery load as it is withdrawn. Photographs. In many the image has retreated into the sepia fog.

Families arranged in precarious little pyramids around garden benches, smarting at the camera-sun. Light enlarges noses astoundingly. Bellies of the children on a brighter plane too. The larger photographs curl around the other ones. Grandma's dynasties of cats. The Mullewa Tom. The Bunbury Cheshire. Tabbies of floral laps on striped deckchairs lightdappled. There he is on the deck of a ship. Shirt blossoming over the belt. Same benign camera-sun squint. The other photographs shuffle him away.

The leg in profile is poised above the other on what must have been a prop of some kind. A few wiry hairs protrude above the horizon of the thigh. This was taken in a gym. The neck is thickly muscular. There is a rush of blood, burns cheeks to a scorch. Carpet imprints floraflora binding me there. The back is arched with great ribspan to where the face nestles, fostered by its curve. The leg must have been lowered after the photograph, the towel unslung from the neck, stretched to a slow whipcrack in the air and then sawtense between the flexed back biceps as he laughs in the steamed up bathroom: Mon! could you fetch my pants. Little beads condense and slow-trickle down the mirror. Is buttock-heavy, calf-heavy, chest tense, eyes puffed as if face were foot-lit. Strokes the overnight beard, engines drone already, heavy-bellied plane. That photograph catches the touch of fatigue, faces of the others darkened too, skeins of cloud rip past, heading for the big one the big one metal belly buffeted in the flux of the canyons of it turbulence turbulence you learn that word at the age of three and cumulo cumulo nimbus as seas receive their human confetti man and man's machine with cloudburst pulverised come on come on collect your speedy particles no full fathom five this just a slight silt absorbed like communion wafer to the flatlapping sea tongue and then the slow ooze osmosis. The journalists blunder past the widow with the sealed face, plunder photographs: sorry Madam we've got a job to do. Headlines, yellow clippings unfurl. Hey! Rita!

The voice cuts hemisphere from hemisphere, wire through the plump cheese. What are you doing there? She is standing in the distended triangle of light at the kitchen door, standing in the crazy whirlpools of illumined dust. Veins stand-out on her hands, knees band-aided, eyes narrowing their glint, face looks convulsed in pain or betrayal. Ah just showing Arlie the fatcotoes the ccccat photos words came out all grated should have cleared throat. She starts towards us and then meditatively lunges at the apple wedged between thumb and fore-finger. Dishclatter. Fridge closed. She knows the pull too but would never display the relics in the cardboard sarcophagus.

Brain revulses. Summon up a catalogue voice. Ah yes. Yes. This is the dog on the farm I told you about. Zozo. Kelpie. Good sheep dog. Remember the flies under the peppermint trees. The yellow eager eyes, the spurt of tongue, and beyond the mean anatomy of the gums, the dust-puffed horizon. The photographs slip one behind the other. Not as obedient as cards. The box reloaded, side gaping wide now. The key droops, back in the lock.

Peepshow. Show you my father's body. And yours, blood still pounding in his ears, still with beard growth overnight, yours the unshowable. Showers behind drawn curtains, closed doors. Can't see Arlie's face, still lowered, hair-curtained. And then she tosses hair back. A little saliva beads, balloons at the corner of the lip. A word inflated, sucked back. She knows now. She knows. It's locked up, nuttight in the neat little skull. Then out it comes, the: Yeah . . . in a five second yawn. Hate her furiously for the drawl of it. She can still get up, walk easily down the entrance hall over the mushroom carpet and through the door. She knows. She can even let the flywire door flap back, crush the superfine with foot after foot. Follow her to a pile of blue metal, weed-infested, left on the edge of the block from the building. She kneels. The nylon dress foams around the dusty ankles, she plays limply with the blue metal, streams it through her fingers. She has it. Turning metal to liquid. Sibyl is closed, no oracles today.

– But that wasn't really like him at all. And he didn't pose for it. It was just taken.

– Oh. Really.

The voice changes register on the 'y', descends the scale as the metal dribbles from the parted fingers. Hair slides. Hers not wiry, massive. Parts like waterveil around the swan-neck. The downy swan-neck.

– Well what was he really like then this father of yours?

This father. As if it were . . . There is a series. Learn the coquetterie of orphans slipping from daddylap to daddylap.

– He was a clown.

– Ha a clown. How can you know . . .

I know. I know when I am a witch the siren airqueen and leap from the jumbled pile of jarrah behind the shed and shout I am Zora born of lightning fed on firefrost and frisky nights I know

– I don't know. That photograph was taken in a gym. He . . .

– Who tells you. Your Mother?

She has a father with workshop and carpentry set, wood-shavings, grows watermelons, makes the toast for Saturday's breakfast, passes the butter for the sweetcorn, calls her Bubs, drives the family in a long and polished car, comes in from work, tie barely relaxed, silk tassles dangling from the dressing gown girdle, leaves the shaving dregs, foam and whisker splinter on the basin sides, calls out from mouthful of food as the front door slams: I'm off, bye Mum, bye Bubs, be good, horn toot, blown kisses.

No clown, no up-side-down acrobat, no shoebox father that. She knows.

Elizabeth Jolley

Woman in a Lampshade

1979

One cold wet night in July Jasmine Tredwell took several sheets of paper and her typewriter together with a quantity of simple food and some respectable wine and, saying goodnight fondly to her dozing husband, she set off in search of solitude.

'I'm going up to the farm,' she said, 'I'll be home first thing on Monday morning,' she promised. But her husband, Emeritus Professor of Neo Byzantine Art, was encased in head-phones listening to Mahler and paid no attention to the departure.

It was not her custom to give lifts to strangers. Indeed, because of reported bashings and murders in lonely suburbs, she had, in an impulsively tender moment, promised the elderly Professor that she would never pick up from the roadside any stranger however pathetic or harmless his appearance.

She saw the young man standing in the dark. He seemed to be leaning rather than standing, the storm holding him up in its force. He was an indistinct outline, blurred because of the rain. It was as if he had come into existence simply because someone, hopelessly lost among words, had created him in thoughtful ink on the blotting paper. Immediately, forgetting her promise, she stopped the car and, leaning over, opened the door with some difficulty.

'Hop in quick young man, you're getting drowned!'

The grateful youth slipped quickly into the warm and secure fragrance. He tried, without success, not to mark the clean upholstery with the water as it ran off him in dirty little streams. Jasmine took the hills noisily, the windscreen wipers flying to and fro flinging off the splashings as if the car boasted small fountains on either side.

'Thanks,' he said, 'thanks a lot.'

'Such a terrible night,' she said, 'are you going far?'

'As far as I can get.'

'Where shall I drop you?'

'Oh, anywhere. It'll do if you drop me off when you've gone as far as you're going.' He gave a nervous little laugh. 'Tah very much,' he said. 'Thank you very much, tah!'

That the young man had no definite destination did not cause Jasmine to wish that she had not stopped to offer him a ride. They hardly spoke. Almost at once Jasmine was touched to notice that her youthful travelling companion had fallen asleep.

'He must have been exhausted,' she thought and she wondered about his ragged soaked clothes. 'He's probably hungry too,' she said to herself.

Jasmine felt safe in the lamplight. And she felt safe in the lampshade, pretty too. She was not a pretty woman, she never pretended to be. But the lampshade, when she put it on, made her feel pretty, softly so and feminine. It was the colour of ripe peaches and made of soft pleats of silk. It was light and it fitted her perfectly. It was like a garden-party hat only more foolish because it was, after all, a lampshade. To wear the lampshade suggested the dangerous and the exotic while still sheltered under a cosy domesticity.

She never guessed the first time she placed it on her head how she would feel. She had never experienced such a feeling before. It had taken her by surprise. After that first time she had looked with shy curiosity at other women in shops and at parties, at the hairdresser's and even while passing them in the street, quietly noticing the private things about them, the delicate shaping of the back of the neck or the imaginative tilt of the ears. She wondered too about all the tiny lines and folds and creases, all the secret things. So recently having discovered something about herself, she wondered what secret pleasures they had and whether they had known them long before she had discovered hers.

She sang softly,

I love my little lampshade
So frilly and warm
If I wear my silky lampshade
I'll come to no harm.

'Are you awake?' she asked the young man later that night. He was buried under a heap of old fur coats and several spoiled pages.

'Are you awake? Hey! Are you awake? God? how soundly you sleep! It's being young, I suppose, hey! wake up!'

'What's that? What the . . .?' he hardly moved.

'Young man, could you move over a bit, my typewriter's falling off my knee, it's giving me the most awful cramp. Also I'm getting a pain in my back. Ah! that's better. No, no further or you'll fall out. That'll do beautifully. Hey!' she laughed, pleased with the music of her own voice, 'don't roll back! You know, if you lie on the edge of the bed, you'll soon drop off!'

He drew the coats closer and made no sound.

'That was supposed to be a joke,' she said noisily rearranging the papers. 'But seriously,' she said, 'it's like this, I've got a young man, he's a bit of a nuisance really. First he's in a suburban post office in Australia. Can you imagine him behind the counter with his pale offended eyes about to burst into tears and all the little veins and capillaries flushed on his crooked boyish face, or something like that?

'Then he turns up again in a depressing hotel in Calais where two lesbians have gone to have a bit of privacy. The younger one wants to get away from her husband and the older one is the husband's secretary, a really boring stuffy old maid. She's quite empty headed and very irritating to be with for more than a few minutes as the younger one discovers quite quickly. In addition, the secretary, the boring one, drinks heavily and is not really very clean. An unfortunate situation altogether. Anyway, my young man's there at the hotel reception desk, in the night, being absolutely useless.'

'Who?' the voice muffled in furs could hardly be heard.

'My young man of course,' Jasmine, preening, fingered her peach-ripe silk pleats lovingly. 'He's left the P.O. to be a hotel receptionist in Calais,' she continued, 'And then, to my surprise, he moves to a cheap hotel in India, Madras to be exact, and I've got him there exactly the same, the pale offended eyes filled with tears, the same blushing capillaries, perhaps he's a bit thinner, more haunted looking and, as usual, he's no earthly use,' Jasmine sighed sadly. 'He's absolutely unable to help the guests when they arrive exhausted in the night. It's two more lesbians, younger than the others and one is very uncomfortable with an unmentionable infection. Not a very nice subject really but, as a writer, I have to look closely at *Life* and every aspect of it.' Jasmine sighed again thoughtfully, her long fingers reaching up restlessly plucked the folds of unexpected foolishness.

'*C'est un triste métier*,' she knew her pronunciation was flawless. 'In all the stories,' she said, 'one of the women is horrible to my young man. Absolutely horrible! I mean one in all three. So that's three times he has a really bad time, in all, he's despised, rejected and betrayed. But I'm glad to say that on all occasions the awful unkind behaviour is deeply regretted as soon as the resulting wretchedness is evident.'

'What's the trouble?' the young man sat up and yawned almost dislocating his lower jaw.

Jasmine banged her typewriter.

'Can't you understand, I'm stuck! I'm stuck, stuck, stuck.' She shuffled the papers across the bed. 'Oh by the way,' she said as calmly as she could, 'would you mind not smoking in bed. My husband can't stand it.'

'He's not here is he?' the young man began uneasily, 'you said, I thought...'

'No of course not,' Jasmine said, 'but the smoke hangs around and he's very sensitive, his nose I mean.' She laughed. 'But,' she said, 'whatever shall I do with them?'

'Who?'

'My characters of course. I suppose,' she paused, 'I suppose they could carry on in bed.' She began to type rapidly.

'Eh? Yeah!' He turned over.

'Mind the typewriter! Oops! I thought it was gone that time. That's better. You know I must tell you I've got a friend, Moira, well she's not a friend really, more of an enemy. Writers don't have any friends.' She settled comfortably against her mountain of pillows. 'Well Moira's trying to get a psychiatric musical off the ground. God! That woman's a Bore when she talks about her work. She never stops talking! All last week she was on about an official speech she'd been asked to write for the ceremonial opening of a deep sewerage system, I mean what is there in deep sewerage?'

'Quite a lot I should think,' he yawned again. 'Have you got going now?'

'No, not at all, it's awful!' she pulled another spoiled page from her typewriter. 'I'm afraid,' she said watching the paper as it floated to the floor, 'I'm afraid, well, you must feel so trapped and cheated. I mean, being here with me in this lonely place. Just think! I brought you all this way and then everything happening like that!'

'What d'you mean, happening,' he said patiently, 'I mean nothing has yet, has it?'

'I didn't expect my young man and the lesbians...'

'I thought they was in Madras,' he interrupted.

'Yes, yes that's right, so they should be, but my young man...'

'Well, where is he then? I thought the idea was we'd be having the place to ourselves and I'd work the farm and –' a note of disappointment replaced the impatience in his voice.

'It's such a nuisance,' Jasmine replied. 'Really I'm sorry. I was so looking forward, you know, to our getting to know each other and,' she paused, 'and there he is, stupid and useless!'

'Who? Where is he?' he sat up.

'In my brief-case. Would you mind awfully? I left it just outside in the porch, I'd be so grateful if you would.'

Reluctantly he looked at the cold floor.

'No stop!' Jasmine cried. 'Stay where you are in the warm. I must be mad! I'm the one who should go. It's my fault he's out there. I should go. I'm going out to get him. You stay in bed. I'm going!'

Jasmine slipped from the bed and pattered with quick bare feet over the boards. He heard the outside door open and slam shut. He heard the noise of plates and cups and cutlery, a plate dropped somewhere crashing and breaking.

'What's that? Who's there?' he called.

'It's nothing,' she replied through a mouthful of food, 'nothing at all to worry about. I'm just having a cheese sandwich.' She came to the bedside. 'Would you like some or are you the kind of person who doesn't like eating in bed? I've sliced up an onion and a hard-boiled egg. Do have some!'

'No thank you,' he said. 'I'm not hungry really no; no thank you, really not hungry thanks all the same.'

Jasmine ate ravenously.

'Have some Burgundy,' she said, 'or would you prefer a beer?' She poured a generous glass of wine for herself and opened a can for her guest.

'Just move over a bit,' she said with her mouth full, 'thanks.' She chewed and swallowed, 'I'm sorry, really I am,' she said, 'about these papers all over the bed. I'd like to be able to make it up to you in some way. You see I should never have picked you up. When I saw you at the side of the road absolutely drenched I simply couldn't help offering you a lift.' She studied the remains of the egg apparently lost in thoughts for which there were no words. 'Ever since I decided to become a writer,' she announced. 'I've been an absolute Pain! You hardly know me really. I mean, take tonight, I've been perfectly terrible. Please, please don't try to contradict me.'

In the silence of his obedience he hiccupped.

'Manners!' he apologised.

'Oh dear!' Jasmine was dismayed. 'Perhaps you shouldn't drink beer in bed. My husband always gets hiccups if he drinks lying down. Try walking about.'

He was not inclined to leave the bed.

'Well,' Jasmine said, 'if you're shy put this old nighty on. You walk about and I'll think up a fright for you.'

Self-conscious and solemn in brushed nylon the young man paced to and fro on the creaking floor boards. He hiccupped at regular intervals. Every minute his thin body jerked.

'Manners!' he muttered, and one minute later, 'Manners!'

Suddenly she screamed, 'Help! Help!'

'What the, who's there? Where the hell are you?' he hiccupped. 'Manners!'

'Help! Hellup!'

He hiccupped, 'Manners! Where the hell are you?'

'Under the bed silly! Help me out there's not much space.' She was out of breath. 'Such a pity it didn't work.' In the brief silence he hiccupped again.

'Look out!' she whispered. 'Look out! There's a spider behind you. A great black spider. S.P.I.D.E.R. Look behind you!'

'Manners! What? I can't hear you. Manners!'

'Oh, it's no good. You'll simply have to wait till they wear off.' She was just the tiniest bit sulky. 'I really can't help it,' she said, adjusting the lampshade with one delicate finger, 'if He visits me in the middle of the night.'

'Who? Here? Who visits you?' He began to search through the heap of furs. 'Where's my clothes? I'd better be off. Look, I shouldn't be here.'

Jasmine laughed. 'Oh relax! The Muse of course,' she said, 'perhaps I should say My Muse.' She paused. 'It's very amusing really Oh!' Her laughter was like a shower of broken glass. 'Oh!' she said. 'I made a pun there. I wonder if I could use it somewhere in here, let me see.' She rearranged several of the papers. She laughed again. 'You look so serious walking up and down in that tatty old gown.' He turned to look at her seriously and steadily.

'I've been wondering what's that, I mean, what's that on your head?'

'It's a lampshade,' she replied.

'If you don't mind my arskin', why do you?'

'Always when I'm writing,' her voice was deep with reverence.

'But I thought we was going to have it away together.'

'Yes,' Jasmine said, 'I thought so too but it's my young man –'

'The one who was in all those places?'

'Yes.'

'Oh, I see,' he paused and said in a flat voice, 'praps I'd better go then.'

'Oh no,' Jasmine said, 'there's absolutely no need. I know,' she said, 'let's dance! My little transistor's here somewhere. I know it's here, somewhere here.' She rummaged among the bear skins and the ancient silver fox. 'Ah! here we are. If we danced, you never know, it might be better. I'll just see if I can get some music. Ah good! here's music. Listen there's a dancing teacher too. What a scream!'

The pulse of the music noticeably caused life to return and the dancing instructor's voice flowed quietly bringing shape and order into the disordered room.

'Now for the stylised step. Starting position,' the Irish voice was kind, 'beat one step up beat two step together beat three step back beat four step together up together back together and up together and back together arms loose relax and smile.'

'Come on!' Jasmine was laughing.

'I don't dance. Really, I don't dance.'

'Oh come on!'

'Not on beds. I don't dance on beds. It's too dangerous and, besides, it's rude.'

Jasmine laughing and breathless reached out and turned the volume on more.

There was a change in the music.

'Now the basic camel walk and step and kick and camel walk,' the instructor's patient voice continued. 'Beat one stub left beat two stub right beat three stub left beat four stub right beat five stub left beat six kick left beat seven stub right beat eight and kick and kick that's just fine you'll make it in time beat one stub left beat two stub right think happy and relax beat three stub left beat four stub right that's great you're great the greatest!'

Jasmine fell off the bed with a crash.

'And now the Latin Hustle,' the dancing instructor's persistent voice changed rhythm as the music changed. 'Touch and one and two and step back three and four forward five and six repeat touch and one and two and step and one and two and one.'

'Now you've properly done it!' The young man fell over the furniture. 'You've knocked over the light. Have you broke it? It's pitch dark!' He stumbled again, knocking over a chair. 'Where are you?' he shouted. 'It's pitch black dark. Yo' must 'ave broke the lamp.'

'Over here!' Jasmine sang, teasing through the music and the darkness.

'Where's the matches?' Panic made him angry.

'Yoo hoo! Here I am,' Jasmine was beside him, and then she was far away. 'I'm over here,' she called, and suddenly she was close again. Both were breathing heavily, gasping even, furniture fell and crockery crashed as if something was rocking the cottage. Jasmine was laughing and laughing, pleased and excited.

'Oh go on,' she cried. 'Don't stop!' she pleaded.

'Repeat these movements till you feel comfortable and confident in your performance,' the dancing instructor's voice, keeping time perfectly, penetrated above and below the sound of the music. 'Follow the beat sequence and turn and turn repeat and turn and repeat,' his patience was endless.

'I'm going outside,' the young man was polite and strained. 'If you'll excuse me,' he said, 'I'll'ave to go outside.'

'Yes, yes of course,' Jasmine said, 'Just through the yard and up the back you can't miss.'

'Thanks,' he let the door slam. 'Sorry!' he called.

'You'll make it in time,' the dancing master's voice consoled. 'Try once more beat one stub left beat two stub right.'

Jasmine switched off her tiny radio. She was laughing softly, breathlessly. 'Now where's the other lamp and the matches? Ah! here they are.'

In the soft light she made herself comfortable with three pillows at her back. She began to type rapidly.

'My story just needs a bit of action,' she said.

A gun shot sounded close by, it was followed by a second shot.

'Splendid!' Jasmine said. 'That's just what I needed. Now I know what happens next.' She continued to type. 'He'd better do it at once. But not in Madras. He'd better get on a 'plane quickly.' Her typewriter rattled on. 'Oh well to save time he can do it at the airport.' She read aloud what she had written in the mincing tones reserved for her work. '*Quietly he took the jewelled pistol from its silky case and held it to his pale crooked forehead. His eyes were full of tears . . .*' She changed her voice. 'That's a nice touch, the crooked forehead, what exquisite writing. I've never written so well before.' She read again in the special voice, as she typed, '*Closing his eyes, he pulled the trigger . . .*'

The young man came in. He hiccupped.

'Oh my God!' said Jasmine. 'What happened?'

'I missed both time,' his voice was flat.

'Oh what a nuisance. So you're still here.' She pulled the page from her typewriter and crumpled it in her hand.

'Of course I'm still here. Where should I be?'

'But the shots,' Jasmine interrupted, 'I thought –'

'Oh that! I tried to get a rabbit but it was too quick,' he gave a shy laugh. 'I've never pointed a gun at anything before.'

'Useless, absolutely useless,' Jasmine was exasperated, 'you've muffed the whole thing. You muffed it, Can't you do anything properly.'

'I don't know,' he was almost tearful, 'I've never had the chance.'

'I suppose you've never tried for long enough,' she said.

'I would be able to if I stayed here. I –' he was eager. 'I've had a look out there. I like your place. It's just beginning to get light out there, I could see all the things that need doing. I'll fix the fence posts and paint the sheds. I think I know what's up with the tractor, I'll be able to get it going. There's all the things I'd like to do out there.' He paused and then rushed on, 'on the way up here in the car you said I could stay and work the farm, you said you needed someone like me.'

'You never stay anywhere long enough, you said so yourself.' She put a fresh sheet in the typewriter.

'Well it's not my fault. Like I said, "I've had no chance."'

'What do you do?' Jasmine asked.

'What d'you mean?'

Outside a rooster crowed.

'Oh never mind!' Jasmine yawned. 'I suppose you're, how do they describe it,' she paused, 'discovering yourself.'

'I'm between jobs,' he shouted, 'That's where I've always been, between jobs. Between jobs. Between nothing!' he paused.

'But out there,' he was breathless and excited, 'I saw it all out there waiting to be done, there's everything to do out there. I'll fix everything, you'll see.'

'We like it as it is,' Jasmine said. 'My husband and I like it as it is, we don't want any change.'

'There's even a turkey yard,' he interrupted her, 'you'd like some turkeys wouldn't you, the yard only needs a bit of new wire netting. I'd have some fowls too.'

'But don't you understand,' Jasmine said, 'we only come here to get away from it all. We like the place as it is. It's only a weekender you know, we like it like this.'

'I'll measure up how much wire,' he ignored her, 'I'll need a bit of paper and a pencil. I'll work out how much paint.'

'Australia, Calais, Madras,' Jasmine said softly, 'what does it matter where I set him, London, New York, Bombay, Paris,

Rome, it's all the same wherever he is. What does it matter where he pulls the trigger. First, I'll get him somewhere alone and then I'll kill him off.'

'What's that,' he said quickly, 'what did you say?'

Outside another rooster answered the first one.

'Oh, nothing,' she fussed through her papers. 'I think it's really quite light outside now. There's a bus down at the crossroads about five fifty. It should get you back to town around eight o'clock.' She paused and then said, 'I want you to know I feel really bad about the whole thing. I mean about bringing you all the way to the cottage like this,' she spoke rapidly, 'because of wasting your time like this, and I do feel bad about it, I'm going to give you this poem I've written. You can keep it. I have other copies.'

'Thank you,' he was only just polite, 'thank you very much.'

'Fourteen stanzas,' Jasmine crooned, 'fourteen stanzas all with fourteen lines and every one all about my adorable little black poodles.'

'What'll I do,' the young man said, 'when I get to the empty town at eight?'

'There's a little refrain,' Jasmine murmured, 'in the middle of every stanza.'

'What'll I do,' he said, 'when I get to the empty town at eight? I mean where will I go? What can I do there?'

'All the stanzas', she continued, 'have this little refrain to include every one of my little black dogs.'

'I mean,' he said, 'where will I go when I get there? I'd rather stay here and fix the fences. Where will I go? What's there to do in the empty town at eight?' He smiled a moment at his own thoughts. 'You know,' he said, 'there's something good about putting new paint on with a new brush. Dark glossy green, I can just see it out there,' he smiled in the direction of the yard.

'When I wrote the poem,' Jasmine said, 'I knew it was good. I was really pleased with it. It's a good poem. I love my poem.'

'Where will I go in the empty town?' he whined. 'I'll have nothing to eat and nowhere to sleep. Can't I stay and paint the shed? Please?'

'I want everyone to be pleased with the poem,' she said.

'Eight's early to reach town if you've no reason,' he shouted.

'There!' Jasmine smiled, 'I've just thought of a wonderful line for a new poem. I must get it down because I forget everything I think up if I don't get it down.' She began to type, made a mistake, and pulling the spoiled page out, started a fresh page.

'I mean,' the young man cried, 'where will I go when I get there? What's there in town for me to do?'

'I never realised before', Jasmine yawned, 'that my young man in Madras is an absolute Bore!'

He went to the door and opened it. 'Well, I'd better be on my way then,' he said in a quiet flat voice. He went out carefully closing the door behind him.

Jasmine sat in bed writing her autobiography. *My father*, she typed, *was the distinguished scientist who discovered heat and light* . She stopped typing to sing to herself,

I love my little lampshade
So frilly and warm
If I wear my silky lampshade
I'll come to no harm.

He wrote, she typed, *in his lifetime, two text books, the one on light was blue and for heat, he chose red.*

Patricia Grace

It Used to be Green Once

1980

We were all ashamed of our mother. Our mother always did things to shame us. Like putting red darns in our clothes, and cutting up old swimming togs and making two – girl's togs from the top half for my sister, and boy's togs from the bottom half for my brother. Peti and Raana both cried when Mum made them take the togs to school. Peti sat down on the road by our gate and yelled out she wasn't going to school. She wasn't going swimming. I didn't blame my sister because the togs were thirty-eight chest and Peti was only ten.

But Mum knew how to get her up off the road. She yelled loudly, 'Get up off that road my girl. There's nothing wrong with those togs. I didn't have any togs when I was a kid and I had to swim in my nothings. Get up off your backside and get to school.' Mum's got a loud voice and she knew how to shame us. We all dragged Peti up off the road before our mates came along and heard Mum. We pushed Peti into the school bus so Mum wouldn't come yelling up the drive.

We never minded our holey fruit at first. Dad used to pick up the cases of over-ripe apples or pears from town that he got cheap. Mum would dig out the rotten bits, and then give them to us to take for play-lunch. We didn't notice much at first, not until Reweti from down the road yelled out to us one morning, 'Hey you fullas. Who shot your pears?' We didn't have anywhere to hide our lunch because we weren't allowed school bags until we got to high school. Mum said she wasn't buying fourteen school bags. When we went to high school we could have shoes too. The whole lot of us gave Reweti a good hiding after school.

However, this story is mainly about the car, and about Mum and how she shamed us all the time. The shame of rainbow darns and cut-up togs and holey fruit was nothing to what we suffered because of the car. Uncle Raz gave us the car because he couldn't fix it up any more, and he'd been fined because he lived in Auckland. He gave the car to Dad so we could drive our cream cans up to the road instead of pushing them up by wheelbarrow.

It didn't matter about the car not having brakes because the drive from our cowshed goes down in a dip then up to the gate. Put the car in its first gear, run it down from the shed, pick up a bit of speed, up the other side, turn it round by the cream stand so that it's pointing down the drive again, foot off the accelerator and slam on the handbrake. Dad pegged a board there to make sure it stopped. Then when we'd lifted the cans out on to the stand he'd back up a little and slide off down the drive – with all of us throwing ourselves in over the sides as if it were a dinghy that had just been pushed out into the sea.

The car had been red once because you could still see some patches of red paint here and there. And it used to have a top too, that you could put down or up. Our uncle told us that when he gave it to Dad. We were all proud about the car having had a top once. Some of the younger kids skited to their mates about our convertible and its top that went up and down. But that was before our mother started shaming us by driving the car to the shop.

We growled at Mum and we cried but it made no difference. 'You kids always howl when I tell you to get our shopping,' she said.

'We'll get it Mum. We won't cry.'

'We won't cry Mum. We'll carry the sack of potatoes.'

'And the flour.'

'And the bag of sugar.'

'And the rolled oats.'

'And the tin of treacle.'

'We'll do the shopping Mum.'

But Mum would say, 'Never mind, I'll do it myself.' And after that she wouldn't listen any more.

How we hated Wednesdays. We always tried to be sick on Wednesdays, or to miss the bus. But Mum would be up early yelling at us to get out of bed. If we didn't get up when we were told she'd drag us out and pull down our pyjama pants and set our bums on the cold lino. Mum was cruel to us.

Whoever was helping with the milking had to be back quickly from the shed for breakfast, and we'd all have to rush through our kai and get to school. Wednesday was Mum's day for shopping.

As soon as she had everything tidy she'd change into her good purple dress that she'd made from a Japanese bedspread, pull on her floppy brimmed blue sunhat and her slippers and galoshes, and go out and start up the car.

We tried everything to stop her shaming us all.

'You've got no licence Mum.'

'What do I want a licence for? I can drive can't I? I don't need the proof.'

'You got no warrant.'

'Warrant? What's warrant?'

'The traffic man'll get you Mum.'

'That rat. He won't come near me after what he did to my niece. I'll hit him right over his smart head with a bag of riwais and I'll hit him somewhere else as well.' We never could win an argument with Mum.

Off she'd go on a Wednesday morning, and once out on the road she'd start tooting the horn. This didn't sound like a horn at all but more like a flock of ducks coming in for a feed. The reason for the horn was to let all her mates and relations along the way know she was coming. And as she passed each one's house, if they wanted anything they'd have to run out and call it out loud. Mum couldn't stop because of not having any brakes. 'E Kiri,' each would call. 'Mauria mai he riwai,' if they wanted spuds; 'Mauria mai he paraoa,' if they wanted bread. 'Mauria mai he tarau, penei te kaita,' hand spread to show the size of the pants they wanted Mum to get. She would call out to each one and wave to them to show she'd understood. And when she neared the store she'd switch the motor off, run into the kerbing and pull on the handbrake. I don't know how she remembered all the things she had to buy – I only know that by the time she'd finished, every space in that car was filled and it was a squeeze for her to get into the driver's seat. But she had everything there, all ready to throw out on the way back.

As soon as she'd left the store she'd begin hooting again, to let the whole district know she was on her way. Everybody would be out on the road to get their shopping thrown at them, or just to watch our mother go chuffing past. We always hid if we heard her coming.

The first time Mum's car and the school bus met was when they were both approaching a one-way bridge from opposite directions. We had to ask the driver to stop and give way to Mum because she had no brakes. We were all ashamed. But everyone soon got to know Mum and her car and they always stopped whenever they saw her coming. And you know, Mum never ever had an accident in her car, except for once when she threw a side of mutton out to Uncle Peta and it knocked him over and broke his leg.

After a while we started walking home from school on Wednesdays to give Mum a good chance of getting home before us, and so we wouldn't be in the bus when it had to stop and let her past. The boys didn't like having to walk home but we girls didn't mind because Mr Hadley walked home too. He was a new teacher at our school and he stayed not far from where we lived. We girls thought he was really neat.

But one day, it had to happen. When I heard the honking and tooting behind me I wished that a hole would appear in the ground and that I would fall in it and disappear for ever. As Mum came near she started smiling and waving and yelling her head off. 'Anyone wants a ride,' she yelled, 'they'll have to run and jump in.'

We all turned our heads the other way and hoped Mr Hadley wouldn't notice the car with our mother in it, and her yelling and tooting, and the brim of her hat jumping up and down. But instead, Mr Hadley took off after the car and leapt in over the back seat on top of the shopping. Oh the shame.

But then one day something happened that changed everything. We arrived home to find Dad in his best clothes, walking round and grinning, and not doing anything like getting the cows in, or mending a gate, or digging a drain. We said, 'What are you laughing at Dad?' 'What are you dressed up for? Hey Mum what's the matter with Dad?'

'Your Dad's a rich man,' she said. 'Your Dad, he's just won fifty thousand dollars in a lottery.'

At first we couldn't believe it. We couldn't believe it. Then we all began running round and laughing and yelling and hugging Dad and Mum. 'We can have shoes and bags,' we said. 'New clothes and swimming togs, and proper apples and pears.' Then do you know what Dad said? Dad said, 'Mum can have a new car.' This really astounded and amazed us. We went numb with excitement for five minutes then began hooting and shouting again, and knocking Mum over.

'A new car!'

'A new car?'

'Get us a Packard Mum.'

'Or a De Soto. Yes, yes.'

Get this, get that...

Well Mum bought a big shiny green Chevrolet, and Dad got a new cowshed with everything modernised and water gushing everywhere. We all got our new clothes – shoes, bags, togs – and we even started taking posh lunches to school. Sandwiches cut in triangles, bottles of cordial, crisp apples and pears, and yellow bananas.

And somehow all of us kids changed. We started acting like we were somebody instead of ordinary like before. We used to whine to Dad for money to spend and he'd always give it to us. Every week we'd nag Mum into taking us to the pictures, or if she was tired we'd go ourselves by taxi. We got flash bedspreads and a piano and we really thought we were neat.

As for the old car – we made Dad take it to the dump. We never wanted to see it again. We all cheered when he took it away, except for Mum. Mum stayed inside where she couldn't watch, but we all stood outside and cheered.

We all changed, as though we were really somebody, but there was one thing I noticed. Mum didn't change at all, and neither did Dad. Mum had a new car all right, and a couple of new dresses, and a new pair of galoshes to put over her slippers. And Dad had a new modern milking shed and a tractor, and some other gadgets for the farm. But Mum and Dad didn't change. They were the same as always.

Mum still went shopping every Wednesday. But instead of having to do all the shopping herself she was able to take all her friends and relations with her. She had to start out earlier so she'd have time to pick everyone up on the way. How angry we used to be when Mum went past with her same old sunhat and her heap of friends and relations, and them all waving and calling out to us.

Mum sometimes forgot that the new car had brakes, especially when she was approaching the old bridge and we were coming the opposite way in the school bus. She would start tooting and the bus would have to pull over and let her through. That's when all our aunties and uncles and friends would start waving and calling out. But some of them couldn't wave because they were too squashed by people and shopping, they'd just yell. How shaming.

There were always ropes everywhere over Mum's new car holding bags of things and shovel handles to the roof and sides. The boot was always hanging open because it was too full to close – things used to drop out on to the road all the time. And the new car – it used to be green once, because if you look closely you can still see some patches of green paint here and there.

Joy Cowley
Apple Wine
1980

Ellen was looking for three perfect roses to go on the table. 'The storm has done almost no damage at all,' she said as she leaned over the bushes, her secateurs probing like the pincers of a large beetle. 'Which do you prefer, Hetty? Pink or white?'

But her sister was in the hall talking on the telephone to Muriel. 'I said the garden, dear.' Her voice came out the front door and rolled across the verandah, every word clear and the shape of a bell. 'We decided to have the reading out-of-doors today. Yes dear. Oh indeed yes. Quite superb. Ellen's put the wicker chairs under the walnut tree and there's plenty of shade, but I suggest you bring your panama. No dear, your hat. Do bring your hat.'

Ellen pulled a pink rose towards the secateurs and waited. Her sister often said things were quite superb. It was a figure of speech which described Hetty's vitality more than anything else, but today the expression was so rightly fitting it had taken on a new sound, magnificent, like a phrase from the Hallelujah chorus. To Ellen's mind, there was no better way of describing the transformation wrought by an overnight change in the weather. It was quite superb.

The lawn was still very damp, of course, but it had risen from the earth as thick as living fur, glistening, patched at the edges with the shadows of trees. And the roses, yesterday half-drowned, had inhaled the sun and expanded until they were almost bursting with colour and perfume.

Ellen touched the face of the pink rose and thought, angel skin, it was like blushing angel skin, then, hearing Hetty on the verandah, she called out, 'Do you remember what Daddy used to say about the rain? How it was the angels weeping for their sins?'

'Did he, dear?' said Hetty, shaking the white cloth over the table. 'No Ellen, those are too pale for the tea set. That red one, dear, growing by the thingummy – yes, yes, that's it.'

'I wonder if it was original,' said Ellen. 'Knowing Daddy, it probably was.'

Hetty didn't comment. She had changed the focus of her spectacles by lifting them away from her nose and was watching Ellen select the flowers. 'Muriel thinks it's time we had a chat to Olive,' she said.

Ellen carefully trimmed a stem. It was an old rose with single petals round yellow stamens and a heavy perfume unrefined by breeding. Too rich for the tea table, she thought.

'Did you hear me, dear? I believe at times you're as deaf as Muriel. I was talking about Olive. Muriel feels we've let it go far too long and the sooner we say something, the better for Olive's sake. Wouldn't you agree? Ellen? Ellen, are you listening?'

She closed the secateurs and brought the flowers over to Hetty. 'They're a nice colour,' she said. 'But I fear everything will smell of roses.'

'Muriel saw Stella last night. Stella says she can't come back to the reading group while Olive's in it.' Hetty flattened the creases in the cloth. 'We should do it today,' she said.

Ellen took the cut-crystal vase from the tea trolley and set it at the centre of the table with the three red roses leaning out from its rim. The light through the walnut tree lay in shivering shapes on the table, striking the vase so that its reflection on the cloth held splashes of white fire extending into rainbows and two red spots like wine stains.

She turned. 'Hetty, let's have a bottle of the apple wine.'

Her sister stopped mid-sentence as though someone had put in her mouth something to be tasted. She smiled. 'What a superb idea. Yes, indeed yes, a bottle of the good batch and we'll serve tea after the reading. Oh Ellen, you are a clever thing with flowers. It's so pretty –' She softly clapped her hands. 'We'll use the decanter,' she said.

It seemed rather frivolous to get out Daddy's decanter for their homemade apple wine and Ellen was surprised that Hetty had suggested it. As she opened the cabinet door she felt her father's disapproval in the stiffness of the hinges and she called to Hetty in the kitchen, 'We'll use the good glasses too, won't we?'

'Of course, dear!' Hetty shouted back and in a voice so reckless that Ellen laughed into the dark corners of the teak shelves.

Muriel came before they had finished setting the table, deliberately early so that she could talk about Olive. She was wearing a white and navy dress with a green silk scarf to hide the cord of her hearing machine, and a hat of yellowing straw. In a brown paperbag under her arm she carried the large-print edition of *Lorna Doone*. For some small time she stood by the verandah to fully admire the garden and exclaim over the stocks and lavender, geraniums, roses, the table under the tree, 'Gosh, Hetty, your apple wine. We are in for a treat.' Then she sat heavily in one of the wicker chairs and pulled off her gloves, finger by finger. 'I came in a taxi cab. Olive offered to bring me, which was jolly decent of her.' She looked at Hetty. 'She's been more than generous with her motor, I don't deny it.'

'We always pay for the benzine, dear,' said Hetty.

'The spirit of generosity,' said Muriel. 'We'll find it difficult to accept the loss of our little excursions, especially the concerts. We'll miss the concert season. I say, Hetty, there must be someone in the village. Are you sure we haven't overlooked the possibility? What about that friend of yours related to the Scott-Turners, Mrs Calder? Doesn't she drive a motor car?'

'She had a stroke,' shouted Hetty.

'Pam Calder? Oh Hetty, what a shame. I am sorry to hear that. Well then – who else? Ellen, do you have an acquaintance with a motor?'

'I'm afraid I don't,' said Ellen.

'Pardon, dear?' said Muriel.

Hetty leaned over Muriel's chair. 'Ellen doesn't want to talk about it. She thinks we're being unfair. Unfair. To Olive. She thinks we're trying to put poor Oliver out in the snow. Muriel, do switch on your deaf aid.'

Unfair?' Muriel fumbled with the pocket on her bodice and her hearing machine whistled like an untuned wireless. 'Does she?' The noise stopped. 'Is that what you really think, Ellen?'

But Ellen didn't know what she thought, only that she believed no one had the right to turn a beautiful day to unpleasant purpose, so she nodded affirmation and sat in the opposite chair, leaning back until Muriel's head was barely visible above the table.

Muriel laughed, 'Olive, I imagine, will be vastly relieved. Of course she will, Ellen. Poor soul gets so fearfully bored with our fuddy-duddy ways, her only refuge lies in sleep or photos of her grandchildren. She'd have drifted away months ago if she didn't have our only means of private conveyance. Loyalty, Ellen. Loyal and generous to a fault, that's our Olive. Years ago Winkie had a batman cast in the same mould. The salt of the very earth.'

Ellen said nothing. The table rose between them like an altar with the white linen cloth, the decanter and glasses, the crimson roses already open to the stage of dropping. There was no sediment in the wine. It glowed in the decanter a pale gold colour but with a look of age to it, as though they had fermented pre-war sunshine in a vintage year. The long-stemmed glasses which had been covered with the fine dust of a locked cupboard were now so clean they looked as frail as soap bubbles.

And, as Ellen had predicted, everything smelled of roses.

'Our poor little group,' Hetty was saying. 'We've been disappearing like the ten little nigger boys. Do you remember, Muriel, the meeting at Cynthia's and how she used to read from that very odd lectern with the carved monkeys on it? Now Cynthia's gone. It was quite sad, dear, very sudden, in a nursing home in Auckland, I believe.'

A stillness came into the garden and a quiet which they held not so much for the passing of Cynthia who had, God bless her, been very trying at times, but for the resurrection of her drawing room and the afternoons they'd spent in it.

After a while Muriel sighed and said, 'I know, Hetty. You told me several times.'

'Did I, dear?' said Hetty. 'I don't remember.'

Olive came late and in a hurry. The moment they decided to pour the wine without her, they heard the little motor car crying out with the suddenness of its halt outside their hedge, and they put the stopper back in the decanter. They heard a car door slam and then immediately, another. Hetty and Muriel looked a question at Ellen who shook her head and stood up, trying to see through the trees. She sat down again quickly. 'I think she has brought a gentleman friend,' she said.

'A what?' said Muriel in a hushed tone, but it was clear from her expression of disbelief that she had heard and understood.

'Oh dear,' said Hetty, and she turned her chair so that her back was to the gate.

None of them got up to greet Olive. She bustled up the path, large in pink and lavender, with a young man following several paces behind her.

Very young, observed Ellen, very tall and so fair his hair caught the sun like thistledown.

He saw them first and said something to Olive, who turned at the point of knocking on the front door, and gave a cry of surprise. She came across the lawn with small quick steps, calling, 'Oh now! Oh my, I mean to say, isn't that just lovely? Isn't it beautiful? Like a scene from the movies, you know, with the garden in the background. Oh, I never in all my born days saw such a picture. You girls, you look just like royalty, don't they, Gareth?' She turned back to the young man. 'Girls, this is Gareth Malleson, my eldest grandson.' Then, taking him by the arm, she introduced him to each of them in turn.

He was only a boy, Ellen decided, tall and well-grown, but with a freshness to his complexion which indicated that a shaving brush was still new to him. He had blue eyes and straight fair hair which fell over his eyes when he leaned forward. His trouser was of a coarse cream fabric with buttoned pockets on the legs and he wore a pink and white striped shirt open at the throat. Round his neck hung a gold chain with some kind of coin or medal attached.

He was unusually polite for a young man of the day, and seemed well enough at ease. 'Nan's always talking about her reading group,' he said. 'I was glad for the opportunity to meet you.'

'Gareth's not staying,' said Olive taking the empty chair. 'He's just dropped me off so he can borrow the car for the afternoon, haven't you, love?' She smiled up at him. 'He's picking me up again at five.'

He would have gone then, but Hetty, perhaps touched by his charming manner or her own initial coldness, held on to the arms of her chair and almost stood. 'Before you go, Mr Malleson, will you please join us in a glass of apple wine?'

'Thank you,' he said. 'Sure, I'd like to.'

'We have extra glasses,' said Hetty, 'and Ellen will get you a chair.'

But the young man insisted he'd rather sit on the ground, no, it wasn't all that damp and no, no, he wouldn't get grass stains, see, he'd make sure he didn't. He unfolded his handkerchief and spread it by the base of the walnut tree, then he came back to the table and offered to pour. 'It's my job,' he said. 'I'm a waiter.'

'Just listen to him,' laughed Olive. 'Of course he isn't a waiter. He's at university. He's going to be a lawyer. Don't let him kid you, girls, he's an awful tease.' And she smiled at him as though he were made of precious metal.

'It is my job,' he said. 'Two nights a week I pour wine and I'm very good at it. I should be. I've been a part-time wine waiter for nearly two years.' He took the stopper from the decanter and held it under his nose. 'Seventy-seven,' he said. 'A very good season for Granny Smiths.'

At that, even Muriel laughed and the sunlight fairly danced across the table.

Olive eased off her shoes and stretched her feet. 'I like a drop of cider now and then. It's got a kick like a mule if you over-indulge yourself, but a glass or two doesn't hurt.'

'This isn't cider, dear,' said Hetty. 'It's apple wine.'

'Oh?'

'They're very different,' said Hetty.

'Well go on, you could have fooled me,' said Olive.

The young man poured the pale wine into a glass, neatly twisting his wrist so that not a drop spilled on the tablecloth. His hands were yet at the bony stage, long fingers, large knuckles. 'What's the difference?' he asked.

'One can make cider of any apple,' said Hetty. 'Oh yes, indeed, any type, any quality. In fact if one leaves the apples to fall off the tree and rot in the grass of their own accord, they will make cider.'

'And wine?' he said. 'How do you go about making that?'

'We use only the best apples,' said Hetty. 'An equal quantity of dessert, cooking and crab apples. Then we add refined sugar. That's another of the essential differences between wine and cider. Cider has no added sugar. The process is the same as for any wine, Mr Malleson, but there is much to go wrong – yeastiness, haze, rope, thinness, acidity. We find that only one year in four produces excellence. This is one of our better rackings.'

'It looks like a sylvaner riesling,' he said.

'Nothing so innocuous,' said Muriel. 'Hetty's apple wine is ambrosia and you'll need the stamina of the gods if you're going to drink it like your riesling.'

'It is – a substantial wine,' said Hetty.

He brought the glasses to them with the small niceties of presentation he'd use in his employment, heels together, a flourish from the waist that turned a stoop into a bow, then he took his own glass and sat with his back against the tree trunk. 'Your very good health,' he said.

'Cheers,' said Olive.

'Good health,' said Muriel.

The wine had only the faintest taste of apples, Ellen thought. Mostly it was flavoured with the season of the picking, the light chill of a mist, the crispness of a little frost and over it all, the warmth of the sun. She leaned back against the cushions to savour better the total effort of the beautifully balanced glass and its straw-coloured content.

'This is a fantastic wine!' the young man was saying. 'It's so smooth on the palate, so – so rounded.'

'Yes,' said Hetty. 'It's quite superb, isn't it?'

'Just goes to show you're never too old to learn something new,' said Olive.

'I assume you're on holiday,' said Hetty. 'From where, may I ask?'

'Christchurch,' he said. 'I don't get up this way very often, not as often as Nan would like. I work most of my vacations and, well, you don't fly five hundred miles just for a weekend visit.'

Olive had her bag open on the arm of Muriel's chair. 'This is the daughter who lives in Christchurch, Edna my eldest, Gareth's mother. I showed you the other day, remember, taken outside their new home, all five of them, the two girls and Gareth standing there by his Dad.'

Ellen sipped in silence. The green shade was spotted and barred with sunlight which moved every time a breeze disturbed the tree so that they seemed to be in the flickering current at the bottom of some woodland pool, like a group of trout or grayling. She watched the shadows move across the young man's face and saw his hair float over his forehead as he nodded, listening.

'I'm so glad I've got Hetty, thought Ellen suddenly. The warmth of the wine had made her feel sad for Muriel living on her own, no one to care for. Poor Muriel, her only daughter had married a dark gentleman from the Islands who had taken her away to live with his family, and Muriel had not seen her in twenty-seven years.

I don't know what I'd do without Hetty, Ellen thought. I've so much to be grateful for.

Muriel had taken the photograph from Olive and was holding it at arm's length towards the young man. 'I say, Hetty, he looks awfully like a young John Ridd.'

Hetty looked and slowly nodded.

'He does, doesn't he?' said Muriel in a deliberately teasing manner. 'What a coincidence. We have a visitation from the hero of this very novel.' And she patted the package in her lap. 'Look, Ellen, wouldn't you say he was none other than John Ridd in person?'

'No,' said Ellen. 'John Ridd was of much broader stature and he had a beard.'

'But I'm sure he didn't always have a beard, dear,' said Hetty, and their laughter surrounded the boy who blushed and put his head down, his composure gone.

Olive said, 'Don't worry, love. John Ridd's everybody's heart-throb. He's a big fellow built like an ox on the outside but a real kewpie doll underneath, kind, as cuddlesome as they come.'

The boy's face was pink and his eyes were down. He tried to say something with hand movements.

Muriel was enjoying herself. 'He gets – John Ridd gets most awfully intimidated by compliments.'

Hetty stopped laughing and turned her glass in her hands. 'Have you read *Lorna Doone*?' she asked him.

He shook his head.

'Oh what a pity,' said Hetty. 'It's a book best read in one's early years. Ellen selected it for the reading group because it was a favourite of her girlhood, but I think it's a mistake to revisit the places of one's youth. Wouldn't you agree? Everything seems so small and so ordinary when one goes back. With *Lorna Doone* one feels that all the best pages have been removed.'

'I don't,' said Ellen. 'I find the story as touching as ever. As for the descriptions of the English countryside, they're beautifully written and quite wasted on a child. I'm sure I didn't appreciate Mr Blackmore's penmanship nearly as much when I was young.'

'Oh yes, indeed yes,' said Hetty. 'He paints delightful little landscapes. But what about the romance, Ellen, that splendid passion between Lorna Doone and John Ridd – how improbable to the adult reader. At no time in the history of men and women since Adam, could friendship exist on such stilted utterances. It's so childish dear.'

Ellen smiled. Hetty, she thought, was getting a little tiddly.

Muriel had taken their large-print edition from its bag and was turning the pages. 'We missed an extraordinary thing, Hetty. Did I tell you? Going back, I discovered an unaccountable change in the character of Mrs Betty Muxworthy. Most extraordinary.' She looked at the boy. 'Betty Muxworthy is a domestic servant in the Ridd household.'

'An unpleasant woman,' said Hetty.

'Embittered by fortune,' said Muriel. 'Here it is. On page 49 when she first appears, she has a lilting Irish brogue. Listen to this: "Men is so desaving," she says, "and so is galanies; but the most desaving of all is books with their heads and tails, and the speckots in 'em lika peg as have taken the maisles. Some folks purtends to laugh and cry over them. God forgive them for liard!" But look here, a few pages further on and for the rest of the book, she has a broad Devon dialect: "Zailor, ees fai! ay and zarve un raight!" There, what do you make of that? Absolutely different.'

'Nothing,' said Hetty, waving her glass. 'He made a mistake, dear.'

'He didn't, said Muriel.

'Oh, he did,' said Hetty. 'Mr Blackmore was not the most gifted of writers in the portrayal of character, but never mind, he was obviously a kindly man. The character of John Ridd assured us that.'

'Assures us what?' said Muriel whose hearing machine was whistling again.

'That he was kind,' shouted Hetty.

Already quite tiddly, thought Ellen, and in fine form. By evening she would have one of her heads.

'I see,' said Muriel, vaguely.

Ellen said, 'Hetty, how do you know John Ridd was an autobiographical portrait?'

'He was,' said Hetty. 'Indeed he was, my dear. When only one character in the book is real, one can be sure he's the author.' She held out her glass. 'Now our young John Ridd is going to help us to some more wine.'

Ellen didn't see what happened next. In standing to take Hetty's glass, the boy somehow knocked over his own. The noise of breaking crystal was loud and discordant as though someone had upset a harpsichord. Ellen heard it in every part of her body.

The boy sucked in his breath with a stricken sound and stood with his back to Ellen, looking at the fragments.

'Jolly bad luck,' said Muriel.

'It's not important,' said Hetty. 'Don't concern yourself.'

'It must have hit the root of the tree,' he said. 'I'm sorry, I didn't see it. I must have kicked – Jees, I'm sorry.'

Daddy's wineglass, mourned Ellen, rocking with pain. Oh, how awful. Daddy's beautiful glass.

'Don't give it a thought,' said Hetty.

Olive got out of her chair. 'Gareth, Gareth!' With her hands on her knees and her arms set like wings, she bent over, looking for the pieces in the grass by the tree. 'You're such a clumsy boy. That was antique, you know, you can never replace it for love or money.'

'Olive, don't make a fuss,' said Hetty. 'There are five of us and we still have five glasses. Olive. Please. You'll cut your fingers.'

'I'm sorry,' said the boy. 'I know they're rare. I feel terrible.'

'All his life he's had two left feet,' said Olive.

'It just happened,' he said.

'No, no,' said Muriel. 'Not in your 'kerchief, that could be nasty.' She handed him the brown paperbag which had held the book. 'Put it in there and do be careful of the splinters. Oh,

I say, cheer up, it's not the end of the silly old world. Bear in mind that John Ridd also had two left feet.'

'All of you leave the wretched thing,' said Hetty. 'Mr Malleson, put that down and we'll attend to it later. Come over here. You may pour us all some more wine, my dear.'

He stood up slowly and brushed his hair away from his forehead. 'Do you trust me?'

Hetty laughed. 'Of course I trust you. When a woman gets to my age, she can trust any man.' She clapped her hands twice. 'We'll have no more talk of broken glass. Ellen, you've been very quiet this afternoon, hardly a word, dear. You can introduce the next topic of conversation.'

Ellen looked away from their eyes. She could think of nothing new, nothing at all. She let the boy take the empty glass from her fingers. 'I don't know,' she said. 'Unless you want to talk about the English countryside.'

'Not of general interest, dear,' said Hetty.

'Gareth's been to England,' said Olive.

'Have you?' Hetty turned quickly. 'Have you really?'

'Briefly,' he said. 'For three weeks last year. We were in London most of the time but I saw a bit of the country. We had a few days travelling round the Lake District, and then for a couple of days we stayed with friends at Great Missenden in Buckinghamshire.' He poured from the decanter into their glasses. 'You'll know it a lot better than I do.'

'Oh yes, I adore the Cotswolds,' said Muriel. 'Did you get down to Aldershot?'

But he was looking at Ellen.

'No,' she said. 'I've never been to England.'

'Haven't you?' He seemed surprised and that pleased her.

'Mother and Daddy were both English, of course,' she said. 'But Hetty and I have never been outside of New Zealand.'

'We were considering a sea voyage a few years ago,' said Hetty. 'People advised us against it. They warned us we'd find the old country changed so much, we'd be disappointed.'

'Terribly,' said Muriel.

'Did you find it changed, Mr Malleson?' said Hetty.

'I don't know,' he said. 'I couldn't make a comparison. Everyone kept telling me the cities had altered beyond recognition but no one told me what they meant by it. Whether you'd be disappointed or not would depend on your expectation, I suppose.'

'But the countryside,' said Ellen, 'is it as green as they say it is?'

'Not when I was there,' he said. 'They were having a drought and the paddocks were burned to a crisp, more like the colour of Spain or Greece.'

Oh no, thought Ellen. Not paddocks. Fields. Fields and meadows, woods and copses, spinneys and hedgerows and thickets.

'These days,' said Muriel, 'you can go from the Bayswater Road to Regent Street and not see a Londoner.'

'Yes,' said the boy, passing their refilled glasses. 'I reckon you could. It's just about possible.'

'You haven't poured one for yourself,' said Hetty.

'No,' he said. 'I'd like to, but if you don't mind, it's time I excused myself.'

'So soon?' said Hetty.

'I'm sorry,' he said. 'I could happily stay here all afternoon.'

'He's taking the car into town,' said Olive.

'Oh yes,' said Hetty remembering. 'You have an appointment.'

He had stepped backwards. 'Thank you for the wine. It was great, really fantastic. And thank you for being so nice about the you-know-what. No, stay there. Please don't bother to get up.'

'Don't be any later than five on the dot,' said Olive.

He had moved beyond the trees but even in full sunlight he looked cool, as though he were made of shade itself. His right hand was palm out towards them, instructing them to remain seated, but when he reached the path he moved it in a sweeping circle and called, 'Ciao. See you later.'

After he'd gone they sat quietly for a while, sipping wine and listening to the sounds of bees in the garden. The air was hot and still and beyond the shadow of their tree the lawn shimmered at an uncertain level as though it were in the process of being dissolved.

On the table one of the red roses made a small noise like a sigh and dropped its petals all at once on to the white cloth.

'You must be very proud of him, dear,' Hetty said to Olive.

'I am,' said Olive. 'But I mean to say, I would be, wouldn't I? There's always something special about the first grandchild.'

'He's charming,' said Muriel.

'He didn't want to come in,' said Olive. 'I had to force him and after all that, I thought we'd never get rid of him. He looked – ha ha. Rid of him. Ridd. Oh, he lapped that up a treat, did you see? See him blush?'

Ellen put her glass back on the table. She felt exhausted, unreasonably tired, and yet at the same time wide awake as though she had narrowly missed some frightful danger. She rested her head back on the cushion and listened to the birds and insects. Somewhere in the garden a grey warbler had started up. It trilled on the upper register like a tipsy flautist, a beautiful extravagant sound.

'Are you ready?' said Muriel.

'Yes, please,' said Olive.

Muriel read in clear and careful tones, 'You may suppose that my heart beat high, when the King and Queen appeared, and entered, followed by the Duke of Norfolk, bearing the sword of state, and by several other noblemen and people of repute . . .'

Ellen shut her eyes.

It could almost have been a nightingale.

Ania Walwicz

Big Tease

1981

She's a big teaser. She took him half the way there. Only one half or a quarter, or even less. Than that. She wore these silk stockings. With a black line down the back. Snakeskin pumps. She's a pretty girl. The only thing she was ever good at. She. She didn't have any men friends. My mother flirts with the tailors. They drop their needles. They laugh with pink, distended faces. She's a big teaser. She's this big tease. Big. She knew what they were after. So she was going to give it to them. Not by a half or a quarter or even less. Not at all. You get some sneaky ways if you can't hit. And angry. He couldn't hardly wait. Broke a box, taking her home. Looked ridiculous. And in one big hurry. You can tell when someone just aims. I was talking to Bruce at an opening. Bruce doesn't like me. And he wants to. I'm talking to this Bruce at an opening. I'm talking. Bruce, this he, drinks this red wine. This claret in a cut glass. Hello Bruce I say and more. Bruce hates me. And he wants to. Bruce doesn't love me. Bruce swings his hand around with a full tumbler. Bruce gets too happy with himself. I watch the hand, the glass describe an arc, and spill the red on someone else's white trousers. I'm this big flirt who put a knife in this man's gut. Made him squirt.

Ania Walwicz

Big Red

1981

Each month. Blood comes. My blood. Comes to me. Out of me. That you are not supposed to talk about. The red. My blood. Each time. She comes. On a Thursday night. Exactly when it happens. Big red. My blood. I'm glad when she does. Yes I am. You know I am. Devil with a red dress. Red dress. Devil with a red dress on. First mark. Little trickle. Makes a stain on me. Then she gets bigger. And brighter. Everyday more. And I'm walking around. Bleeding. That's what I'm now doing. And I don't talk about it. Don't talk about it. First time I saw. My mother told me. It was chicken. Somebody killed a chicken here. That's what they did. Yes. My sister. Drew a diagram. That doesn't tell me what it is. I was so young when it first happened. First time. School showed me pictures of clean clean girls. This girl thinks she will bleed to death. How many buckets. At me. In me. How many and how large it is. This bleeding. Each time I'm so glad that it does. First used to hate it. Walking with a trickle. Blood down my leg. Everyone could see. Maybe. Could. To be bleeding. Yes. Bleeding. I cut my finger. It bled. My mother killed the fish. He bled. We all have so much blood in us. It's unbelievable. To have so much blood. And I am so glad. Each month. That there is nothing growing in me. That I'm free of it. That there is no swelling in me. No foreign growth. In me. That there is just me. In me. Once I thought that I was. Yes. I waited for my blood. All the time. All day. Leaking. And looking. And hoping. And dreaming. Won't get you into his heart. I was looking for my blood. When it came. It was bliss. To see. All the big bright red. In me. Coming out. All clean. Now I like it. I like this. I like it. I like the way you hold me. I feel soft with this. I get tender with this. I get so soft with this. These Jews. They drain their meat. And I want blood. Raw steak. Big red. Red claret. A bottle of. A bucket. Red big. Once I saw them kill a policeman. There was all this blood. Everywhere. Down all steps. Of Flinders Street Station. All way down. Like a waterfall. Brightest red you ever did. Really poppy. And shiny. So lovely. It was lovely. That we have so much of it. That every month I see it. That it used to frighten me. That it makes me quicken. That I like to see my blood. That I see it on a sheet. Pink sheet. With red spots. All elegant. That red is my favourite colour. That I like red. That I am so red. Now. That she used to show it me. Show me. That I did it. That it doesn't scare me anymore. That I live with it and in it. That I'm at one with the bleeding. That I bleed. That it goes out of me. That I am bleeding. That I am now bleeding. That this is my child. I didn't want to have. That I like red. That I like big. That this is what is happening. That it never ever hurt me. Never. That it makes me feel softly, softly, for myself. That I am bleeding. That now I am bleeding. That my blood makes the nicest mark. That there were spots on the road. That it doesn't hurt. That I like it. That this is what I've been waiting for. Some red paint. A red raincoat. A scrap of red plastic. That I like to see it. That I like to bleed. Every month. That I live with this. That I am now bleeding. That I live with it. That it used to frighten me. Now I live with it. That I am bleeding. That now I am bleeding. That my blood. Is brightest red. Red satin. Red feathers of a reddest bird. Red sequins. Red glass beads and red beads. And rubies. Yes. Rubies. That it is coming out of me. That it make me soft. That it makes me tender. So tender. So soft. It makes me so soft. That it makes me juicy. And red. All over. That it makes me glisten. And full rounded. That it make me better. That it makes me a rose. Red rose. Reddest, reddest rose. That I open up. That I am a red rose. Red rose.

Anna Couani

Xmas in the Bush

1981

Running along far away from the road. Along the shallow creek bed, the wide flat rocks just below the water, creamy brown. The creek is wide here and open for hundreds of yards until it makes a turn. And straight ahead above the blackberry bushes and foliage along the water's edge is the typical country house with a row of yellow pines up one side, white walls and a red roof. The mother, the father and the children are here. With friends. The adults stand on the beach made of river stones or on the big rock in the middle of the creek or on the bank, talking, talking. All day. They made sandwiches while they talk. They smoke cigarettes. They point at things. The sight of a parent's eyes following the pointed finger across to the bank on the other side of the creek or into the branches of a nearby tree. They gesticulate sometimes. The men put their hands in their pockets and take them out again. The women fold their arms or put their hands on their hips. They go for a walk very slowly while they talk. Along the road, across the ford, up the hill, round the corner. They stay away for hours, talking. The shadow of the hill falls over the creek. It grows cooler. They come back and organise dinner while they talk. The women talk to each other. The men talk to each other. The men talk to the women. They all talk at once. They set out the card table under the trees, light the kerosene lamp and play 500 while they talk. They miss tricks while they talk. The children go to sleep in the tents and wake up in the night and hear them talking. Then later they wake up and everything's quiet.

In the morning the father throws the dog in the water. The dog paddles madly to the shore. The father talks about snags in the river. They all discuss the difference between snags as in water hazards and snags as in sausages. Sausage dogs. Smoke. Children who've drowned. Bushfires. Snakes. Carpet snakes. The long grass. The blackberry patch. The tar baby. Was there such a thing as Brere Bear. The Pyjama Girl. Bullrushes. Flash floods. Flying foxes. The hazards of flying foxes. High tensile wires and electricity lines. Broken electricity lines hanging down into creeks. Fords with cars on them washed away in flash floods. River snakes. March flies. Bot flies. The difference between bot flies and sand flies. Maggots in sausages. Maggot stories. Meat safe stories. Ice chest stories. Milk delivery when milk was in pails. The bread cart. The sound of the bread cart. Draught horses. Old draught horses. Horses being sent off to the blood and bone factory. Horses in the city. Sewerage. The sewerage works. Polluted creeks. The correct drinking sections of creeks. The aeration process. Stagnant water. Boiling the billy. Billy tea. The Billy Tea brand name. The inferior quality of Billy Tea. Swaggies. Gypsies. The cleverness of gypsies. Poverty. Bread and dripping. Sausages. Home grown vegetables. Out door toilets. Improvised toilet paper. The long summer nights. Mosquitoes. Marshes and bogs. Moonee Moonee and Brooklyn. The possibility of a mosquito breeding in the dew on a leaf. Playing the comb. The mouth harp. The bush bass. Bottle tops. The corrosive qualities of Coca Cola. Big business. Monopolies. Bigger and Bigger monopolies. Free enterprise. Russia. The idea of women working in men's jobs. Suez. American election campaigns. The Ku Klux Klan. The colour bar. The Iron Curtain. The Cold War. The ideals of communism as distinct from the practice. China. Industrialisation. Cuba. Atheism and agnosticism. The idea of the supreme being. The church in Russia. The Jews. Israel. The world wars. The next one. The fatalistic approach. The end of civilisation. The end of the human race. The inexorable continuation of the universe in spite of the human race. Humans as microscopic and trivial beings. The frailty of humans. The stupidity of humans. The innate badness of humans. Animal life and animals' code of behaviour. The rationality of animals. The fowls of the air and other biblical quotes. And now I see as through a glass darkly.

At the end of the last hand of 500, they remember other discussions they've had and that they always concluded with politics. The father turns down the tilly lamp.

Anna Couani

The Train

1981

You show me your child. You're standing so close to me, whispering. I can feel the hard material of your harsh black suit and your bony elbows underneath it. You are controlled. You look controlled. You're about to tell me the tragedy. We look at the child with dark eyes and dark hair. I look at your wife standing behind you. She's blind. This must be the tragedy. I grab your elbow out of pity. The wife and now the child. But you smile and say, No, the child can see, isn't she beautiful. The child isn't tragic, you and I are tragic.

You keep talking. 'You can't run away from the past. You carry your memories with you always.' This is something you say when you expect remorse and penitence from me. You want to see me as the escapee with the head wounds. Scarred by love and still limping. Childless and alone.

The sun streams into the room through the doors onto the balcony. I sleep for days and days to forget. I dream about the train where we all lived together. You said the train always stands for the past. Our homes were the carriages joined together. The train stopped outside the town in the countryside. We jumped off and ran around in the long grass shouting and laughing. One man set a fire through the train and burnt all the unnecessary things. A purification. You can't run away from the past, you said. I tried to light the fire but I didn't have the knack. I burnt the blue chest of drawers and scorched the timber panelling. Only one person could light the fire correctly. He was the escapee who never felt remorseful or penitent. He was always forgiven and never carried the past with him.

But if the train was all our houses joined together from the past and through the present into the future, the train is not the past but our lives as they run together. And the man who changed our lives without destroying us has gone away and taken his secret with him. You stand beside me now, more gentle than you've ever been because the kid didn't have to carry our own afflictions.

Bub Bridger

A Wedding

1982

In the year nineteen hundred and thirty-six, Aunty Prue married our insurance man. His name was Mr Armitage. He was an Englishman, a widower, tall and fair and always beautifully dressed in pale silk shirts and salt-and-pepper suits. He came to see us more often than his job warranted, but nobody minded because we all liked him. He was clever and kind and funny in a gentle way and he brought Cotton and me cigarette cards and paper twists of acid drops. They got married in our front room. Aunty Prue wore a honey coloured dress and blue coat with a little feathered hat and blue shoes that hurt her. She looked plain and nice and she looked happy. Mr Armitage looked a complete stranger in a dark suit and white shirt. It was the first time we'd ever seen him in anything other than a donegal tweed.

We had no idea about him and Aunty Prue at first. We had no idea about anybody and Aunty Prue. She was nearly forty – quiet and ordinary and selfless. Not like Mama. Beautiful laughing Mama who turned men's hearts over with a look. I guess we thought it was really Mama Mr Armitage came to see. Then when Aunty Prue told us she was going to marry him, we were shocked. She was ours – and now she was going to marry the insurance man.

'Who'll give her away?' Vanny wondered.

'What do you mean, "give her away"?' I asked.

'She has to have someone give her away at the wedding.'

I knew nothing about weddings – 'What for?'

'It's traditional,' Vanny explained, 'the bride is always given away to the groom. It's usually the father.'

'Oh well,' I said, 'there's only Mama and Gram. It had better be Gram.'

Vanny looked pained. 'It has to be a man – you loony twit!'

I quailed from her scorn. And then I thought about it.

'One of the fathers, then.'

She pursed her mouth thoughtfully, then she shook her head.

'Their wives wouldn't like it,' she said.

'But they're our fathers,' I persisted.

She nodded. 'Yes, they are,' she said, 'but this is Aunty Prue's wedding, not ours.'

I went to ask Aunty Prue who would give her away. She said Mr Green from the office. Mr Green was a small grey man with a stoop and I would much rather it had been one of our handsome fathers.

'Why can't it be a father?' I asked.

'No,' said Mama, 'that wouldn't be right. It's up to Prue to choose. And anyway, I wouldn't know which one to ask.' Mama never did know which one to choose.

Until she was a girl of eighteen, Mama and Aunty Prue lived with their parents in the same street as the gas works. The Heron twins worked for the gas company. Every day they walked past the house and eventually they saw Mama. And they fell in love with her. And Mama fell in love with them. Both of them. They were exactly alike and she never bothered to discriminate. When she found out about Vanny they both wanted to marry her but she couldn't bear to choose. Grandfather insisted that she marry one or the other and in desperation she ran away. Aunty Prue and the twins found her in a tiny room in the city and Aunty Prue said she would run away too, and they would find a house together. Aunty Prue was twenty-one and she had a good job, so they would manage, she said. And they did. Grandfather never forgave either of them. He forbade Gram to have anything to do with them, but when Vanny was born Gram sneaked away to the nursing home with lots of things she had been secretly making ever since Mama ran away. The Heron twins were there, both delirious, and Mama held a hand of each. In the background, Aunty Prue held Vanny. She didn't care what Grandfather thought or which twin was the father, she just held Vanny and let the love flow. Five years later, I was born and Aunty Prue went through it all again. Mama and the Heron twins made the babies, but Aunty Prue made a home for us and filled it with comfort and love. In between me and Cotton Grandfather died and the twins got married. They waited a long time for Mama to make up her mind, but she never could. So they married sisters which was the closest they could get to the relationship they had with Mama and then they went right back to the old setup. Mama loved them more than ever and when I was seven, Cotton was born. She is Mama's favourite. Vanny and I are both redheads like Mama, but Cotton, with her grey eyes and thick dark hair is the image of our fathers. Vanny has always been Aunty Prue's favourite, I think, but Vanny says I am. So I guess we both are. And that's nice.

Everybody got new clothes for the wedding. Or nearly new. Vanny bought a yellow wool dress that cost her three weeks' wages. Mama couldn't decide and kept putting it off. The fathers gave her a pound note for Cotton and me and Vanny took us down to Mrs Barrett's 'GOOD AS NEW' shop. Straight away I saw a shiny red dress and grabbed it, but Vanny hit my hands away.

'What the hell's wrong with you?' she hissed. 'You want to look like a bloody toffee apple?'

So I knew I'd have to go to the wedding looking sensible. At school I wore a sensible gym dress, a sensible cardigan and sensible shoes. And I hated the lot. Only the hard up kids had sensible clothes. The lucky ones wore frills and bows and patent leather shoes.

'When I grow up,' I muttered, 'I'm going to wear what I like and nothing's ever going to be sensible.'

'Shut up,' Vanny breathed 'or you'll wear your gym dress to the wedding.'

She chose a brown corduroy jacket and skirt and herded me into the cubicle. There was a cracked mirror on the wall that showed me a lopsided picture of myself, but Vanny stuck out the tip of her tongue and nodded her head happily.

'That's it!' she said. 'That's lovely!'

I looked sadly in the mirror.

'I don't think I look right in this,' I said.

Vanny didn't even hear me.

'You can wear my cream blouse with it and I'll buy you new shoes and socks.'

Mrs Barrett put her head around the curtain and instantly Vanny became a countess.

'I'll take this for my sister Hazel and I'd like something as nice for Rachel.'

Mrs Barrett almost bowed. Cotton flashed her a radiant smile and Mrs Barrett beamed.

'What a lovely child Rachel is!'

She bustled away. I stared at the floor. I still wanted that red shiny dress. I felt the tears starting.

'Look happy you stupid sheep!' whispered Vanny, 'or I'll tell Aunty Prue you're out to spoil her wedding!'

She gave me a stinging clout over the ear and grabbing Cotton's hand, she swept out into the shop. She came back a little later with a fluffy yellow jersey and a green plaid skirt. Mrs Barrett hovered behind her watching Cotton with melting eyes.

'Really Vanessa – what a little princess!'

She was. I nodded at Vanny, open-mouthed in admiration.

Vanny forgot about Mrs Barrett and gave me a cross between a hug and a shove.

'You're a princess too. Now hurry up and put your other clothes on.'

All the way home Cotton danced and twirled and skipped her delight thinking about her new clothes, but I lost out, even with the new socks. I wanted the pale pink lacy ones to the knee, but Vanny shuddered and bought us both plain white ankle socks.

We had a dress rehearsal for Mama and Aunty Prue. I looked in the long mirror and it wasn't me at all. They said I was going to be a beauty. I laughed and poked my tongue at the red haired girl in the mirror. She poked hers right back at me and her dark eyes danced.

The August days grew warmer and we were sure the sun would shine for Aunty Prue. Cotton and I could hardly wait. And then one day at school it hit me that after the wedding she wouldn't be living with us any more. I thought I would faint. I put my arms about my head to shut out the awful reality but it stayed and then I was sick. I went home in the headmaster's car. Mama was frantic.

'What is it? What's wrong with her? Oh!'

The headmaster couldn't tell her and I wouldn't until he had gone. When I told her Mama leaned against the kitchen dresser and turned her face away.

'Mama?' I said anxiously, 'Mama?'

'I don't want to talk about it,' she whispered. She began to sob and it terrified me.

'Mama –'

She pushed me away.

'Go away and leave me alone!'

I went outside and sat on the back step. The wedding was no longer a joy to look forward to. It was a black shadow that would ruin all our lives. I stared at the garden without seeing it, without seeing anything but the terrible emptiness that living without Aunty Prue would bring. I was still sitting there when Cotton came around the corner of the house.

'Why are you home this early?'

'I was sick.'

'Were you?' Her small face tightened in concern. 'Shall I get Mama?'

'No, don't worry Mama. I don't think she's very well either.'

She sat down on the step beside me. After a while she slipped her arm through mine and rubbed her cheek against my shoulder.

'It's all right Hazel,' she said, 'Vanny will be home soon.'

But Vanny came home with Aunty Prue and they were both full of excitement because Aunty Prue had the material for her wedding outfit. So I went to bed. I stayed awake till Vanny came and then I told her. She didn't say anything at first and I thought she had fallen asleep. Then she rolled out of her bed and came over to mine.

'Move over,' she said, 'and give's a hug.'

In the safety of her arms I let all the fear and pain go. She held me, rocking and murmuring sounds of comfort. It was quite a long time before I realised that she was crying too. In the morning I heard her singing in the bath. There was a note on the chair by my bed.

'Hazel' I read, 'you have to realise that sooner or later everything changes. Nothing stays the same even though you might think it does or hope it will. We've been lucky having Aunty Prue all our lives but now she's going to make a life of her own. We won't be happy about it but she will and that's what matters. She's always looked after us but now we have to mind ourselves. And Mama. We'll have to mind Mama. The fathers will help. They're always very good. Probably Gram will move in with us – I think Mama would like that. Anyway Aunty Prue won't be far away. We'll see her often and we can have turns to go and stay.

'I didn't have time to talk to you about this so I wrote it down. And I think it's better written down then we won't cry over it. Can you understand what I'm trying to say? I hope so because I don't know how else to explain. Love – Vanny'
When she came back from the bathroom I said,

'Thanks for the note.'

She smiled. 'That's okay,' she said.

Every night and weekend Aunty Prue shut herself in her room and sewed. We played cards and ludo or read. Usually one of the fathers was there and Mr Armitage, but it was odd without Aunty Prue even though she was only in another room. Mr Armitage was so delighted about marrying her, he grew handsomer by the hour. He was a tall thin man with thick curly hair the colour of his suits and his eyes were blue as the sky. At first the fathers hadn't trusted him. They thought he was after Mama. But when they saw his blue eyes following Aunty Prue's every move, they relaxed. Not that they understood him. How any man could look at another woman when Mama was around was beyond them. Especially Aunty Prue. When fate doled out the good looks she certainly didn't do Aunty Prue any favours. Mama got the lot. Every man ogled Mama, from college boys up. Except Mr Armitage. Aunty Prue's plain face and pale whispy hair, her plump body and legs, were only the packaging as far as he was concerned. Her light blue eyes twinkled with intelligence and her laughter was merry and innocent as Cotton's. He saw her as she really was. He saw the strength and the love and the wisdom in her and he knew he was a lucky man.

Two weeks before the wedding Vanny decided which boyfriend she'd invite and I was sick with jealousy. She had about a dozen to choose from but the only boy who fancied me was Ernest McCutcheon and I towered over him by about half a head. Secretly I longed to ask the school heart-throb because along with the rest of the girls at school I was in love with him, but I decided against it. My being in the third form and his being in the upper sixth didn't help, and there was the sad fact that he didn't know I existed.

I took my misery to Vanny but she was unmoved.

'For god's sake! You're twelve years old! Just be patient. In a few years you'll be fighting them off. And remember – it's Aunty Prue's day – pull a long face at the wedding and I'll flatten you!'

I didn't always understand Vanny.

The fathers bought Mama a green velvet dress and she was ecstatic. She tried it on for them and they could only gaze at her. She looked like a tulip on a stem. I had a sudden thought that in a few years I could very possibly look a little like that and my stomach turned right over. I stopped being jealous of Vanny having a boyfriend for the wedding right then.

Aunty Prue took the week off before the wedding and she and Mama were like giggling girls about the house. It shone as it never had before and the garden glowed with spring flowers. Gram came over every day and baked till all the tins were full and then she brought all her tins over and filled them too. On the last day she roasted a ham and Mama and Aunty Prue made sponges and little layered sandwiches which they wrapped in wet towels. I went to bed at ten but I was too excited to sleep. Vanny came home from the pictures with her favourite beau of the moment and I could hear them talking and laughing softly on the front steps. That's another thing I'll have to look forward to I thought. I fell asleep imagining myself in Mama's green dress and pale shoes, queening on the front porch to some tall beautiful young man who could only whisper my name and cover my two hands with burning kisses.

I awoke in the early hours because somebody was moving about in the kitchen. It was Aunty Prue making a cup of tea.

We lit the gas fire and pinched two biscuits from the laden tins. We didn't talk much.

She said, 'Aren't your feet cold without slippers?'

'A bit,' I said, and held them out to the fire. We sipped our tea and smiled at each other.

'You'll have a room to yourself after tomorrow.'

'Yes – unless Gram comes.'

'Would you like a room of your own?'

'Yes – no. I don't know – I'd miss Vanny.'

'Of course. And I'll miss you all.'

I slid down on the floor at her feet and she put her arms around me. Her whispy hair bristled with curlers and her plain plump face streamed with tears.

'I love you,' I said, 'I love you more than anyone in the world.'

Later I made another pot of tea and just when Aunty Prue was opening another biscuit tin, Cotton came padding in. We laughed and Mama called,

'What are you doing out of bed?'

Then she came into the kitchen with Vanny in her wake and I got three more cups.

We were still sitting there, talking and laughing and sipping tea when the sun came up in a great blaze on the perfect spring morning of Aunty Prue's wedding day.

Olga Masters

On the Train

1982

The young woman not more than twenty-seven slammed the gate on herself and the two children both girls.

She did not move off at once but looked up and down the street as if deciding which way to go.

The older girl looked up at her through her hair which was whipped by the wind to read the decision the moment she made it.

Finally the woman took a hand of each child and turned in the direction of the railway station.

'Oh goody!' cried Sara who was nearly five.

'The sun's out,' the woman murmured lifting her face up for a second towards it.

Sara looked again into her mother's face noticing two or three of her teeth pinning down her bottom lip and the glint in her eyes perhaps from the sun? She felt inadequate that she seldom noticed such things as sun and wind, barely bothering about the rain as well, being quite content to stay out and play in it. The weather appeared to figure largely in the lives of adults. Sara hoped this would work out for her when she was older.

The mother bent forward as she hurried the younger child Lisa having difficulty keeping up. Her face Sara saw looked strained like the mother's. Sara hoped she wouldn't complain. The glint in the mother's eyes was like a spark that could ignite and involve them all.

She saw with relief the roof of the station jutting above the street but flashed her eyes away from the buildings still to be passed before they reached it.

The ticket office was protected by the jutting roof.

Sara was glad of the rest while her mother had her head inside the window and laid her cheek lightly against her rump clad in a blue denim skirt.

The business of buying tickets went on for a long time. Sara's eyes conveyed to Lisa her fear that the mother's top half had disappeared forever inside the window. She clutched her skirt to drag her out and opened her mouth to scream. Lisa saw and screamed for her.

The mother flung both arms down brushing a child off with each. They dared not touch her when she turned around and separated the tickets from change in her purse.

She snapped it shut and looked up and around in a distracted way as if to establish where she was.

It was Sara who went in front taking the narrow path squeezed between a high fence on one side and the station wall on the other. She swung her head around to see that her mother and Lisa were following her bouncy confident step.

On the platform waiting for the train the few other passengers looked at them.

Sara's dress was long and her hair was long and she was not dressed warmly enough.

The people especially a couple of elderly women noted Sara's light cotton dress with a deep flounce at the hem and Lisa's skimpy skirt and fawn tights. They looked at the mother's hands to see if there was a bag hanging from them with cardigans or jumpers in. But the mother carried nothing but a leather shoulder bag about as large as a large envelope and quite flat.

'She's warm enough herself,' one of the women murmured to her companion with a sniff.

They watched them board the train noticing the mother did not turn her head when she stepped onto the platform. It was Sara who grasped the hand of Lisa and saw her safely on.

'Tsk, tisk,' said the watching woman wishing she could meet the mother's eyes and glare her disapproval.

The mother took a single seat near the aisle and let Sara and Lisa find one together across from her.

Dear little soul, thought the passenger on the seat facing them seeing Sara's face suffused with pleasure at her small victory. Lisa had to wriggle her bony little rump with legs stuck out stiffly to get onto the seat.

Sara read the passenger's thoughts.

'She doesn't like you helping,' she said.

This was almost too much for the passenger whose glance leapt towards the mother to share with her this piece of childish wisdom.

But the mother had her profile raised and her eyes slanted away towards the window. The skin spread over her cheekbones made the passenger think of pale honey spread on a slice of bread.

She's beautiful. The woman was surprised at herself for not having noticed it at once.

She returned her attention rather reluctantly to Sara and Lisa.

She searched their faces for some resemblance to the mother. Sara's was round with blue worried eyes under faint eyebrows. Lisa's was pale with a pinched look and blue veins at the edges of her eyebrows disappearing under a woollen cap with a ragged tassel that looked as if a kitten had wrestled with it.

The passenger thought they might look like their father putting him into a category unworthy of the handsome mother.

For the next twenty minutes the train alternated between a rocking tearing speed and dawdling within sight of one of the half dozen stations on the way to the city and the passenger alternated her attention between the girls and the mother although at times she indulged in a fancy that she was not their mother but someone minding them.

'I can move and your mummy sit here,' she said to Sara with sudden inspiration.

I'll find out for sure.

Sara put her head against the seat back, tipping her face and closing her eyes with pink coming into her cheeks.

The passenger looked to Lisa for an answer and Lisa turned her eyes towards her mother seeing only her profile and the long peaked collar of her blouse lying on her honey coloured sweater.

Lisa looked into the passenger's face and gave her head the smallest shake.

Poor little soul.

The passenger stared at the mother knowing in the end she would look back.

The mother did her eyes widening for a second under bluish lids with only a little of her brow visible under a thick bang of fair hair. There was nothing friendly in her face.

The passenger reddened and looked at the girls.

'Your mummy's so pretty,' she said.

Sara swung her head around to look at the mother and Lisa allowed herself a tiny smile as if it didn't need verification.

'Do you like having a pretty mummy?' the passenger asked.

The mother had turned her attention to the window again and her eyes had narrowed.

The passenger felt as if a door had been shut in her face.

'Are you going into the city for the day?' she said to the girls.

Sara pressed her lips together as if she shouldn't answer if she wanted to. Lisa's mouth opened losing its prettiness and turning into an uneven hole.

There's nothing attractive about either of them, thought the passenger deciding that Lisa might be slightly cross-eyed.

She sat with her handbag gripped on her knees and her red face flushed a deeper red and her brown eyes with flecks of red in the whites were flint-hard when they darted between the mother and the girls and vacant when they looked away.

After a moment the mother turned her head and stared into the passenger's face. The girls raised their eyes and looked too. The train swayed and rushed and all the eyes locked together. The mother's eyes although large and blue and without light were the snake's eyes mesmerising those of the passenger. Sara swung her eyes from the passenger to the mother as if trying to protect one from the other. Lisa's face grew tight and white and she opened her small hole of a mouth but no sound came out.

The mother keeping her eyes on the passenger got up suddenly and checked the location through the window. Sara and Lisa stumbled into the aisle holding out frantic fingers but afraid to touch her. Sara stood under her mother's rump as close as she dared her eyes turned back to see Lisa holding the seat end. The train swayed and clanged the last hundred yards slowing and sliding like a skier at the bottom of a snow peak stopping with a suddenness that flung Sara and Lisa together across the seat end.

This was fortunate.

The mother level with the passenger now leaned down and sparks from her eyes flew off the hard flat stones of the passenger's eyes.

'I'm going to kill them,' the mother said.

Kerryn Goldsworthy

Female Friends

1982

Jackie arrives on her bicycle. It's raining, and she's very late. I'm not ready.

'You don't want to go to this party either, do you,' she says.

'Of course not,' I say. 'But you know what'll happen if we don't'.

She follows me into the bathroom to talk to me while I have my shower. I can feel her watching me curiously as I tip my head back under the steamy torrent to wash the shampoo from my hair. I have stood and talked thus in her bathroom and know that her body is perfect, smooth and brown even in winter, lean where it ought to be lean and rich and soft where it ought to be rich and soft. Her face, atop this monument, is a surprise. She is younger than me, but not much. My own body is nothing like hers: fair-skinned, over-indulged, abused and tired from too much wine and not enough vitamins, too many cigarettes and not enough early nights. When I tell her that I feel cheated, that no one ever told me that you start growing old before you've even finished growing up, Jackie laughs. She thinks I am being witty.

I have reservations about Jackie. But she needs me, and this butters my vanity. We define ourselves against each other. She cries, and I soothe. When she drinks too much, she collapses and demands to be looked after, long before she needs it; when I drink too much, I am still damagingly on my feet, long after I ought to be unconscious. She wears the clothes I help her choose, clothes that emphasise her legs and breasts, the features she is proudest of. I am the one men talk to and she is the one they take to bed; and if I sometimes, only sometimes, wish it were the other way round, it is perhaps because then I would not be so frequently subjected to her full-frontal traumas of aftermath. She thinks I am indestructible.

The bathroom interlude does much to upset this balance of power, for it is the first time she has ever seen me undressed. I have always been nothing to her but indomitably maternal; suddenly she's being forced to acknowledge vulnerability and sexual threat, interlinked, unmotherly. She's no fool, and cannot now evade the knowledge that her own youth and beauty and erotic brand of helplessness can't always be counted on to put me out of the running as a rival. She is, in short, shaken by the sight of my naked back, and is clearly relieved when I dry myself, put on my clothes and shake the water from my schoolboy hair. ('Men like long hair,' says Jackie often, as she flips her own, with a variety of emphases for my benefit and instruction: *men* like long hair. Men *like* long hair. Men like *long* hair.) Now we are ourselves again: she kittenish and anachronistic in a tight woolly turtleneck for which I am not responsible; I prudent and matronly in burgundy and black. And we are united in our common desire to get out of going to Julia's party.

There is no getting out of going to Julia's party. It has stopped raining, and Julia only lives three streets away. I lock my door, she chains her bike to the lamp-post, and we walk off slowly down the road.

We should have stayed away. Julia is already mad with us, and Julia is already drunk. She is our workmate, but she pulls rank often by virtue of her thirty-nine years, more than ten years older than the oldest of the rest of us, in the group of friends at work.

She has invited the entire staff of the department to her party, but only our group – from the lower echelons – has turned up. This, and the prodigious quantities of claret it is clear she has already downed, have put her in an ugly mood. Some of her other friends, several of whom I have met and disliked, are sitting round the kitchen table self-consciously smoking dope, engaged in a conversation whose dominant note is arch, dated, sexist, middle-aged smut. Jackie and I begin to feel very uncomfortable and very superior indeed. 'Get yourselves a drink,' says Julia crossly, and leaves us to our fate.

We exchange glances and head for the soda water. Greg and

Richard, we discover, are also hanging around the soda water, looking unhappy. So we collect the drinks and the boys and the four of us are retreating up the hall to the deserted front room when Muriel arrives, shining, at the front door. This completes the little group from work: Julia, Richard Muriel, Jackie, Greg and me. Without Julia, we go into the sitting-room, shut the door, and sit, and laugh, and talk, and hope fervently to be left alone.

But no, the door bursts open. It is Julia's door, after all. Our hostess is now very drunk, and weeping. She takes up her actress stance in the middle of the room and begins, very quietly, to speak. About the party, about us, about herself. We all know from experience that she will quickly ascend the scale to a fully fledged shriek in the course of her recital, and we know, more or less, what she will say. Still and silent in our seats, we watch.

Julia is in every sense enormous: bloated and ungainly from twenty years of compulsive eating and unchecked solitary drinking, a physical and emotional omnivore, she is also a dynamic and large-hearted presence, witty, generous, intelligent, and as we sit and listen to her climb the ladder of hysteria we are all trying desperately to remember this. The face of her beautiful nineteen-year-old self smiles sweetly down from the mantelpiece on the demented harridan she has become; the photograph is a merciless mockery of the face that is beginning to scream at us, unrecognisably distorted by tears, rage, fat, and the fine red lines that you see on the face of the fair-skinned alcoholic.

Her accusations are incoherent, and of course could not be otherwise. We are, after all, guilty of nothing. Why should she be angry with us? We are the only workmates who have *come* to her party. Of course we all know, on a subterranean level of awareness that has no truck with logic, that she is angry with us because we are the *only* workmates who have come to her party. She would have been even angrier, had we failed to arrive; but we are not the important ones. not the ones who still need to be impressed and wooed. She is angry because we are us and not them; because we have come, and seen that they have stayed away. She is angry because we are not drinking, because we are not impressed with her other friends, because we have shut ourselves apart.

She doesn't say any of this. She is too proud to admit it, and too drunk to follow it. Instead she tells us, not for the first time, how much she has done for us, and how little we have done for her. What she means is that she hates us because we are young and she is not. We have over her the power of youth, of laughter, of turning away.

Turning away is in fact what we begin to do, since by now she is an awful, awful sight. One of the aging smut merchants from the kitchen table comes into the room to see what all the shouting is about, and staggers backwards as she hurls herself into his arms. He recovers, and strokes her hair, and makes soft little noises. We see that the doorway, and beyond it the hall, are blocked with people.

Richard gets up, opens the window, and climbs through it into the garden. We follow him, one by one.

This is what she hates us for. We are the people who can escape through windows when the night gets too old and turgid. We are young, we are healthy, we are hopeful.

Except me. As I wait my turn at the window, last in line, she turns on me and I'm transfixed. I'm the one; I can see that. I'm the one person in this bunch of infant defectors that she's picked as a prematurely seedy cynic, a spiritual derelict, a sister. 'You!' she says, stabbing a trembling finger at me in a gesture I recognise from her gifted amateur performances as the First Witch in *Macbeth*, as Hecuba in *The Trojan Women*, as Martha in *Who's Afraid of Virginia Woolf*?

'You, you!'

Does she mean, Stay? Go? Pay? Don't leave me?

I climb out the window.

Greg is caught on rose thorns. Richard, sober but seriously upset, is being sick. Jackie is crying. Muriel is looking resigned. I untangle Greg, Muriel holds Richard's head, Greg gives Jackie his handkerchief, and we all trail back to my place, which has never looked so nice, and shut the door.

Jackie, reminded of the similar endless tirades that she still endures from her awful mother, tirades she still reacts to like a naughty child, has not yet managed to stop crying. Richard, the vague and halo-headed lover of all things transcendent and ephemeral, is pale with postnausea and disbelief; Richard shares with Keats the conviction that truth and beauty are all ye need to know on earth, and Muriel and I have never had the heart to point out to him that Keats never got to be thirty. Greg is still punching and kicking his way out of the caul of a protracted adolescence, but he's better at pity than the rest of us, and he is, for once, silent.

That leaves Muriel and me. Muriel is serenely detached: old enough (like me) not to be surprised; different enough from Julia (unlike me) to remain, at least on her own account, unperturbed. Muriel has her own weaknesses like everybody else, but none of them has a place in the occasion. My own vision, of Julia betrayed, is too private to share. Even with Muriel.

Here, now, it is urgently necessary to make some statement about what we have just seen, some counter-declaration of innocence. So since Greg has suggested it, and nobody has had any dinner, I make hot Milo and toasted Vegemite sandwiches and we eat the food of happy children.

But we're not happy, and we're not children. We still feel accused and repelled, and guilty, and terrified of the things that the next ten or fifteen years might do to us. And then Greg, given to such things, gets the bright idea of deliverance by psychodrama. 'Now, we'll re-create it, act it out,' he says. 'Jackie, lie down.' Jackie lies down, there being nowhere else, on the floor. Greg gestures to me. 'You be Julia,' he says.

I cringe. Muriel is watching from the chair where she's curled up graceful as a cat. She raises one eyebrow at me in bright mockery; I accept the challenge and fling myself into the role of Julia, improvisation, observation, empathy, memory, it isn't difficult, the style, the stance, the lack of grace, the failure of control –

I hear myself produce a sound that turns my bones to glass. Jackie hoots, the boys applaud, Muriel sits up alarmed and straight and sends me an urgent, silent message: Oh, my dear, *stop now*.

Greg speaks and Muriel turns to try to shut him up, but it isn't possible to shut Greg up. 'That was *brilliant*!' he shrieks. 'You sounded *exactly like* her!'

'I know, Greg,' I say. 'I know.'

Helen Garner

Postcards from Surfers

1983

> One night I dreamed that I did not love, and that night, released from all bonds, I lay as though in a kind of soothing death.
>
> *Colette*

We are driving north from Coolangatta airport. Beside the road the ocean heaves and heaves into waves which do not break. The swells are dotted with boardriders in black wet-suits, grim as sharks.

'Look at those idiots,' says my father.

'They must be freezing,' says my mother.

'But what about the principle of the wet-suit?' I say. 'Isn't there a thin layer of water between your skin and the suit, and your body heat...'

'Could be,' says my father.

The road takes a sudden swing round a rocky outcrop. Miles ahead of us, blurred in the milky air, I see a dream city: its cream, its silver, its turquoise towers thrust in a cluster from a distant spit.

'What – is that Brisbane?' I say.

'No,' says my mother. 'That's Surfers.'

My father's car has a built-in computer. If he exceeds the speed limit, the dashboard emits a discreet but insistent pinging. Lights flash, and the pressure of his right foot lessens. He controls the windows from a panel between the two front seats. We cruise past a Valiant parked by the highway with a FOR SALE sign propped in its back window.

'Look at that,' says my mother. 'A WA number-plate. Probably thrashed it across the Nullarbor and now they reckon they'll flog it.'

'Pro'ly stolen,' says my father. 'See the sticker? ALL YOU VIRGINS, THANKS FOR NOTHING. You can just see what sort of a pin'ead he'd be. Brain the size of a pea.'

Close up, many of the turquoise towers are not yet sold. 'Every conceivable feature,' the signs say. They have names like Capricornia, Biarritz, The Breakers, Acapulco, Rio.

I had a Brazilian friend when I lived in Paris. He showed me a postcard, once, of Rio where he was born and brought up. The card bore an aerial shot of a splendid, curved tropical beach, fringed with palms, its sand pure as snow.

'Why don't you live in Brazil,' I said, 'if it's as beautiful as this?'

'Because,' said my friend, 'right behind that beach there is a huge military base.'

In my turn I showed him a postcard of my country. It was a reproduction of that Streeton painting called *The Land of the Golden Fleece* which in my homesickness I kept standing on the heater in my bedroom. He studied it carefully. At last he turned his currant-coloured eyes to me and said,

'*Les arbres sont rouges*?' Are the trees red?

Several years later, six months ago, I was rummaging through a box of old postcards in a junk shop in Rathdowne Street. Among the photos of damp cottages in Galway, of Raj hotels crumbling in bicycle-thronged Colombo, of glassy Canadian lakes flawed by the wake of a single canoe, I found two cards that I bought for a dollar each. One was a picture of downtown Rio, in black-and-white. The other, crudely tinted, showed Geelong, the town where I was born. The photographer must have stood on the high grassy bank that overlooks the Eastern Beach. He lined up his shot through the never-flowing fountain with its quartet of concrete wading birds (storks? cranes? I never asked my father: they have long orange beaks and each bird holds one leg bent, as if about to take a step); through the fountain and out over the curving wooden promenade, from which we dived all summer, unsupervised, into the flat water; and across the bay to the You Yangs, the double-humped, low, volcanic cones, the only disturbance in the great basalt plains that lie between Geelong and Melbourne. These two cards in the same box! And I find them! Imagine! '*Cher Rubens*,' I wrote. '*Je t'envoie ces deux cartes postales, de nos deux villes natales . . .*'

Auntie Lorna has gone for a walk on the beach. My mother unlocks the door and slides open the flywire screen. She goes out into the bright air to tell her friend of my arrival. The ocean is right in front of the unit, only a hundred and fifty yards away. How can people be so sure of the boundary between land and sea that they have the confidence to build houses on it? The white doorsteps of the ocean travel and travel.

'Twelve o'clock,' says my father.

'Getting on for lunchtime,' I say.

'Getting towards it. Specially with that nice cold corned beef sitting there, and fresh brown bread. Think I'll have to try some of that choko relish. Ever eaten a choko?'

'I wouldn't know a choko if I fell over it,' I say.

'Nor would I.'

He selects a serrated knife from the magnetised holder on the kitchen wall and quickly and skilfully, at the bench, makes himself a thick sandwich. He works with powerful concentration: when the meat flaps off the slice of bread, he rounds it up with a large, dramatic scooping movement and a sympathetic grimace of the lower lip. He picks up the sandwich in two hands, raises it to his mouth and takes a large bite. While he chews he breathes heavily through his nose.

'Want to make yourself something?' he says with his mouth full.

I stand up. He pushes the loaf of bread towards me with the back of his hand. He puts the other half of his sandwich on a green bread and butter plate and carries it to the table. He sits with his elbows on the pine wood, his knees wide apart, his belly relaxing on to his thighs, his high-arched, long-boned feet planted on the tiled floor. He eats, and gazes out to sea. The noise of his eating fills the room.

My mother and Auntie Lorna come up from the beach. I stand inside the wall of glass and watch them stop at the tap to hose the sand off their feet before they cross the grass to the door. They are two old women: they have to keep one hand on the tap in order to balance on the left foot and wash the right. I see that they are two old women, and yet they are neither young nor old. They are my mother and Auntie Lorna, two institutions. They slide back the wire door, smiling.

'Don't tramp sand everywhere,' says my father from the table.

They take no notice. Auntie Lorna kisses me, and holds me at arms' length with her head on one side. My mother prepares food and we eat, looking out at the water.

'You've missed the coronary brigade,' says my father. 'They get out on the beach about nine in the morning. You can pick 'em. They swing their arms up really high when they walk.' He laughs, looking down.

'Do you go for a walk every day too?' I ask.

'Six point six kilometres,' says my father.

'Got a pedometer, have you?'

'I just nutted it out,' says my father. 'We walk as far as a big white building, down that way, then we turn round and come back. Six point six altogether, there and back.'

'I might come with you.'

'You can if you like,' he says. He picks up his plate and carries it to the sink. 'We go after breakfast. You've missed today's.'

He goes to the couch and opens the newspaper on the low coffee table. He reads with his glasses down his nose and his hands loosely linked between his spread knees. The women wash up.

'Is there a shop nearby?' I ask my mother. 'I have to get some tampons.'

'Caught short, are you?' she says. 'I think they sell them at the shopping centre, along Sunbrite Avenue there near the bowling club. Want me to come with you?'

'I can find it.'

'I never could use those things,' says my mother, lowering her voice and glancing across the room at my father. 'Hazel told me about a terrible thing that happened to her. For days she kept noticing this revolting smell that was . . . emanating from her. She washed and washed, and couldn't get rid of it. Finally she was about to go to the doctor, but first she got down and had a look with the mirror. She saw this bit of thread and pulled it. The thing was *green*. She must've forgotten to take it out – it'd been there for days and days and *days*.'

We laugh with the teatowels up to our mouths. My father, on the other side of the room, looks up from the paper with the bent smile of someone not sure what the others are laughing at. I am always surprised when my mother comes out with a word like 'emanating'. At home I have a book called *An Outline of English Verse* which my mother used in her matriculation year. In the margins of *The Rape of the Lock* she had made notations: 'bathos; reminiscent of Virgil; parody of Homer.' Her handwriting in these pencilled jottings, made fortyfive years ago, is exactly as it is today: this makes me suspect, when I am not with her, that she is a closet intellectual.

Once or twice, on my way from the unit to the shopping centre, I think to see roses along a fence and run to look, but I find them to be some scentless, fleshy flower. I fall back. Beside a patch of yellow grass, pretty trees in a row are bearing and dropping white blossom-like flowers, but they look wrong to me, I do not recognise them: the blossoms too large, the branches too flat. I am dizzy from the flight. In Melbourne it is still winter, everything is bare.

I buy the tampons and look for the postcards. There they are, displayed in a tall revolving rack. There is a great deal of blue. Closer, I find colour photos of white beaches, duneless, palmless, on which half-naked people lie on their backs with their knees raised. The frequency of this posture, at random through the crowd, makes me feel like laughing. Most of the cards have GREETINGS FROM THE GOLD COAST or BROADBEACH or SURFERS PARADISE embossed in gold in one corner: I search for pictures without words. Another card, in several slightly differing versions, shows a graceful, big-breasted young girl lying in a seductive pose against some rocks: she is wearing a bikini and her whole head is covered by one of those latex masks that are sold in trick shops, the ones you pull on as a bandit pulls on a stocking. The mask represents the hideous, raddled, grinning face of an old woman, a witch. I stare at this photo for a long time. Is it simple, or does it hide some more mysterious signs and symbols?

I buy twelve GREETINGS FROM cards with views, some aerial, some from the ground. They cost twenty-five cents each.

'Want the envelopes?' says the girl. She is dressed in a flowered garment which is drawn up between her thighs like a nappy.

'Yes please.' The envelopes are so covered with coloured maps, logos and drawings of Australian fauna that there is barely room to write an address, but something about them attracts me. I buy a packet of Licorice Chews and eat them all on the way home: I stuff them in two at a time: my mouth floods with saliva. There are no rubbish bins so I put the papers in my pocket. Now that I have spent money here, now that I have rubbish to dispose of, I am no longer a stranger. In Paris there used to be signs in the streets that said, '*Le commerce, c'est la vie de la ville.*' Any traveller knows this to be the truth.

The women are knitting. They murmur and murmur. What they say never requires an answer. My father sharpens a pencil stub with his pocket knife, and folds the paper into a pad one-eighth the size of a broadsheet page.

'Five down, spicy meat jelly. ASPIC. Three across, counterfeit. BOGUS! Howzat.'

'You're in good nick,' I say. 'I would've had to rack my brains for BOGUS. Why don't you do harder ones?'

'Oh, I can't do those other ones, the cryptic.'

'You have to know Shakespeare and the Bible off by heart to do those,' I say.

'Yairs. Course, if you got hold of the answer and filled it out looking at that, with a lot of practice you could come round to their way of thinking. They used to have good ones in the *Weekly Times*. But I s'pose they had so many complaints from cockies who couldn't do'em that they had to ease off.'

I do not feel comfortable yet about writing the postcards. It would seem graceless. I flip through my mother's pattern book.

'There's some nice ones there,' she says. 'What about the one with the floppy collar?'

'Want to buy some wool?' says my father. He tosses the finished crossword on to the coffee table and stands up with a vast yawn. 'Oh – ee – oh – ooh. Come on, Miss. I'll drive you over to Pacific Fair.'

I choose the wool and count out the number of balls specified by the pattern. My father rears back to look at it: this movement struck terror into me when I was a teenager but I now recognise it as short-sightedness.

'Pure wool, is it?' he says. As soon as he touches it he will know. He fingers it, and looks at me.

'No,' I say. 'Got a bit of synthetic in it. It's what the pattern says to use.'

'Why don't you –' He stops. Once he would have tried to prevent me from buying it. His big blunt hands used to fling out the fleeces, still warm, on to the greasy table. His hands looked as if they had no feeling in them but they teased out the wool, judged it, classed it, assigned it a fineness and a destination: Italy, Switzerland, Japan. He came home with thorns embedded deep in the flesh of his palms. He stood patiently while my mother gouged away at them with a needle. He drove away at shearing time in a yellow car with running boards, up to the big sheds in the country; we rode on the running boards as far as the corner of our street, then skipped home. He went to the Melbourne Show for work, not pleasure, and once he brought me home a plastic trumpet. 'Fordie,' he called me, and took me to the wharves and said, 'See that rope? It's not a rope. It's a hawser.' 'Hawser,' I repeated, wanting him to think I was a serious person. We walked along Strachan Avenue, Manifold Heights, hand in hand. 'Listen,' he said. 'Listen to the wind in the wires.' I must have been very little then, for the wires were so high I can't remember seeing them.

He turns away from the fluffy pink balls and waits with his hands in his pockets for me to pay.

'What do you do all day, up here?' I say on the way home.

'Oh . . . play bowls. Follow the real estate. I ring up the firms that advertise these flash units and I ask'em questions. I let'em lower and lower their price. See how low they'll go. How many more discounts they can dream up.' He drives like a farmer in a ute, leaning forward with his arms curved round the wheel, always about to squint up through the windscreen at the sky, checking the weather.

'Don't they ask your name?'

'Yep.'

'What do you call yourself?'

'Oh, Jackson or anything.' He flicks a glance at me. We begin to laugh, looking away from each other.

'It's bloody crook up here,' he says. 'Jerry-built. Sad. "Every conceivable luxury"! They can't get rid of it. They're desperate. Come on. We'll go up and you can have a look.'

The lift in Biarritz is lined with mushroom-coloured carpet. We brace our backs against its wall and it rushes us upwards. The salesman in the display unit has a moustache, several gold bracelets, a beige suit, and a clipboard against his chest. He is engaged with an elderly couple and we are able to slip past him into the living room.

'Did you see that peanut?' hisses my father.

'A gilded youth,' I say. '"Their eyes are dull, their heads are flat, they have no brains at all."'

He looks impressed, as if he thinks I have made it up on the spot. '*The Man from Ironbark*,' I add.

'I only remember *The Geebung Polo Club*,' he says. He mimes leaning off a horse and swinging a heavy implement. We snort with laughter. Just inside the living room door stand five Ionic pillars in a half-moon curve. Beyond them, through the glass, are views of a river and some mountains. The river winds in a plain, the mountains are sudden, lumpy and crooked.

'From the other side you can see the sea,' says my father.

'Would you live up here?'

'Not on your life. Not with those flaming pillars.'

From the bedroom window he points out another high-rise building closer to the sea. Its name is Chelsea. It is battle-ship grey with a red trim. Its windows face away from the ocean. It is tall and narrow, of mean proportions, almost prison-like. 'I wouldn't mind living in that one,' he says. I look at it in silence. He has unerringly chosen the ugliest one. It is so ugly that I can find nothing to say.

It is Saturday afternoon. My father is waiting for the Victorian football to start on TV. He rereads the paper.

'Look at this,' he says. 'Mum, remember that seminar we went to about investment in diamonds?'

'Up here?' I say. 'A *seminar*?'

'S'posed to be an investment that would double its value in six days. We went along one afternoon. They were obviously con-men. Ooh, setting up a big con, you could tell. They had sherry and sandwiches.'

'That's all we went for, actually,' says my mother.

'What sort of people went?' I ask.

'Oh . . . people like ourselves,' says my father.

'Do you think anybody bought any?'

'Sure. Some idiots. Anyway, look at this in today's *Age*. "The Diamond Dreamtime. World diamond market plummets." Haw haw haw.'

He turns on the TV in time for the bounce. I cast on stitches as instructed by the pattern and begin to knit. My mother and Auntie Lorna, well advanced in complicated garments for my sister's teenage children, conduct their monologues which cross, coincide and run parallel. My father mumbles advice to the footballers and emits bursts of contemptuous laughter. 'Bloody idiot,' he says.

I go to the room I am to share with Auntie Lorna and come back with the packet of postcards. When I get out my pen and the stamps and set myself up at the table my father looks up and shouts to me over the roar of the crowd,

'Given up on the knitting?'

'No. Just knocking off a few postcards. People expect a postcard when you go to Queensland.'

'Have to keep up your correspondence, Father,' says my mother.

'I'll knit later,' I say.

'How much have you done?' asks my father.

'This much.' I separate thumb and forefinger.

'Dear Philip,' I write. I make my writing as thin and small as I can: the back of the postcard, not the front, is the art form. 'Look where I am. A big red setter wet from the surf shambles up the side way of the unit, looking lost and anxious as setters always do. My parents send it packing with curses in an inarticulate tongue. Go orn, get orf, gorn!'

'Dear Philip. THE IDENTIFICATION OF THE BIRDS AND FISHES. *My father*: "Look at those albatross. They must have eyes that can see for a hundred miles. As soon as one dives, they come from everywhere. Look at'em dive! Bang! Down they go." *Me*: "What sort of fish would they be diving for?" *My father*: "Whiting. They only eat whiting." *Me*: "They do not!" *My father*: "How the hell would *I* know what sort of fish they are."'

'Dear Philip. My father says they are albatross, but my mother (in the bathroom, later) remarks to me that albatross have shorter, more hunched necks.'

'Dear Philip. I share a room with Auntie Lorna. She also is writing postcards and has just asked me how to spell TOO. I like her very much and *she likes me*. "I'll keep the stickybeaks in the Woomelang post office guessing," she says. "I won't put my name on the back of the envelope."'

'Dear Philip. OUTSIDE THE POST OFFICE. My father, Auntie Lorna and I wait in the car for my mother to go in and pick up the mail from the locked box. *My father*: "Gawd, amazing, isn't it, what people do. See that sign there, ENTER, with the arrow pointing upwards? What sort of a thing is that? Is it a joke, or just some no-hoper foolin' around? That woman's been in the phone box for half an hour, I bet. How'd you be, outside the public phone waiting for some silly coot to finish yackin' on about everything under the sun, while you had something important to say. That happened to us, once, up at –" My mother opens the door and gets in. "Three letters," she says. "All for me."'

Sometimes my little story overflows the available space and I have to run over on to a second postcard. This means I must find a smaller, secondary tale, or some disconnected remark, to fill up card number two.

'*Me*: (opening cupboard) "Hey! Scrabble! We can have a game of Scrabble after tea!" *My father*: (with a scornful laugh) "I can't wait."'

'Dear Philip. I know you won't write back. I don't even know whether you are still at this address.'

'Dear Philip. One Saturday morning I went to Coles and bought a scarf. It cost four and sixpence and I was happy with my purchase. He whisked it out of my hand and looked at the label. "Made in China. Is it real silk? Let's test it." He flicked on his cigarette lighter. We all screamed and my mother said, "Don't *bite*! He's only teasing you."'

'Dear Philip. Once, when I was fourteen, I gave cheek to him at the dinner table. He hit me across the head with his open hand. There was silence. My little brother gave a high, hysterical giggle and I laughed too, in shock. He hit me again. After the washing up I was sent for. He was sitting in an armchair, looking down. "The reason why we don't get on any more," he said, "is because we're so much alike." This idea filled me with such revulsion that I turned my swollen face away. It was swollen from crying, not from the blows, whose force had been more symbolic than physical.'

'Dear Philip. Years later he read my mail. He found the contraceptive pills. He drove up to Melbourne and found me and made me come home. He told me I was letting men use my body. He told me I ought to see a psychiatrist. I was in the front seat and my mother was in the back. I thought, "If I open the door and jump out, I won't have to listen to this any more." My mother tried to stick up for me. He shouted at her. "It's your fault," he said. "You were too soft on her."'

'Dear Philip. I know you've heard all this before. I also know it's no worse than anyone else's story.'

'Dear Philip. And again years later he asked me a personal question. He was driving, I was in the suicide seat. "What went wrong," he said, "between you and Philip?" Again I turned my face away. "I don't want to talk about it," I said. There was silence. He never asked again. And years after *that*, in a cafe in Paris on my way to work, far enough away from him to be able to, I thought of that question and began to cry. Dear Philip. I forgive you for everything.'

Late in the afternoon my mother and Auntie Lorna and I walk along the beach to Surfers. The tide is out: our bare feet scarcely mark the firm sand. Their two voices run on, one high, one low. If I speak they pretend to listen, just as I feign attention to their endless, looping discourses: these are our courtesies: this is love. Everything is spoken, nothing is said. On the way back I point out to them the smoky orange clouds that are massing far out to sea, low over the horizon. Obedient, they stop and face water. We stand in a row, Auntie Lorna in a pretty frock with sandals dangling from her finger, my mother and I with our trousers rolled up. Once I asked my Brazilian friend a stupid question. He was listening to a conversation between me and a Frenchman about our countries' electoral systems. He was not speaking and, thinking to include him. I said, 'And how do people vote *chez toi*, Rubens?' He looked at me with a small smile. 'We don't have elections,' he said. Where's Rio from here? 'Look at those clouds,' I say. 'You'd think there was another city out there, wouldn't you, burning.'

Just at dark the air takes on the colour and dampness of the sub-tropics. I walk out the screen door and stand my gin on a fence post. I lean on the fence and look at the ocean. Soon the moon will thrust itself over the line. If I did a painting of a horizon, I think, I would make it look like a row of rocking, inverted Vs, because that's what I see when I look at it. The flatness of a horizon is intellectual. A cork pops on the first floor balcony behind me. I glance up. In the half dark two men with moustaches are smiling down at me.

'Drinking champagne tonight?' I say.

'Wonderful sound, isn't it,' says the one holding the bottle.

I turn back to the moonless horizon. Last year I went camping on the Murray River. I bought the cards at Tocumwal. I had to write fast for the light was dropping and spooky noises were coming from the trees. 'Dear Dad,' I wrote, 'I am up on the Murray, sitting by the camp fire. It's nearly dark now but earlier it was beautiful, when the sun was going down and the dew was rising.' Two weeks later, at home, I received a letter from him written in his hard, rapid, slanting hand, each word ending in a sharp upward flick. The letter itself concerned a small financial matter, and consisted of two sentences on half a sheet of quarto, but on the back of the envelope he had dashed off a personal message: 'P.S. Dew does not rise. It *forms*.'

The moon does rise, as fat as an orange, out of the sea straight in front of the unit. A child upstairs sees it too and utters long werewolf howls. My mother makes a meal and we eat it. 'Going to help Mum with the dishes, are you, Miss?' says my father from his armchair. My shoulders stiffen. I am, I do. I lie on the couch and read an old *Woman's Day*. Princess Caroline of Monaco wears a black dress and a wide white hat. The knitting needles make their mild clicking. Auntie Lorna and my father come from the same town, Hopetoun in the Mallee, and when the news is over they begin again.

'I always remember the cars of people,' says my father. 'There was an old four-cylinder Dodge, belonging to Whatsisname. It had –'

'Would that have been one of the O'Lachlans?' says Auntie Lorna.

'Jim O'Lachlan. It had a great big exhaust pipe coming out the back. And I remember stuffing a potato up it.'

'A *potato*?' I say.

'The bloke was a councillor,' says my father. 'He came out of the Council chambers and got into the Dodge and started her up. He only got fifty yards up the street when BA – BANG! This damn thing shot out the back – I reckon it's still going!' He closes his lips and drops his head back against the couch to hold in his laughter.

I walk past Biarritz, where globes of light float among shrubbery, and the odd balcony on the half-empty tower holds rich people out into the creamy air. A bare-foot man steps out of the take-away food shop with a hamburger in his hand. He leans against the wall to unwrap it, and sees me hesitating at the slot of the letterbox, holding up the postcards and reading them over and over in the weak light from the public phone. 'Too late to change it now,' he calls. I look up. He grins and nods and takes his first bite of the hamburger. Beside the letterbox stands a deep rubbish bin with a swing lid. I punch open the bin and drop the postcards in.

All night I sleep safely in my bed. The waves roar and hiss, and slam like doors. Auntie Lorna snores, but when I tug at the corner of her blanket she sighs and turns over and breathes more quietly. In the morning the rising sun hits the front windows and floods the place with a light so intense that the white curtains can hardly net it. Everything is pink and golden. In the sink a cockroach lurks. I try to swill it down the drain with a cup of water but it resists strongly. The air is bright, is milky with spray. My father is already up: while the kettle boils he stands out on the edge of the grass, the edge of his property, looking at the sea.

Kate Grenville

No Such Thing as a Free Lunch

1984

It's a fancy place in the way places are fancy here. Dim yellowish walls which anywhere else you might take the liberty of calling shabby. Ah – but the paintings! One doesn't like to look naive and peer too closely, but clearly they're originals, little gems dashed off by the masters, signed with a flourish. My compliments to the chef and to Claude for his wonderful restaurant. The lights are dim but of course no mere vulgar pink. This, my dear, is the dimness of quality. Among the sparkling white linen and the shadowy old chairs – old but good – large elegant men sit back at ease with a bottle of de Rothschild still half full in front of them. Poised women sparkle discreetly, leaning languorously, laughing in streams of silver bells.

Oliver does not, of course, expect me to exclaim aloud my awe or to shame him by clumsy colonial enthusiasm. Super cool now behind the black cummerbund of the maître de. Skirt round this chair, don't brush the tablecloth as you pass and for heaven's sake try not to knock those flowers over. Chin up, back straight, now. No scurrying. Well done.

The chair is being pulled out for me and the oily face inclining with bogus respect. Madame? Slide in slowly now. Weight on the balls of the feet so that he can slide the chair in under me. Well done. What a team.

Oliver is of course totally au fait and absolutely au courant with this place. Evening Luigi, how are you this evening glad to hear it. Where's Claude tonight I don't see him. A few new faces I see. Well now what do you recommend tonight Luigi? The plovers' eggs in sauce de la maison? Plovers' eggs it shall be. That is, unless, of course . . . he inclines his smooth polished Public School face towards me . . . no that will be fine Luigi, two plovers' eggs. And I think a bottle of the '68 don't you? Yes. Fine.

Of course I come here pretty often you know. The odd business lunch and pleasurable um dinner. Nice quiet place. Bit pricey of course but utterly worth every penny.

At the next table a young man with pale eyes like a blind fish in a dead-white hairless face is talking steadily, calmly, without the slightest shadow of a doubt, to his companion who is elegant in black silk and blond coiffure. Her perfect face framed in the bell of her hair stares at him. She nods, murmurs. Absolutely oh yes. Quite. How amusing. Quite. Her dark eyes never leave his decomposing-flesh face. Oh how splendid. How absolutely. She leans forward to him, one hand supporting an elegant cheekbone, the other resting, forefinger pointing, on the table.

Oliver unfolds his napkin and arranges it in his lap.

Now we were talking were we not about *Lear*, without a doubt the greatest play ever written. Genius with a capital G. That strange quality not so very far from madness which we like to call Genius.

His voice is properly reverent in the face of Genius with a capital G.

I venture to differ. *Hamlet*, perhaps?

Oh no dear. You're quite wrong about that. Without any argument his masterwork, his chef d'oeuvre as it were. Definitely his greatest. No. I was just talking to Hall about this very subject last week and he was telling me. No, I'd say you'll have to look at it again. Ah the wine thanks Luigi.

The correct half-inch in the glass. Lift it to the light and peer at it with one eye. Swill it round in the glass. Sniff. Close eyes the better to appreciate this really remarkably fine aroma. Tilt the head back, toss it in and swill it around the back teeth before finally swallowing. Purse the lips. Yes lovely. Not quite up to the '65 naturally but what would you?

At the next table the food has arrived. The long slender fingers delicately grasp the knife and fork and convey dainty morsels to the perfect mouth. Chewing discreetly, she nods and leans forward, swan-like, between mouthfuls, all intelligent interest. Her companion picks petulantly at his food and lifts a disdainful forkful to the blank hole of his mouth.

Well now what were we saying yes the Theatre. Of course the Theatre is without a doubt the highest form of art. No doubt that a fine piece of theatre played by truly professional actors well there's nothing can touch it in terms of sheer artistry. Now the films. I know you work in the films. Well I'm sure there's a lot of merit in certain films but you won't convince me that it's a medium in which art can flourish. Fine for a night's simple entertainment of course absolutely. Quite hits the spot at certain times. And of course for the mass of people, the bulk of the population, well I don't of course want to sound snobbish or in the slightest degree elitist but I'm sure you'll understand when I say that some pleasures require an educated palate.

Another swig of wine hits his educated palate and he closes his eyes and leans back.

Now what would you call a really good film, I mean a film that's not simply a piece of entertainment now I did see a good film a while ago, what was the name of it now. Remarkably fine film within the limitations of the medium. Now a film like that takes the medium to its highest point and there's no doubt there's a lot of merit in it, without a doubt that film is one of the masterworks of that particular medium. But compare it with a piece of true theatre and you'll just have to agree with me.

The plovers' eggs arrive and look distinctly nasty.

I think you'll find that these are really remarkably fine. You'll enjoy these, no question of it.

Now you're obviously an intelligent girl I'd be interested to hear your views on this. Clearly you're not just a run of the mill type of person. Obviously you're more intelligent than most and I'll be interested in your opinion. Now the way I see it is this, you've got two distinct and separate things going on and only one of them can rightly be called Art. And of course there's not a shadow of a doubt in my mind that.

The plovers' eggs are like the insides of golf balls.

Yes the chef here really is remarkably fine no-one to touch him in the whole of London. Now I was talking to Claude last week and I said Claude your chef is a treasure. I think you'll agree that this is the finest food of its kind you've ever tasted.

Absolutely tip top Luigi up to the usual high standard do convey my felicitations to Pierre. I think you'll have to agree that burp. Pardon me.

Now if you'll just excuse me a moment. Bows slightly the embodiment of breeding.

The dead fish at the next table is also making his way to the door at the back. When he's out of sight the immaculate blond slumps forward at the table and covers her face with her hands. Under the table I see her kick off a shoe and scratch the back of her leg with her toes. She sits for a few moments with her face in her hands hidden by the bell of her hair. She looks up at last, straightens her back, resumes the graceful listening attitude, takes a sip of wine. She catches my eye. Without cracking the perfect symmetry and beauty of her heart-shaped face, she gives me a slow patient wink from one brown eye. Then with a wide pink cat's mouth she yawns – tremendously, tonsil-exposingly, eloquently.

Sue Reidy

Alexandra and the Lion

1985

Not long after midnight the lions begin to roar. Maybe they feel the cold. The temperature has dropped to almost zero. Pacing distractedly backwards and forwards in their confinement, they vent their fury at the full moon.

A mile away, Alexandra tosses and turns restlessly in her sixth-floor bed. Effortlessly, she absorbs the sound into her dreams. Falling, falling deeper into cold velvet depths. Above her, waves smash and roar their way to a waiting shore. Her arms flap and flounder as she thrashes her sheets into knots. Inadvertently a flailing hand strikes Narron as he sleeps tidily beside her.

Sleeping the sleep of the dead, his eyelids barely flutter. A gentle breath escapes his mouth as small, perfect teeth sink into a fleshy rambutan. Followed a second later by a hiss, as the rambutan dissolves into a limp butterfly struggling to be free. Deeply asleep he spits, desperate to rid himself of the taste of dry leaves which suddenly fill his mouth to the brim.

A gob of spittle falls on Alexandra's face and she plucks anxiously at it, trapped by a sheet which has wound itself about her with the tightness of a shroud.

A cloud passes. Released, the moon shines brightly into the room. Alexandra wakes abruptly, her heart thumping. Gradually she becomes aware that the roaring which fills her ears has not abated. Not only that, but the sound appears to be getting both louder and closer.

She shivers with the cold and untangling the mess of sheets and blankets huddles closer to the still form of her tiny husband. Only his face registers his dreams. His body remains immobile. Narron gives off little body heat and there are no soft fleshy hollows in which to nestle.

Wrapping her arms tightly around her chest and bringing her

knees up almost to the level of her chin, she burrows deeper into the bed. Very soon she submits to sleep.

The lions pursue her into dreams. Relentlessly she strides with them around the absurd prison. Her own throat opens to emit a shout.

A call of anger and dismay. A cry for the banished earth and sky. The wind blows and dulls the roars to a whisper.

A sudden draught and a door silently swings open. A dozen dark shadows leap into the void and disappear.

A solitary shape remains. From opposite ends they stare and then with one accord move towards each other. Without making a sound, a diminutive Alexandra climbs upon a firm broad back. She has barely grasped handfuls of rough woolly mane before he jumps.

Velvet paws swallow miles. A sharp intake of breath and with a lunge they're cloud bound. Over the monument at One Tree Hill. Past a volcano. Near an island. By a sea. Past a ship with winking lights. Lime-green eyes shining and red hair flying, Alexandra is transported swift as thought.

Alone in an apartment Narron waits. At the foot of the bed a heater, freshly activated, warms an ice chamber. Slender olive fingers drum against the mattress. He turns over onto his side – and there she is. He has not heard her return, but she is there.

Tentatively Narron reaches out a hand for reassuring flesh. Upon contact, he flinches, scorched from the touch. Alexandra is burning as if fevered. He nuzzles against a long red curtain and smells damp strands of salt water and sea air. He lifts himself up onto one elbow and gently brushes the hair away from her face. He looks down at her closed eyes, knowing better than to ask where she has been.

In the morning they perch doll-like upon their breakfast stools and consume bowls of cold brown rice, sprinkled with a selection of chopped nuts and slices of hard-boiled egg. Narron liberally drenches his with a dark sweet sauce.

Alexandra is buried in a manuscript for a new novel her

company is planning to publish. She is chief editor at a large publishing house. Half-heartedly she picks at her rice with her spoon, keeping one eye on the clock and another on a typewritten page.

Narron thinks already of his orchids, waiting for him in his glasshouse on the roof garden. Today he has an important client coming to visit. He is accepting bids for his new award-winning hybrid, which he has named 'Singing Swan'. No one but Narron knows why he names his orchids as he does. He expects to receive up to $800 for the rights to 'Singing Swan'.

He has a great deal on his mind. Usually he is completely absorbed by the maintenance of his huge greenhouse and his other great passion – cooking. He runs a catering business in Indonesian food as a sideline.

Now, however, there is the mystery of Alexandra's nocturnal disappearance and – more worryingly – 'The Book'. Alexandra has asked him, on behalf of her company, to write a book on his especially rare orchids, as well as detailing growing techniques. She is to edit it and Narron's good friend James is to design and do the photography for it.

Alexandra has told Narron that whenever he feels so inclined he is to speak into the miniature tape-recorder she has given him. He wears it around his neck and most days he feeds it a few sentences, usually while he is in the throes of cooking a meal. Away from the demanding presence of his orchids, he seems somehow to be able to think of them more clearly.

Alexandra has no memory of the night before and wonders why she feels so exhausted. Narron anxiously notes the smudges of mauve under her eyes. 'Tonight we will be very warm,' he promises her. You will be so warm you will not vanish again, he tells himself.

That night the temperature drops further. Unprecedented low temperatures for that time of the year. Coldest June for fifty years, headline the newspapers, radio and television.

Narron is in the kitchen preparing the peanut sauce for a simple Sumatran-style gado-gado. He quickly fries the crushed onion, garlic and shrimp paste together and then tosses in the ground peanuts and red chillies.

Alexandra is also in the kitchen – all but sitting on top of the heater. Her long red hair is spread fan-like around her to dry. She finds it comforting to watch Narron as he cooks. He is very neat and economical in his movements. Unlike Alexandra, who sketches the air with wild extravagant gestures, and often leaves a litter of chaos behind her, Narron always stacks his pots and dishes into formidable piles ready for her to wash after each meal.

'And how is "Singing Swan"?' she enquires.

'It awaits the right owner,' he replies, adding a pinch of salt, a generous squeeze of lemon juice and a small amount of brown sugar to the swirling mass.

'And who is the right owner?' she enquires mischievously, raising an eyebrow.

'I'll know the person when I see him. Or her,' remarks Narron cryptically. Swiftly he pours in coconut cream. 'Now don't interrupt me any more, or I'll burn the sauce,' he says, momentarily exasperated.

Alexandra trudges wearily into the lounge, dragging the heater behind her. Narron has complained of the excess heat in the kitchen.

She notices immediately Narron's tape-recorder lying neglected on the sofa. Curiously she picks it up and winds it back.

'. . . The Paphiopedilum family is found not only in Indonesia, but also in India, China, Burma, Malaysia and New Guinea . . .' emerges Narron's thin reedy voice.

Alexandra switches the tape on to fast-forward and quickly listens to random pieces in order to assess Narron's progress.

'. . . Man-made crossings between the species and/or hybrids have been produced in the Paphiopedilum family for more than a century. The Paphiopedilum hybrids today are very different from their delicate exotic parents. The plants are stronger with larger, fuller flowers and their colours are richer and better defined. Their appearance, which seems glossy, almost lacquered, is very distinctive . . .'

'Well, what do you think so far?' enquires Narron, appearing suddenly in the doorway.

'I like it. It seems to flow quite well. I especially loved the bit about the "delicate, exotic parents". Keep going, you're doing well,' she enthuses.

Narron, resplendent in large white apron, takes a bow. 'Dinner is served, Madam.'

Alexandra drops the tape-recorder and, very much like a child, hastens to the table.

'*Selamat makan!*' She grins at him.

Narron takes a swallow from a glass of cold water and observes Alexandra with pleasure as she greedily spoons up her dinner. Alexandra adores her food piping hot, whereas Narron prefers his slightly lukewarm and gains his heat from extra chilli. Finally, he serves himself some gado-gado, a little salad and *lots* of rice.

'Mmmm. I'll never, never tire of your cooking, Narron,' comments Alexandra enthusiastically, her mouth full.

'And I'll never tire of you doing the washing-up,' replies Narron with equal enthusiasm.

After dinner, Narron watches the Tuesday Documentary – 'The Wandering Company'. He is a great fan of Ruth Prawar Jhabvala's novels and he is interested to hear of her partnership in films with director James Ivory and producer Ismail Merchant. He dreams of one day visiting India.

Alexandra divides her time between her book and the television. Before the documentary is finished she rises, yawning and rubbing her eyes, muttering something about having an early night. Narron is glued to the set and doesn't respond. It is only later, when he has plunged the television into silence with the portable remote-control, that he remembers Alexandra's words.

He swiftly turns off the lights and makes for the bedroom. In the darkness he can see only the glowing red spot on the Goldair heater. It whirs away comfortingly, drowning out any sound of human breathing. Narron cautiously prods the bed till he makes contact with the sleeping form of his wife. Reassured, he begins to undress. He dons a pair of fine red woollen longjohns and a baggy red T-shirt. He climbs, flinching, into the cold bed.

Alexandra is curled into a small foetal ball in the middle. He gently rolls her off to one side and then hops out again to pull on an old sweatshirt – also red.

He curves his body around Alexandra's and waits for sleep to claim him. 'I must buy an electric blanket . . .' is his last conscious thought.

The clock strikes midnight. As if on cue, the lions once again begin to roar. How they howl. The wind blows more and more furiously, but does not succeed in drowning their sound. Windows rattle and open gates swing crazily backwards and forwards on their hinges.

Alexandra stirs, but she does not wake.

At about one o'clock the noise reaches a crescendo and Alexandra sits bolt upright in her bed. She stares straight ahead – her eyes wide open in the darkness, straining towards she knows not what. She only knows that she is filled with a terrible sadness, which becomes a great yearning. Though she is awake, she gets up with the jerky movements of a marionette and puts on a violet, velvet dressing-gown. Mechanically, she adjusts the quilted satin collar and tightens the belt. She twists the handle of the door gently and silently closes it after her. Behind her, the small lump of flesh that is Narron releases a soft snore. In his dream he is reliving his first sighting of Alexandra.

Narron is in his second year studying for a Bachelor of Commerce and hating it. He has in addition been sponsored by a New Zealand family. Narron is not in the least bit interested in his degree but his country needs qualified people so desperately, and his parents over in Jakarta have put enormous pressure on him. If he could decide on an appealing alternative he would forfeit it all – but his background has not allowed or prepared him for the luxury of choice.

In order to take his mind off his worries his sole friend James, a Malaysian student, has dragged him to see the annual university capping revue at the Maidment Theatre. Most of the humour floats easily over Narron's head. It is not until

Alexandra appears on the stage in the guise of Cinderella that it absorbs a great deal of his attention.

It is a humorous parody of the old fairy-tale and the audience is soon shrieking with laughter. Narron alone is completely silent – his lips parted slightly in disbelief. His entire concentration is directed towards a tiny red-headed figure in centre-stage. He is deaf to all sound. He can only drink in the sight. So does a starving man look at a banquet. The rest of the performance passes by in a blur. He stumbles into the night half-dazed.

In his sleep, Narron permits himself a small smile.

Alexandra, meanwhile, is already in the lift, swiftly sinking to the ground floor. Through the lattice-work of the metal gates, she can see a ghostly blue flicker of light as she passes each floor. She is not afraid, for she believes that she is dreaming.

As she emerges she glimpses a powerful dark shadow waiting silently, through the glazed double-doors of the foyer. She feels no shock or surprisc. Shc knows cxactly what shc must do, as if she has been reherased a dozen times.

With practised ease she slips the lock on the front door and glides through. A great draught of cold air rushes up at her. She is oblivious. She has eyes only for the familiar, oh so dear shape attentively nuzzling at her hand. Trustingly, she grasps a clump of mane in one hand and resting the other on the broad tawny back, lifts herself up onto the beast. No sooner has she settled herself astride than with a heart-stopping leap they are swallowed up by the thick fog.

Narron fights against the waves of sleep which threaten to engulf him. All is not well. Slender fists batter cool, stiff sheets. To no avail. Overcome with weariness, he drops back into a dreamless slumber.

Alexandra is many miles away in the far north. The storm increases as she journeys further. Yachts drift from their moorings and smash into a thousand fragments against the rocks. Mandarins and lemons are flung helter-skelter into the air. A shower of sparks pierces the blackness as a large old tree spontaneously combusts. Alexandra droops low over the lion's head as a volley of citrus fruit is hurled at the leaden clouds.

Then – as suddenly as it had begun – the storm ceases. The absence of sound is almost as frightening as was the storm itself. The air smells sweet and fresh and the lion, in an abrupt about-turn, heads for home.

Alexandra is almost unconscious. She drifts in that trance-like state between wakefulness and sleep. Her petal-like face collapses over its fragile stalk-like neck, combining to unbalance her torso, which nose-dives into the lion's mane. Her spirit rushes to greet temporary oblivion.

Closer to home they pass over a deserted park. The swings whine and squeak in the breeze. Discarded beer cans litter the ground. Over the road the Market's brick chimney looms large. Alexandra's dangling feet brush within millimetres of it.

The sudden silence as the storm abates in the city at last brings Narron to his senses and to the realisation that he is alone. With a shrill cry of panic he flies from the bed. He wildly searches the apartment, calling Alexandra's name.

Desperately, clad only in his red bedclothes, a barefoot Narron rushes to the lift. Dancing with impatience at what seems an impossible slowness, he finally reaches the ground floor. Flinging aside the heavy metal grille with almost Herculean strength for his tiny frame, he lunges towards the front doors. A few persistent droplets of rainwater plop intermittently from the roof onto the concrete steps.

Narron is inconsolable. Dawn is still an hour away and he peers frantically into the garden from his vantage-point on the steps. His eyes narrow. A slight breeze has caused a dull piece of cloth to flutter under the lemon tree. The cloth continues to flap about bravely, as the wind playfully tosses it this way and that. Hardly daring to hope, Narron makes his way over there.

A sodden, discarded bundle has been placed as an offering to the heavy old tree. With a cry of horror Narron runs towards the crumpled figure. He gently eases her onto his back. The rag doll's arms flop over his shoulders and swing crazily onto his chest. A slipper falls and an icy white foot is exposed.

Even rag dolls can become a dead weight. Narron crawls over the garden at a snail's pace, terrified of dropping his precious burden. He heaves a reluctant form up the steps and, pausing only to draw breath, once more tackles the cumbersome metal grille.

Back in their apartment, Narron with a beating heart directs a spotlight onto his beloved's face. Not a cry escapes his frozen throat as he gazes at Alexandra under the harsh glare. There is no time to be lost.

After wiping the perspiration from his forehead, Narron quickly switches on a couple of heaters and relieves Alexandra of her garments. He briskly towels her dry with sure, even strokes and wraps her up in the warmest clothes he can find. Afterwards, he seals her firmly in the bed. She utters a low moan.

Concerned, Narron bends over Alexandra and her eyelids snap open. There is no sign of recognition in the glance she gives him. Soon, her eyes drift shut again and her breathing resumes its normal rhythm. Scarcely relieved, Narron bustles about, rearranging the heaters and then dealing with the wet garments. He remembers Alexandra's drowned hair chilling her head on the pillow and, grasping a blow-drier, attempts to dry the more soaked tresses. Despite the drone of the drier, Alexandra does not reawaken.

Narron sits on the bed beside the still form. He keeps watch on her till daylight.

Every hour he brews up a fresh pot of strong, thick coffee. His little face is grey and pinched with worry. He plans to ring a doctor at 8.30 a.m. In the meantime, he ponders over Alexandra's nocturnal activities. He is too astute to attribute them to mere sleepwalking.

His mind in a turmoil, Narron is eventually driven to phone James. It is many years since student days and Narron and Alexandra both have a wide circle of friends. Yet James, his first friend, has remained, aside from Alexandra, his closest confidant. In a halting, confused sort of way, Narron relates the events of the past couple of days. James paces up and down his lounge. He jabs at his cigarette, stubbing it out in the ashtray.

'Possession,' he states. 'Something or someone has some sort of hold on her.'

It all makes sense to Narron. He frowns and pulls at his lower lip.

'What do you suggest?' he asks.

'You say you found her in the garden. Have you searched it in daylight to see if there's some sort of clue as to how she got there?'

'No,' replies Narron with excitement. 'No, I haven't.'

The problem assumes more tangible proportions. They hasten downstairs.

They both notice at once, as they prowl about, that several smaller shrubs appear rather battered. One or two seem to have been completely crushed.

'These bushes could have been damaged in the storm, though,' Narron reminds James.

James gives a sudden shout and Narron rushes over to the lemon tree again. James is pointing to a muddy area at the very base of the tree. An animal's footprint can clearly be seen.

'The sort of animal that made that mark would be pretty heavy,' speculates Narron.

'It's the print of a lion,' replies James quietly. 'I'm absolutely certain.'

A piece of the jigsaw silently clicks into place in Narron's mind.

Thoughtfully they return to the lift. They have managed to discover only one other footprint. More blurred than the first, but nevertheless made by the same creature.

'You know what you must do, don't you?' says James. 'You must not let her out of your sight for the next few days. You'll have to lock her in the apartment and hide the keys.' The thought seems distasteful to Narron, but he can't think of a better idea.

'I'll be back this evening, though. I'll even stay over and keep you company if you like.'

Narron accepts James's offer with gratitude and persuades him to swallow a quick breakfast.

A long day looms ahead of Narron. He checks on Alexandra. Her face appears bloodless against the black sheets. The doctor comes and goes. 'Warmth and rest, warmth and rest,' she assures Narron heartily, patting him on the shoulder.

'Don't let her get up too soon. We don't want to catch pneumonia. Ring me if there's any change for the worse.'

Narron phones the publishing company and speaks to Alexandra's secretary, who asks if she may visit. 'No, no,' replies Narron, horrified at the very idea. 'She is much too sick. I will phone you again.' The secretary, puzzled, slowly replaces the receiver.

The hothouse is out of the question for the day, so Narron seeks to divert himself with his tape-recorder.

'... It is difficult to grow the hybrid Paphiopedilum satisfactorily without a glasshouse.'

Narron sighs deeply and then recommences.

'... Ideal ventilation often incorporates a fan system and maybe perforated polythene tubing. Any rapid drying out which occurs can be counteracted by ...' Here Narron pauses, momentarily losing the thread of what he was about to say. With an effort, he takes a grip on himself and continues. 'Counteracted by automatic foggers or vapour jets ...'

A shrill series of rings punctuates the air. Narron jumps.

'Is that Narron's Indonesian Catering Service?' enquires a recognisably eastern suburbs voice.

'Yes,' replies Narron listlessly.

Undaunted by Narron's seeming lack of response, the woman rushes on, 'Would you be available to cater for ten people this Saturday? I know it's short notice being Wednesday already – but could you ...?'

'I think so,' replies Narron dolefully. He takes down the address and phone number and they discuss menu details. Narron requests a deposit in advance and the woman promises to mail a cheque to him that very day.

He shuffles into the kitchen to retrieve his large diary and transfers his phone notes into it. Out of habit, he methodically checks his stock of spices and ingredients and begins to make a list of the items he will need to purchase. He observes that he has run out of terasi (shrimp paste) and also kemiri (candlenuts).

His business details thus arranged, Narron once more attempts some recording. It's a slow process. He regularly tiptoes into the room to look at Alexandra.

A weak and sickly sunshine gradually begins to filter through the windows. This cheers Narron somewhat. After his last phone call he has activated his answer-phone and when the rings pierce his concentration for the second time that morning, he is able to sit back and listen to his recorded message. James's comforting tones penetrate the room. Narron jumps up and quickly switches off the machine.

'James, James, I'm here after all,' he says.

'I'm just phoning to see if Alexandra has woken yet,' explains James.

'No, not yet,' replies Narron.

They discuss the situation for some moments more and then James rings off. He is not having a good morning. He has a presentation to a major client in a couple of days and there is still much to be done. He has put an amount of work out to free-lancers but there are some aspects of the advertising campaign which can only be dealt with by himself. He doodles onto his layout pad with his felt pens and the shape of a lion emerges. He tears the drawing off the pad and places it under a fresh sheet of the thin paper. He traces over his first drawing and extends the legs so that the lion appears to be running. He draws the small figure of a woman on its back. Long red hair streams behind her. The woman's eyes are firmly closed and she has a beautiful smile on her face. Threadlike fingers grasp handfuls of mane and the lion's eye appears to burn. James erases the mouth he has drawn and replaces it with teeth that are bared in a terrible grimace.

James stares at his drawing for some moments and then he reaches over and picks up the phone book and looks up Auckland Zoo.

He doesn't have much luck with his phone call. He can tell that he is viewed as a crank. Nevertheless he has, through his persistency, established that yes, all lions are present and correct, they're all sleeping now but have been unusually restless over the past few days. James suddenly taps his head excitedly and dials the same number again. He discovers that the zoo has only recently brought in a new lion from Central Africa – one of their largest lions in fact. When James thinks back, he does actually recall glancing over a small article in the *Inner City News* about the new arrival.

He picks up his two drawings and carefully places them in his briefcase, wedged between the pages of a magazine.

Narron is finding it progressively more difficult to concentrate on his dictation. His heart is simply not in it. He has just re-entered the lounge from yet another check on Alexandra. He has managed to spoon a little warm orange juice and honey down her unresisting throat.

Narron decides to cheer himself up by making a sop kembang kubis, or cauliflower soup. All this worry and excitement have made him hungry.

Soon he is quite absorbed as he boils up some chicken stock, onion, cauliflower, black pepper, nutmeg and salt. He stirs dreamily and remembers back to how he finally got to meet the Cinderella he saw on stage all those years ago.

His studies were neglected for a few days as he loitered about the university grounds, hoping for a glimpse of Alexandra. After a couple of days, his patience was rewarded and he espied her in the student cafeteria. She was laughing with a group of friends. Her hair thrown back over the chair, exposing the slender white column of throat. Narron swallowed nervously.

He sat down at the next table and stared, not even bothering to camouflage his activity behind a screen of sipping coffee. She didn't notice him and when she got up to leave, Narron followed behind at a discreet distance.

It was not difficult to discover the pattern of her lectures and movements. Narron pondered as to how he could actually meet this glorious creature. She seemed totally unapproachable, always surrounded by friends.

'Do you know anyone vaguely connected with her who could introduce you?' James had suggested.

'No,' admitted Narron in despair. 'It's hopeless.'

'Don't give up,' comforted James, 'there must be a way around it. Somehow.'

Alexandra acquired a faithful shadow. On an edge of consciousness she sensed an intense concentration directed inexorably to her. Signals indicated the presence to be benign. She waited. There was an inevitability about the collision.

On a crisp autumn morning patience was rewarded. A slight

figure, walking for once towards her, glanced up. Discomposure. He tripped and fell, literally, at her feet.

A freckled white hand pulled him to his feet with a surprising strength.

His thoughts, like birds, flew right out of his head. She took the initiative.

'Don't you think it time you introduced yourself?'

Narron smiles as he tosses noodles into the steaming broth.

Alexandra wakens very weak and Narron spoonfeeds her some soup. He doesn't wish to upset her by clamouring for explanations at this point.

Her gaze is clear and open, expressing only gratitude and love. She displays no curiosity or memory of the previous night. Soon she falls asleep again.

Narron is relieved a few hours later, when James cheerfully arrives.

'You look a bit washed out,' he comments as he bounces in and throws himself on the sofa. He points to the bedroom and mouths, 'Is she okay?'

'Not sure,' replies Narron and he makes a seesaw gesture with his hands. 'It could go one way or the other.'

'I've brought you a drink,' says James and passes over a bottle of chardonnay. Narron brightens. 'I'll fetch some glasses.' James attempts to divert Narron and launches into an hilarious piece of gossip about one of his clients. In spite of himself, Narron begins to smile and look a little more cheerful.

'. . . He was wearing a crotchless spiderman's outfit,' continues James, 'trying to climb on to the wardrobe in order to jump off it, when the thing overturned and fell on top of him, breaking both his legs . . .'

Narron's eyes gleam. He pours them both another drink. 'And then what happened?' he encourages.

'Well!' replies James. 'His wife, meanwhile, was still tied to the bed, so *she* couldn't do anything . . .'

Narron laughs, imagining the expression on the nighbour's face after he had responded to the cries for help.

Narron turns up the heat and stretches out full-length on the sofa. A wave of exhaustion sweeps over him. For a brief moment he closes his eyes.

The ever-observant James gets to his feet and offers to cook dinner. Narron smiles in anticipation. Each has tried to outdo the other over the years in creating spectacular culinary delights.

Alexandra lies perfectly still in the bed. Only the feverish fingers plucking at the bedclothes betray her inner turmoil.

She is in a dimly lit movie theatre, seated in the front row of the lower level. Two enormous golden plaster lions flank either side of the screen. Their cavernous eyes are lit from within by fierce red bulbs. Alexandra becomes mesmerised as the eyes flicker on and off, on and off.

In that blurred dimension of dreams, she is both watching herself in the seat and at the same time tentatively reaching out to touch the gleaming muscular flanks. There is a swift intake of breath as her hand encounters the chilled surface of the statue. She explores further. Seen from a distance the skin appears smooth, satin and wonderfully modelled. To her dismay, however, some of the plaster falls away in her fingers. The rippling flesh is an illusion. Gold flakes attach themselves firmly to her hands. An icy buttock peels away and crumbles onto the stage.

Frightened and tearing at her hands to remove the gold foil, she finds herself once more in her seat. Slowly, the great head swivels and a fiery eye fixes her in its gaze. Alexandra's teeth are clenched with fear. Her breath comes in short gasps.

Mercifully, the creature finally averts its eyes and once more faces its twin. Rhythmically they flash signals across the stage.

Alexandra tosses and turns then, as the darkness grows deeper. She doesn't hear James clattering about in the spare room. She doesn't feel Narron's pliant little body slip quietly in beside her.

The moon is at its zenith. Despite having vowed to keep awake, both James and Narron quickly fall asleep as the wine takes its toll of their bodies.

All night long, sure footsteps pad softly around the small apartment block. A velvet shape rests briefly under the lemon tree before resuming its regular circuit. Daylight advances stealthily.

It is the milkwoman who first observes the trespasser and raises the alarm.

Up on the sixth floor, Alexandra's consciousness faintly begins to stir. The lion on her right slowly stretches and emits a huge yawn. Alexandra scarcely dares breathe. A burning look passes between them before it begins to cross the stage towards her. The audience, which until now she has been unaware of, breaks into a confused babble all around her.

Alexandra grips the seat tightly with both hands and clamps her knees firmly together. Her heart is beating so hard it drowns out all the noise. The beast is almost upon her when suddenly all the lights are turned off and the theatre is plunged into darkness.

She screams.

A loud cracking sound splits the air. Two human cannonballs hurl themselves at the door of the top apartment and negotiate the stairs in a series of leaps and bounds which take them to the ground floor and finally to the front lawn. A small crowd has gathered around the body. In daylight the teeth appear yellow and tarnished. The splendid mane, a tangle of matted twine. In spite of himself, Narron's heart contracts.

James and Narron, remembering Alexandra, leave the scene of all the excitement down below and rush back to Narron's apartment. They peep around the bedroom door and see Alexandra beaming and rubbing her eyes.

'I've had such an odd dream . . .' she murmurs.

Beverley Farmer

Home Time

1985

By late afternoon the sky is a deep funnel of wind, damp and white. She remarks as she passes through the lamplight around his desk on her way to the bathroom: 'Doesn't it look like snow!'

'Do you think?' He squints out the window.

'That hollowness of the light.'

'It's early for snow.'

'*Casablanca*'s going to be on TV tonight at eight,' she says before he can look down again. 'Why don't we go to that bar and see it and then have dinner somewhere after?'

'Mmm.'

The room is grey; only the light around him is warm and moving with shadows. The steam pipes are silent. Whenever will they start clanking and hissing and defrost the apartment? '*Isn't* it cold, though!' she says brightly.

'Mmm.'

'Maybe I should go for a walk downtown, take some photos of the lights coming on,' she says.

'It's a lot colder outside.'

'Walking would warm me up.'

'Okay.'

'Oh, maybe not,' she says. 'I might write letters home instead.' Home is Australia. It's summer there. 'Until it's time for *Casablanca*.'

He sighs and waits for silence.

She has an electric radiator on in her room – the sitting-room really, but she works in here. She has twin lamps of frilly glass at twin tall windows inside which wasps sizzle and cling and trap themselves in shreds of cobweb. The table she writes at faces the windows. Three times a day she pushes books to one side and turns papers face down, since this is also the table they eat at. The kitchen is next to it, bare and icy, smelling of gas.

She pulls her radiator over by the couch and lies curled up in the red glow with her head on a velvet cushion.

Later she half-wakes: he has walked past into the kitchen. When he switches her lamps on and hands her a mug of coffee she is stiffly sitting up to make room. 'Did you get much written?' She yawns, stretching an arm warm with sleep along his shoulders.

'Fair bit.' He grins. 'Did you?'

She is glad she stayed in. 'No. What's the time?'

'Hell, yes.' He looks. 'Ten past eight.'

'Oh, we've missed it!'

'No, we haven't. Only the start.'

They gulp their coffee and help each other drag coats and boots on. 'You must have seen it, haven't you?' he says.

'Oh, yes. Hasn't everyone?'

'Then what's the –?'

She shuts his mouth with a kiss. 'I want to see it with *you*. In America.'

He smiles at that. They fling open the door and stop short. Snow is falling, must have been falling for hours, heavy and slow, whirling round the white streetlamps. 'Oh, *snow*!' She dashes back inside for her camera and takes photo after photo from the stoop, of fir branches shouldering slabs of snow, drooping in gardens, and elms still with gold leaves and a fine white skin all over, and lawns and cars and rooftops thickly fleeced. Passing cars have drawn zips on the white road.

'Now we're really late,' he says. Hand in hand they tramp and slither the few blocks to the bar they like, bright as a fire with the lamps on. Outside it two young men are throwing snowballs. She gasps as one leaps on the other and they flounder giggling at her feet.

'Pussy cat!' one jeers. 'That's *all* you is!'

Her man is holding the blurred glass door open. Heads along the bar turn away from *Casablanca* to stare at them. He leads her to a stool, orders a red wine and an Irish coffee and stands at her back. Ingrid Bergman's face fills the screen.

The door opens on a white flurry and the young men stamping in, shaking the snow off. The heads turn and stare. 'Celebrate the first *snow*!' one young man announces. 'Have a *drink*, everybuddy!' A cheer goes up. The barman brings her another red wine and him another Irish coffee. The young men have flopped crosslegged on the carpet and are gazing at the screen.

'Oh, they're *so* young,' a voice murmurs in her ear; the grey-haired woman beside her is smiling. She smiles in answer and gives herself over to *Casablanca*. He is at her back with his arms round her. When it ends he goes to the men's room.

The old woman is dabbing her eyes. 'Oh dear!' She makes a face. 'Do you come here a lot? I do. We live just down the road.'

Do you come here a lot? I do. We live just down the road. You can see this bar from our stoop and I tell you it's a real temptation, glowing away down here. With that lantern at the door with snowflakes spinning round it and the way the elm leaves flap against it like yellow butterflies – it's like some place in a fairy tale. And here inside it's as bright and warm as inside a Halloween pumpkin. Those lamps everywhere, and the bottles burning in the mirror. And whenever the door opens, a breath of snow blows in and the lights all shift under and over the shadows. Even if *Casablanca* wasn't on the TV I'd have come tonight.

What'll you have, honey, another one of those? What is that, red wine? Jimmy, another one of those red wines and I'll have a Jack Daniels. Yes, rocks. And wipe that silly grin off your face, have you no soul, what kind of a man laughs at *Casablanca*? Thanks, Jimmy. Keep it.

Look through that archway, the couples at their little tables, all so solemn and proper with their vintage wine and their candles – look, their heads are hollow, like the candles burnt their eyes out. They might all have stories just as sad as *Casablanca*, but who cares? It's *Casablanca* breaks our hearts, over and over. You cried at the end, I saw you. So did that nice man of yours. Oh, a bar's the place to watch it, a bar's the perfect place. I cry every single time, I can't help myself, it's so noble and sad and innocent and – hell, you know. I couldn't watch it home, anyway. Bill, he's my husband, gets mad when I cry. He walks out. 'Why, am I supposed to stay and watch you slobber over this shit?' he said last time it was on. 'Most people got all they need to slobber about in real life.'

'You're what *I* got,' I said right back.

That's him there, over at the pool table. That your man he's talking to? I thought so. They're lighting up cigarettes and getting acquainted. Isn't that a coincidence? He looks a nice easy-going kind of a guy. But then so does Bill. I love Bill, I love him a lot. I've known that man thirteen years, I could tell you things . . . I'm not blind to anything about Bill, I love him anyway. He loves *me*, though it doesn't feel like being loved much of the time. He needs me. He has to punish me for that. There he is, an older man than he acts. His hair has a grey sheen and his skin hangs loose all over, see the crazed skin on his neck. He's affable and a bit loud with the drink, everybody's pal. Well, when we get home there won't be a word out of him. Under the skin and the smile he's a bitter, fearful man and nobody gets close to him.

He's a second comer, for one thing. He can't forget that. He's my second husband. Yours is a second comer too, is he, honey? Don't mind me sticking my nose in. It's just I can tell. You two are a mite too considerate, too careful with one another, know what I mean? It shows, that's all, if you can read the signs. So what if you are Australians. Oh no. Look, I don't mean you haven't got a nice relationship. But it's only the first time you give your whole self. After that, like it or not, you hold back. You've gotten wise – and you can't pretend *other*wise!

We've been married ten years this Thursday – Thanksgiving Day. You got to laugh. Cheers. Isn't that something, though. My first marriage never got to double figures. I had twenty years alone in between.

Do you remember the first time you saw *Casablanca*? Mine was in 1943, when it first came out, on my honeymoon with Andy. That's reason enough to cry. Bill knows. It's something he can't stand to be reminded of. He pretends it's only Rick and Ilsa making me *slobber*. Men – you tell a man the truth about your life, you end up paying for *ever*. Remember that.

1943! Andy was nineteen, I was seventeen, his ship was sailing for Europe in a week. Our parents said no, you're too young, but we said we'd only run away, so they gave in. We had one weekend for a honeymoon in New York City. The hotel was an awful old ruin – it still is – full of cockroaches and noisy plumbing. We were so embarrassed, you could hear every drop, every trickle. Our room was on the top floor. Through the fire escape we could see the river, and the moon in the mist like a brass knob behind a curtain, and the lights of Manhattan. So it's not a bed of roses, Andy said: it's a bed of lights instead. We saw *Casablanca* and we cried. We were such babies. He was going to be a hero and I was going to wait... We danced round the room like Rick and Ilsa did. We sure didn't sleep much. We didn't even know how to *do* it, you know. We were scared. Oh, we soon got the hang of it. And then his ship sailed.

He came back, oh, he came back. He'd won medals in Italy, he was a hero. But he wouldn't ever talk about it. Whatever happened over there, it finished Andy. He started drinking, then he lost his job, and soon he couldn't hold down any job, he just drank and gambled and played the black market. He'd come home once, twice a week, then sleep for days...

One night he started hitting me. Everything was my fault, he said. Then he cried. He promised he never would again. I was fool enough to believe it. If they've hit you once and gotten away with it, honey, you're in trouble. It can only get worse.

So, one night I woke up on the kitchen floor. The table lamp was still on, the beer that he spilt looked like butter melting under it. I remember I saw the pattern of brown triangles on the linoleum every time my eyes came open, they looked wet and red, but I couldn't see sharp enough to be sure. The window was black – so it was still night time – and had silver edges like knives where he smashed it. The curtain was half torn down, sopping up the beer on the table and moving in the wind, a white curtain like a wedding veil. *Help me*! I called out. My head felt crushed. The wind must have blown my hair on my face, hair was stuck to it. A long way away something was – snuffling. My nose was flat on my cheek, red bubbles blew out. Andy *wasn't there*. I held my head still and pulled myself up by the table leg: broken glasses, slabs of the window pane, the wet curtain, but no note. No nothing. The room was going all watery and dim as if the floor was hot as fire and yet it was so icy when I lay down, I pulled the curtain down over me to keep warm.

It wasn't till morning that I saw he'd taken all his stuff. God knows there wasn't much, poor Andy. Then I got started all over again: *Don't leave me! Don't leave me alone now! I love you*! Even now I dream – I wake up and for a moment I'm on that floor again knowing I've lost Andy, he's gone for *ever*. Oh, I've never gotten over it.

I'm sorry. Don't be embarrassed. I'll be all right in a moment. Thank you, yes, another Jack Daniels would be nice. Yes, thank you.

Funny thing was, when I got up off the floor next day and my nose was smashed and my eyes looked like two squashed plums and I was shaking so hard I thought my teeth would crack – I ran out into the street in case I could see him and maybe catch him up and all the time I was whimpering, *After all you've done to me, you just get up and go*? I looked in the kitchen window. It was empty, all shadowy gold behind the edges of glass.

Another funny thing – I had a vision in the night, a ballerina came in. (I wanted to be a dancer, I was good, but first the War started, then I got married . . .) Anyway, this ballerina in white was waving her arms and bowing. It must have been the curtain that I saw. She bent down to lift me then she lay beside me, sobbing, I remember that.

Look at us there in the mirror, like two ghosts among the whisky bottles. Okay, Jimmy, laugh. He thinks I'm admiring myself. I'm not that far gone, though I'm getting there. Cheers. Is that really me, that scrawny thing with the spiky grey hair? You'd never think I was a ballet dancer. Bill hates ballet. He says that because the pain and exertion and ugliness aren't allowed to show, it's one big lie. Tinsel and sweat, he says. Dancers smell like horses, someone famous says, so Bill has to read it to me out of the newspaper. Horses aren't any less beautiful for the way they smell, I say. Horses are dancers too and dancers love them. Anyway, I say, I like the way they smell. You would, he says, you're not what you'd call fussy, are you. Now wasn't that asking for it? *No, well, I married you*! I let it pass, though, and he gives me points for not saying it: just a flicker of the eyelids, but enough.

Most of our quarrels end like that. They're harmless. Nothing Bill says or does can get to the quick of me like it did with Andy whether he meant it or not. Bill can make me ache with misery when he wants, but somewhere deep down inside me now there's this little tough muscle braces itself so the barbs can't go too far in. Bill knows. He's the same. Maybe by now it would have been like that with Andy, who knows? I don't even know if he's alive or dead. My parents came and made me get a divorce. They told him I said he couldn't see me or the kids ever again.

Let me tell you the *worst* thing – let's have another drink? – the worst thing – oh, God, I've never told a living soul this. Jimmy, more of these and have one on me, okay? The worst thing is, when he had me on the floor that night – just pushed me down – and started smashing things and yelling that he wanted *out*, I rolled over and hung on to his trouser leg for dear life and begged him not to leave me. I just wouldn't let go. I – slobbered, and howled and – and I kissed his muddy shoe. So he slammed his other shoe in my face. That's when my nose got broken. I mean, that's why.

I thank God the kids weren't home, they didn't see that. They saw him hit me other times, but not that. They were only little. Rick was about five, Ilsa was just a baby. Something like that, though – if they saw it happen, it'd leave a scar on them. 'I won't let Daddy hurt you,' Ricky used to say to me. They were at my parents' place in New Jersey because I had to get a job so I couldn't look after them. We called them Rick and Ilsa – well, *you* know why! Ilsa's married, she's in Alaska now, she's a nurse. Rick's dead. He got killed in Vietnam. Got a medal doing it, too. If his Daddy ever heard about it, I suppose he must have felt proud. Or maybe not.

Don't get me wrong, I believe in sacrifice, and love and honour and loyalty, even if it turns out they were wasted – else why would I love *Casablanca*? Rick and Ilsa, they had something or someone they'd give up everything for. I only wish I still did. Real people have their moments of glory. Time goes on for them though, they can't live up to it. But the glory lives on in memory. Bill won't see that. Face facts, he says. You and your glory and your wallowing in the past. It's shit, that's all it is, shit preserved in syrup. That's better than shit preserved in vinegar, the way yours is, I say. Oh, that's good, he says. Make with the witty repartee, babe, you know I dig that. (Bill can never let go of anything. All his past is still there inside of him, pickled.) Why better, honey? Shit's still shit, he says then. Who knows the truth? I say. You refuse to, *he* says, and round and round we go.

What you never really get over, I suppose, is finding out love's not enough. Loving someone's no *use*. And you only find out the hard way. No one can tell you. You believe in love when you're young, you believe it's forever, it's the only thing that matters, it'll save you both, if you just hang in there and give more and more. I wonder if Ilsa would have gone with Rick – given up everything and gone with him – would it have ended up with her on the floor with her nose smashed? You never know.

Here they come. Look, they're wondering what we're saying. Look at those suspicious eyes and butter-wouldn't-melt smiles of theirs! Your man's been watching you all this time. Here's looking at you, kid! Easy to see you're new. It's great while it lasts, make the most. The couples have had their wine and candlelight and now they're leaving. Don't you just love a black and white night like this after snow, when it echoes? And you slide and fall down on top of each other all the way and rub each other's feet dry and warm once you're inside. Okay, fellers, home time? I've lost my coat. Thanks, honey. I feel so lit up it's a wonder you can't see me shining through it! I'm sure I don't know why I've been telling you the story of my life. You cried at the end of *Casablanca*. I suppose that's why.

'Can I read that?'

'Read what?'

Her hands have instinctively spread across the pages of blue scrawl. He raises his eyebrows: 'What you've been writing half the night.'

She passes them over her shoulder. The couch creaks and the pages rustle until at last he tosses them back on the table and goes to make coffee. She stares at them, sweat prickling her. The heating is on full.

'Thank you,' she says when he brings her mug.

'Is this finished?'

'Oh, for now, anyway. I was just coming to bed – I'm sorry. Haven't you been asleep?'

'I used to respect writers rather a lot,' he murmurs. 'Now I'm not sure.'

'You're writing your thesis on one.'

'Mmm. There's writing and writing. To my mind this –' he points – 'is more like scavenging.' He waits while she swallows hot coffee. 'Perhaps if you wore a badge, a brand on your forehead that meant: *Beware of the scavenger*? Then people would know they were fair game.'

'You think *that's* being *fair*?'

'She trusted you, it seems, with the story of her life.'

'I hope I can do it justice.'

'Justice.' He sighs.

She has nothing to say. He finishes his coffee sip by sip, takes his mug and rinses it, then comes back to stand behind her chair. Her mug is clenched in both hands; the light of the two lamps blurs in her coffee.

'I am not to figure in anything you write,' comes the smooth voice again. 'Never. I hope you understand that.'

Hardly breathing, she cranes her neck forward to have a sip of coffee, but he grabs the mug from her and slams it down on the table, where it breaks. Coffee spurts up and splashes brown and blue drops over her pages. This time she knows better than to move until his footsteps creak away across the boards. His chair scrapes. She hears a match strike in the room beyond, and a sigh as he breathes smoke in.

Yvonne du Fresne

Christmas (Shirley Temple is a Wife and Mother)

1985

We are on our Christmas journey, north, home, at the end of term. Sometimes I have been able to think of the car, the dog and me like the Three Wise Men, journeying on in noble simplicity, but heat, petrol stations, ice cream wrappers, etc., render this nearly impossible.

This Christmas will pass like all the other Christmases. With a brisk infant mistress's trot I make for the car. The dog collapses on the foothpath and pants desperately, eyeing me shrewdly. There is no water anywhere. I rehearse: Could I have a drop of that water you have in that handy can behind that petrol-pump there? No, I haven't got a saucer, perhaps you have an old bucket, an old fish-tin, perhaps I could soak my hanky and squeeze some moisture into that poor dehydrated mouth?

How do mothers cope? I bite one piece off a warm Wellington tomato and place it neatly by the dog's front paw. Lovely, juicy. *Eat it*, I say. The dog stiffens, and pathetically removes both paws from dangerous contact.

O.K., I say heartlessly. No water from here to home.

We take off, and soon float rather than drive into an alien world of paper-thin leaves and grass in the cruel sun, as if they have been pressed between the pages of a Bible – an old, black, long-ago Bible.

As we drive, a forgotten memory almost jabs through. Some routine I learned last Christmas to fix all Christmases to come, for ever. I must have been very tired last Christmas to have to learn a *routine*.

Now I remember. The first hairline crack in the placid mirror of my year is suddenly here. No husband. No child. Christmas is coming. The Festival of the Mothers and Babies is about to begin.

Daddy, Daddy – she's here. Our little girl.

All right – all right – don't tell us all the punctures you had.

Daddy, she's only just arrived and you are at her the *minute* she steps in the door. The dear little dog, then. Look at her frisking about. Not a bit ruffled by the long trip you've had.

Well, how many broken hearts did you leave behind? Any exciting visitors suddenly dropping out of the skies – unable to bear your absence a moment longer? Any mysterious male voices on toll for this Christmas?

Now leave her alone, dear. Don't nag her the minute she's stepped in the door.

Still, Daddy – our girl – home at last!

Can you still be their girl at forty-five?

The only toll call I'll get will be, 'Madam, we regret to inform you that your house burned down last night. The fire appears to have been started by two six-year-olds.'

We have had tea. The dog has had two biscuits and is lying – freed from terror at last – log-like under my father's chair. There is no news except interesting titbits about my house.

Did I tell you that the geraniums came out after all? I got twenty-three cuttings off that bush I found and now I've got twenty-three geranium bushes all exactly the same colour. All sisters – well – brothers and sisters I suppose you'd say.

There is a short silence.

Nancy has new slip-covers, says my mother. Dark. It'll keep Clara's children from dirtying them. Just fancy – two children and there, Nancy is a grandmother already.

Entering very dangerous ground here.

We say to them, don't we, Daddy – grandchildren! Wouldn't be bothered with them. Upsetting everybody. And the furniture! This way we've got you every Christmas. Come next year and Nancy and Bob will be cooling their heels – an empty house – he'll have *his* parents and off they'll go. Clara wouldn't think twice about the loneliness here.

It is my turn.

Clara's *young* isn't she! She hasn't any proper job qualifications has she? Not like you, dear – with all those exams you've got. We look at them and we say Huh, don't we, Daddy? Keep your grandchildren. We wouldn't be bothered with them.

Clara was nine when I was twenty.
Clara is a wife. Clara is a mother.
Shirley Temple is a wife and mother.
And Princess Margaret is a wife and mother.

It is very hot. But I go to the library to get out Stone and Church and *Aspects of the Gifted Child's Development*, etc. so that I will go back to work remembering the meaning of dichotomy and so on, when I am using them in spirited conversation in the staffroom.

I am getting out Stone and Church and *The Gifted Child*, etc. to show the librarian, my parents and any visitors picking up a book after I have carelessly strewn the lot about the house, that I have a mission, almost a vocation, to teach. The word will go around again. Oh, no – she has a vocation for teaching. Not marriage for her – she is a brilliant teacher, they say.

The high soft singing is beginning. 'What Child Is This?', 'I Wonder As I Wander'. I check the defences. No secret photograph album full of little godchildren and cousins. No desire to linger by other people's prams. A thankful getting out from under at end of term.

Ho, I say. Bring on anything you may have in your bag. Even a lost Child in the snow.

I see myself unguarded in the bathroom mirror, a dangerous Lorelei wreathed in steam, luring the traveller to his death.

I don't want to feel like the Lorelei.

I don't want to meet any more travellers, all brave as bulls, and running to their mothers at the most desperate moment. When do we stop thinking we are princesses in disguise? There I am, rather fat, sitting at the breakfast table drinking coffee in the early-morning sun with my dear love, rather lined, rather fat. Who was it who said I'll build you a little sod house by the Waimakariri, I'll build you a little slab house by the Manawatu? Someone who said Let us seek the wild cattle in the scrub when the sun is high, let us sit and sing lullabies to our sheep when the sun sinks in the west.

Oh, we would have been honoured as the most famous pioneers in all of New Zealand. You for the invention of a revolutionary shearing shed. And me for general excellence in the management of the camp-oven.

Tonight is the night of the lighting of the Christmas tree. The Christmas tree is thin and going brown. We closed the deal at fifty cents with the Minisuper Market. Now Father is draping the vigorous green fairy light cord over it and tying everything down strongly. The tree seems to give no more heartbeats under this last burden. Father switches on the lights and there they are as if new. Once again I am swept over by the pink light. It is terribly pink. You should have outgrown me, it signals.

Is ours the prettiest tree in the street? Mother goes out into the dark garden to judge. There are no lights anywhere in the discreet house over the street – shrouded in sensible trees. They probably wrap all their rubbish carefully in newspaper over there. No nonsense with fairy lights for *them*.

The anonymous battered State houses still have their front curtains tied in knots and half a car by their front doors. Father, coming back from his observation post in the kitchen, reports that the Mayor's house on the hill has not only a Christmas tree that switches on and off by itself but an extra row of coloured light bulbs lining the downstairs windows. Confusion reigns and out of it Mother's voice says clearly that of course he would have access to the city decoration equipment and has just used some illegally on his own house. She judges our tree the most natural – lights in clusters here and there, and not artificial rows of coloured light bulbs making a vulgar show and nothing else. We eat supper, observing our tree narrowly. The pink light still signals to me.

Christmas is just a new problem in each year, and I've licked it, I think. I've got over the lullabies, we've got over the Christmas decorations with babies in. I've got over the neighbour's children's excitement; I've got over the dog's trusting eyes, as if he too wanted me to take him to town to see Father Christmas. Please God, we'll get over Christmas. The house, when I go outside, looks just the same ranch house set in browning Christmas grass as it ever did, except I am no longer riding my bike round and round the lawn to stem my dangerously rising excitement.

Today I took twenty minutes to make my bed. Tomorrow I'll take even longer, sitting around mooning at my two feet. So now, all right, it's the day of Christmas Eve. The shops are telling us that soon they're shutting, and are we ready? Never ready, me.

We look anxiously at the sky all morning. What's it going to do? Is it going to rain or is it going to blow?

Oh Cecil, we can't have a blowing Christmas. I couldn't bear that. Can you think what it would be like now? Hmm? Can you just imagine it with all that wind blowing and the back lawn muddy and nowhere for the dog to run? All of us cooped up inside? All fighting. Do you think I should bake some more little cakes – some Nutty Chews?

The telephone rings. It is my younger aunt. She asks How are we getting on? Are we tired yet? She is very tired. She has been working all morning and now she just thinks she'll do out the cupboards. Do we think it would be a good idea if she tidied the cupboards? We urge No, think of all your visitors coming, be bright for them, Nancy. Yes, the says, she must be bright for them, and not exhausted.

Over the road some children are starting to run senselessly in and out of one of the houses. It is a very dirty house with curtains knotted at the windows, not new-washed, new-ironed for Christmas. They look up at the sky almost as if they're going to run into their mother any minute now with the signal, He is here, Mother; just the hooves of the first reindeer we can see, coming over the sheep at the top of the hill.

Now, are we going to make some Nutty Chews? Where did we find that last good recipe?

I have a new recipe, here it is in my glossy new book of Kiwi Cooking that I brought all the way from Wellington just for you to bake Nutty Chews from for us all.

But that's not the same recipe, dear, that hasn't got condensed milk in it. They must have hundreds of recipes for Nutty Chews by now, all different. I know I have the right one. Think of the Nutty Chews, think of them when we had them years and years ago, when they always tasted better four days after they were made. It's the condensed milk makes them like that.

I go into the sitting-room and check just once more to make sure we haven't forgotten one tiny little thing, and to see if the Christmas tree is looking slightly different. Nothing's going to happen to that tree. The lights are going to come on and that's going to be all. But I still go into the sitting-room just to check up. The room is so clean that it threatens us. It says, I am waiting for the signal that tells me that the moment is about to begin. What are we going to do? I think All right, we are going to come in here, and the TV announcer is going to tell us Merry Christmas, and we'll smile back and then we'll look at the Christmas tree and the pink light is going to save me again by making me see in my inward eye the 1933 pink striped pencil, the 1939 candy floss. And I will think, happily, This is the world's birthday, then I think No, only two thousand years of birthdays, and I think back to the Greeks and the Egyptians before that, and the thought catches me by the throat again, What is going to happen when we all die? Where are we going to go? Where are all those slick smooth answers I knew when I was fifteen and playing Chopin? They've temporarily gone. I must go to the library and look up P for Plato and A for Aristotle, and no skipping, read right through them, so that I can shelter behind those great men. And I think O God, here I am *wanting to stay* for the first time in my life, and now I have to think of shuffling off this globe with a calm and happy heart. And I may never find the shoulder of my dear for my weary head.

The phone rings early. It is my older aunt. And she says How are we all getting on with The Work? We reassure her that we're just bearing it. After all, she says, even though you have only got one child coming home for Christmas you still have *something*. Oh hell, here we go again. I frown at my cup of tea. When I see the next crib I will think O.K., there you are a baby, but you'll be mine when you're five. You'll be in my room and I'll teach you reading and when I'm feeling especially strong I'll pick you up in my arms, and say Whose girl are you? or Whose boy are you? All forty-three of you.

It isn't only lullabies that come thick and fast on every radio – but lullabies for a *lost* child outside on a snowy night. The feelings of the parents at birth I dare not even think about. Peace, peace, after this tremendous moment. How would I drift into sleep with my dear one's shoulder protectively *there*, not bolting away.

I am *useless* at self-discipline about dangerous thoughts.

Oho, I rage.

What about that picture long ago in *The Family of Man* of a pregnant woman a still centre in a street that was a blur of rushing cars and people? Only herself at peace? What about that years-ago pregnant woman in a grey pinafore holding a woven bag and her children's hands peacefully waiting for the lights to change by Kirkcaldies? Why did I witlessly imagine her home and the children playing and her dear coming home from work and their both having the secret look of love that she had by that traffic light?

Why, why, why did I put myself there, keep those pictures in my mind, *let myself drift?*

Hide me O my Saviour hide me – hide me hills – make a thick blanket of folded hills around my unpainted house. And let the rooms be soft and warm – and the windows frosted over with salt so that a parchment glow warms the plants in their pots, and me. I will never complain again, oh Lord – even if you unleash the strongest northerly gales and we can't see out of the sea windows for weeks. I start a helpless imaginary wander through my house, mooning out of windows at blonde summer grass, sheep lying in the hollows for their afternoon nap. I have lost myself. *Who am I?*

Miss Taylor – he has taken my pencil.

Who has taken your pencil Helen?

That Richard – he has taken my pencil and licked my name off.

I didn't take no pencil Miss. This is my pencil, my pink pencil.

Helen, wasn't your pencil green?

My old *pencil green Miss Taylor – not my new* pink *one . . .*

I'll have to concentrate on busily writing new ideas for Social Studies and Language in Action when I get back, if I ever get out of Christmas.

And why haven't I new ideas for Social Studies and Language in Action written down in fat bursting notebooks? I've been lazy. I haven't covered acres of pages daily with little ideas, nitty-gritty slog. I'll have to do it – spade by spade. I can see my pen slowly moving like an ant on a plain.

There, the neighbours will say. Do you see that woman in the sunporch of that house on the hill? It's her holiday really, but she sits down regularly every afternoon and you just see her writing page after page. Never nibbling fattening toast and spying on her neighbours with binoculars. Just working.

And *here* is the Queen. Mother gets right down in front of the screen – crouched like a worshipper – but only to give Her Majesty's carved chair a raking inspection. Father gives a helpless vulgar trapped snore. But I sit dully on, recollecting that we were girls together. Both of us wore tweed coats, felt hats, long socks and stout walking-shoes. But – ah me – she has had four children and one husband. I have had forty-three children a year, and no husband. We both look worn out. And still only halfway to senility. I think of the stream of work-books I will have to invent before then. She is thinking of all the luncheons and smiles ahead. She clears her throat and sets her lips in a way that tugs at my memory. She is not pleased, she tells us severely, with the situation in Ireland. I feel guilty that we have caused her such worry. Then my memory clears. It is my old head prefect giving us a wigging. We have not *worked* hard enough, we have not pulled together. We politely sit. A Merry Christmas to you *all*. The very same vowel sound. I remember with shame the many merry occasions when I did my successful imitation of her broadcast to the children of the Dominions at the beginning of the war. Higher and higher – like piglet's voice – over all that gunfire of static.

How lovely, says Mother. She looks *so* nervous. And tired. Still. Never mind.

Tired, scoffs Father. If she were out, holding down a decent job somewhere, or just democratically biking through the streets.

Mother bridles with imperial langour. You don't under-stand, I hear as I bolt to the kitchen, and soothing cups of tea for all.

The visiting to all the family starts. My old, new country house is dragged up. It sounds, says an uncle solemnly, like a good place for a homicide. An old house like that perched on a hill by itself and only the sea in front. Did you, he asks Father, as one who never neglects these things for *his* children, did you consider that when she took it? I presume there is thick cover right up to the house?

A tiny picture flashes into my mind. I see a white-haired sixty-year-old child of nature, me, come wavering up my path. She talks to birds hopping ahead of her; she brings in the escaped convict she finds shaking with fever behind the spare water-tank. The birds and the convict stay with her for ever. Thunderbolts never fall on that house ever again.

Well, bluffs Father, she's a big girl now, Henry. She should be able to ring the police by herself. He bares his teeth in a hostile smile at me.

It's so *lonely*! cries my younger aunt.

She could be hit on the head, shrills my older aunt, and left for a week! She only has that dog, and that useless cat! cries Mother. And they don't need much money to hit anyone on the head for these days. Just the thrill. A loud whistle – a loud whistle's the thing! shouts Henry. Just one blast.

The gentle little old lady of the first pictures turns into a tough little old lady dressed in a track suit and tennis shoes, crouching behind the spare water-tank, gripping a whistle.

What does homicide mean again? (Say lady, ring Homicide – there's been a –) Ah yes, now I recollect.

The visiting to the old family friends begins.

I should swallow my fright and go. I should be able to keep my head at my age and not smile too much, not talk too quickly, and sit, occasionally smiling with that old wing of silver-blonde hair sheltering my gently experienced face, and lean against a veranda post, not the shoulder of my dear. For will he be there? Not anywhere there, I fear. I will speak with the fed-up husband and his wife, answering me with their eyes searching for their missing children. Oh yes, they will gladly cry, we know Wellington! Did you ever know Dustin Crescent in Wadestown? A little house with a dear little plum tree? The usual death sweat breaks over me. I was in the next street to them, those days. *I must not ask them*: Did you ever see a man and a woman walking down your street – amazed and silent with love – and see a lamp go on, and hear Mozart, and see even the outside of that awful green concrete house on your corner grow solid with midnight love and constancy?

And how is your little house? they all ask vaguely, handing the plate out to my father with a merry smile, while he pops his eyes and blows his cheeks out at yet more rich Christmas cake.

All right, I'll tell you, I rage, biting cake.

It has peaceful white walls and a solid floor. I have almost forgotten it! Then my alarm ceases. I can see a streak of winter sun lying across its stone hearth. A fire is burning. There I am, writing on my very own writing block in my very own armchair. Very settled. Then *who* is this nervous woman eating fruit-cake and smiling too much?

I go to the library to take back Stone and Church and *The Gifted Child*, etc., from where they have been lying under my bed, eclipsed by all the news about how to eat more and weigh less, and ways to redecorate a mews cottage, from my mother's magazines. The sad tourists and I lethargically pass each other in the sun-scalded street. O Lord, I say, as I see a cross-section of all of our faces in Woolworth's regrettable street mirror. It is not mothers and babies we should be thinking about at Christmas – it is all of us – all shot to pieces by shovelfuls of damaging Christmas.

Oh, I hadn't planned all this at all. Not having to think about life and death. I just wanted to lie in a warm chair and dream over comforting Christmas magazines, full of paintings and diagrams of galleys and Victorian trains.

How could we plan a new Christmas next Christmas? Have trees in our streets laden with our gifts for each other? Manage to lure out the invisible gentleman with the stiff leg and his silent housekeeper from their lair behind the trees that shroud their windows and say Happy Christmas my dears to us all? And then sit and talk and touch each other's hands for comfort against the year to come? In the library the word 'Depression' on a magazine catches my eye, as it has over the past few days. My wet fingers leave clumsy dark marks over all that clean organised print.

> This is the time of the year in many parts of the world when the affliction of depression cuts deepest. Psychologists are so familiar with the phenomenon of Christmas depression that they have given it a name – The Holiday Paradox. There are a number of obvious reasons why the depression occurs. The season inexorably stirs up deep-seated childhood and family traumas.

It wasn't me, just me. It wasn't me alone!

> Christmas celebrations stimulate a desire to regress to childhood innocence and normal expectations in life. And when this is contrasted with painful realities, psychic crisis results...

Thousands of us, reaching for the telephone for a psychiatrist, praying for one to appear at the other side of the table, ready and waiting, and paid for by Social Security.

> Even the most well-adjusted personalities suffer the pangs of the Holiday Paradox at one time or another – and then go on to an uneventful recovery...

And soon, with all the other well-adjusted personalities, I find my Holiday Paradox is over. The endless summer world arches over our blonding hair. We stray through long dry grass, staring and dreaming. The summer clicks and hums about us. Soon we are specks, dots, lost in the long, droning summer afternoons. O Lord, if not a dramatic conversion to religion this Christmas, in place of a family could you not give us – the newly-ageing – a space before we have to go; a little more time to sit and talk and be together, in the tender evening light by the sea?

Joan London
The Girls Love Each Other
1986

The girls love each other these days. That's what I told Beth last week. She'd just got back from Bali and we were having one of our catch-up sessions: Beth comes into the salon at eight and we talk our heads off while I give her a shampoo and brush-up before work. By half past there's cold coffee and cigarette ash and photos all over the bench. We're always frantic – that's our word – but it's our only time to really talk since Beth moved in with Douglas, and I've got Morveen at home most of the time. With friends.

That's what I was trying to talk about with Beth. That was my news. After she'd shown me her tan (she was worried she was *too* dark), and given me my carving and the batik for Morveen and gone on about all the tourists who'd been after Mardi's body and even hers – I told her that I was sharing my house with *three* unemployed teenage girls.

'Jan, you're too easy-going,' Beth said, for about the thousandth time. Two weeks alone with Mardi (her daughter, Morveen's age) had been enough for her, thank you, though they'd had their good times too, some good talks. I started to say that yes, so had we, it was interesting in a way.

'Actually', Beth went on, bending her head away from the blower, 'it's not the girls so much I mind, it's all the boyfriends hanging round.'

'There's no boyfriends', I said. I was standing over Beth, layering up her left side, she's got lovely hair, coarse, blonde, shapes up beautifully. Then I found myself saying it, as if it had been on my mind all the time: 'The girls love each other these days.'

There was just that moment when Beth looked up and caught my eye waiting in the mirror, and looked down again. Ticking back over ten years like I'd been doing.

'First I've heard of it', she said.

Morveen and Mardi practically share a birthday – they're both Leos – but it took Beth and me quite a time to give up on pretending they were friends. They learned ballet and tap together until Morveen just wouldn't get into the car one day. And in the school holidays Beth and I would take a day off and drag the girls round town to lunch and a matinee. 'Go on your own', they told us in the end. Then by the time Mardi was fourteen you'd have thought she was twenty: she's working out at Channel 9 now and the trip to Bali was the prize for the Beach Queen heat last year.

Morveen's like me, no show pony, she doesn't even try. But up to now there's always been this little thing between Beth and me, that our girls were in the same race, only Morveen was shy and young for her age.

I suddenly remembered how different Beth and I were. How when we used to work together at Max's she wouldn't talk to any of the clients she thought were 'weirdos', and called old Max 'the poofter' behind his back. And how she just doesn't say anything about Morveen going on the dole when she could have got a place in the Teachers' College. Morveen had said she wanted a break to think things over, and I know what she means. I'd wanted that too once, and then when Johnny my son left, I'd *had* to have it – Morveen's had a lot to handle, one way or another. There are some things Beth doesn't understand.

'You know', I started, though I didn't know what I was going to say. But Beth jumped up, she had to rush, she was frantic, she had to be in Perth by nine (she's a cosmetic rep these days) and Douglas had asked all these people over for drinks that night.

'Sure you won't come?' she asked, patting her hair in the mirror. 'Bring Bradley? How is he these days?'

'I haven't seen him for a while', I said, 'since the girls came.'

'Take care', she said (it's one of Douglas's expressions). We kissed each other at the door.

Friday is our busy day at the salon, but every time I turned on the blower I was taken back to what I'd said to Beth. I thought about the girls. How they just seemed to appear in my life, sitting round the kitchen table. I'd been to a movie with

Bradley: we nearly fell over a couple of duffle bags in the hall. Then we saw these three cropped heads turning towards us at the kitchen door. Morveen had a little glittery catch in her eyes that she gets when she's pleased about something.

It turned out that Steph is a sort of cousin by friendship. Lily Carson, her grandmother, was my mother's best friend. I just remember Lily before she moved to Sydney, but something about Steph's neat sharp face and her quick way of talking reminded me of her.

'Yeah, everyone says that', Steph said. It seemed that Linda, Steph's friend, who's got a soft baby face and smokes a lot, had been having hassles with the Youth Hostel. They'd been telling Morveen about it. They wondered if... So I said they could have Johnny's room.

Bradley didn't stay long. It didn't feel right somehow, to go into the lounge with the whisky and close the sliding doors like we usually do. He stood up and straightened his jacket and said: 'Goodnight... girls.'

'Night', they said, hardly looking at him.

At the door he said: 'Be careful Janet. Don't let them take advantage of you.' We didn't make any plans for the next weekend.

It soon became clear that the last thing those girls wanted was to take advantage of a fellow woman. They decided that since I was the worker they would do all the shopping and cooking and washing-up.

'That's how a co-operative works', Linda explained to me.

'In some circumstances', I said, 'it's also called marriage.'

'We're not asking you for sexual favours', Steph said with a little smile.

But it worked out pretty well. In fact shopping and cooking seemed to be all they did do.

'It's such lovely weather', I said, 'and you've hardly seen anything of Perth.'

'Depends what you're interested in', Steph said. She smiled at Morveen and me. She's got a lovely smile.

Some nights they borrowed my old Torana and went to hear some music in a pub or see a film in Fremantle. Mostly they sat around talking. On nights that we were all at home I seemed to be expected to join in. I must say there was something about the way Steph gave you all her attention, with big nods at everything you'd say, that really got you going. I'd never heard Morveen talk as much either.

Steph tackled me about my job. How did I feel, she asked, that as a hairdresser, I basically 'exploited the beauty trip' that men laid on women? I said that most of my clients at 'Janette's' were older women coming in for a trim or a perm. 'Nobody wants hair down to their ankles', I said.

'Come on Jan, I'm talking about fashion.'

'Look at you three, that's a fashion isn't it? Who cuts your hair anyway?'

'It's not fashion, it's anti-fashion. It's cut by a friend in Sydney who's dropped out of the straight hair-dressing scene.'

'And it *feels* good', put in Linda.

'So does my hair', I said. 'And I can blow-dry it in a few minutes.'

'Whether you know it or not', Steph said, 'you wear it like that to attract men.'

'Yeah', said Morveen.

'Well who are you trying to attract with your hairdos then?' I said 'Each other?'

They seemed to think this was a huge joke. Linda started to clap and knocked her drink over Steph's record.

'By the way', Steph said, grabbing the record off Linda and wiping it without looking at her, 'I need a trim. You wouldn't. . .?'

'No I wouldn't', I said.

It was good for Morveen and me, having the others there. It was a relief not to come home and find her sleeping with five apple-cores beside her bed. Or hear the fridge door open and close all evening while she ate as if she had to save her life.

When had I last heard her hum like she did when she was cooking the co-operative meals? I guess it was when she was a kid and she'd come in after Johnny had taken her for a ride on his bike. She's never been one for smiling much – all chins and frown as a baby – but when we'd all been talking and it was getting late, she had this sort of sleepy soft look about her, and she'd rest her head on the nearest shoulder. When it was mine I wanted to stop talking, everything, and put my arms around her, but I'm not that silly.

I found out that all this time she'd never liked her name.

'It was your grandmother's name', I said. 'It's Welsh.'

'So?' she said. 'I don't like it. *Mor – veen.*' She beat her fist on the table in time and and glared at me. 'Mor – veen – Jones.' Bang, bang, bang.

'I never thought of it like that', I said. Lennie had wanted it, and then it had become part of a different sound, 'Johnny and Morveen', the sound that kept me going.

But the next time I came home I heard Steph say quite casually as she put on a record, 'Do you know this one Veen?' From then on it was 'Veen this' and 'Veen that'. No one said a word about it.

The story of my marriage went down very well. They sat there shaking their heads through the saga of Lennie and his disappearing act. Linda jumped up and started massaging my neck. Not that their own family histories sounded much better. Though I must say it surprised me that a son of old Lily Carson would be a 'mental wife-beater' and an 'alcoholic capitalist exploiter'. His wife's only sin seemed to be that she 'freshened up before hubby came home'. I don't suppose I came off any better when I'd gone to work.

Then the last Saturday before they went, I was lying out the back in my bikini, soaking up the lovely late summer sun. Even my face, though Beth's told me off about that often enough. I still get a kick out of my backyard after all those years in the flat. It's just a big square of brown grass sloping down to an old peppermint tree by the fence.

Then I heard the crying. It was coming from Johnny's room on the back verandah. Not just crying, but an awful rising wail that seemed to curl around my stomach. I picked it out, like you do with little children, as Linda's voice. I sat up and everything went blurry. I heard the other two run in to her. She screamed 'You!' There was talking, and the crying dropped away.

It was all over in a minute. I lay down again but my stomach kept on tightening. I could see our washing dancing at me on the line, the girls' big clown clothes flapping against my uniforms and panty-hose and bras. After a while I made my way inside. I just kept thinking, I don't know, I don't know anything.

I took the girls out to the bus station on Saturday afternoon, as soon as I got home from work. The co-operative had been winding down that last week, the girls had gone out a lot more. I was glad, I was tired: even at work I seemed to be hearing their young voices all day, back and forth with mine.

They didn't talk much in the car. Every time I'd say something to Morveen next to me, she'd say 'What?' She kept looking out the window, humming.

At the bus station Steph fished out their tickets from the little purse she wears looped around her waist, and Linda queued with their bags. There seemed to be a rhythm going round between them all. I watched Steph, standing there with her head just nodding and one foot tapping away in its old tennis shoe. I thought, she's so sure. She's dangerous.

They stood waiting for the call then, the three of them, with their arms around one another. When it was time to go there were big serious hugs all round.

'Jan, thank you', Linda said through tears. I watched them darting off behind the other passengers, like children. When I turned, I found that Morveen had already set off. I saw her striding ahead of me towards the car.

It seemed so quiet at home that afternoon, you could hear the peppermint tree tossing about in the wind. Morveen went straight to her room. I couldn't settle on anything. I put a few things back to their old places in the kitchen. In the end I jumped in the shower. Then Morveen stuck her head round the door and said: 'It's the big B for you on the phone.'

Bradley's voice seemed to come from another world. I stood there watching the mist spread out from my hot toes over the polished boards. He was trying to let me know how busy he'd been these past weeks.

'Are you all right?' he asked.

'I've missed you.'

There was a pause. Then very gruff he said:

'Pick you up at eight then – sweetie.'

Morveen came into the hall.

'Are you going out tonight?' The same old question.

'Yes', I said. 'Are you?'

'I'm not into socialising, just for the sake of it.'

'Some of us actually enjoy a man's company from time to time. Drinking and talking like you've been doing every night.'

'We had real talk. But Bradley's a shithead. They've all been shitheads, you know that.'

'Don't you think', I said at last, 'that there's any good men around?'

'Well one thing's for sure, she said, walking off. 'I don't need them.'

I headed outside then and sat on the front steps, still in my dressing gown. There are no houses in front of us, just a lovely stretch of sky over the railway line. The street lights had come on and the evening traffic was starting up. I watched the cars, joined up by headlights, filing towards the subway.

Saturday nights. The city. Morveen always hated me going out in the old days. She'd scream and scream so Johnny'd have to take her for a ride around the block while Beth and I drove off. 'She's just jealous', Beth would say, accelerating. 'You deserve a bit of fun.'

Morveen hated me talking on the phone too, those long sessions picking up the pieces after all the fun. Every two minutes one of us would have to break off to hiss and slap and bribe with biscuits, just to stay on that life-line, just to say: 'Do you know what that bastard said to me?'

And now here was Morveen saying she could do without all that. You could hardly blame her. I think her view's lopsided: she thinks mine is. We're opposite each other like a pair of scales. But for a long time my side carried the weights. Maybe Morveen was pushed out of balance, right from the start.

I *had* learnt some things. Not enough for Morveen now, not enough to even up. But I learned to pay my own way. In the beginning, when I married Lennie Jones, I thought that from then on I'd be taken care of. Even afterwards, when I was alone, I had my sheikh dream. I'd be walking to the bus-stop after work (Jan, you get along now, Max'd always say, dead on five, I'd spend all year wondering what I could buy him for Christmas), two buses I needed to get the kids home, and I'd think that if a big fat sheikh pulled up beside me in a limousine, I'd just crawl right in. 'Come on kids', I'd say, 'We're going to live in a harem. Won't that be fun?'

Beth came along and she taught me: you always pay your own way. Now I didn't ask for much, just my own place, and a chat with Beth, and Bradley turning up from time to time.

Bradley's a shithead. Well I know what she means. You think he's good-looking, so clean and well-cut, till you get up close and there's something missing in his face, he has to practise looking you in the eye. And practise having what he calls his 'R and R': he fits me in between badminton and bushwalks, and then cuts everything short to get a good night's sleep. He can't cope otherwise, he says. Well, that's how he is.

So why do I bother? Just sometimes, out of the blue, driving home late, or having breakfast, once when we were standing in a queue, I start to tease him, I can't stop myself, I'm laughing like nothing matters any more. And he bends his head to me (he's very tall) and calls me a terrible girl, and keeps looking at me sideways in a shy, pleased way . . . So I hang in there, while the weeks build up again between us, work and the telephone, dinner and a show. Waiting for those real times again.

Morveen was sitting beside me in the dark.

'Jan. I'm going to Sydney.'

'When?' The stars seemed tiny above the lights on the road.

'As soon as I can get my act together.'

'What'll you do there?'

'Live with the others. They've got a big place, there's six of them.'

'Six girls', I said.

'I'll look for work of course. I'm not going to bludge forever.'

'Six girls, in a house. Don't you think that's a bit . . . narrow?'

'People come and go a lot, Steph says. Anyway, what are you trying to say?'

'I dunno love. It's not my way I guess.' *You pay for your choices*, I wanted to say.

Morveen had put her arm around me.

'Mum, why don't you come over when I'm settled and have a holiday? We'd have a good time I know. We could look for Johnny . . . Steph and Linda reckon you should.'

'Thanks love. I'll think about it.'

Morveen jumped up soon and went inside. She couldn't keep still for long that night.

I felt very tired out there. Too tired to get ready for Bradley. It was getting cold.

The phone rang. Beth.

'I know this is an awful time to ring', she said as usual. 'It's just that I'm feeling so *flat.*'

'That makes two of us.'

Then she was off. Douglas hadn't come home yet, he was on his high horse, he said she drank too much when she was with his friends. Who were so boring anyway . . .

'Honestly Jan, sometimes I miss the old days. When you and I used to hit the town. I think I'm a romantic at heart.'

Also her tan was peeling, and Mardi was off looking for a flat. 'God knows what she'll get up to then', she said.

In the kitchen Morveen had switched on the light and the radio. I smelt scrambled eggs and I felt like a glass of wine. This was something that seemed to stretch right back to Mum and Lily Carson. A kind of talk. I'd been speaking it for years now at the back of all the heads of those faces in the mirror.

'Hold on a sec Beth', I said. I whipped into the kitchen and filled up a glass from the cask with a wink at Morveen.

'Anyway, how's things with you?' Beth asked. You always have to remind her that you've got a life ticking away there too. 'How's Morveen and the girls?'

'The girls have gone back to Sydney', I said, 'and Morveen's going to go over there too.' I took a deep sip while Beth went on about how they all leave us and how we'd probably end up in a Home together.

'Morveen wants me to come over for a holiday.'

'Yeah?' said Beth, listening.

'I dunno, I'd have to get someone in at the salon, and it might put Bradley out a bit, and I'm tired, there doesn't seem much point . . .'

'Well hang it all', Beth said, out of the silence. 'Hang it all, why don't you go?'

Anne Kennedy

The Road to Damascus

1986

My greatgrandmother who couldn't suck eggs. Oh she was hopeless, a mope and a malcontent. She was tardy and truculent, vague and vain, but her main failing was – she could NOT budget.

She could scour she could starch she could sew she could knit, she could stew up the meat and boil fat to make soap. But could she behave? Could she be thrifty? Could Greatgrandmother be satisfied with *anything* in this *world*? Oh no she was chronically covetous spendthrift and shiftless.

What was the matter? they asked on the Coast. (That's where they lived, there was only one Coast.) She had a husband a house nine children to fill it, a cat and a dog and a goat and some geese. Chooks – bits of fluff that blew round in the yard – rabbits to boil, turnips to bake. What, what more could she possibly want?

Her husband's employment was not of the ilk of the typical man on the job on the Coast. He wasn't a shoveller he wasn't a groveller he didn't get black and take baths in the yard. He earned more than most he took home more than most. But Greatgrandmother said she didn't see more than most.

He said *she* couldn't budget.

Her husband (Greatgrandfather, 'Kennedy' to her) was not an unreasonable man he was not a bullying man. He adored his wife. But from the very day they were wed he saw he'd have to keep a tight rein on Greatgrandmother. And he did.

Each week there was the ceremony of the breadwinnings. Greatgrandmother received on her tongue what Greatgrandfather deemed necessary for food clothes bills and unforeseen, and she blessed herself. The rest – one of the great mysteries – went into a fund for the education of a son at a seminary in Sydney.

There was James there was John there were Frank and Vince. There was poor little Joe who drowned one grey day. And there were Molly and Annie and – then they lost count – till they came out at the end with nine mouths to feed nine bodies to clothe. School shorts to be bought woollen stockings and socks sturdy shoes for the boys pinafores for the girls. Nightshirts and nightgowns, longjohns and petticoats. And two suits of clothes for the man of the house, one workaday grey, one black for the sabbath, with white winged-collar shirts and gold cuff-linked cuffs and a soft-knotted tie of funereal silk.

On Sundays Greatgrandmother laid out this suit. She laid it out as if it were dead with a reverence reserved for not-of-this-world. She had laundered the shirt on Monday mended on Tuesday starched and ironed on Wednesday and brushed and aired the whole outfit on Saturday ready for reincarnation on Sunday.

On this day, the seventh day, she also put away her husband's weekday clay pipe and replaced it with his Sunday birchwood.

Then Greatgrandmother made the beds aired the rooms stoked the range laid out the breakfast prepared the joint for dinner put the vegetables in to soak and mixed the dry ingredients for the pudding. She fed the chooks fed the cat fed the dog fed the youngest. She got the children ready got herself ready by flinging on her coat and pinning on her battered flat black straw hat, and the whole family went off to Mass.

Greatgrandmother couldn't behave. She could not would not pray. She'd sit in church and look along the pew filled with her children all clean and shiny and pressed and she would feel proud. She'd kneel down and look at her husband all clean and dull and pressed and feel – fond. She'd stand up and look at the other people in the church, the boys with their sailor collars, the girls with their sashes, the men in their grave suits and the women in their coats. At last she would pray.

It was the year of Our Lord 1894. The fashion was for cape collars big sleeves caught in at the wrist and Mary-Mother-of-God a bell-shaped fall from a tapered waist. There were some beautiful coats Amen-Amen oh there were, some magnificent specimens among the worshippers. Linen mohair camelhair wool. And the furs in that church! Not just lapin, sinners, but real furs, lynx and skunk and Russian fox, sable seal marmot goat. There were furs among the faithful.

Greatgrandmother's coat didn't have much of a pile. It was a thin greenishgrey gaberdine with a shine and it hung on her back like a streak of slime. The hem had been altered so many times it was now puffed up with a fat false pride. She'd bought it as part of her wedding trousseau – a married woman must have a serviceable coat, one that can take the good with the bad – and there'd been little to spend on frivolities since, what with nine mouths to feed nine bodies to clothe and a son to send to seminary school.

But all the same she was ashamed of the coat.

After Mass she would scuttle away from the throng and walk quickly home with her flat black straw bowed and there would be glad to unspike her old hat and shake off the hideous green gaberdine, to be safe in the kitchen and warm near the range and clean shiny and pressed in her work overall. She blew up the fire sliced up the bread dished up the porridge brewed up the tea. She was here she was home and away from the world who would jeer at the state of her gaberdine coat. Her husband updated himself with the news.

Her husband (Greatgrandfather, Kennedy, the same) stayed in his Sundaysuit all the day through. The boys wore their longs their best shirts and their ties, and in order to keep their velvet frocks clean the girls played outside in their smocked petticoats. If there were visitors that afternoon the family of course would want to look neat.

Greatgrandmother cleared the breakfast dishes away. She put the joint and the potatoes in the oven. She boiled the pudding in a muslin cloth. She stewed some plums she made sweet sauce she made Yorkshire. She turned the potatoes. She steamed the greens. She reset the table and made the gravy. Finally she dished up the dinner.

But typically the meat was tough and as usual the potatoes were underdone and the silverbeet lukewarm, the pudding was gluggy and the sweet sauce – sticky. Oh she was hopeless. Look at her sitting down to Sunday dinner and still in her apron! But they all ate and they all worshipped the ground she walked on.

Now Greatgrandmother was not a working woman. She didn't earn money for her labours like any common drudge. Why should she with a husband to keep her? Greatgrandfather certainly wouldn't approve of his wife selling herself. No wife of mine will work! No wife was Greatgrandmother.

She deceived her husband, not because she wanted to but because she had to. She hid from him, in full knowledge of her wrongdoing, the fact that she was operating a little business.

Each week day she would go down to the gate to meet the children as they came from school. Hordes of children running shrieking like locusts ravenous children her own seven youngest amongst them, and her own would rush up to the house and into the kitchen, seven curses, and ravage the bread bin the cake tins the cheese cooler and milk pail.

One afternoon Greatgrandmother baked a tray of her mother's cupcakes. She baked in her sleep, in her childhood, she dreamed and sang as she baked. She dreamed of things fuzzy and snuggly and tapering ever so slightly at the wrist and she dreamed of herself as adored. Greatgrandmother took her tray of cakes down to the gate where she set them on a table and put up a sign: Cupcakes ½d each.

Soon a plague of children arrived. Some of them had ha'pennies and they bought cakes and the other children stood on tiptoe to watch with currant eyes and to beg for a taste just a nibble *please* and then they ran home to ask for ha'pennies ha'pennies Mum can I have a ha'penny for a cupcake tomorrow they're bosker cupcakes.

Tomorrow Greatgrandmother baked two trays of cakes. She dreamed and she sang, she sang *Mama's little boy* and *O Bread of Heaven*. More children had ha'pennies and she sold all the cakes. The next day Greatgrandmother baked *three* trays of cakes and mothers had given their children sixpences to buy cakes for the whole family a round dozen Betty get me a round dozen of Mrs Kennedy's cupcakes. Greatgrandmother put up a new sign: Cupcakes ½d each, 6d a baker's dozen. They were famous cupcakes.

All the same Greatgrandmother was ashamed. She was ashamed of her peddling her greed and her wile. Wasn't she already vague and vain? Now she was voracious as well. Greatgrandmother was nothing but trash. She hid the evidence. By the time Kennedy came home in the evenings all trace of the cakes – the table the sign the baking's takings – had been whisked away and the children sworn to secrecy with threats of no cupcakes and rewards of – of course – cupcakes, and although Mrs Kennedy's cupcakes were known all over the valley and although her husband must have known he could not *but* have known, he never mentioned the matter. Perhaps he too was ashamed, deeply ashamed that his wife was a known woman.

Though she was half-tramp half-man being gainfully employed Greatgrandmother after a few years had a respectable sum. Not a large sum but a tidy one. Greatgrandmother at last had a pile.

It was the late 1890s. She had been laundering and starching and airing and laying out all the while. She had been preparing and stoking and cooking and baking and sweeping and keeping the sabbath holy. But Greatgrandmother wasn't quite as hopeless as she had once been. The girls now washed up and peeled and scrubbed. The boys gardened and chopped. Kennedy had once heated the water for a bath but for this last Greatgrandmother was remorseful. She may have turned into a tartar a shrew a vixen, but there were limits.

Greatgrandmother kept her cache in a crock that was supposedly full of cucumbers in brine. One morning she flew through her chores, she washed and she cleaned, she cooked and swept, then she went to the crock and unplugged the cork and emptied the contents into a drawstring purse. She put on her green gaberdine. She skewered her black straw hat. Greatgrandmother walked into town. She went straight to the bank and changed the ha'pennies and sixpences into notes and suddenly she was light-as-air and heady and girlish and she tripped across the street to the furriers where the window was full of dancing bears. She went in.

Madam, said the furrier appearing, You require a fur?

Oh there were furs! There were furs upon furs the whole shop muffled and stuffed with fur. Greatgrandmother was overwhelmed she was stifled and pushed back by a million a billion waving shafts of hair. She prayed briefly Lead us not into temptation Oh Lord deliver it. And she pointed, bending her finger in an unaccustomed arc, to the most delicate of the bears a creature with a coat the colour of her three-fruit marmalade.

Yes, I think I require... And immediately it was before her. It was as if she wore red leggings and brass buttons and cut the air with a whip and cried out Marmalade bear! and the ludicrous animal lumbered away from its companions and reeled for her pleasure. It was as if she had power, Yes I require.

Greatgrandmother peeled off her cold gaberdine. The furrier took it and ran it up a pole like a flag for all to see, then he invited her to slide into the garment she had chosen. Compare compare! and Greatgrandmother did, breathlessly. The fur was cool inside it was warm. It was heavy and buoyant at the same moment prickly to the touch and silken to stroke. It was sensuous and skinlike.

As if it were made for Madam, said the furrier, as if she were Madam.

Greatgrandmother turned seductively as if she were naked in front of the large oval mirror. The coat had an angry collar, petulant sloping shoulders, determined catches and an arrogant swagger below the waist. Oh she was vain wanton wasteful avaricious.

I'll take her thank you and I'll wear her, said Greatgrandmother and it was like a land transaction. She handed over 14,000 cupcakes her labour her childhood her sleep and her small ruth voice. The furrier swept them all away and counted them. Then he took the gaberdine down and folded it reverently in tissue paper and placed it in a great box for Greatgrandmother to carry home.

She didn't go straight home she walked about the streets. She walked because she bore a weight on her shoulders and she liked the feeling of it, a little woman with a large weight. She walked because she enjoyed the sensation of creatures swishing about her legs, animals and children, and she walked because it was a marmalade coat and the autumn day was of marmalade light.

As she walked she told herself You're a vain woman you're a wanton wasteful avaricious woman and you're a virago. But she didn't really believe it. She believed the fur coat was all these things and the fur coat was the sweet fruit of her secret labours. (No wife of mine will work!)

I don't work, she told herself. I don't work I only carry bricks. *I don't work I only carry bricks.* The idea of a little woman carrying bricks was more than she could bear and for some reason she cried. She walked along in the marmalade coat and her funny battered black straw hat, happy, crying.

As she was nearing home a man appeared on the road ahead of her and she was startled because you didn't see many people out walking in the middle of the day and she felt conspicuous wearing a fur, a fur coat indeed in this neighbourhood. She felt herself to be glowing in an aura of fur and she feared the man might see her from the distance as brilliant and daunting and as if it were Saint Paul he saw and this the road to Damascus might fall down before her struck and adoring. Hail hail! The adorned!

Greatgrandmother shrank a little, she shrank inside the marmalade fur but she walked on and she and the man drew nearer and nearer and presently she saw that he smoked a pipe and the smoke brushed his cheeks. They came together closer and closer and Greatgrandmother saw that it was indeed Greatgrandfather, her husband, Kennedy.

Oh she was afraid aghast and adither! Shesheshe – leapt through the nearest gap in the roadside hedge and crouched down behind it trembling like a small ginger animal caught in a trap. She stayed low until she had heard Kennedy draw level pause and continue on his way. Then she shuddered, a long enduring shudder that worked its way around her shoulders down her spine and her legs and out through her toes sweeping before it greed vanity wastefulness ambition – sins, sins. When the shudder had left her she tore off the marmalade fur. Fool thing, vacuous shallow and worldly! And straight away a new peace came over her, a goodness she had not known before when she had desired to be eminently desirable in ermine or fox or sable or seal. She wrapped the fur with veneration as if this were a dead child and leaving the box under the hedge went home clasping her gaberdine coat about her.

Greatgrandmother didn't bake any cupcakes that afternoon nor did she dream nor did she sing. Wearing the green gaberdine and the flat black straw she combed the length of the hedge on the way into town thinking to retrieve the fur and return it to the furrier. (I'm so sorry, I made a mistake. I'd like you to take the coat back if you will . . . Madam, I . . .) But there was no box. There was no marmalade fur.

In later years Greatgrandmother's daughter-in-law, my grandmother, acquired a grey squirrel necklet. She went into Kirk's one autumn day and put it on her husband's account, never thinking to mention it to him and when the bill came he paid it. My other grandmother had a silver fox fur, a gift from her husband. It had piercing glass eyes and hard little paws that trailed pitifully down her back and her grandchildren thought that because it had eyes and paws it also had a soul.

Her daughter, my mother, wore a 1950s-length swirling musquash coat that drew the hands of children hungry for tactility and the admiration of her husband, my father, who paid a hundred pounds for it. Three furs. Three women. Not one cupcake did they bake.

Greatgrandmother got it all wrong. It's the men who buy the fur coats.

Keri Hulme

The Knife and the Stone

1986

Every morning before it was light, just before the alarm went off, she woke with a jolt. Not from a bad dream: it was as though her body had a prescience of pain and responded with a sudden hurtful wakening.

This morning was no different.

She lay quiet a moment, feeling her heartbeat slow down to normal.

It is today.

She sighed. Shuffled off the eiderdown, shuffled into her work-clothes. Stood a moment by her warm disordered bed, touching it with one finger, her mind a blank. Then, like every morning, she went straight to the lavatory. Her bowels never worked until after breakfast but it was her father's belief that everyone should empty themselves on rising. And her mother was listening.

She banged the seat. The noise echoed. She stood a moment, not thinking. Letting whatever was around imprint itself. The stink of Jeyes fluid and excrement. One hinge off the door ever since she could remember. The old map showing English ley lines. Ahh! said the Guests.

Hand-adzed walls!

Rain-stained walls.

She touched them, briefly.

Five minutes after she'd risen, she was stoking the range. Like every morning. The rata-chips caught alight: the coal dust flared. Ten minutes to boil the kettle. She hated the range.

She set out milk-jug and honey-jar, china spoon and tea-mug on the wooden tray while waiting. She hummed, automatically, a tuneless wavering no-song. 'You have no idea how much it means to me,' her mother had said, often, 'hearing you cheerful and busy at dawnlight. It's only then I know I have survived another night, that another day has truly come.'

She picked up the tray with care and carried it, still humming to herself, into her mother's lair.

The room is dazzling with lights her mother never turns off. It is crammed with boxes piled with scraps of materials, with large pots and huge pale dusty plants. It is foetid. Full of blood-stink, like old menses or meat on the turn. Incense-smoke eternally spirals, boring into the blood-cloud. Today, as well, there is the rank sweetness of lupins, bunches of them jammed into the Ali Baba pots.

She drew a deep breath.

Past the harsh stares of the bed-lamp, side-lamp, signal-lamp. Past the duelling flickers of the thousand fragments of mirror sewn into the canopy over her mother's bed. Concentrating on the intricate stepping needed to carry a laden tray through the maze.

The breath ran out by the bedside.

Her mother smiled at the sound. With her pallor and enormous grey eyes, she looked a nocturnal carnivore. Her smile menaced.

'My darling daughter.'

Never, thank you.

'You had good dreams, my bantling?'

Never, how did you sleep?

'Yes mama dear.'

Another smile.

'Alas, no visitors,' said her mother.

What a menace you are, Maeve! laughed the Guests. An Aldis lamp. Imagine if some ship sees your flashes . . . Maeve the wrecker!

Her mother answered dreamily, 'Imagine if some starship sees them, and we have visitors . . .'

'Maybe tonight, mama.'

'The blind hope of youth,' said her mother and sucked at the mug of tea.

She put the tray down carefully. She thought, No more mama.

So charming, some of the Guests found it. How charmingly old-fashioned, said one, with a lop-sided smile. Natural word, said her father then. Better than you lot with your Mum and Mummy. Bloody old dead gyppos. He'd barked with laughter.

You can call me my given name now, said her mother a year ago, but o how I shall miss being your mama.

She waited for the next cue.

'Your father will be home soon dear one. Back from the wearying sea. Perhaps you could have something ready for him?'

My mother is mad. She knew that wasn't true. She sounded mad, with her artificial stilted language. She looked mad in her scrambled light-ridden den. She was frighteningly sane.

Today, she said

'I'll put something on for him.'

As I've put something on every morning since I was eight. Mainly the same sort of something. Last night's spuds, chipped and fried. Two fried eggs, two onions carved into rings.

And he'll say

'There you are,' said her father, and

'Good. Breakfast,' and

'There's about a case on the lawn.'

That last could change.

Sometimes he'd stamp in, snarl over breakfast, grunt after every mouthful of tea, then rush into her mother's bedroom and slam the door.

On that kind of day she could steal back into her room and strip off her work-clothes; have a proper wash in water now warmed by the range. Get rid of the stinks. Then, no sneers from whoever sat next to her. Gidday Fishy, how's it goin' Gutbucket? Life okay down on the dope estate, giggle giggle.

Unless it was Mark. If it was him next to her, he'd grin his hesitant badteeth grin and whisper, Today, your eyes are like *pure* Marmite. Or something equally fatuous.

Which was worse, she wondered, turning the eggs and onions and chips with precision, which was worse?

If there was nothing. They sulked or did something horrid. If there was a case, it was bad because there was time to process it but not enough time to get properly ready. Inevitable scales on her hands, a feeling of slime all over her. Yet the times her father came in jubilant, shouting Hey a dozen cases! Hear that! We're riiccchhhhh! the rich sounding like coarse cloth tearing – those times were probably worst. It meant taking the day off, because a dozen cases took her hours. It meant her father could do the full round, paying something off the grocery bill, a bit off the petrol account, even some to the hardware store. But then he'd waltz into his favourite pub and drink his way into instant friendships. He never seemed to see the sly nudges, Could be on to a good thing here Mac, that she felt on her skin as though it were raw and they were hard knocks. And later, buying a crate or two of beer, a quart or two of vodka – 'Vodka my girl!' he'd roar. 'No congeners, remember that!' – he'd collect the drink friends and they'd all come rolling home. And he'd stand in the front door yelling You're Guests in my home, everything's yours my Guests! his dark face suffused with a purple wash, his lips loose and wet. And he'd take his dobro off the wall and twang it; sing old and pseud songs and the Guests would sing along. And some would vomit and some would wander curiously around, admiring or puzzled, and some would lie in a stupor on the livingroom cushion pile. And sometimes, her mother would limp out, swathed in one of her quilts, her face glowing, the blood aroma trailing heavily after. The singing would gather a mellowness, the bottles lower more slowly. She would have finished making tea for the drunker Guests by then. She would steal away to bed before her father noticed her, because otherwise he would come lurching and whispering God I love you girl love you girl, fumbling, delving.

The jubilant times were very much the worst, she decided, sliding breakfast onto the three plates.

Yet, some times, rare times, she would get safely to bed by herself, and wake, she never knew how much later, and hear the end of the party. Her mother's thin perfect soprano winding like a flute above her father's velvet baritone, the dobro a sure melancholy underlining third voice. The songs were real, unknown to her. They were beautiful. She would cry, at the way the good dreams had come to die, and crying, sleep.

She ate quickly, as she did every morning. About a case, waiting on the lawn. She picked up her knife and stone and went to meet them.

The stone was a wedge of fine-grit sandstone, white and worn. A gift, like her first knife. One Guest, reeled in like all the rest, stayed until morning. He watched her awkwardly using the butcherknife. He didn't say anything. But when she had finished half the case, he'd gone inside and brought out a tableknife. He took the whetstone out of his pocket and beckoned to her. Warily she came. Still not talking, he broke most of the plastic handle from the knife. He bound what remained with tartape so it fitted edgeless and easy in the hand. He honed the blade to razor thinness, razor sharpness, after snapping it in half. He showed her how.

He took one fish out and demonstrated the right way, carve, scoop, flick, slice. He was slow and deliberate. Then he handed her the knife and the stone, and went back inside to finish off the remaining crate. He was a noisy drunk but he never touched or spoke to her. She still thought of him with love.

She also thought, bitterly, My fifth knife.

In the case on the lawn they waited, their murky golden eyes bulging in the heavy deeps of air. The slime was running out of the plastic slats.

Think of us as a team, her mother had said two years ago, picking her words with care. Don't *respond* to those ignorami at school. We are an elite, a tiny chosen venturing band. Do you remember the Company of the Nine Walkers? No? She had sighed. I never understood why your heart didn't thrill . . . let it be. We are heart people, special, tied by love, supports each for the other. If Gareth had lived . . . she sighed again. Not to mind (a brave smile). We are the team. Your father fishing our daily bread and maintaining the house. Myself, labouring over these quilts for all our extras. And thyself my dear one the helpmate, doing the little things to assist each of us. *Being* the reason it is all done for.

Hi team, she said, to the knife and the stone. We're the winning side, you know that? Couldn't be anything else because he always checks his nets even if he has to crawl to the boat. And look at the other side.

Flat, sticky, and already defeated. Among them, occasionally, a stargazer; rarely, silver-bellied eels, and most rarely, a glorious coral-fleshed salmon fresh run from the sea. But those he took care of. His ruined hands took infinite care boning them. He soaked them in brines of his own composing. He nursed them through the drying stage, gauzed against flystrike. He travelled long roads in the battered van, selecting manuka and silver pine for sawdust. He hovered nervously while they smoked. He sold the beautiful results and bought records and grog. Any spoiled results he ate for breakfast.

She never ate fish, least of all them.

First cut, just below the belly fin, slip through a vertebra and sever the spine. Out the other side in one smooth slice to arrive just above another scarlet-edged fin, in line with the gill case.

She remembered little of before. Before she was eight. Before Gareth died. Before the close warm world fell apart. She did remember the night they brought her father in, howling, bleeding, cursing, bleeding. Drunken, he had lifted the outboard motor from the water. Drunken, he had slipped, knocking the gear from neutral to fast forward. Drunken, he had slipped further, and grabbed the prop. Healed to grotesque stumps and scars, he'd growled at her, 'That fiddly work is woman work. In the old days, that was the proper way. We men do the catching. You women clean it up. That's what you're for.' He'd handed her the boning knife and yelled at her until she had learned, clumsily, to carve up flounders. Second cut, quick flash to the anus careful not to rupture any sacs of roe. Then hold up the slimed thing and quickly slit down the other side to the arsehole again. Arsehole was Mark's word. Right in the arsehole from my old man, slight emphasis on the 'my'. His tall thin body twitching, as normal. The locker bay was crowded. They had their heads close together.

Why? she had asked. Why tell me?

Because. He had brown eyes too, but not as dark as her own. Because I know about you. His eyelids flickered, a similar beat to his twitching body. Now you can destroy me if you want, he said. He shrieked out in a hun yell REVENGE. No heads turned. Mad Mark at it again.

The momentum of the cut and the weight of the newly-severed head made it fall, dragging the guts neatly behind it slop into the gut bucket. Slice: the lower intestine freed. Chop the tail off in one fluent cut. Throw the bloody thing into the wet bucket, ready for later washing.

I know it's not easy but we make do, crooned her mother. We're not rich in material terms, but we make do. We planned for this when we were not much older than you are now. O the sun and flowers of being sixteen! We planned a good place out away out of the corrupt system, a clean strong place for strong new people. If Gareth . . . her voice became throaty. But you're strong, she keened, fondling her daughter's arm, wiry but strong. And so rich in your mind! Far more rich than we were at your age, poisoned by the garbage they taught *us*.

She remembered hearing a Guest burst out, O you've given her such riches but you've sacrificed so much! Her mother had looked out the windows, over the beam of the Aldis light. We have riches too, she said strongly. Natural food and holistic medicine and freedom from city pressures. Strong Guestly murmurs of support. And we have a *good* child. God yes, said another one, you want to see my little monster fat and pasty and deathrays all day long and god the language! Yes! Yes! Yes! they top each other's monsters as her mother's smile grew wider, tighter.

Am I rich in my mind?

I have words for every colour under the sun. Weird gobbets of knowledge from weird Guests. I can hate. I can gut. I know all about dead and dying flounders. The fibrillation, the strange and beautiful fluidity of their rippling fins as they try to gain purchase on air. The mottling of their skins, mosaics of rust and olive-green and sepia on the back; mushroom and grey and terracotta and lemon-blotched cream on the underside. The pout of their lips as you hit their heads with the hammer.

She did that surreptitiously to the livelier ones. Her father sneered, 'Afraid they'll bite? You're bigger than them.'

She knew all about the occasional parasites, pinholes in the white flesh with black writhing cupheaded worms extruding. Sealice pecking away like bloated pink slaters. Colours, she thought, colours.

The pale yellow granular roe. Faintly blue gluey strings of slime. Grey blurred crabs in the anus tubes. Green fragments of annelid worms in the guts. Matt rusty liver. Pink veined coils. The delicately irridescent inner skin. The brilliant viridian of the gallbladder.

Today, she was halfway through the case.

It's not really work, said her mother to her complaint last week. You cannot, my sweet, truly call it hard labour now can you? I remember working twelve-hour days, on my feet all that time, waitressing for slobs. And your father, immersed to the heart in the gore at the freezing works, a sensitive singer breaking apart with all that pain. But we earned the money for here that way. That's work, my girl!

Now she thought.

Every morning for the last eight years. Unless nothing has been caught. Maybe a day a week. 300 days a year. 2400 days. Normally an hour of blood and guts, sometimes much much longer. In the wind. In the rain. In the frost. In the sandfly hordes of summer. 'Allergic to sandflies? But she was *born* here,' exclaimed a Guest, a hundred years ago. 'Surely she'll grow out of it?'

Not so far. The bright welts keep coming, each marked with a watery red centre. The sandflies know her hands are full. They feast with impunity.

Cover yourself with treacle, said Mark. They'll have a bloody hard job biting through that.

Then he said, I have a cousin who can get us out.

Her heart had seemed suddenly huge, forcing the air from her lungs.

I have a cousin with a fish-shop in Auckland. Don't wince. There is a restaurant attached, and a flat attached to the restaurant. I can cook in my poofy way. You can process. He will send the fare.

He said, carefully.

If you want, we can make it?

She whispered.

I can't hear that, said Mark.

I said, it has got too hard. And your teeth are horrid.

Long lean body, long lean hands, long lean smile, all suddenly beautifully still.

Tomorrow then, midnight eyes.

She had shivered.

Why don't your friends ever come? she asked her mother yesterday. She remembered the afternoon light fighting through the lamps: her mother's hands stitching polygon to polygon: patchouli incense at war with the omnipresent reek of blood. Her mother gave a high sharp bark of laughter. 'O dear heart, we are friends of all the world! The house positively *vibrates* with our friends. Our hospitality is acclaimed far and wide – my darling sweetsullen child, you must have noticed!'

Slither. Cut. Scarlet floods or slow upwellings or a cold dark ooze. Slice. Slap of body in the water. Heads with eyes unchanged piling up amid the coiling innards.

It was time to cleanse them; scrub off the outside blood and slime, and force out the inside jellied clots from the secret cavities by the spine. A final inner sluice. Marketable goods.

As on every morning, she came to the last one.

She looked at it a long time, not thinking of anything.

Then she staggered to the porch with the basket of cleaned gutted fish, left it covered with a sack.

She scrubbed down the gutting block and the fish case. Slow cold-drowsy blowflies lifted away reluctantly from the streams of water. She picked up the shovel and the gutbucket and went to the burying-ground. The tin banged against her leg: the wire handle creased her palm painfully. She dug the hole, emptied the tin savagely down it, stared at the mound before covering it over.

Then she hurried inside. Washed her hands, pulled comb through her hair. She watched her father pull off his boots, awkward and slow, and tramp into her mother's room.

She picked up her heavy schoolcase.

On impulse, she took the knife and the stone and slipped them into a side-pocket.

She thought, I don't have much to offer. A body and a baggage of words. A hate. A knowledge of how to gut things. But it must be better.

'I'm late,' she called to the shut bedroom door.

This morning, she didn't say goodbye.

Marion Halligan

Blood Relations

1986

Martha climbed slowly up the steps, pressed between fellow travellers. She had a good view of the plane's flank, the shabby aluminium patched and riveted. It was her first flight. She knew the theory but the practice was still a mystery. Why did it stay up? A boat floated in the bath or on the sea; she had travelled 12,000 miles and danced away the small hours in the sliding bowels of an ocean liner with never a minute's panic. But how could the air hold up this small metal object, with its stiff and impotent wings?

– It does work, said Richard.

– It's still scary. And so are strange in-laws.

– *Strange*'s probably the word. I can't imagine them changing much.

The steward brought orange juice. Richard opened the bag of duty free shopping: cigars for Ron, scent, sunglasses, a small radio.

Martha thought: families are like transistorised circuits; you need to know what you're doing before you fiddle with them. She couldn't even tune a radio properly.

– We'll be there before you've had time to think, said Richard. The Tasman's only a puddle.

The plane took off. Martha gripped the seat arms and thought the only part more dangerous is the landing. But when they got to Wellington the plane darted down between the hills in a series of swooping glides, comfortably, like a bird. Perhaps its flight was logical, after all.

There were houses at the end of the wings' span: elaborate eyries. To the eye in flight it seemed the only means of access must be airborne. Ron lived in such a house, she knew, hung on a cliff face; Cecily was too terrified to drive the car down to it.

Ron and Cecily were waiting. He was delighted to see his brother.

– Ten years. After ten years. And a lovely new wife into the bargain. A child bride, I'd say.

He stood with his arm round Martha and squeezed her.

– Hardly new, said Richard. We've been married for five years, you know.

Ron took them on a scenic drive home, sitting Martha in the front so she'd have a good view. The Daimler climbed up and curved down, careful on tight bends and sharp corners. Whenever there was anything special to be seen Ron patted her leg to point it out.

– What do you think, eh? Different from Australia.

– Yes. It's so new, so rough, all fresh and jagged.

She'd never realised before how soft her country was. The lovely long curves of the Brindabellas, the low fuzzy hills around Canberra, blurred and gentle, stroked smooth by the tireless hands of millennia, they were all so muted. So old.

– This country will never be old, said Richard. Its own seething guts won't give the centuries a chance.

The wind buzzed, the sunshine flickered, clouds zoomed their dark chariots across the landscape.

– Wellington's famous for its wind, said Cecily in a quiet proud voice.

When they reached the house Martha understood her feelings about the driveway; the car dropped down the cliff like a slow-motion replay of a death plunge, but landed safely in the garage.

Lesley and June were out playing tennis. Bruce had the kettle boiling ready for tea. He was a slender boy, not tall, beginning his last year of school, and shy; he didn't say much, but Martha noticed how his eyes watched them, and his ears listened to every word, and the accenting of it. Unlike the girls; they dashed in and hugged and kissed, and sat down briefly, and chattered streams of questions, and reeled off all the amusing details of their tennis game, and had only time to gobble a bit of tea before rushing off to get ready for a dance at somebody's house.

Ron was opening a bottle of champagne.

– Not everyday a brother comes from Australia, he said. Make sure it's not so long next time. In fact, what about making it an annual event, eh?

– What about your coming to see us next? said Martha.

– I'd love that, said Cecily.

– Have to see about the business, said Ron. Difficult to leave, you know, especially when you've built it up yourself.

He poured the champagne into large hollow-stemmed goblets and carried them one by one to his guests.

We've got a great little programme lined up, he said. Starting tomorrow night. New Year's Eve party. Just across the way. Drinks the next afternoon – hair of the dog, eh? Barbecue here at the weekend, just a few of our closer friends. And of course the usual: golf, fishing, and I daresay the girls'll want their shopping. How does that sound, eh?

– Great, said Richard.

Ron was a wine merchant. He'd started off as a suburban shopkeeper – Ambrose's Corner Store – had turned it into a small wine supermarket, and then a big one, right at the start of that sort of thing in Wellington.

He took Richard to see his own cellar, good and cool in the side of the cliff. Martha offered to help Cecily.

– Oh no. I'm all organised. If anybody helps me I take twice as long.

Martha wandered around the pale bare spaces of the living room. Nothing in it could compete with the view. She was staring out at sky and sea pearling in the evening light when Bruce came in. He stared for a while too.

– Would you like a little walk along the cliff?

Looked at close it was a delicate cliff, with tiny flowering plants in crevices and icy threads of waterfall, fern-hidden. Bruce could show her all its minute details. Then wave his arm and offer all the grand scope of bay and headland. Martha imagined his looking at landscapes with the same serious attention he gave to people, and continuing to think about them afterwards.

– You're a schoolteacher, aren't you? he said. What do you teach?

– English, she said, with the diffidence of one offering a classical conversation killer.

Bruce smiled.

– I love English. I don't get very good marks, but I like it. Shakespeare, he said, looking sideways at her.

Martha dabbled her fingers in a thin cold stream beside the path, and wondered if he meant it. Perhaps he was just trying to please her.

It began to get cold on the cliff with night coming up from the sea. Time to go inside.

– You've made quite a conquest of that boy of mine, said Ron at the New Year's Eve party. Next thing you know he'll be following you round like a mooncalf. Not that I'd blame him, eh? Gorgeous creature like you around.

Ron had been making lascivious remarks all evening, his pink hands patting her, his round red face leering beneath its speckled dome. He seemed to be hinting at swapping partners. It must be a joke, but only Ron got any amusement from flirting with the idea.

Martha was glad to make conversation about Bruce instead.

– He's a very charming boy. I like talking to him.

– Charming, eh? Bone idle, I'd say. You should see his marks.

– I get the impression he works very hard.

– Not a chance. He'd get better marks if he did. Never mind. Next year – this year, already! – work, results, or trouble. That's my New Year's resolution.

– What does he want to do when he leaves school?

– God knows. Some airy fairy notions. A boy like that needs somebody to make up his mind for him. Medicine, law, they're the ticket. Respected professions, and you don't get stuck on a salary. Otherwise, the business.

– What if he's not suited to medicine or law or the business?

– Suited? You don't get on in life by being suited. You get stuck into the job in hand and make something of it. You're a teacher, you should know that.

– And the girls? Are they clever?

– Oh, they're pretty bright. But it doesn't matter for girls. It's just a matter of time until they get married. And of course they've got their secretarial courses.

He smiled.

– Pretty, aren't they?

– Very.

– I wouldn't have minded if they'd have wanted to go to university. I'm not narrowminded. But it stands to reason, a boy can't have the same leeway.

Yes, thought Martha. It takes more than a suitable marriage to furbish the family honour, where a boy is concerned.

Ron didn't want to leave the party. The New Year was long in and much drunk to and everyone else gone home before he would come away. He kept trying to kiss Martha Happy New Year, grabbing her and smacking his lips, as though making a lot of noise about it made it acceptable. Martha dodged and Cecily looked unhappy.

When they got him away he stumbled and sang, so Richard took one arm and Cecily the other and they marched him along. Martha wanted Richard's arm for herself; the night was immense and still, she would have liked to walk home beside him, waist entwined, lust growing sweetly in the sea-scented dark.

She dawdled behind, thinking how mysterious and full of accident was the parenting of children. Here were two brothers, seed of the same loins, fruit of the same womb, and yet hardly of the same kind at all, in mind or body or nature. One she loved, the other she could hardly begin to like. It was chastening to think that had her parents made love the night before or the night after, had the sperm hooked to the egg at a different moment, she might be as different from herself as was her husband from his brother. How nearly her personality had never been formed. The essential *her* . . . *she* . . . Martha, walking along this dark New Zealand road. God's eye on the fall of a sparrow was the most routine of sentry duties compared with his hand in the conception of his children. Easier to imagine blind fates spinning threads, knotting genes; or laughing-eyed gods making sport from the arbitrary collisions of cells. Perhaps laying bets, throwing dice; inveterate gamblers in the sky.

Cecily took motherhood very seriously. Raising her children had been the business of her adult life, and was not over yet. Bruce would be around for a long time, and the girls would simply convert her role to doting grandmother.

The girls were working hard, laying the foundations of it.

Martha could see why people would call such girls 'birds'. Lesley and June fluttered in, perched, chattered, swooped about the room, fluffed plumage and, dazzling display over, darted off. Conversation was a series of bright offerings, like the tawdry treasures of magpies, of significance only to themselves. Ostensibly compliant, were it not for the smiling charm of self-satisfaction with which it was offered.

– Beastly wind, practically blew us off the court.

– Oh my hair. I can't go anywhere looking like this.

– Damn, this hem's coming down.

– Oh hell. Can I wear a purple scarf with a green dress?

– It's sure to rain, since we're going to the beach.

There were also brief character catalogues: Sam's gorgeous. Jan's a slut. Sally gets drunk. Gary's got hands like an octopus. Sue chases anything in trousers.

They lived in a bright mosaic of a world, and knew where all the pieces went.

They laughed at Bruce. Cecily tried to admire him, but found it hard. She showed Martha a painting that had won him a prize. Her pride was eroded by distrust.

– It's not very well drawn, she said. The proportion's all wrong. And look at that woman's bulgy head, and the unnatural colours. Of course, I don't know anything about art.

– But you can see the emotions, said Martha. It's not meant to be a painting of real objects, so much as an emotional response to them. That's why the teacher's so big beside the class – that's how kids feel about some teachers. And look at her face: bilious yellow, jealous yellow. Didn't you ever see somebody like that, in your mind's eye? I think it's brilliant. I can see why it won a prize.

– Oh, can you? said Cecily. She peered at Martha, trying to decide whether she was honest, or mistaken, or right, or polite.

– Well, as long as he gets something out of it, I suppose, she said.

Cecily spoke in a slow fruity whine, which held certain words as though they were notes she was singing. Martha longed for an exuberant maestro to speed the whole thing up, or better still change the tune to something happier. To provide a new burden to her song.

Martha was ironing in the laundry under the house. Bruce put his head round the door and came in. She thought he was pretending he hadn't been looking for her.

– You're off tomorrow, he said.

– Yes. Time passes, as they say.

– She hung the shirt on a hanger. He rubbed the silk between his fingers.

– Your dresses look so nice to touch. Mum's aren't. They make the tops of your fingers feel blunt.

Martha had noticed that Cecily was always body-guarded in crimplene.

– I like real things, she said. Silk and wool and cotton. They feel good on the skin. Not chemical, or plastic, like synthetics.

Bruce was still stroking the silk shirt, his fingers sensuous, his eyes sly.

– Can I come and look at them? he asked, in a voice conscious of the oddity of his request.

Delicately she carried the ironed clothes upstairs, silk not so practical for travelling as crimplene. All her belongings were spread over the bed, ready for packing. She'd left everything dull and scruffy at home, so there was nothing to be ashamed of. He ran the fabrics skilfully between his fingers, smoothed the leather of her handbag, picked up her shoes, felt their weight and balance, snuffed their polished leather smell, and went back to the silk shirt.

– Jane's got one like this, only green.

– Who's Jane?

– Oh, a friend of mine. She's gone to Napier, or you could meet her. We get around together, when we can. Go to plays and things. Mum and Dad don't know about that – *sheer waste of time, lad* – and as for girlfriends, wow. They'd have a fit. What are you going to wear tonight?

– What do you think?

He chose a long caftan of dark red silk. A lot of Martha's salary went on clothes, even though she sometimes made them herself.

Bruce was looking at her dressing table, and fingering the pots and jars and sticks and pencils she used to paint her face. He unstoppered the scent Richard had bought her on the way over and snuffed it, drawing it right into his lungs, thinking about it.

– Try some on your skin. You get the full effect that way. Mm. *Ma Griffe* quite suits you.

– Jane's going to be an actress. She's rather good, I think. And pretty good-looking.

– And what about you? Would you like to act too?

– Oh well, you know, I wouldn't be any good at putting myself across on stage. But I'd like to work in theatre. I'm quite good at painting, you know. I mean, not good enough to be a great artist or anything, but I'm quite clever at designing things.

– Does your father know anything about this?

– Oh no. Dad doesn't take things like that seriously. You couldn't tell him that.

Bruce looked at the make-up pots.

– I'd really like to be a theatrical designer, he said. Do sets and costumes, even make-up. He looked at Martha's face; it was already painted. His own was virgin territory.

– Have a go, she said. He sat in front of the mirror, outlining his eyes with black, shadowing them with brown, darkening the hollows in his cheeks so that the bones stood out, rubbing his lips with dull crimson colour. He turned to the long mirror by the door, took the ruby caftan from its hanger, and held it against him.

– I look like Othello, he said. Jane was Desdemona in the school play last year. I saw it three times.

He threw his head back. *Put up your bright swords, or the dew will rust them . . .*

The door was open. Cecily put her head round, took the brunt of perfumed, painted, silken son, and retreated. Martha and Bruce grinned at one another.

– What about your father's plans for university? said Martha, watching Bruce examining himself in the mirror.

– There's not a hope. He's got more imagination than I'd have given him credit for if he thinks I'll make it into one of those classy careers. Though I expect there'll have to be some hideous showdown before he'll admit it. I mean, look at me, Martha. Can you imagine me as a doctor? *Now, Mrs Twiggywinkle. Stick out your tongue and say ah.*

– Sounds like a terrific bedside manner.

– Yeah. But you have to pass exams before they'll let you near any beds.

– Well, what about the business?

– I'd die.

– You'd better use some cream to get that lot off. I don't think your father would be too impressed.

Bruce stood before the mirror, raising his chin and turning his head as he smoothed cleansing cream into his skin, and there, in the curve of his cheek and the almond of his eye, Martha saw Richard. Cecily she'd seen before, and Ron. But the transient image of Richard was a surprise. She felt suddenly jealous of his lineaments in anyone else's child. One day, not yet, not for a long time yet, she and Richard would have a baby. Eventually, they wouldn't be able to resist the reach into the next generation. For the first time she imagined this idea as a fact. This young man with his troubles would be their child's cousin; he gave it a sudden reality that was a weight in her chest. One day, or the next, she and Richard would make love, would make love and make a baby, and it might be gentle and odd and not very bright like this nice boy, or it might be tall and thin and clever like its father, or none of these things, perhaps blonde and plump and short-sighted and a girl: endless possibilities and so out of her control she was frightened. She put her arms round Bruce and gave him a strong hug; she didn't know whether she was comforting him or herself.

He looked a bit surprised but didn't seem to mind; he even gave her a kiss on the cheek.

– It's nice to find a family all ready made, she said, in a clumsy attempt to explain, which he didn't need.

When he was gone, and she was dressing herself in the red silk for the last celebratory night, she felt the thrill of this late blossoming of blood relationships. She thought of them as strange neglected growths, uncultivated, uncherished, growing lightless and pale under the weight of the long separating years, yet nourished by some secret vitality of their own. And belonging to her too. *Husband and wife is one flesh* said sarcastic Hamlet; it seemed to be true. Bruce was her nephew just as much as Richard's. She wanted to express some practical love for him.

When Richard came back from Ron's ritual fishing trip she said:

– You know, Bruce wants to be a theatre designer. Perhaps he should come and stay with us, just for a bit, I mean, to get started.

– Do you think that's a good idea? Canberra's not much of a place for theatre. And I don't know about having somebody else living with us . . . still, it's a thought. Though I must say, I can't see Ron letting son and heir go into the theatre.

– Yes, well, funny things can happen. Ron must get the message sooner or later. He won't make medicine or law, and his talents would be wasted in the business.

– Try telling Ron that.

– You're his brother. You should be able to talk to him.

Cecily's cooking was Kiwi international. She and her girlfriends swapped ideas, outdid themselves at parties, and were always putting one another on to some goody just discovered, usually in magazines which told them how to entertain glamorously. Much had been carefully prepared against the day of the visiting relations and stored in the freezer. Cecily had her provisioning campaign all mapped out, with lists and menus and defrosting timetables stuck to the fridge door. Martha was touched by all the trouble taken. But she was surprised at how short and busy meals were. People came and went, late and early; despite the organisation, food was mainly fuel.

But Ron insisted on the sanctity of the pre-dinner drink. He liked to relax and talk about his day. And on this occasion it was apparent that his day was ruined. There would be no relaxing.

They caught the tale's end: Bruce in make-up and a dress posturing before a mirror.

– The boy's a bloody poofter, said Ron.

– Oh, but, it's not that at all, said Martha.

– I think this is our problem, Martha.

– Yes, I know, but I can explain, it's not what you think. There's nothing at all . . . homosexual . . . (Cecily and Ron looked at her as though she'd seduced him to arrive at this certainty.) The dressing-up was theatre . . . he wants to make it his career, he's good . . .

– The theatre, gasped Ron. That garden of fairies. Over my dead body.

– Oh dear, said Cecily. P'raps they're not all like that. We don't really know, do we . . .

– Dad, you're wrong, you know . . . was all Bruce managed before his father rushed at him and hit him hard across the face with the palm of his hand, knocking him backwards across a sofa. Blood flowed from his nose. He cupped his hands around it and ran out of the room, careful not to bleed on the vast spaces of beige carpet and cream silk upholstery.

– Po-faced little prick. I should belt his bum for him.

– Ron! breathed Cecily. Her scandalised face tried to convince the guests that this was a novelty.

– Alliterative as ever, I see, said Richard, meaning to amuse and defuse, and entirely forgetting the ancient power of his vocabulary to infuriate Ron.

– Dear, there's no need to upset yourself like this, said Cecily.

Ron took deep breaths, staring straight ahead with apocalyptic eyes. No, he said finally. He poured out more wine. We'll drop it now. I'll talk to Bruce tomorrow.

He kept pouring more wine for the rest of the evening, and eventually everybody had drunk enough to manage parting toasts.

– You must come and see us again soon, said Cecily. Now you've found the way.

– Yes, my word, said Ron.

They drove off next morning in a hired car. Martha sang:

> We've been to see the rellies
> The wonderful rellies of . . . Niz.

and Richard groaned as he always did because Martha always sang flat, and they both laughed like idiots as the red Mini scuttled north.

They enjoyed their fortnight's touring in perfect selfish unison. They swam in sulphurous yellow pools and water heavy with iron. They drank old boiled coffee and ate triple-decker sandwiches in wayside cafes. They wandered through blasted thermal landscapes and stayed in hotels which could no longer match the magnificence of their conception, and had a habit of burning down, Richard said. Or in practical modest motels where they fed themselves on bacon and eggs. They decided against visiting forgotten aunts and uncles in Te Aroha and Hamilton. They went to Coromandel and the delicate bays of the north, and laughed at Bavarian bagpipes. They made love in indifferent fresh-sheeted beds the length of the country, so that their daytimes were glossy with the nights' desires.

And they got pregnant. Martha often wondered how accidentally she had left behind her contraceptive pills in the motel at Lake Taupo. She hadn't meant to forget them, she didn't think. But they didn't stop making love afterwards, so that was a kind of choice.

The holiday ended, and they came home, feeling like different people. Life went on, in both countries. The busy nieces soon alighted on suitable husbands; they were both married in the next summer.

– It's a pity New Zealand girls get married so young, said Martha. They can't possibly know what they're doing.

She and Richard with a new baby didn't go to the weddings but sent presents.

Bruce saved himself from the twin disasters of medicine and law by failing to get university entrance. He is involved in amateur theatricals. He writes sometimes to Martha and tells her about them, and of his plans for getting out of the business. She leans over the basket and watches the round bald head of her sleeping son, and thinks of the curve of Bruce's cheek and the almond of his eye, though she can see nothing of them or of the lineaments of herself or Richard in this plump mysterious baby grown from their flesh. He is essentially himself.

She makes passionate promises to herself and the child.

Shonagh Koea

The Dancing Master

1986

Thorstensen came threading through the crowd just before half past ten, when the music started. By that time a stag's head the decorators had brought in wore festoons of hired bow ties, silk evening scarves, a top hat and Mrs Bradford's own black stockings. The evening had decayed away into a never-never land of chicken skeletons and dessert gateaux.

'Will you dance with me? Would you care to dance with me?' said Thorstensen. His outstretched hand across the table might have been sly or shy, she was not sure. 'Won't you dance with me?' said Thorstensen and the slim ovals of his gold cufflinks were as thin as the covering on a man's soul.

'Watch out for Thorstensen,' Bernard had said, but that was hours ago when they ran out their own front door to the waiting taxi, its peremptory hooting like a preliminary call to battle. Bernard had forgotten all that now and sat chin in hand as he idly ate some fruit salad, talking to Wevers about the next board meeting and complaining that the champagne tasted like creaming soda.

'You mean the alleged champagne,' said Wevers and tapped his hairy nose.

'Right,' said Bernard. 'The alleged champagne it is. I stand corrected.'

'You steer very well clear of Thorstensen, little lady,' Bernard had said earlier. 'Thorstensen's a dangerous man. Thorstensen's put the skids under more men than you've had hot dinners. Stay away from Thorstensen.' Thorstensen was the new company head.

The taxi hooted again as one of her high heels caught in the doormat.

'Blow old Thorstensen,' she said then. 'Who cares about old Thorstensen, anyway? Blow these shoes, blow the whole thing, Bernard. For two pins, Bernard, I'd stay at home, I'd be like old weasel-faced Madley's wife and send you off by yourself. Blow company parties,' and she tore the lacerated heel from the rope matting. 'Never mind about old Thorstensen. It's the dancing I'm terrified of, Bernard. At the school I went to you could only have dancing lessons if you had a partner and nobody ever asked me. What will I do, Bernard, if someone asks me to dance?'

'They won't,' said Bernard, tramping towards the far gate-post.

'Thanks,' she said. 'Thank you, Bernard. What a lovely evening I look forward to.'

'No need for sarcasm, my dear,' said Bernard and gave the address to the driver who looked at them in the rear vision mirror with hooded calculating eyes as they drove through sudden rain.

'I knew it rang a bell,' said the driver as he drew up under the office veranda. 'You've got that Thorstensen.' Eight floors of the company premises reared above them, the windows brilliantly lit for Thorstensen's gala evening. 'I've got you slotted now,' he said. 'I've read about your Thorstensen in the Sundays.' Thorstensen sounded like an illness.

'Excuse me,' said Thorstensen now and Bernard's small spoon remained suspended over the last slice of banana, 'I'm asking you to dance. Wouldn't you like to come and dance with me?' and he held out that inviting hand again.

Beside them the company engineer, dressed as a fusilier, plunged his hands down the neckline of somebody's wife, a thin girl with a sharp little face like a wedge of cheap sweet cake.

'I must thoroughly investigate how this superstructure is kept up,' he shouted and the sound of her laughter was wild and shrill as she threw her corsage of violets at the stag's head.

'I think the party's getting rough,' said Thorstensen. 'Won't you dance with me?'

Earlier, the empty foyer had an air of forgotten excitement as though crowds had already passed that way and while they waited for the lift she watched the taxi driver fill in his notebook outside. The silhouette of his humped figure held a peculiar and unintentional menace and his radio splattered through the night, words distorted so it seemed more like distant gunfire than messages about innocent journeys.

'It's not going to be a pleasant evening,' said Bernard. 'Lunches last week and a ball this week – I don't know how they expect me to find the time. We're late, and I'm not sure yellow's your colour.'

'Yellow and pink,' she said, 'and it's not and my shoe's nearly ruined as well.'

The lift bore them upwards and smelt faintly of cigars as though somebody, anxious to have a jolly evening for the entire time, had anticipated later pleasures.

They passed accounts and advertising on the first two floors, computer programming on the third and flashed past the wider hinterland of middle management on the upward journey. Beyond the serpentine lengths of executive corridors lay office suites with drinks cabinets and tweed sofas, oil paintings. There secretaries were called personal assistants and had secretaries of their own. They all nurtured bright-eyed young men under forty-three who did aerobics.

The lift spilled them out on the eighth floor, usually a staid boardroom, and they stepped forth into an instant baronial hall with plastic beams and flashing electric candle bulbs in the candelabras.

'Oh my God,' said Bernard, 'they've had the decorators in. Oh my God, it's fancy dress. I thought they were joking.'

'Thorsty won't be pleased with you,' said a fat man as he passed. 'Didn't you get the memo from the lovely Caroline? Thorsty said it was to be fancy costume. Thorsty said it was to be a Victorian evening with everyone joining in the spirit of the thing. Don't you like my dress kilt? It's Black Watch.'

'It would be,' said Bernard.

'Who was that man, Bernard?' she tugged at his arm. 'Who was that fat man?'

'That's Wevers,' said Bernard, 'and keep your voice down, Bridget. Wevers is a dangerous man. You watch out for Wevers. Wevers is the axe-man. Wevers fires the bullets.'

'Show me Thorstensen, Bernard. Which one is Thorstensen?'

'I can't see him.'

'Where would they have got those lovely dresses, Bernard?' There seemed to be a parade of crinolines.

'Hired them, or made them – how should I know.'

In a corner a woman with ringlets and a black lace dress sat on a man's knee and began to sing light opera, trilling on the high notes till her curls fell askew.

'Oh my God,' said Bernard, 'Mrs Bradford's well on the way.'

Mrs Bradford began another song, waving one hand in time to the waltz. Her ringlets tumbled farther down and her rings flashed, massive diamonds in trios on the left hand and on her right a large ornate offering that might have been a signet ring, a man's ring. She tossed the hand that wore it with a careless insolence as though the ring were a reprimanding gift, even a legacy, from an admonishing father, worn now to acknowledge an influence that must be defied.

'Did Mrs Bradford's father die recently?' she asked.

'How should I know. I can't keep up with your questions. Who's Wevers and where's Thorstensen and where do people get their dresses and did Mrs Bradford's father die? How should I know?'

Dinner was a forgettable two hours, but soothed by meat and wine and cake, the crowd parted for a moment and Bernard suddenly said, 'There, there, look now – that's Thorstensen at the top table, in the middle beside the woman in red.'

For a moment she saw him clearly. One hand shaded his eyes as if the light were too bright or, she thought later, he was bored.

'But Bernard,' she said as the woman in red stood up, blocked that clear view of a thin dark face, 'he's quite a young man. Thorstensen's quite a young man. I always thought he was an old, old man with an ugly face. Why didn't anyone tell me Thorstensen was young? You never tell me anything.'

'How many times must I ask you?' Thorstensen had withdrawn his hand now. 'Won't you dance with me? Please, won't you come and dance with me?' The big clock beside the stag's head said twenty-eight minutes past a mis-aimed black sock. 'I think the party's getting rough,' said Thorstensen again as Mrs Bradford screamed. 'Please, for heaven's sake, won't you come and dance with me?'

'I can't,' she said. 'I can't dance. I've never learned. There are lots of other people who'd love to dance with you.'

'That's all fibs,' said Thorstensen. 'I think you're a fibber.'

Bernard stirred uneasily, put his spoon down.

'I suppose you've noticed we're not in costume,' he said, 'and I don't know if you've met my wife.'

'No,' said Thorstensen, 'and yes, I have now,' and he took her away through the crowd, holding her hand in an imprisoning grip, to where the orchestra was beginning to play. They wore red velvet coats and the music hung in the air, full-bodied and luxuriant, like the scent of peonies.

'You could dance with someone else,' she said and tried to pull her hand away. 'I can't dance, truly. I've been terrified all night.'

'Fibber,' said Thorstensen.

'No, really. At the school I went to you could only have dancing lessons if a boy asked you to be his partner and nobody ever asked me. Bernard never dances. Bernard never danced with me in his life.'

'I don't believe you,' said Thorstensen.

'Why couldn't you just have a cocktail party?' They were beside the dance floor now. 'That other man only ever gave cocktail parties or dinners. I can manage cocktail parties and dinners and lunches. I've caught up on everything except dancing. Why did you have to have dancing?'

'I like dancing,' said Thorstensen. 'I love dancing. I used to like dancing with my wife.'

'I wish,' she said, 'that you'd just given a dinner. That other man used to have things flown in for dinners – salmon and oysters and blueberries, things like that. Blueberries,' she said, 'are horrible. I remember he had blueberries flown in once, when blueberries were new, and I saw them squashed all over the floor.'

'Did you, indeed,' said Thorstensen, and they glided away across the floor. 'I knew you could dance,' he said.

'I tripped over your toe.'

'No,' said Thorstensen, 'I tripped over yours, and you're a fibber.'

'I'm not,' she said, 'honestly. I was a very dull, common, ugly, graceless girl and nobody ever bothered about me. It took me years to catch up.'

'Where was this?' He gave her a suspicious look then and when she told him the name of that small old town he straightened his arms, held her away so he could look at her again. 'I can't believe that. You're a terrible fibber,' and she skipped round the corner beside the grand piano, joyful that the old bitter life had left no mark, that it was not apparent it had been lived at all.

'I saw you at the lunch last week,' he said. 'Why did you have a hat on?'

'I saw you too. I thought you were that new traveller they've got. You know the one they all talk about, that one who's supposed to have been married to someone in a soap opera.'

'But why did you have a hat on?' So the traveller did not interest him, she thought.

'It was only an old black beret I wear in the rain. It was raining when I went to catch the bus into town. I don't have a car any more.' But would he be interested in that either?

'Why didn't you take it off?' he wanted to know. 'Nobody else had a hat on.'

'I know,' she said. 'That's why I left it on.'

'Ah,' said Thorstensen as if he understood and he swung her into a large clear space that seemed to have been left for them by the others. They left a clear space for Thorstensen, she noticed, as hens put a space between themselves and a predator.

'Do you see that man over there,' he said, 'that man with the yellow hair? That's Abrams. I hate Abrams. Abrams swindled me. He's dancing with his wife. Do you know his wife?'

'I know hardly anybody.'

'Wise,' said Thorstensen. 'Very wise. They're both awful. You wouldn't like Abrams.'

'He's very ugly,' she said. 'I wouldn't worry about him if I were you. All that money couldn't make him beautiful. Money can't buy beauty,' she said, 'or charm, can it?' and she looked up into his bright face as, laughing, he danced them off the floor into the old upper vestibule, decked for the evening as a garden room.

'Mind the step,' he said but she still tripped, laughing and looking up at bright brave Thorstensen. 'I knew you could dance,' he said. 'I knew you were a fibber. You're as light as a feather and your hands are so cool.'

'I'm terrified,' she said. 'That's why my hands are cold,' but he laughed and swung her round again.

'Fibber,' said Thorstensen. They seemed to hang in that conservatory with its silk flowers and artificial trellis like people on a swing.

'I love dancing,' he said. 'I used to dance when I was a gravedigger. I went to dancing lessons on Friday nights. I started off as a grave-digger, did you know that?' The worst thing was, he said, when the old bones were scattered, when one grave had to be dug on top of another.

'The first job I had was in a hospital kitchen,' she said, and they changed the dance then from a foxtrot to a quickstep as if to get away from the graveyard and her old sink.

'I like your cuffs,' she said. 'I like those double cuffs turned back like that.'

'They're French cuffs,' said Thorstensen. 'Have you ever read Hartigan? You'd enjoy Hartigan. Hartigan explores the relationship between work and luxury. French cuffs are my luxury and I can look at them while I work. Hartigan, you see? You must read Hartigan.'

'I will,' she said and as the music changed to a waltz he suddenly stood still in the middle of the floor like a lost boy. 'But this is a waltz,' he said. 'I've forgotten how to waltz.'

'Waltzing's easy.' She grasped his elbows and swung him lightly round. 'I'll teach you how to waltz. One two three, one two three.'

'I knew you could dance,' said Thorstensen. 'I knew you were a fibber.'

'All wallflowers know how to waltz, silly,' she told him. 'They learn how to waltz round their own kitchen tables, all alone.'

As they passed Abrams again Bernard called from beside a potted palm, 'I've got your coat. It's after eleven. The taxi's waiting.' A quick and greedy half an hour had passed already.

'He's a nice fellow, is he?' asked Thorstensen. 'Bernard?' Oh very nice, she told him, on a good day, at the right moment, when viewed with the light behind him.

'I see,' said Thorstensen and she thought he did.

As their taxi drew away from the kerb Thorstensen stepped from the shadows, tapped on a window.

'You don't mind, do you,' he said, 'if I hitch a ride? We could sing all the way home. I know the first hundred and four verses of "Eskimo Nell".'

They dropped him at the beginning of an oak avenue and she watched him out of sight, the sound of his whistling sharp and clear on a westering wind.

'He seemed in an odd mood tonight,' said Bernard. 'What was he saying to you? I saw you talking. I saw you laughing.'

'He was only laughing about my hat, Bernard, my old black beret, that's all. He just asked if you were a nice fellow and I said you were, and I said why did he have to give a ball because I'm terrified of dancing. I said why couldn't he just give a cocktail party or a silly dinner like that other man. That's all, Bernard.'

'Oh my God.'

'Bernard, I do wish you wouldn't keep saying "Oh my God" all the time.'

Towards November that year, when the Christmas decorations were starting to be put up in the shops, receivership loomed after boardroom infighting and two takeover bids by the multinationals. The company shares dropped overnight and Thorstensen's house in the avenue of oaks was found empty one day with its big front door swinging open in the breeze. At an entailed auction of the contents a big brass bed with Sevres plaques fetched three times the estimated price and an antique dealer, of hitherto irreproachable reputation, had to be hustled out the back door to a waiting ambulance after behaving with marked peculiarity during the sale of the silver.

The gossip writers of the financial columns dug deep but found Thorstensen's sudden departure was worth only a paragraph or two. No one knew his friends or his foes.

'I hate Abrams,' he had told her, 'but I'm very fond of little McIndoe. I rely on McIndoe. I get very fond of people sometimes,' he said, 'do you?' and she said she did. 'I never let them know, though,' said Thorstensen. 'I hide it. I keep it a secret. Do you do that?' She nodded again.

He was called a workaholic, a self-actualisation man who studied under a guru whose name nobody knew. That very afternoon she ran straight to the library to find Hartigan.

'We'd have him on toast,' they said, 'if we knew where he came from, if we could just find out where he started off, if we could dig up some mud. Was he ever married?' they wanted to know.

That night she said to Bernard, 'Do you remember the night Thorstensen hitched a ride in our taxi? If you ever told anyone about that, Bernard, I'll go, do you understand. Is that quite clear?'

The rumour surfaced then that the Mastersons' grandmother, on the trip of a lifetime, had seen Thorstensen walking through a shopping plaza in Vancouver. His name was reputed to be on the books of a worldwide executive employment agency. Somebody else said he had been glimpsed on a KLM flight from Singapore to New Delhi, in business class eating lobster off a tray. Later the same month a short paragraph appeared in some of the financial pages announcing he had gone to Burundi to work for the Aga Khan.

'Would the Aga Khan be a nice man to work for?' she asked at the next company party. 'Would the Aga Khan be kind to him? Would it be pleasant living in Burundi? Would he like it there?'

'That's it in a nutshell,' said Wevers, tapped his hairy nose again and held out an oily hand. 'Put it here, lady.'

'What do you play off?' That would be someone at the other end of the table. 'What's your handicap? Whoops, Bernie old chum, we've lost your good lady. Not a golfer, is she?'

It was safe then to wander away, easy to find another table with a vacant seat or two, simple to sit talking to the flowers in the middle of the crowd.

'I liked Thorstensen,' she could say then. 'Thorstensen taught me how to dance. I was a wallflower all my life till Thorstensen asked me to dance. He made up for all the years when no one chose me. I loved him. You couldn't imagine how bright and brave he was,' she would say, drawing on the tablecloth with a fork, little runnels that led to nowhere, and wearing Thorstensen's secrets like jewels.

Jessica Anderson

The Late Sunlight

1987

As Gordon crossed the park on the way back to his chilly rented flat, and felt the stored warmth of the day's sun rising from the terra cotta paving, he was tempted into turning aside and sitting next to an old woman on a sheltered bench. He put his folder and notebooks beside him, let the sunlight settle on him, and felt his body sigh. The old woman said, 'You are taking the sun?'

He did not try to define her European accent, knowing only that it was not French or Italian. Nowadays he tried to provide against his tendency to be too friendly too soon; in his youth it had led him into so many long useless conversations, had wasted so much of his time; warring couples whose only aim was to condemn each other had made him their confidant, and evangelists for the more unusual religions had scarcely been able to believe their luck. Without looking at the woman he murmured an assent.

'The sun in winter is like the medicine.'

Gordon gave the slightest of nods.

'You need the medicine of the sun?'

Gordon had had such a disappointing day at the library that he could not help saying that at the moment, he certainly felt he did.

'You have been sick?'

This was how it had always started. He tried to retreat by shutting his eyes, as if his eyelids especially needed the sun.

'You look as if you have been sick.'

Such a voice, so loud and acid, gave him a choice. He could get up and go, or he could turn and talk to her. His old tendency was always inclined to revive when he was away from his wife and family.

Her eyes were a faded black, lustreless yet intense, perhaps hostile. But to their stare she added the smile of long painted lips, the vivacity of eyebrows drawn far above her natural browline, and a sociable inclination towards him of her thick body. 'You are too pale,' she said. 'You have none of the pink.'

Neither had she. Her skin was olive with undertones of lead. He saw now that she was dressed in what his two elder children called 'money-money clothes'. Richness glistened in her fur collar, in the velvety pile of her elaborate asymmetrical hat, in her narrow finely-crafted shoes, and in the handbag, made of the skin of some reptile, which lay rigid and sharp-angled in her lap. 'A young man,' she said, 'should have a little of the pink.'

The inclination of her body seemed ingratiating, but her tone was still acid. Forty may really seem young to her; Gordon absolved her of flattery. 'I suppose I'm so thick-skinned,' he said lazily, 'that no pink can get through.'

'Thick-skinned? No.' She shook her head in absolute negation. 'No, no, no, no, no.' She leaned back on the bench. 'You are refined,' she said, and gave a single sharp nod.

Scottish ancestors had given him a lean gingery ascetic look, and he supposed it was this she called refinement. But from her generation to his, it could be a dubious compliment. He made an ironical mouth and said, '*Am I*?'

Below the thin black arcs, the two lumps of her hairless brows drew together in a scowl. 'You think I don't know?' she said. 'You think I can't tell? When I see these others, all around me?'

Her little gloved hand, curved downward, stabbed towards the other occupied benches, towards the sunburst fountain, where people were taking photographs, towards the paths on which they were daring to pass up and down.

'They are so common.'

The last word was delivered on a guttural of hatred and contempt. Gordon's recoil was swift and instinctive. His parents had put an absolute embargo on this epithet, assuring him that his own inferiority, and possibly wickedness, was all its use would prove. Nor had the sympathies of his maturity tempted him far in a contrary direction. Indeed, if blasphemy existed for Gordon, this painted old woman had just committed it. He folded his arms and raised his face again to the sun. There was no point in anything but politeness. 'Excuse me,' he said. 'I'll take a bit more of this curative sun.'

He knew she would speak again. But now the sun was holding him, as was a reluctance to face the depressing flat. When she asked if he was a writer, he prepared to pay for a few more minutes of the sun, and replied that he was a teacher.

'Those papers,' he said patiently, guessing what had prompted her question, 'are notes I've been taking in the library. I've got time off to do some research.'

'You teach in a school?'

'I teach in a university.'

'You are a professor?'

The word was pronounced with respect. 'I am a tutor,' said Gordon. 'I teach history in Canberra.'

'Ah. Can-*bair*-ah.'

The respect this time sounded false. She asked him what history he taught, and when he said Australian, she asked with dangerous playfulness whether there was such a thing. But the sun was her enemy; it was easy not to reply. Behind his closed lids, light motes sweetly floated. Her voice, like the footsteps on the path, changed timbre, became muffled, retreated. And sweet as a light mote, there drifted into his brain the knowledge that his thesis should not be on the colonial institution he had chosen, but on one man, the one whose character had permeated that institution. There that man stood. Details, so carefully gathered by Gordon, worried over, mauled, but stubbornly disparate, flew to assemble round him. The voice at Gordon's side, continuing to speak of Can-*bair*-ah, still sounded distant, but he knew it was not. Begging his man to stay, not to fade, he jumped to his feet and picked up his papers. 'But what does Can-*bair*-ah matter,' cried the woman, giving her little gloved stabs, 'when there are no real cities in Australia anyway?'

Gordon wished he had a hat to raise, something to placate her for his abrupt departure. But he could only apologise for leaving so suddenly, and hurry away. 'You are a gentleman,' she called after him, loud enough for half the park to hear.

In the depressing flat, which he had taken unseen, Gordon sat down immediately to his books and notes. He worked, with a short break for dinner at the Indian restaurant three doors down, until midnight. By that time his excitement was tamped to a sober hopefulness. More information was needed to confirm that vision. But Gordon thought he knew where to find it.

The next day in the library, he crashed. The information in which he had trusted diminished the man's importance. Yet his vision had made it impossible to return to his old institutional subject, which now spread itself out like so many lumber rooms. He dropped again into the dullness and perplexity that had brought him to search in Sydney. The library, because in his boyhood and youth it had often been a refuge from the enthusiasms of his family, had always rested in his mind like a point of peace. But now even the library was uncongenial to him. He left early, crossing Macquarie Street with the hunched gait by which his wife Marion said she could detect his low moods.

In the park the old woman sat in the same seat. Seeing her before she saw him, Gordon recalled the words she had called after him yesterday – 'You are a gentleman' – and speculated on their meaning: they were a sarcastic reproach for his abrupt departure; they were flattery to make him come back; they were simply wild and heedless. He intended to pass her by, but she saw him, and gave him her slow red foxy smile, and for some reason – perhaps because disappointment had made him apathetic – he went and sat at her side. 'Today I will tell you of my son,' she instantly announced. But then she turned the red smile downwards, brooded, and said, 'No, I will not.' She eyed his notebooks, became sociable. 'You have been at your library.'

He nodded. He kept the notebooks in his hand, and did not relax into his seat. Today she was dressed with a richness that at four thirty in this scrap of a park amounted to grotesquerie. Her jacket and cap were mink, he was sure. Only diamonds could have the flashing power of the stones in her dangling ear rings, and in that case, the stones surrounding them must be – yes – rubies. That was to say nothing of the rings on her fingers, perhaps six. She wore no gloves today. The handbag was the same one. She opened it, shook a pill from a tiny round silver box, and shut the bag with a satisfied snap of its double clasp. In some recess of his mind he had already decided she was middle European, and now, from those turbulent countries crushed together on the map, Hungary stood out.

She rolled the pill in her mouth and eyed him sideways. Both her painted and real brows were at rest, but the smile of her sucking mouth was anticipatory. She was waiting to finish the pill before speaking. Her legs were shapely; she crossed them and kicked out the upper one. Had she been a performer of some sort? An actress? Perhaps she had even ridden a white horse round a circus ring. He could see it. And then had married a rich man, and puffed herself up with jewels and furs, and begun to call people common. He wondered why he rather liked her. She finished her pill.

'You are married?'

'Yes.'

She was at her most ingratiating. 'You have the look of a man nicely married.'

'Well, I am.'

'Your wife's name?'

'Marion. And,' he said, before she could ask, 'we have three children. Peter, Tess, and Joel. Twelve, eleven, and seven.'

'I once knew a Marion.' She deepened her voice and drew a hand downward from her chin. '*Such a chin*! That was when I was first in Australia. Has your Marion – *such a chin*?'

He foresaw an analysis of Marion's appearance; he would not encourage it. 'Have you been long in Australia?' he asked.

She subsided into disgust. 'One hundred years.'

'But actually?'

'But actually, since during the War.' She was watching him keenly. 'No, I am not Jewish, in case you will now want to forgive me everything. Yes, that is what some people do. My husband, who was also not Jewish, acted in a political way, so we had to leave.'

He knew from experience that if he replied to this, the conversation would certainly be long, and if not useless, infinitely knotted. He put down his notes and leaned forward with his elbows on his knees. 'What part of Europe do you come from?'

She spread a hand on her breast. The stubby little ringed fingers sank in fur. 'I am Viennese.'

He made a swift mental appraisal of his inaccurate guess, and another of his passing thought that it had been near enough.

But now she said, with sudden prim finality, 'And you, sir? You are Australian?'

He said he was.

'Of Australian parentage also?'

'On both sides.'

'From one of the big country estates perhaps?'

He could not help laughing. He thought of the little bungalow, so flimsy that in memory it shook with the thump of argument and exhortation, and threatened to burst with the people who had nowhere else to go. Worthy causes had slept on the verandah or on a mattress in Gordon's room, and a victim of society had stolen his Cambridge histories. Leaning back on the bench, he gave a long soft laugh not only at the contrast of the suggestion with the reality, but in tribute to his dead parents, so good, tireless, and indignant. But she was looking at him with her long mouth shut as tight as the clasp on her handbag. He stopped laughing and said, 'Sorry. In fact I was born right here in Sydney. My father was a teacher too. Only he taught little kids, in primary school.'

Her hard angry calculating look did not waver. She said, 'You should not tell anyone. No one would ever know.'

He could have laughed again, but did not want to anger her further. Nothing she said could matter. He half-shut his eyes against the sun, and at that moment knew at what point in the day's research he had taken the wrong direction. He saw his own hand as it wrote the request for the misleading material. She was speaking, but he shut his mind to her words, while quickly he allowed to enter the knowledge of the path he should have taken. But he could not help hearing that he was the very model of an Englishman she had once known, who was a very great aristocrat, and a model of refinement, so that when he rose quickly to his feet, and picked up his notes, he gave her a little bow of farewell. He had never bowed in his life before, but he wanted to please her. Today's insight, like yesterday's, was without doubt the result of relaxation after hard mental work, but she had been present on both occasions, and though he knew he was not superstitious, he could not afford to take risks. Bowing, he explained that he must hurry back to the library. She gave her consent with a nod, but did not let him go until he had told her his name, and she, again with that precise gesture of hand on breast, had given him hers. It was long, and he was too distracted to listen with his usual care, and all he retained was her Christian name, Vera.

On his way back to the library he bought a pack of chicken and gobbled it up behind one of the advertising fixtures on the railway platform. He was glad Vera could not see him. He did not have much time in the library before it shut, but enough to assure himself that this time he was not mistaken, and to reserve his material for tomorrow. When he got back to the flat he rang Marion. While he waited for an answer he envisioned her walking through their pleasant haphazard rooms, wearing the padded black Indian dress and the boots she had hardly changed out of lately. Her fair hair would be loose on her shoulders, and as she walked she would slip a hand beneath it and massage the back of her head, where the knot had been pinned all day. When she answered she sounded tired.

'Darling,' he said with a rush, 'I'm sorry I didn't ring before. Is everything okay? Kids okay? You?'

'Everything's fine. How's your work?'

'Oh – all right.' He knew she would understand, from his guarded yet airy tone, that at this stage he wanted to keep it to himself. She would recognise it as a good sign. 'What about yours?' he asked.

'Guido is sick, and I'm taking one of his tutorials. But don't worry. Don't hurry home. Peter and Tess cooked dinner tonight, and Joel set the table. How is the grisly flat?'

He had not even noticed it tonight. 'I guess it serves its purpose.'

'I long to see you, Gordon.'

'I long to see you, my love.'

'How much longer?'

'Two more days.'

'That's not bad.'

'At the most. Has Joel got his glasses yet?'

'No. Tomorrow.'

'Home on Friday, then. I'm fairly sure.'

'Try hard. Goodnight, darling.'

'Goodnight, sweet.'

He felt deeply contented as he undressed. He sometimes felt more genuinely a part of his family when away from them than when at home. There, he occasionally had the curious feeling that he had had no part in their making, but that he had come gambolling to their door one day, and they, calmly, smilingly, kindly, had taken him in and given him a good home. Marion was a mathematician, and so, potentially, were all three children. All passionately loved music, though never to dance to, as he had once done, and none read fiction for pleasure. They disregarded their own beauty, and in their cupboards hung few more than the essential garments. Interchangeable hats hanging on pegs in the hall guarded their fair skins. The oddest thing of all about them was that on Sundays all went to the Anglican church, Marion simply insisting when he teased her about it that that was how she had been brought up.

But when Gordon was away, none of these differences caused him the alienation (which sometimes became resentment) that they caused him at home. The contentment with which he went to sleep continued into the next day. In the library he proceeded with absolute certainty to find his material. It was one of those rare days when nearly everything he turned up was useful, and could be accepted without surprise. The congeniality of the room – the peace of its polished timber and high pale panes of glass – was restored to him. Flickering only on the margin of his consciousness were the morbid shadows on Vera's skin, her disquieting eyes and the long red lips sucking at her pill. As he walked to his train in Martin Place, these settled into a conclusion that she was very sick.

The first sight of her seemed to contradict it. She sat in the same place, and when she saw him, she kicked up a leg and patted the seat at her side. She had no pill in her mouth, and again her smile was mocking, deliberate, and foxy. She was dressed entirely in black, on her coat an astrakhan collar, on her head an astrakhan toque incredibly twisted to one side in a kind of cockade. 'So today you carry the brief case,' she said as he sat down.

She took no notice of his explanation that he had had some documents copied. She seemed excited, bursting with talk. 'My son also carries the brief case. He is like a good little doggie, carrying the brief case. I do not mean you are like a doggie. You are so tall. But he is little and neat, and should not carry the brief case.'

'Is your son here in Sydney?' asked Gordon.

'Of course he is here in Sydney. He is Australian. His wife is Australian. His children are Australian. He is a little Australian doggie. And now my neighbour tells me how I must see him, this doggie, how I must ring him and tell him to come.'

It disturbed Gordon that she had only a neighbour to tell her this. 'You have no other children?'

'I have no children at all. I do not count doggies. He will get everything. That is the law. That is enough. I will not see him also.'

Her handbag was again the same one. She shook out a pill from the little silver box. 'Last time I see him was two years ago. He comes to me and he says, "Mutti, you must do this thing for your health, you must do that thing." I say yes, yes, and now go home, good doggie, to your *Sand*-ra.'

She pronounced the name with even more hatred and contempt than she had used for the word common, but because this time it was merely personal, it did not shock Gordon so much. The late sunlight was having its usual benign effect. His thoughts settled contentedly on his work. His colonial man stood before him in promise of full life. He estimated that tomorrow about three hours of work would give him enough to go on with for months.

Vera finished her pill. 'Now I wish to speak of your wife.'

He was good-humoured but wary. 'What about her?'

'You have her photograph?'

'Not here.'

'Please to describe her.'

Gordon laughed. 'She is slim and fair. You want to know if she is beautiful, don't you?'

She gave one of her consciously dignified nods. He had changed his mind about her having been a circus performer, but the suggestion of theatre lingered. He said, 'Yes, she is beautiful.'

'And – excuse me – is she common?'

'I'm amazed that you excuse yourself. I don't quite know how to answer you, but if in your opinion I am not common, then neither is Marion.'

'That is good then. I would like her to have the dark beauty, but the fair is also good. Though not so good for the men to have.'

Her son, she went on to say, was of that fairness they call washed-out. Gordon was not attending. He was thinking of the tick Marion had found the summer before last in her pubic hair. They had been bush walking, and that night she had found it, and had lain on the bed while Gordon anaesthetised it and plucked it out. Now he could never hear darkness and fairness contrasted without seeing again, in the light of the halogen lamp drawn down to the bed, the black tick in the curling shining flaxen hair, its head already embedded in her white skin. Nor could he ever think of it without feelings of tenderness, lust, and romance. The prospect of an early start at the library tomorrow, his certain return home in the afternoon, made him tolerant of Vera's vehement wanderings about Sandra and the doggie, for both of whom he felt a humorous sympathy.

'Before that last time he came to see me, he would come every Friday. Alone, of course, without his *Sand*-ra. He would make the conversation. First he would want to speak of the old days, as he would call them. But I do not speak of the old days to doggies. And then there is the weather. Or the news. He would make the long face. "The news is bad, Mutti." And I would say, "If it is Australian news, do not tell me. Here is no news." My husband used to get the European papers, you understand. And when they would come, he would put away your *Heralds* and *Telegraphs*, and he would say, "Now we will have some real news."'

Gordon wondered how often she must have been asked why, since she hated Australia so bitterly, she didn't go back where she came from. So many times, he guessed, and with such hostility, that she now scornfully invited the question. He said, 'Have you never been back?'

'We went back, but it is here my husband makes the money, so it is here we must stay. Then my husband dies,' she said, with one of her angry looks, 'and it is too late to go back.' With one gloved hand she stabbed the air. 'And of Vienna what is left anyway?'

'I have never been to Vienna.'

She said with calm contempt, 'Of course you have never been to Vienna, my dear. In your lifetime is no real Vienna left.'

He was about to reply that he knew people who said there was no real Sydney left, when a voice above them said, 'Well, Vera, you look happy enough today.'

A tightly stout and smiling woman stood beside the bench. She was perhaps not much younger than Vera. 'All the same, Vera,' she said gently, 'I wish you would come home with me.'

Gordon got to his feet and picked up his briefcase.

'This is my neighbour,' said Vera, beginning to kick up her leg again, to smile and to mock.

'Mildred Reed,' said the woman. 'Vera and I have lived next door in Charton Towers for ten years.'

'Gordon Harbage,' said Gordon.

'Well, Mr Harbage,' said Mildred Reed, 'I suppose it's no good asking if you have any influence with Vera, but I wish someone had. I wish someone could persuade her to see Arthur.'

'Arthur is the name of the little doggie,' said Vera complacently.

'I understand your concern, Mrs Reed,' said Gordon, 'but as for influence, I've none. We've simply met a few times here in the park.'

'He is the very image of that Englishman I was once talking you about.'

'Talking me? Vera, you're tired. And it's getting cold out here.'

'Yes, I will come,' said Vera calmly.

'I think we'll get a taxi.

'Wait,' said Vera. 'First I will give my new friend this. I will not see him again.' She opened her bag. 'I wish for him to take this little gift to his beautiful wife.'

The little parcel she offered was wrapped in a twist of red paper, tied with a crumpled red ribbon. 'It is one of my pill boxes.'

'Those pill boxes are solid silver,' said Mildred Reed with respect.

'Well, thank you,' said Gordon, taking the little parcel, trying to imagine Marion using a pill box.

He got the two women a taxi. He was surprised that Vera did not look at him after he had helped her into it. It was Mildred Reed who smiled and raised a hand, while Vera sat hunched, her face turned away, as if offended. He had, he supposed, omitted some ceremony natural to a great gentleman.

At the flat he rang Marion. 'Three hours is all I'll need tomorrow. I'll go straight from the library to the airport.'

'The two o'clock plane?'

'For sure. I'll be home before you. Has Joel got his glasses?'

'Yes. He keeps screwing up his face. He says he can't forget those things are on it.'

'Poor old boy.' Gordon suddenly clapped a hand to his pocket. 'I've got a present for you.'

'What?'

'No. Wait.'

'All right. A surprise.'

'It certainly surprised me.'

The next morning, when Gordon was getting ready to go to the library, he saw the little red parcel among his papers, and impulsively opened it. He knew by the worn embossing that the box was very old, and he smiled to see that, small as it was, room had been made for minute cherubs to loll about it here and there, linked by garlands. Marion would probably become fond of it, and keep it on the shelf with the sea shells, pieces of blue glass, and the Chinese figurine with the missing hand. He opened it and took out a piece of stiff paper which he thought may be a note, but from which fell into his hand the diamond and ruby earrings Vera had worn in the park on the second day.

He felt himself flush hot with anger. Now he must get them back to her; now he could miss the two o'clock plane. And now, above all, the precious steadiness of his investigation would be disrupted. He stamped about dressing, he cursed, scowled, chucked papers into his case. Then he abruptly checked himself. Like this, he was compounding the danger. Instead, he could congratulate himself on remembering the name of Vera's building. It would not take long to go there and return them – nothing, nothing, would induce him to argue or talk – and if he maintained his steadiness, kept his goal immovably in sight, neither his research nor his return to his family need suffer.

A taxi took him to Charton Towers in five minutes. The directory in the foyer showed M. Reed in 99, but both 98 and 100 were shown only as occupied.

Without more than a few seconds of grinding his teeth, he took the lift to the ninth floor. As he walked down the corridor he saw Mildred Reed coming out of a door. She saw him, and stood with the knob in her hand for a moment before shutting it. She waited until he was within close speaking range. 'Vera is dead,' she said then. 'I found her two hours ago.'

He breathed out an automatic 'Good heavens'. The door behind her was marked 98. When she moved towards her door, 99, he followed her, not wanting to, yet not knowing what else to do. 'Will you come in?' she said.

'For a few minutes.' As she opened the door he looked quickly at his watch.

They sat on opposite chairs in her hall. 'It could have happened any old time,' she said. 'It was just good luck it didn't happen in that park.'

'Her heart?'

'Yes. Hopeless. Hopeless. But when it came to the last, she wouldn't take advice. The moment they told her she would have to go to hospital, she went straight to the bank and got all her jewellery out, and every day after that she had to get dressed up and go wandering about talking to people in shops, and sitting in that park.' Mildred Reed grimaced, close to tears. 'I'm going to miss her. I'll tell you that.'

Though still uncertain what to do, Gordon had drawn his case on to his knees. He took out the pill box. 'There's this,' he said.

'It's valuable, do you mean? That's right. But Vera wanted your wife to have it. I heard her myself. But if it puts your mind at ease, ask Arthur.'

'Her son's here?'

'Of course. I got in touch with him at once.'

'Good. Splendid. Because there are these, too.'

He tipped the earrings into the palm of his hand. She plucked one of them out, held it dangling, and smiled while she shook her head.

'They're not genuine?' he asked.

'Oh, they're genuine. I was just thinking of the time Sandra had the cheek to try them on. Which, I might mention, was the absolute end.' She smiled again, dropped the earring back into his hand, closed the fingers of both her hands around his, and put her face near his like a plotting schoolgirl. 'That's what Vera was doing. Making damn sure Sandra wouldn't get them. If I were you, I wouldn't ask Arthur anything. He never stood up to her, that was his trouble. If I were you, I would do just as she wanted.'

Gordon disengaged his hand. 'No chance.'

'It was her last wish.

But now Gordon was standing, looking openly at his watch. 'I want to see Arthur, Mrs Reed.'

'Well, all right.' She sighed and laughed as she hoisted herself out of her chair. 'But I only wish you could see Sandra too.'

Vera's furnishings were as rich and weighty and tortuous as her clothes had been. They dominated the man who stood among them. Gordon found in him no resemblance to the little doggie projected by his mother. He was of medium height, slender, with grey among his fair hair, and a finely moulded and thoughtful face. In other circumstances, Gordon would have liked him on sight, but at present he knew what he had to hold on to; he knew what was threatened; he would not divert himself by taking one of his sudden likings. He noticed that the man had been crying; the flesh about his eyes was puffed, the eyeballs were inflamed. He did not offer his hand, but stood straight, his arms hanging.

'Of course you must keep them.' He spoke coldly, or perhaps only distractedly; Gordon could not tell. Gordon's explanation had been too much interrupted, too much vouched for, by Mildred Reed, and to his great irritation, he saw that she was now about to burst out again.

'Mrs Reed,' he said, 'please let me speak for myself.' He turned to the grieved man. 'The point is, I simply don't want these. I'll give the pill box to my wife. That's okay. I consented to that. But I won't keep these.'

'I understand,' said Vera's son. But he did not extend his hand to take the earrings, and Gordon was forced to lay them on the nearest surface, which was a small inlaid table. He did this gently and with great relief. 'I wouldn't have chosen to come now,' he said, 'only I leave Sydney early this afternoon. I'm sorry about your mother's sudden death.'

Tears filled the eyes of Vera's son, and he turned away. 'I am sorry about her whole life,' he said. He opened the door of an inner room. 'Goodbye. And thank you.'

In the corridor again with Mildred Reed, Gordon saw by his watch that he had lost less than half an hour. He had remained steady; the day was fine, and taxis would be easy to get. He said, 'I liked her son.'

'Arthur's all right.' She lowered her voice. 'She did have a cruel streak.'

'Still, I can quite see how you will miss her. She had such a strong presence. Was she an actress of some sort?'

Mildred Reed drew in a breath of half-pretended shock. 'Lucky you didn't ask her that. She was a countess. That's why she used to go about saying everyone was so terribly common.'

'I thought they didn't,' said Gordon.

'What, countesses? Titled people? Well, she's the only one I've ever known, and she did, no doubt about that. And no doubt about the title either. It was in her own right. I saw the documentation. I suppose there are lots of them in those countries. Her father was Hungarian. But still.'

'Well,' said Gordon. 'I see I've been badly educated.'

He was alone in the sealed lift on the way down. At the rim of his steadiness he knew there was some disturbance, some little clamour. He said aloud, 'May God rest her soul.' The words dying away left him surprised. She had made him bow, she had made him pray, and each time for the same purpose.

In the two o'clock plane, with the morning's solid work behind him, Gordon allowed himself to wonder what would have happened if he had agreed to keep the earrings. He imagined Marion, in front of the mirror, laughing as she held them up to her ears. He imagined one of the children – it would be Joel – saying with anxiety, 'But they're worth a lot of money.' He imagined Marion saying, 'Then we can sell them, and buy Tess her violin.' Beyond that, he would not allow himself to imagine. He knew he would never regret having refused them.

Fiona Farrell Poole

Footnote

1987

Kirmington. Page 63 in the *Motoring Atlas of Great Britain.* There is no store in Kirmington. No public telephone. Nowhere to buy a magazine or a drink. The church stands stolid in couch grass overlooking a raggle-taggle bunch of inter-war cottages, an early Victorian rectory and a light-electrical firm. The air is filled with the agitated humming of Euro-executives jetting in and out of the Hull International Airport down the road. Only the verges are beautiful, pink yellow-white, thick with Queen Anne's lace. She walked round the church twice before she found them. There were eight Quickfalls. Their stones were stacked one against the other in a corner by the rectory. Joseph, Elizabeth, Francis. Another Elizabeth. Brothers, sisters, cousins, aunts. But not Jane. Jane had gone away.

It's so little to leave behind. A scrawl, 'Jane Kendall' (born Quickfall), a photo. A faded fleshy woman in a dark dress. How could anyone live so long and make such a tiny mark on the earth? It's the scratching of a nomad. The imprint of a transient. Skilled trackers are needed to tell where such travellers have stood. Where they have eaten. Where they have lain down.

. . . all morning she'd been watching him from the creek where she knelt, scrubbing. Keeping up appearances, keeping down the bugs. They'd abandon ship temporarily, but give them a week and they'd be back. Peppering her linen, crawling and biting and hopping and breeding. She stood up amongst the ferns to straighten her back, feeling her knees cold against the heavy wetness of her woollen skirt. Looks up through leaves and branches to see him bending in full sunlight, cutting wood. He is a short man. Square. With thick red-brown hair. He lifts his arms. Brings them down and a piece of mahoe springs in

two, clean as new cheese. He bends, gathers one and chop chop chop it lies in neat straws to kindle the fire. Sweat runs down the crevice along his spine. Sunlight on his arms and shoulders. She kneels on the stone and draws the white linen towards her against the current . . .

How could anyone have endured it?

Here
lies interred the body of
THOMAS QUICKFALL
who died 24 January 1810
Aged 71 years

and underneath, the limestone peels leaving sudden patches:

blank some by blazon'd heralds shine
And backwards trace their ancient line;
blank heaps of blank and others raise
blank monuments of blanking praise;
Let others boast their pompous state,
of merit void, ignobly great:
One truth, o'er these remains below
Inscribed, more honour will bestow,
Than lineage, wealth or grandeur can.
Here lies interr'd an HONEST MAN.

She traces the words with her finger, kneeling on damp earth threaded with purple worms, snail slime and the white veins of bruised grass. The Quickfalls, square and grey, stand ready for the last trump under the hawthorn.

Tickling. Like a moth caught in cupped hands.

. . . she lay under the table looking up at rough wooden planks and thought, 'So this is it. This is adultery. The seventh commandment.' But no angel drew back the blanket over the door and stood with flaming torch directing her out into consuming darkness. There was no thunder. No lightning. The table stood solid over her head. She reached an arm up and ran her finger along the grooves left by her husband's adze. And with her other hand she traced the deep cleft down this other back (he was asleep), still damp and warm. Outside Kereu kereu, pigeons drunk on soft red puriri berries, the creek and sea

sighing, moaning, in and out, in and out. 'So this is adultery,' she thought and waited for dogs to howl and Jezebel to be torn to pieces . . .

They had been driving for two hours. Rain poured against the car, sealing them into a small grey world. Vivaldi on the radio, buzzing advancing and retreating. Jeff liked long drives, liked pointing the car north and driving through. 'It'll be a long day,' he'd say apologetically, knowing she hated this rush, wanted to potter up side roads, inspect cathedrals, or stop for picnics. He always promised a slower pace next time. But when next time came round, there they'd be, driving at 70 over hundreds of miles of motorway. She'd sit and read the Guide as they passed the road signs: 'Rievaulx,' she'd say. 'A monastic ruin in a secluded valley.' Or 'Lincoln: cathedral city, noted for its Roman gateway . . . the oldest house in England . . .' But he'd have a meeting to get back to, or an appointment which couldn't be made for any other time. They'd leave with just the time necessary to make the journey direct and arrive, tired. Tired of each other and sitting in the same place, tired of motorway meals because there was never time to look for somewhere better. (And it was cheaper too, she thought. Another characteristic she was coming to hate: his stinginess. As he got older he earned more and spent less. Wore the same clothes year in, year out, bought books he never read from bargain bins. Saving for what?) But enough. They were caught in the car together, two more hours to go. It wouldn't do to start worrying at grievances as one prods at a throbbing tooth. Vivaldi pranced nearer dum *de* dumdum, dum *de* dumdum and the rain swept down.

. . . she had a baby to him of course. Lay on a bed and brought forth her 'spurious brood'. The sheets were covered with blood. The baby lay on a piece of cloth, legs waving frantically like an insect's. 'Hold me, hold me.'

Who helped her? Did one of her country-women buttoned against contamination venture into that house heavy with the smell of blood and sin, to boil linen? Tightlipped by the fire bathing her beautiful boy? Did they give her brandy to restore her strength? Was her husband somewhere near, or off bobbing about half-seas over babbling guilt and guns on some trader? Impossible to know. No letters, no diary. Just a scribble on sand . . .

Kirmington was her idea, of course. They'd left London at one (Jeff had an appointment at LSE and no, it couldn't possibly be made for any other time). 'We'll just make it,' he said as he accelerated onto the motorway, pleased at the urgency of it all. But there were roadworks near Stevenage, and on the A15 past Peterborough. They crept in single file behind lorries, Jeff cursing monotonously and repetitively. She saw the sign-post by accident when they were nearing Hull. There was another diversion. A truck jack-knifed on the motorway, a collision, a petrol tanker perhaps? She could see a dense column of smoke rising to the west as they snaked off through the countryside following the scarlet arrows along smaller roads. The car moved slowly in heavy traffic, Wrawby, Barnetby-le-Wold, past fields, pubs, houses with peas on crossed sticks. Jeff muttered. They'd be late he'd arranged to meet Gordon at five they were all going to have a drink together and now look at it they'd be hours late Jesus Christ get a move on did you see that? just cut in . . . Then there was Kirmington 9 miles. She'd insisted. 'We're late anyway,' she reasoned. 'You can ring and tell Gordon not to expect us. Ring from Kirmington.' Besides, it would be useful background for her book. Jeff gave in. So they came to the village, the raggle-taggle cottages and the church and its heap of Quickfall dead in the late afternoon, and the rain cleared and the clouds rolled back and she walked round the church with its plain tower and its plain windows, her jeans wet to the knees in the long grass. And found the Quickfalls stacked for heaven like the Sunday bread. Jeff couldn't even find a telephone. A desert place. Surely Paternoster Valley couldn't have been worse than this?

Tickle. Tickle. Twitching under her navel.

. . . rum is the answer. At night, in the dark, clinking of cup on bottle as the children slept, wrapped in rows in blankets. She sits on the bed drinking slowly. Fire in the grate, banked up for the morning, blanket round her shoulders. Fumble, pour, drink. Fumble, pour, drink. At

least she always uses a cup, hasn't yet descended to drinking straight from the bottle. One of the children cries out, flings an arm out of his blanket warding off some other smaller devil. Husband away for months, the community prying. God looking into her very heart, and if not God then one of God's delegates, alert to the slightest falter, eyes bright behind their prayer books at morning service. And no words. No letters. No diary. Who can she talk to who can guess at Kirmington and despair and the exact nature of temptation? She's the woman with no head in the joke; the silent woman. Fumble, pour, drink . . .

Back on the motorway and her turn to drive . . . Rain again, and the wipers move back and forth. Jeff seems to doze but when she brakes suddenly his foot jams against the floor, driving with her. They don't talk. Strange that. Once they drove to Auckland from Dunedin in his old VW and talked all the way. That first time. They camped near Kaikoura. His wife had packed him a picnic dinner. They ate Shirley's chicken, drank Shirley's coffee, then tumbled into the tent and she made love to Shirley's husband while a sudden gale nipped at their bare bodies and threatened to lift them and the tent clear away. By the time they reached Auckland Jeff had said, 'I'll leave her,' and he did. As he did anything he'd decided on. It was what drew her to him at first, his decisiveness. She would spend hours, gnawing her pen, looking out the window at the harbour, trying to decide which essay to write for his economic history course. 'Which dress will I choose?' she'd ask him, buy one, and instantly regret it. Not Jeff. He wanted her. He didn't want Shirley. So it was clear. He left his home, left his children who were teenagers anyway and old enough to cope (almost as old as herself she remembered, as she changed gear and they climbed towards the Humber Bridge). To begin with she loved his sureness. The way he drove from A to B. The way he stood in the mornings, still wet from the shower simply putting on his clothes; no dither, no agonising over this shirt with these trousers. He was strong, loved her with vigour and pleasure. He cooked when it was his turn without consulting a recipe book, adding spices, herbs, a glass of wine, tasting. Always certain.

. . . 'And they called Rebekah and said unto her, Wilt thou go with this man? And she said I will go.' But how was it really for Rebekah among the Canaanites? And Ruth? 'Whither thou goest I will go and where thou lodgest I will lodge.' Ruth the Moabitess? What was she thinking of, there amongst the alien corn?

They'd discussed babies of course, back then on the way home from the Auckland conference. 'No,' he'd said. He didn't think he'd want any more. He'd had four, was too old. And she wanted a job, didn't she? Babies and jobs didn't mix easily. Shirley could tell her that. (Poor half-a-BA-Shirley. Poor-part-time-librarian-Shirley . . .) 'OK,' she'd said, that young girl driving down the Desert Road through tussock and skylarks, one hand warm between Jeff's thighs, her hair whipping in the cool wind off Tongariro. She loved him. He loved her. She'd given a good paper. She was a Young Professional Woman, on her way, intent on a Career, and that was that. Soon after they began living together, Jeff went out one Saturday morning and had a vasectomy.

. . . when confronted with her sin she'd confessed of course. Anyone who could count to nine could tell anyway. Husband gone 11 months, belly swelling under her black dress. (The delicious tickling of hands and feet in her belly . . .) She was pregnant, no denying it. And pregnant to the hired man, an exconvict. Two of the women come to her house one morning, stand in the doorway: 'You are a shame to us all how can we preach the Christian faith when one of our number openly flouts all the values we profess? a fornicatress an adulteress.' They spit chapter and verse at her. She holds onto the table for support. And when she has had enough she picks up a wooden beater and they step back. Two dark shadows. Two angels flying from her sunlit door. 'We shall pray for you' their final threat . . .

Across the Humber, river oily and the wet road. Tomorrow she'd visit York, gather more pieces for the puzzle, her book on missionary wives in the South Pacific. She'd unpack her neat white file cards, add a fact here, a name there. Kirmington. Those gravestones might be useful. They were stone. They were certain. They gave dates and places. No eminent grey-beard would be able to lift himself from his rock at some conference and woof, as one had woofed already, 'Yes, but is it history?' Jeff takes out the conference folder and fumbles for his glasses. 'He's old,' she thinks suddenly, watching him from the corner of one eye as they wait at the toll booth. 'His hands have grown old.' Stiff-fingered, he fights with the glovebox catch. She puts out her hand and rests it on his thigh. He pats her, spreads the conference map and peers at names and numbers. It's getting dark. Soon too dark to see.

She loved him she supposed. Simple, 'Jane loves Tom', something carved on a tree with an arrow through. She lived with him for years, had his children, watched one of them die. 'I will go,' she'd said. And meant it. 'Till death us do part,' she'd said. And meant it. But there are difficulties. You find yourself alone, pitching about on a place they said was a fish, where charts and rules run slap against despair. In a harsh new light where old certainties fade. Or you find yourself wanting a baby so much you can't bear it any longer. You have a Mature and Loving Relationship. Your work is going well. You even have a Reputation. You receive grants to do research abroad. Students leave notes in your box at the end of the year, 'A stimulating year. Thank you.' And you're 37 and one day your period, always so reliable, never any bother, doesn't come on time. It's early. You're at the beach for the weekend to get some writing done away from the telephone, and you're not prepared. Two days of making do with torn dusters (no shops for miles), and it stops again. Nothing to worry about, though. Your body, it seems, is preparing for The Change. This is it. So what do you do? If you are Liz you raise the matter with Jeff (one must be honest with one's partner) and he says (because she cries), 'If you want it so much, I'll see about having the vasectomy reversed.' And finds it might be possible. But the night before he is to go to the hospital he wakes you. Lies there in the early morning half-light, sea breathing, one bird calling. 'No. I can't go through with it.' He won't explain. But when she turns over to look at him, he is shaking. And since this is an adult relationship (no one has any rights over another's body) she can't press. She walks alone on the beach and cries of course. But it is his body the doctors must cut and snip and rearrange. So there you are. Then, if you are Liz, you go to a party three weeks before you go to Britain on study leave. Jeff is away tramping with his younger son. You talk to a German *lektor* out for the year. You offer him a lift home. He is an efficient and pleasant lover, and thanks you for the coffee in the morning. ('The only good coffee I have had since I am in New Zealand.') And you throw up in the Ladies Room at LA airport. You eat nothing but Indian food for the first three months in London.

The car is approaching Hull. Jane sits in her whare playing with her baby. The boys are swimming in the creek, their brown naked bodies whiplash from the tree and splash. 'He who would valiant be,' hums Liz to keep their courage up and switches on the headlights. The tickling starts again, a moth in her belly and unmistakeable. In Hull they'll talk, they'll sort it out in their rational adult fashion. But in the meantime, she asks Jeff for a peppermint.

Carmel Bird

Buff Orpington and the Disasters of Middle Life

1987

Carrillo Mean, Californian guru, did not write his definitive work, *Buff Orpington and the Disasters of Middle Life*, until well after Stanford Fox, Melbourne barrister, had suffered some of those disasters.

THE PEOPLE

Stan Fox – a barrister
Maureen – his wife
Melanie – his girl-friend
Tony – his partner
Margaret – Tony's second wife
Barbara – Tony's first wife

THE STORY

At one time, it was fashionable, in Melbourne, to have spent the years of childhood in a working-class inner suburb where everyone had a chook house down the yard.

Chook house nostalgia gripped the hearts, the hearts of all the barristers and of all the wives of all the barristers in Carlton. Long and narrow channels of their brains were furnished with rusting sheets of corrugated iron, lacy panels of chicken wire, pollard and bran, and shell grit. White Leghorns and Rhode Island Reds tark-tark-tarked through their dreams. They began to collect large paintings by artists about to be famous. Poultry appeared in these paintings. Men who could be seen by day wearing jolly little wigs and crossing William Street, their black gowns flapping, sometimes catching at the knee, by night lay beneath Danish quilts on Japanese beds beside Indian rugs, gazing up at a few hints of stars through new curved skylights, thinking, every now and again, about the straw in the nests. There was the colour and shine and smell of the straw, and the gleaming hint of the china egg which they had hidden there to encourage the hens to lay.

The wives of these dreamers also gazed up through the skylights in the renovated terrace house, as proud visions of the White Leghorn rooster, his long tail-feathers curving, his comb standing up like play-dough, strutted across the skylights of their minds. Mistresses, generally speaking, were spared these farm-yard scenes, for they were as a rule too young for chook house nostalgia. In fact, they were inclined to have been born in wealthy suburbs in times when Rhode Island Reds no longer tark-tarked at the bottoms of gardens, but lived, still and quiet with hundreds of their sisters, their beaks and legs useless, laying eggs for rich farmers. Those who had studied biology at the most expensive schools had, of course, been given an egg to hatch and a chicken to carry round under their pullovers, but there was no connection whatsoever with the farm-yard.

So by now you are beginning to imagine the kind of life led by Maureen (known, by the way, as Buffy) and Stanford Fox.

They were about forty, and were building up a collection (amongst all their other collections of wines and paintings and Limoges china) of books about the crisis of the middle years of mankind. No book in their collection made any reference to the important part which

> the chook house of childhood plays
> in the crises of the middle lives
> of Carlton barristers and their wives.

Stan lay on his futon, underneath his doona, next to his dhurrie, thinking of money, and of Melanie, and of what it was like when he was four. All he had wanted for his birthday when he was four was a little black hen. He had got that hen, and her feathers glittered in the sun which shone all day every day when he was four. There he was in his tartan shirt and his khaki overalls.

In the books – *You and the Mid-life Adventure, Professional Man at the Crossroads, Births, Deaths, and The Ageing Process* – eminent psychologists explained that at any time after the age of thirty-five, Stan would probably grow 'dis-enchanted' with the Law. Had he ever been enchanted, he wondered. The books went on to tell him that he would be seduced by any one of about four fantasies:

There would be the sailing-around-the-world fantasy, or the becoming-a-creative-artist fantasy, or the running-away-with-the-girl-from-the-milk-bar fantasy. Or the back-to-the-earth. The title of this last one worried Stan. He was about to be forty-one, and he was staring at the skylight and working on the back-to-the-chook-house fantasy which was not described in the books. It escaped Stan's notice that back-to-the-chook-house was but a variation of back-to-the-earth. And that being in love with Melanie was the running-away-with-the-girl.

Carrillo Mean wrote of the function of nostalgia for childhood and the obsession with nursery foods. He dealt briefly with the phenomenon of back-to-the-school-room as a misdirection sometimes taken by men in middle life when they seek, as Mean put it, 'the authority of the dominant schoolmistress figure'. As noted earlier, it was going to be years before Mean would write *Buff Orpington and the Disasters of Middle Life* – a name adopted, incidentally, by a group of feathered singers. In fact, Mean would cite the case of Stanford Fox Q.C. in a detailed footnote to the third chapter.

Stan lay in bed planning to find a little place in the hills. There was a tall pine tree at the front, rather like an illustration in *The House at Pooh Corner*. Water babbled over nearby rocks.

Look, look, there are clumps of bluebells, and carpets of wild freesias in the spring. Rabbits peer from behind the stumps of trees. On green wicker chairs beneath an apple tree, sit Stan and Melanie. Oh, Melanie is wearing a sort of transparent nightgown which might have appeared in a film in the forties. Her hair, a mixture of corn silk and soft ripples of amber with flashes of topaz, is long and ruffled. Her feet are bare in the dewy grass. They are drinking russian caravan tea from dainty cups with violets painted on them. The cups belonged to Stan's grandmother. The teapot is blue and fat. It has a little chip in the spout, just where Stan's mother's teapot, also blue, had a chip. As Melanie gestures to emphasise a point, the Milk Arrowroot biscuit between her fingers is snatched away by one of the hens which fidget around her feet.

Buffy lay in bed and thought about the fountain which she planned to put in the courtyard in the middle of the house. She stared up through the skylight and thought about the Italian fountain, and about money, and the children, Bib and Bub, and about Tony.

Every Monday, in reality, Buffy met Tony at the beach house. She had been doing this for five years and had seen Tony through his divorce from Barbara and his marriage to Margaret. If, as sometimes happened, Tony was unable to get to the beach house, she went there by herself. She would make avocado dip, and lie on the old sofa reading Doris Lessing and listening to the sea. And still after all this time, she had visions of Tony. She lay in bed in Carlton and Tony would float across the fashionable skylight. His outline would, it is true, occasionally recede as sharper apparitions of the two Italian boys from the bike shop pedalled into view. Buffy would imagine herself feeding imported chocolates into their open red mouths. She would buy the chocolates in little gold mesh bags from the coffee shop just down the street, and, dangling the bags from her fingers, she would stroll into the bike shop to buy a taillight for Bub's bike. And there they would be the boys, wiping the grease from their fingers with a grubby cloth.

As she lay in bed, Buffy decided that she would ring the plumber tomorrow. She would have the fountain in the central courtyard, the babble of its water echoing the sound of the stream on the country property blooming in Stan's head.

For Stan's birthday, they had a dinner party. Tony and Margaret were there. And so was Barbara, Tony's ex-wife who was married to the orthopaedic surgeon who had put her bones together again after Tony had pushed her down the stairs.

'When I was four, I got a little black hen for my birthday. It was all I wanted. And I really loved it. I called it Natalie. I was madly in love with a girl called Natalie.'

'We had about a dozen Buff Orpingtons at one time. When we lived in Northcote next-door to the Italians that were supposed to have shot the man in the TAB. God, they were pretty little things. The chooks I mean. Like corn silk with ripples of amber and flashes of topaz. In the sun.'

'I was famous for my chook imitations. Tark-tark-tark-tark.'

'But that's wrong. It's puck-puck-puck-puck.'

'It is not. They go cluck. I know it sounds like something out of a school reader, but they really do go cluck. I know. We had about twenty fowls, and ducks as well, and the hens definitely said cluck and the ducks, believe it or not, said quack.'

'French ducks say coin-coin. I've heard them. When we were in Brittany last year, Madame Thing kept the most fabulous ducks in the sort of basement part of the house. And they all said coin-coin. All the time. You could smell them in our bedroom, whatsmore. It was just above them you see.'

'But really, don't chooks say a sort of mixture of tark and quick?'

'What sort of chooks did you have, that said that?'

'Well, Australorps. You know, little black hens. Tark-quick, they said. Always.'

'Oh, Australorps.'

'My sister took a photo of me with the little black hen, and she won a fountain pen in a photographic competition.'

'Have you got the photo?'

'No. When I was about sixteen, I think I tore it up.'

'Oh, what a pity. We could get a little Australorp though, and we could take some more pictures of you. And it. We might all win fountain pens.'

'Buffy does a really good imitation of a rooster. Go on Buff.'

'Cock-a-doodle-doo.'

It was then that the discussion moved on to talk of the bouquets of the wines, and the effect on the middle palate. We may record that the Mouton Rothschild was really quite delicious, and everybody became rather drunk.

It was on a sunny day in spring that Buffy took Bib and Bub onto the bike path by the river. The children had yellow helmets with scarlet straps. Flags on tall stalks fluttered behind them as they rode. They looked rather like little soldiers in some modern and yet medieval war. The boys from the bike shop whizzed past on a bright red tandem, almost knocking Buffy from her bike. They waved, and kept going, shouting something cheerful in Italian.

On this same sunny day in spring, Stan and his sweet Melanie were inspecting a small property in the hills behind the city. A dusty pine tree grew by the front gate. There were bluebells in clumps by the tap at the back door. Water trickled over the pebbles of the stream which marked the northern boundary. And an asthmatic sheep-dog dozed in the dust.

That night, at Melanie's house, Stan had a heart attack. The books had warned of this.

They had been sipping Chateau Neuf du Pape, and leafing through a poultry catalogue.

'Let's have one of everything,' said Melanie, her hair a ripple of corn silk, flash of amber, dash of topaz.

Buff Orpingtons, Rhode Island Reds, Australorps, White Leghorns pecked cheerfully at grain in the pictures in the catalogues.

'*The birds must be induced to take sufficient exercise in the house.* That would be their own house, wouldn't it?'

Stan drained his glass, smiled at Melanie, embraced her, caught his breath, and fell onto the peach velvet settee.

It was while Stan was in Intensive Care that Italian workmen came to install the fountain in Buffy's courtyard. Water gushed from it in a shiny cone which overflowed like a melting ice-cream. In the sunlight, droplets of water winked like stars.

'Stan will find it soothing, won't he, watching the water and listening to it. When he comes home.'

Buffy was talking to Tony on the telephone.

'You've done a great job, Buff. Hold the phone up to the water again for a minute. It sounds great. Just great.'

'Come round later,' said Buffy, 'I've just put the Veuve Cliquot on the ice. And you must see what I've bought for Stan. It's the sweetest little statue, just like Natalie, the hen he loved so much when he was four.'

Barbara Hanrahan

Lily

1987

Poor old Mum used to work like a man because Dad was away. You had to have a lot to feed ten children on. But you wouldn't have got Mum into trousers – she was too ladylike. I was born up the country and Dad was a rabbit inspector, working for the Government on vermin destruction out on the farms. He was away weeks on end.

My sisters and I used to walk two miles to church of a Sunday night. When we walked into church, we thought we were great. There was Madge, then me – Lily, then Hilda and Francie – they were twins – and then Ev; and my brothers were Ron, Henry, Norm, Wal, and then Vic was the last one. There's six years between Mum's last two. She thought she wasn't going to have any more and then she had Vic.

Mum had a big garden and we grew tomatoes. She had to plough the land and make the rows for the tomatoes to grow in. My sisters and I had to do the housework, but we never did the washing; we could do the ironing but not the washing (she was a very fussy person, my mum). Madge and I, or Hilda and Francie, did the cooking. Us girls wore white starched aprons. At night we played cards and if somebody called in we'd have a sing-song. Madge could sing nice.

I was only young them days. I was only seventeen when I met him. Stan came up the country to give his sister away: she married my brother. Stan stopped at our place while he was over for the weekend when Ron and Harriet got married. Then, when Stan was going he kissed me and I thought, Well, that was funny.

I got a surprise when he sent me a letter – I hadn't thought of him after he left. I had other boyfriends at the time. Mum let me go on writing to them for a while, then when Stan wanted to come over to stay with us again she said I had to give them up. Mum said to me, 'After Stan's been over and you see him, you've got to make up your mind whether you're going to have the other boys or him.' He had dark eyes and dark curly hair (I had ginger hair). He was very nice but I didn't like him to begin with.

I had a glory box, Mum saw to that. We had to start when we were fourteen. We were always working with our hands, crocheting things. And I had towels and sheets. I always thought I'd be getting married. But I had two aunties who were old maids, Aunty Nance and Aunty Jean.

Sometimes you'll go down the beach and the sand's all out – the water's taken it out; then the sea'll come rough again and bring all that sand back. We've had some terrible storms here and yet the houses still stand up. When the sea's rough and making a hang of a noise in the night I lie awake listening, I love it. I first saw the sea when I came over here for a holiday before I was married. I just stood there, down towards the sea, and I couldn't believe it, though Stan had sent me some photos. We courted two years. I had an embossed satiny dress and two bridesmaids – one pale pink and one pale blue and I had white roses; it's a long time ago.

I lie in bed and things come to me. We had a lot of relations up the country and one'll just pop into my mind that I haven't thought of for so long. I often think, I wonder if she's gone or not. Aunty Beatrice, Aunty Grace, Aunty Nance, Aunty Jean. Aunty Grace had eight children and then she got ulcerated legs. I'll never forget her legs. She always had to have her legs bandaged up, she nearly went mad with the pain. Mum was old when she died; she was well in her eighties and she'd worked like a man out in the garden. She'd ploughed her land with a horse and plough.

My husband died years ago. I don't remember when; I forget a lot of things. It must be twenty years ago or more. I couldn't put anyone in his place. Never. No. We were very close. We had our family and we were happy with them all. I can't remember how old he was when he died, I can't think sometimes. He had cancer very bad in the throat. He was a heavy smoker in his early days. Nobody could catch it so they sent him home from the hospital. He was pretty good right up to the last, really.

Meals on Wheels comes and I like stewed steak and gravy but I can't eat greens: beans or peas or cabbage give me pains in the stomach. Doctor Whelan was growling at me for days and months to get Meals on Wheels. I said to him, I feel so lazy getting Meals on Wheels when I'm on my feet. He worries about me.

I'd like to go up the country to see my people, but Doctor won't let me go. I have tablets all the time. From what he's saying now, I think he knew I had it a fair while back. He comes to me any time, but all he can give me is pain relievers and sleepers (but I still hear the dog across the road). So I've just got to live as long as I can, that's all. The pain's worse now. I've had a lot of operations – seven: appendix and hernia and I've had my innards taken out, the womb and everything. I had my six children first, thank goodness. One little boy died but I've got the others. But it's just that I haven't spoken to my children about it, I haven't told any of them. I don't want them going round thinking, How long's Mum got to live? I keep it to myself as much as I can. I don't know whether to tell them or not. Those close to you worry, so I'm not saying anything, but I might tell my eldest daughter when she's down, because she's very worried about me. It's getting worse and worse. I've been having spots taken off my face for years and I thought if it's been on my face it could be inside – in my stomach where this big lump is. You can feel it, it's all puffed up. This morning it wasn't very good, it gives me a lot of pain. And it's been paining more lately than before, but the pills help.

My youngest brother writes to me, he never forgets. Some families split up and that's the end of them – we're all very friendly but I'm a lousy letter writer. When you're not well, you don't like sitting down writing about your troubles. I've got an older sister but she had thirteen children and she's in the hospital; she's been in there for months. She doesn't know anybody and they sit there and talk to her; they think it might sink in, but it doesn't.

I went out in the garden the other day to see if the Easter lilies were coming through the ground, because I knew I had some out there, but I couldn't see any and then I did see one or two, so I gave them a good water, and this morning I went out to water the garden and I've got ever so many up. And some of them's up that high and yet a few days ago I couldn't see anything. So I picked two and put them in a vase on the TV, but they've got to go outside now, they've had it. And the yellow rose is out – I'm going to get my son to come down and prune it when it's time – and I've never had the oleanders grow like that, I've never had them high like that before and a woman asked me the other day what kind they were but I couldn't tell her. I brought them down with me from the country a long long time ago. I don't know what in the world struck them to come up like that. And I've got a white geranium and a pink rose; I've got plenty of things. I want to get a film for my camera and take a photo of the garden before it all flops down. I didn't think the oleanders'd grow so tall. The sea air's on them, but they've grown lovely.

I say my prayers every night. Mum'd go mad if she thought we didn't kneel down by our bed and say our prayers. I don't kneel down now, I can't get up – the old knees are too bumpy. All the things you can get wrong with you. I've had everything under the sun. Oh well, I've lived my life, haven't I? Doctor Whelan won't let me die. He said I put him in mind of his mother.

Thea Astley
Right off the Map
1987

'It's everywhere,' Harry said – chanted really. He chucked his stained work hat down on the kitchen table and a swarm of flies rose.

Harry stank of cane and sweat and a sicklier, subtler, aromatic failure.

All month and the month before that the men on the road had been going through looking for work. Their humility was stunning, corrosive. They would do anything, anything, for a few bob. He'd had to turn all of them down. After the first dozen or so, he got tired of explaining that the crop had failed that year with unseasonal rain. He got tired of telling them he was nearly through himself. He couldn't bring out the words to describe the week there'd been nothing to eat but pumpkin. Couldn't. He simply couldn't cry poor mouth when he had a roof over his head.

The men stood hopelessly before him, their eyes with that dead look peculiar to long hungers, their clothes baggy around the skinny bodies.

He simply waved his arms in an emptying gesture that took in the flattened soggy fields.

There was always a sandwich up at the house, he said. And a cuppa.

Most accepted. Some didn't. Those who followed him to the kitchen nibbled at Clytie's 'doorsteps' as if the sight of food made them shy. 'Thanks, missus,' they mumbled, looking past her, because this beggary had reduced them below humanity. One of them had even wept.

The last one had been more insistent, a lash-thin man of forty or so, though at first Harry had thought him older, with blank puddle eyes. His swag was the thinnest Harry had ever seen, the blanket so worn, so lacking in essential fluff, the threads that composed it had the clarity of hopsack fibres. A skillet and billy and mug were tied to the outside rope and a little canvas pouch for sugar and tea.

Not that he was insistent verbally. He had merely stood there in his amazing thinness, his eyes without emotion as they looked back at Harry without seeming to absorb his refusals. He might have had no shadow and there was only the sickening heat of later afternoon walloping the landscape.

This one wouldn't get much farther, Harry decided, apart from the fact that the track up the coast petered out to a horse trail beyond the next farm. There was nothing there. Nothing. And 'There's nothing there,' Harry said again, dragging a forearm across his own sweaty essence. 'Sorry, mate.'

He began to turn away but the man went on standing as if Harry hadn't moved, standing in an abstract of himself, refusing the clichés of knock-back, his own substance left in some southern squalor when the jobs gave out, the susso law keeping him on walking and walking until he might tramp light-headedly and empty-bellied off the tip of the Cape. Months of hunger had driven him to the stage where he did not take his body very seriously at all.

So the man stood watching Harry Laffey turn away, and the small girl who had been hanging about could see her uncle didn't want to do this, that he felt uncomfortable, and she kept staring from one to the other, twisting her yellow hair about one finger; and when her uncle turned round and said sharply, *Come on, Connie. Come on*! she looked right into the man, who didn't seem to notice at all, and then Uncle Harry came back along the fence, the sun exploding in his face, and he took her hand and said to the man, 'You'd better come on up, too. No sense getting sunstroke.'

Clytie was putting out the tea things on the kitchen table just as usual, but when she took a look at the man wavering in the doorway, she went back to the safe and hauled out the last of the corned beef and began cutting slabs.

The man's eyes at last acknowledged surfaces, the shine on crockery, on kettle and pot, the light slicing along the bread knife, and his lips moved, struggled with thanks that couldn't come out loud enough for anyone to hear. He sat upright at the table as if plenitude frightened him.

But he couldn't eat much.

His mouth laboured with the bread and meat and he tried a smile of apology. Crumbs dropped from his lips and fell unnoticed on his lap. *He was beyond it*, Uncle Harry said later in the kids' room, *poor bugger. The poor devil needs a hospital.* And Aunt Clytie whispered quickly, *If you send this one off, Harry, I'll never forgive.* And then she shut her lips tight.

He managed the tea. He drank three big mugs of it and finally got half a sandwich down and when Harry said, forgetting, that he could take the rest of the food with him if he liked, Clytie slammed a plate on the sink top and said she didn't like to interrupt but he could doss down in one of the sheds where they kept a shakedown for casuals. The man told him his name then and young Will, who hadn't said a word all through the meal, grinned at this and said, 'That's my name too.'

'Hullo, mate,' the man said. He heaved himself up and thanked them, pulling his face into what was meant for a smile, picked up his swag and walked slowly across the paddock to the shed.

Harry watched him go, stared after him through the kitchen window while the sound of plates being washed and put away went on behind him, the back of his mind taking in the comforting permanence of soap and hot water and Clytie's voice weaving in and out the voices of the kids. Later that evening he took a lamp across to the shed to see if the tramp wanted anything and found him lying stiff and silent on his blanket, unfocused eyes gazing out at the fireflies.

'Nothing,' the man said. 'Thanks.'

'Where are you from?' Harry asked. 'You got a family some place?'

What little energy the man had seemed to expel itself in a sigh. He turned his starved face towards Harry's and the lamplight picked out cheekbones and nose above the straggly beard and pocketed the eyes.

'I've been walking since Adelaide,' the man said. His voice was soft and listless.

'God Almighty!' Harry cried. 'That's a helluva way, mate. How long have you been on the track?'

'Two years,' the man said. 'Two whole years. It was all right for a while. In the fruit country. It was all right there.'

'What about your family?'

The man was silent. His bony fingers picked at the edge of the blanket with a rasp of torn nail and fabric that set Harry's mind on edge.

'I don't know,' the man said at last. 'There was a wife and two kids. I tried. I tried a long time. Then I got tired of trying.' There was another small sigh. 'Real tired right through the bones of me. So she took the kids and went back to her people's farm. God knows how they were coping. So I just hit the road.'

'I'm sorry, mate,' Harry said. 'There's been dozens like you through here this past year but they always turn back. There's nothing up at Charco. It's the end of the line here. Well, just about.'

'I won't be turning back,' the man said. He kept seeing the long hot stretch of the Hop Wah road and the Chinese gardens along the creek.

He had tried every cane farm on the way in, the dairies, the slaughter-yards, and at the end of the day a man he met on the waterfront took him back to the showground where the unemployed were camped. He hung around there for a couple of days, long enough to be driven out by police. He kept seeing the horses, hearing the shouts, feeling the crack of pick-handles and rakes turned into weapons. The man who'd helped him kept cursing through broken teeth and blood, spluttering his hate as they stumbled off in the darkness. His own face was torn open along the cheekbone but the pain became distant as he staggered away, his unrolled swag shedding most of the last few things he owned. There'd been nights on the beaches north of town and then he rode a goods train up the tablelands to Molly and started walking again. Somewhere down the Bump road a farmer's wife gave him tea and bread. But no work.

There was never any work.

He ran one finger across the scar on his cheek. It was puckered and red like bad stitching.

'Memento of the north,' he said to Harry. 'Something to take with me.'

'How did you get that?' Harry shifted the lamp so that the light flooded the gaunt face beneath him. The man's eyes winced from the glare and he flung an arm across them.

'The law,' he said. 'The law and some earnest townsfolk. They don't like beggars up this way. They don't like them much anywhere, come to that.'

Harry set the lamp down. 'I heard about it. Where were you? Squatting out at the showgrounds?'

'Squatting!' the man replied bitterly. 'I thought this country was founded on squatting. It's all right if you squat on a bit of land big enough. They respect you then. All we had in Reef-town was tent space. A few lousy feet of tent space, less than I had on Gallipoli, somewhere to doss, and they begrudged us that.'

'Gallipoli!' Harry said. 'You were there too?'

The man nodded. 'That's how the wife and I got the farm. Soldier settlement from a grateful government. It wouldn't grow a bean. Squat!' the man said. 'They treated us like blacks in Reeftown.'

'It's the same everywhere,' Harry said. 'People are scared.'

'Scared!' the man scoffed. 'I could tell them about scared.' He shoved out both hands and the knobs on his wrists stood out so sharp they hurt. 'Most of us were too weak to run. It was a massacre.'

Harry nudged the lamp and the movement swung an oily glow on the nothing outside the shed.

'Look,' he said, 'it's no use going on. Charco's a closed shop. They've been coming down from there too. It's worse than here. You'd be wasting a lot of footwork. You can stay on a couple of days, rest up a bit. I can't pay you anything, mind, but we're right for tucker at the moment. What do you say, eh?'

The man closed his eyes against this effusion. Outside the thud of night animals tracked spoor across his despair.

His eyes were still closed when Connie and Will crept over to inspect him before breakfast. The sound of their whispering woke him.

His eyes had lost their muddy look, although they were still prowling feverishly the perimeter of moonscapes.

'There's eggs,' the small boy said, 'for breakfast.'

'Is there?' the man said.

'And bacon,' the girl said. 'You have to have bacon with eggs.'

'Christ,' the man said. 'Bacon and eggs. Oh Christ!'

'You're crying,' Connie accused.

'I could be,' the man said, 'if I had any juice left.'

He talked to them over the meal, telling them stories of life on the track. He ate slowly and carefully between words and was still mopping up yolk long after the others had finished. 'Can't tell you, missus,' he said to Clytie, 'I just can't tell you what that means.'

'You don't have to.'

Clytie's mouth had gone all funny, Connie noticed. And then the man did something she had never seen a man do before. He got up and stacked the dishes and filled the washing-up dish with hot water from the stove and beat the water into a lather with the old wire soap-saver and started washing the plates.

Clytie sprang up as if she were outraged by trespass and then she began to laugh.

'All right,' she conceded, 'you can do it and thank you. It'll be the first time in twenty years I've had a man help me.'

He stayed the rest of the week after that, working in the vegetable patch, splitting kindling for the stove and giving Harry a hand with the clearing of a back paddock. Every afternoon after the children rode back from school, he spent a while yarning with them and he showed the small boy how to build a gunyah out of saplings. It was finished by the end of the week and on the next morning after he had dried the dishes for Clytie and burnt off the rubbish, he said he'd best be going.

'I don't know how to say thanks,' he said, standing there, his roll hitched over his shoulder, his old felt hat crammed down on his head.

'I'm the one,' Clytie said, 'who should say thanks. You've given me a holiday. All of us. Things have got to get better.'

'They have already,' the man said, and raised a laugh.

Clytie had packed him a small bag of groceries. 'There's some eggs in there,' she warned. 'Careful how you carry them.'

'I won't forget,' the man said. 'Not anything.'

Harry walked down the track with him as far as the first gate and warned him again against turning north. 'There's nothing out there. Not for the next hundred miles.'

'That'll do me,' the man said.

They raised hands to each other in that old bush signal of recognition, the sign that transmits arrival or departure and recognition from one being to another, and then the man hoisted his swag a little higher and trudged off along the track.

The children were waiting for him out of sight of the house where the home trail met the packway going north. Their hands gripped small newspaper parcels.

The man stopped and wrenched up a smile for them, for the girl – pretty, he'd noticed, her swag of bright hair drooping straight beside her face, but especially for the boy who reminded him so much of his own kid. The boy's eyes trod ahead of the present. The man understood that.

They pressed their small packages onto him. He could feel the weight and shape of pennies.

'Go on,' the girl urged. 'We want you to take them.'

He stared down at them both a long time.

'There won't be any shops,' he said at last. 'Your uncle said.'

'Why don't you stay then?' the boy asked.

'I can't do that.'

'Why?' the boy persisted.

'Because,' the man said, remembering the old childhood answer. 'Just because.' He looked at the girl and knew she understood. 'I've got to keep going now.'

'It's an adventure, isn't it?' the boy asked, hoping.

'I suppose it is,' the man said. 'A sort of adventure.'

'I like adventures,' the boy said. He was kicking one foot eagerly against a clump of guinea grass.

The man kept looking at them, and the space and the distances, the dark puddle looks, seemed to have come back to his eyes.

'Would you like to come with me?' he asked, looking at the boy. He heard his words and was surprised that for the time those words took he meant them. His loneliness was crashing in again, and the awful solitary crawls between towns, along with the lack of responsibility for any human except himself. He needed that most. Responsibility. Foolishly he thought their presence might stop the inevitable. Yet even as he thought that, he knew the inevitable was what he wanted.

They didn't laugh at him. They didn't shy away. He was

grateful for that.

The girl treated his question with an adult seriousness.

'I'm afraid it's not possible,' she said. She looked straight into his face, unsmiling in the clarity of her understanding. 'We can't do that. Not yet.'

'When can we?' the boy demanded. 'When can we, Con?'

'Soon,' she said. 'One of these days.'

The man was already drawing away from them down the track. He felt their terrible comprehension overtake him as he put one hand to his hat in a kind of farewell.

'I'll remember that,' he said.

Wendy Pond

Journal of a Hanger-On

1988

A Birthday Party

In the late afternoon Jane Bowers cycled over the Wharf Road to rig her sailing dinghy, but there was only a trickle of breeze in the bay with meanders of placid water and reflections along the cliff edge. Instead, she walked up through the pines to Millie and Kate's where they gathered cherry plums from the tree outside the living-room window. Jane packed a dozen plums to take to town for Gillespie's birthday.

On her way home, she stopped at the phone box and rang Gillespie. What was he up to? she asked. Sorting through the litter they had collected, he said.

'Where from?'

He said they had been to Miranda to empty the pitfall traps. Had a picnic and went to the hot springs, she thought. She pedalled on up the hill. So that's how it is. Picnics with Crowhurst each weekend.

Jane shopped and made the trifle with peaches and cream on a jelly base. She iced the cake, placing it in the middle of the table with the cherry plums around it, and was looking out the kitchen window when Gillespie drove up the drive. He sat for a while in the car, reading, and then slowly got out and unloaded the boot without looking up.

'Happy birthday!'

'Is there time for a jog before tea?' he asked.

'It's very lovely evening. Drive to the park and I'll come with you.'

'Oh. Oh well, all right then,' he said.

The trees stood widely spaced, lofty, European. Jane slipped through the strands of number-eight wire, circling the hill to reach the summit. She saw the western suburbs concealed in haze, locked in the vision imported by nineteenth-century painters. Tiny figures of joggers bobbed along the stone-walled drives.

In the north-east, the hill's shadow stretched across the greensward of the archery range, through the line of lombardy poplars, and on into the houses and streets. She imagined the birthday tea. Gillespie, Crowhurst and herself sitting at the table round the cake with the cherry plums, and the raspberry jelly at the bottom of the glass bowl glowing in the late afternoon light.

Gillespie was waiting at the car, damp from his run. His towelling hat shortened his forehead, erasing the aura of a scientist. Jane turned towards him in her bucket seat.

'Through friendships we open new vistas,' she said. 'I grew up on stories of foxes and rabbits. Your knowledge of native insects reveals a hidden fauna. Gillespie, why haven't you invited me to join your expedition?'

'Because you're not a naturalist. You wouldn't have anything to do.'

'Why not invite me for my sake, for the landscapes I could paint?'

'I don't know. It just didn't crop up. You can come if you want to,' he said.

At Frankton Airport they stood on the tarmac like early aviators. Rita Angus hung around them, in the slant of the slopes, the yellow, the blue. The great adventure was afoot.

'Gillespie,' she said, 'you would have left me out.'

* * * *

The leading protagonists of this journal are Terrence Gillespie, Fellow of the NZ Entomological Society, Dr Henry Crowhurst of Carnegie Institute, and the artist, Jane Bowers.

Gillespie's Nightmare

The Remarkables, the Remarkables, so blue, so black, so stark. The shout of triumph, the gasp of sharp air. From Queenstown they drove through Arcadia to Paradise and entered the red beech forest. They spread their parkas on the picnic bench and ate their packed lunch. She was there beside the open boot in her red sandshoes and navy boilersuit. She was there at the foot of the waterfall, where the water dashed on the mossed ledges and dripped from the mossed clefts. She was there by the rotted log where they lifted the mossed bark and shook the crushed wood through their canvas sieves. She stood in the crowd of sandflies and laughed as they scowled and swatted their tender skin, those two entomologists in mental disorder from the naonao, the naonao, the little black blighters, the sharp biters, the shout of outrage, the welds on their fair skin, at Paradise.

Gillespie came back to the car with his heavy canvas sieve and bags of debris. It was drizzling. He stood by the boot, placidly wiping his glasses with his handkerchief.

'We'll pick up Crowhurst down the road.'

'Give me the keys, I'll drive.'

'It's all right, thanks,'

'Oh, but I'd like to.'

'You're not an official member of the party.'

Oh! the splash of water on the mossed cleft.

Oh! the slam of a car door.

Late into the night Crowhurst sat working at the microscope with a bare bulb lighting the tray of insects. He worked with both hands, moving the tray with one and holding the tweezers in the other, sorting the insects with mechanical manoeuvres. Dreaming, Jane was woken by a yowl from Gillespie. Crowhurst was standing stock still in front of the table, his skin sallow, his hair lank, a northern raider. Gillespie was sitting up in bed.

'I was having a nightmare,' he said. 'Pursued by wild cattle. A beast charged me.'

They established that as Crowhurst rose from the microscope, he had stepped in front of the bare bulb and cast his shadow across Gillespie.

The yowl of fear, the heart's leap.

Jane's Oversight

In the morning, Jane got up and made three lunches. Then she cooked three breakfasts, cleared the table, washed and dried the dishes, cleaned her teeth, packed her bags, put on her tweed jacket and walked into town to get the grocery order. The Remarkables were bitumen blue.

They set out for Makarora. From the back seat Jane saw that they crossed the Crown range. At the brow, the naturalists stopped to beat the native broom and gather tussock litter, while

Jane sketched in the sun, in the crotch of those yellow hills. She watched them move across the hill face: Crowhurst in a short-sleeved shirt and straw hat, purveying his imported vision, and Gillespie winding along a sheep track, unaware of her perspective.

In the Cardrona Valley they caught up to a herd of Hereford cattle. Horned cows with calves at a loitering pace, three men with sticks and a pack of dogs. On the river flat they stopped for lunch. By the viper's buglos, by the roadside broom, Jane laid out her parka and opened her paper bag. By the yellow hawkbit, by the roadside tarragon, Gillespie heard the cattle mooning. Jane closed her sketch book, she snatched up the lunch bags, she grabbed her shoes.

They drove to Lake Wanaka, to the grassed banks and the picnic seats and swings, to the populars and willows that grace our lakes' edges. At Hamilton, at Karapiro, at Taupo, at Queenstown, mown grass and willows right to the water's edge. Postcards of golden poplars, postcards of lake reflections, postcards of green swards. At Wanaka, Gillespie asked for his vials.

'I gave them to you at lunch,' he said. 'I asked you to put them in my brief case.'

'If that's what you asked me to do, then that's what I did,' Jane said. Then she recalled that at the sight of the cattle she had sped from the crushed grass, seeing herself shunted by a front runner, mooing for her lost calf.

A Debate

They drove on, along the shores of Hawea. The putrid shores, the wracked shores, the adjustable shores of Hawea.

'Crowhurst,' Jane said. 'Why did you come here? Can't New Zealand scientists do it themselves?'

'Crowhurst is a world specialist,' said Gillespie. 'He has brought new methods of collecting which add greatly to our knowledge of the fauna.'

'Do you mean New Zealanders aren't doing their job properly?'

'There aren't enough of us,' said Gillespie. 'There are ten thousand species of insects to describe.'

'But a northern hemisphere vision is holding us up. Take these forests of moths. In every New Zealander's childhood is a story of a lepidopterist with a butterfly net in the meadows, instead of a high wattage light bulb in a beech forest at night. The museums have displays of gaudy Brazilian butterflies and ignore our subtly marked moths, camouflaged to lichens and barks. Isn't it better for us to proceed ourselves, for the fauna to be observed and described with our own vision, our own sense of this country?'

Gillespie drove steadily along the loose metal road. 'We don't know yet what's in this country, and it is the scientists who are demonstrating its uniqueness in terms of world fauna. Its particular eccentricity: the number of flightless species, for instance. It's precisely the scientists who are overcoming the northern hemisphere bias.'

'Science is international,' Crowhurst confirmed. 'It has no preference to vision.'

'Just your one ubiquitous vision.'

Gillespie glanced at Jane in the rear vision mirror. 'We developed the microscope. We've looked more closely than any other culture,' he said.

Nature at Risk

At Makarora, they took a motel unit and shortly set off along a nature walk on the edge of the Mount Aspiring National Park. This walk traversed a small island of podocarp forest.

'A good track for night collecting,' said Gillespie, and they returned to the motel in the mid-afternoon.

The Memory Log of G. M. Hassing,
Sailor, Pioneer, & School Master,
died 1928.

. . . The Makarora valley was at that period covered by an entangled, impenetrable mass of cabbage trees, flax, and fern, growing to a height of 8ft to 10ft and the ground a jungle of dried and decayed vegetation over which it was utterly impossible to make any headway. The only access to the bush was by following the river beaches and fording the river wherever obstructions presented themselves. To get over the difficulty in our attempt to reach the bush we started a fire at the head of the lake. This soon developed into one unbroken, seething ocean

of flame from hillside to hillside, and fanned by a southerly wind, it raged for three days and nights, travelling up the valley 20 miles. It was a terrific blaze, that levelled everything in its course, and disclosed the charred remains of an old Maori pa near the bush, the old Maori Kaika Paikai (the place of abundant food).

'This great fire transformed the appearance of the country, so that in March 1865, when the late explorer William Docherty and I started on our exploring trip by way of lake Wanaka, the Makarora valley presented a beautiful carpet of luxuriant grass, over which it was a pleasure to travel . . .

That night, Gillespie went back into the forest. On the outskirts, he stood listening for the hum of chafers. Then he opened out his beating tray and hit the overhead branches sharply, searching the tray in the light of his headlamp. He shook the debris off the tray, folded it up, and walked further into the forest. His headlamp picked up the shining wing-covers of tiny beetles feeding at night on the moss. It caught the spread of the canvas tray, the front of his check woollen shirt, his face lined and absorbed as he ran his beating-stick lightly down the trunks of the trees, gathering on to his tray the gallers, the strippers, the cambium borers and shoot destroyers, the diverse weevils, the byrrhid beetles, the phytophagous moss insects.

They travelled west over the Haast Pass. The grey-green forest slopes slid apart, the blue-grey river bed broadened, and they ran along fence lines of mossed posts and swampy paddocks where inroads of pasture ambled round trees and heaps of stumps. They got out at the coast and ran through the dunes to the sea. The black swells, the sinking sand, the undertows: the West Coast confronting the Tasman Sea.

From Haast they drove north through the iron-pan belt of pakihi swamp, stopping for lunch at Doughboy Creek. Crowhurst went westwards with his litter tray and cloth bags, heading for the forested dunes. Gillespie simply ducked into the trees beside the car. In the wet moss meadows of that seething forest he heard the sound of trucks along the main road, and through his sieve went the archaic Nothoderodontus.

A Glimmer

Their crib in the pakihi swamp had wirewove beds with candlewick bedspreads, lino floors, and batten conduits for the electric wiring. At home, they hung the extractors in the wardrobes and their damp clothes on the verandah, placed the microscope on the kitchen table, and agreed to keep the door closed on account of the naonao, the ubiquitous naonao.

In their crib in the pakihi swamp there was a large glass, a medium-sized glass, and a small orange plastic tumbler. Gillespie placed them on the kitchen table with two bottles of beer.

'Jane, do you mind,' said Gillespie, 'having the orange glass?'

'I've got the vege water to drink.' Later, Jane said, 'Gillespie, why did you offer me the plastic beaker?'

'I thought you might like the colour.'

'Why didn't you have it yourself?'

'You usually drink less than me.' Hapless, Gillespie asked, 'Is that why you didn't want any beer?'

A Search for Flightless Beetles

Travelling on, they came to the Franz Joseph glacier. Gillespie's attempt was to reach the slopes of Mount Moltke where he would search for flightless alpine beetles, isolated during the last glaciation. Crowhurst would continue to collect litter in the lowland forest. At dusk they would rendezvous in the pub.

Jane climbed with Gillespie. She caught the sweet scent of native broom in flower and glimpsed flares of red rata on the hillsides. As they came round on to the south face of the saddle, the canopy of bush gave way to tussock and the ridge rose into a white wall of vapour. Its southerly trend was consistent with the bearing of Mount Moltke, so Gillespie set out.

Alone in the mist, Jane strolled in an alpine garden of giant buttercups and daisy heads. At hand, the silver tussock blades warped across each other and between the clumps were patches of piebald mosses. Through the drizzle the tussock gave off a vibrant mustard glow.

Clambering up and down the hummocking ridge in the course of the afternoon, Gillespie came to a cleft. In a lifting of the vapour, he faced a forested wall towering vertically above him, and a second peak rising behind. Gillespie lay back amongst the tussock in the yellow cocoon of his wet-weather gear. As he slept, orographic cloud swirled up the cleft.

Plodding back, Gillespie recounted his dream. He was heading for the Mahia peninsula in the Ford Eight. Sheer walls of conglomerate rose beside and ahead of him. He reached a look-out point near the summit and got out of the car. The open ocean was slate green. Below, the sea was groaning in the rock caverns. The ferry was due to leave. He drove at speed down the hillside to the wharf. The tide was washing in around the motor spirit pumps and he had to dodge the waves to reach the ticket box. It was empty. A fisherman told him that the Cook Strait ferry had left the day before and would no longer berth at this wharf, owing to the rise in sea level. He recalled the leather suitcases strapped on to the carrier, and the labels saying 'Christchurch'.

As it turned out, the Franz Joseph settlement didn't have a pub. They picked up Crowhurst walking resolutely north along the main road through the pakihi forest. Old kahikatea stood raggedly against the orange sky.

Crowhurst Clinches the Debate

That evening, Crowhurst proceeded as he had every night, with the microscope on the kitchen table and a reading lamp directed on to the tray of insects, picking out each creature and dropping it into a vial. He had a specimen of Heterojapey, a missing link connecting earwigs to springtails. Crowhurst got up and stood aside. Gillespie, without sitting down, looked through one eyepiece of the microscope.

'Crowhurst,' Jane said, 'there are some naturalists in this country who don't want Maori names to be used in the binomial system.'

'Well, of course,' replied Crowhurst, 'scientists at Carnegie Institute, with an African name here, a Javanese name there, don't know the meaning of those names.'

'Scientists give each other's names to insects,' Jane said, 'with less meaning than a Maori name.'

Gillespie was refocusing the eyepiece. 'On the contrary, that's how we scientists record our ancestors.'

'Then who is New Zealand's fauna being classified for? World scientists or ourselves, the indigenous people?'

'You can use Maori names yourselves,' said Crowhurst.

'The categories are different. The old store-keeper at Te Puru uses papapa for things that scuttle away, like slaters and cockroaches.'

Gillespie began filling the vials, and Crowhurst returned to the microscope. 'People prefer the finer distinctions of science,' he said.

Crowhurst worked on through the night, adjusting the dish of specimens and advancing the tweezers, with the fractional pauses of a hydraulic lift changing from one position to the next.

During the course of next morning, Jane saw in the sky a thick cloud, segmented like the mouldering skin on sour milk, gaining height above the trees. The lower cloud boiling up was bruised with lime and purple: smoke from a Forest Service burn-off. Rita Angus had seen it too, and when Gillespie and Crowhurst returned at dusk they likewise stood in the yard, their gaze lifted towards the hills.

Homeward Bound

With the week's end, they began the homeward leg through Arthur's Pass. They took a cabin on Camping Flat, corrugated iron painted romany red. It had belonged to the railway engineer. Blue lupins were flowering around it, and through the four-light casements the beech forest towered over the roar of the river. Gillespie lit the pot-belly stove, Crowhurst hung the calico bags of litter to dry on the fire surround, and Jane made a stew which they ate on their laps.

At nightfall, she watched the sheets of rain move across the hill face, striking the green-black forest with a sharp hiss. In those landscapes, waterfalls break the cover of every valley.

Gillespie was up at seven to empty the pitfall traps. The beech forest was clean and light. He worked round to the eastern face and climbed steadily up the ridge line. Then the tide of cloud covered the pied snow peaks and he stood on his own tussock ridge, turning stones.

They drove back to Christchurch through Rita Angus country, Cass and the Craigieburn range. Jane's heart sang. How sinuously the lines portray those austere yellow hills, those blue mountains, those braided river plains.

Janette Turner Hospital

Isobars
A Fugue on Memory

1988

Where does a circle start? Wherever one decides. All these circles begin and end in Melbourne.

And what is an isobar? An isobar is an imaginary line connecting places of equal pressure on a map. All lines on a map, we must acknowledge, are imaginary; they are ideas of order imposed on the sloshing flood of time and space. Lines on a map are talismanic and represent the magical thinking of quantitative and rational people.

These particular isobars connect points where the pressure of memory exerts an equivalent force.

And how is a storm front plotted? The detection of warm fronts, cold fronts, rainstorms, cyclones, and other such assorted cataclysms and disasters requires the intuition of the scientist. If the meteorologist has received sufficient advance training in oceanography, statistical mathematics, Jungian archetypes and dreams, he or she will be able to read the signs correctly. Such a meteorologist will watch for the figure in the surface disturbance of water (though to what purpose, discerning the gust in a shoal of lake breezes, no one is ever certain).

Water.

The Ringwood Lake and the Ballarat Lake were separate bodies of water in the Jurassic Period, early 1940s, when M (for Made in Melbourne, maid in Melbourne, for memory itself, for meteorologist-in-training, for...) But perhaps we should be more conventional and call her Em? Or even, more decorously, more appropriately, buttoning our gloves and keeping our knees together in the approved Melbourne manner, Emily. Yes, Emily will do very nicely...

The Ringwood Lake and the Ballarat Lake were separate bodies of water when Emily floated the leaves of childhood on them, when she threw breadcrusts to swans now several generations gone. But those two ponds, infinite as oceans in a bygone era, are one puddle now. Statues clutter the walks that surround them. Sometimes the English grandfather comments on the statues, sometimes the Welsh grandfather. The Ringwood town hall and the Ballarat cathedral and the Ringwood railway station push through bullrushes.

The English grandfather's hand is soft and pale, a schoolmaster's hand; the Welshman's is callused. With a grandfather at each side like charms at her wrists, Emily flexes her toes, she sinks her bare feet into gurgling mud. Already she is learning that the property of water is sameness, Ringwood shimmering, Ballarat dreaming, the future sighing at its own reflection.

Once, the English grandfather says, there was a picnic by the lake and afterwards you vomited chocolate in the back seat of the Bishop of Ballarat's car. Your mother was mortified.

The Welsh grandfather says: Don't lean so far out from the edge of the jetty, the swans will snap at your fingers. Once there was a picnic – don't you remember? – where a little boy fell in doing that and got drowned. His mother sobbed and sobbed, she could not be comforted, she had to be taken away.

The English grandfather scoops up lakewater and pours it into Emily's palm. One little drop of memory, he says, can hold everything at once, and forever. It's like having a thousand eyes.

Grandpa, she says. Why is that lady crying? And what is that man doing?

What lady? both the grandfathers say. What man? Where?

There, she says. There. Over there by the gum tree. Is she the little boy's mother?

Oh, they say, maybe. Or maybe she's someone else. In any case, it's nothing, it's nothing that little girls need to worry their pretty little heads about.

But Grandpa, Emily persists, why is she crying?

No, no, she's not crying, they say. (Their voices are fearful, embarrassed, harsh.) She's laughing. Trust us, they say. Don't look.

And they take her hands, playful, and lift and swing, this is fun, they swing her to kingdom come, out out over the water, over the Pacific, over the Atlantic, over the Arabian Sea

where, briefly, the fisherman offers his hand as she steps into his boat. She is in South India, Pleistocene era, 1970s, the coconut palms throwing spidery shadows on Kovalam beach. When she takes the fisherman's hand, brown flesh white flesh interlaced, he giggles with embarrassment, waits for her to settle herself between the lashed logs, pushes off with his bamboo paddle.

Blood warm water bathes her from the waist down. The boat is stable and buoyant, not watertight; she and the fisherman ride just below the water's surface, passing through the sides of waves as a knife through butter, as spirits through walls, as memory through time. She sees Ringwood swans and a row of little fishes suspended like bubbles in a green flank of the Arabian Sea.. The Bishop of Ballarat, concerned, leans forward with his bamboo paddle. You won't be sick, will you? he asks in some unknown tongue. The ways of God are inscrutable, he says; it is not our place to question why. Don't lean so far, he says. Someone was drowned doing that.

Why is that woman screaming? she calls, her mouth full of water. And what is the man doing with the knife?

What knife? the fisherman shouts back. (Bubbles and tiny fish stream from his lips like ribbons.) Where? he calls.

There, she points. There. On the beach.

No, no, you are not understanding, the fisherman says. Man is cleaning fish and woman is laughing, isn't it?

Relieved, she smiles through the fluid green belly of the wave as the fisherman casts his net. His eyes and hers are both amber as cats'-eyes in the water, salt crusts their lashes, branches of their seaweed hair float into the mouths of crabs. Bubbles of laughter fizz from her throat, it's a champagne baptism, euphoric, surf foaming through her lips, and the woman on the beach is laughing too, thank God, (yet it is odd the way a laugh or a scream seems defined by the ears of the hearer). Still. The fisherman knows the local tongue, he must be right, though people do tell lies, Thoreau warns. Especially the avoiders, especially those fearful of being held accountable for what they have failed to do, especially those ashamed of their own fear.

Thoreau is sitting at the edge of the water, his hut behind him, nine beanrows and a hive for the honeybee to one side, Walden Pond flashing sunlight in his eyes.

The man over there under the trees, she says. The one talking to the woman who is crying. . . .

Thoreau looks and looks away. They say she has lost a child, he says. They say she has never been quite right since. And the man is claiming it's his loss too, he's offering comfort, he's promising extravagant things. Thoreau shakes his head and warns: But men rarely mean what they say. Still, he adds, the woman wants to believe him. Can't you hear her laughter?

It's such a strange laugh, Emily says. It doesn't sound like a laugh at all, it sounds more like a –

Thoreau puts a finger to his lips. If you hear a different drum, he says, you have a choice. You can march to it, though this will certainly get you into difficulties with the authorities. Or you can pretend you didn't hear it, like everyone else. You have to weigh the consequences, you have to choose, you have to balance costs, balance is essential. Left foot on one ice cake, right foot on another, no one should be too far from shore when playing this game. Five minutes, so they say, at these temperatures, and the body shuts down.

But warmth is on the way, April is here, the Ice Age is over, spring has come to the frozen St Lawrence, a rubble of ice with a Great Lakes postmark is floating past Emily's dock and should reach Montreal by the middle of this May. A puzzled loon, the first of the season, touches down, disappears, surfaces, watches the mad balancing act.

Don't lean so far when you throw him a crust, the Welsh grandfather says. A boy was drowned doing that.

Do I hear a woman scream, Emily asks herself, puzzled. Or is it simply one fractious chunk of ice shrieking up against another?

Newspapers.

The Melbourne *Age*, the *Sun*, the *Argus* all have pictures: of the little boy who drowned, of the mother weeping, of the murdered woman. Was this all the same event? Emily remembering a picnic by the lake and much panic, is confused. Her parents and grandparents press their lips together and shake their heads. Her mother says: 'Don't ever lean out from the dock, don't ever ever *ever* go in the water unless someone is with you.

A man on the Ringwood railway station tells Emily's grandfather: I expect she asked for it. (The mother? Emily wonders. Or the woman with the knifestripes on her stomach?). Newspapers flutter from carriage windows and shout from their stands beside the ticket grille. These are the facts, the newspapers say. Women and children are always asking for trouble. They get it.

Brisbane *Courier-Mail*, circa 1953. BETTY SHANKS MURDERED. This happened just an eye-blink away from Wilston State School. In the playground, rumours fly. *She had boyfriends, she talked to strange men.* From the school gates, the children can see the police, the reporters, the chalk outline on the footpath.

It seems, the teacher tells the frightened (yet strangely excited) children, that Betty Shanks rode home on the tram late at night. She was all alone. She spoke to a strange man. This was madness on the part of Betty Shanks.

Don't ever speak to strange men, the teacher warns. Don't ever go out alone at night.

That's right, the nice constable tells the class. If you do, you're asking for trouble.

The *TLS* (May 5, 1988) has reviews and scholarly reminders that the victim is always to blame. 'Tuberculosis attacks failures,' declares medical expert of 1912. (TLS, page 463, a review of a book by F. B. Smith, the Australian medical historian.) 'It is just the ignorance of millions like yourself that causes the miseries of mankind,' Smith reports that a grieving mother was told over the body of her dead tubercular child.

The woman weeps and weeps. She's a difficult woman, the doctors and experts say. Probably over-protective, stifling, the usual thing. Probably *caused* it, in a way; more or less programmed the child for death. A difficult woman.

CBC, Canada, the national news, May 6, 1988: A recent survey of attitudes of high school students toward rape indicates that most boys think girls who are raped were asking for it.

Air. And circles within circles.

Curses fly through the air, and sometimes fists, and sometimes broken bottles. Emily stands in a circle on a street corner somewhere in the heart of Melbourne or in the vortex of Brisbane (they are one circle now: covered wagons, rampart, the ring of accusers, prison wall, ghetto, all the same circle). There are drunks and traffic in all directions. In the air above Emily's head, catcalls collide with Biblical codes. *Come unto me all ye who are weary*... leaps out of the megaphone. *Aaah, shut yer fucking mouths* comes winging back into the circle. Emily watches the words eddying together, twisting, full of cyclone danger.

This particular evening (Jurassic Era again, the Japanese defeated but black paint still being scraped from the windows of Melbourne), this particular evening of Circle Time, which is every evening, a ragged mother and a dirty little boy stop to watch, leaning against a shop window. The boy licks an icecream and watches Emily who stares back hungrily. It is his safety she wants; being part of *that* crowd, the circle outside the circle, one of the watchers. Whatever happens, the boy can stay or go. The boy is safe.

Emily wonders when the lots were drawn, when the circles were allotted, and by whom. The kind of thought that comes from beyond the margins, from who can say where? from outside the lines that form the edges of maps, the kind of question that can change worlds asks itself inside Emily's five-year-old mind: Is anyone allowed to change places? Is it against the rules? What happens if the rules or the circles are broken?

The boy licks his icecream and watches her. What is he thinking? She sees him suddenly suck in his breath, sees his eyes widen, sees the man with the knife. A cry with no sound to it flies from Emily's mouth.

Girls! the boy says, exasperated, as he disappears behind scuffling bystanders, police, circle people. The police are angry. *Holy Rollers*! they say, disgusted. *Just asking for trouble.*

Nobody sees what happens, nobody hears.

Nobody saw, nobody heard, nothing we can do, the police tell Emily (Brisbane now, the seedy West End, 1965).

But everyone must have heard the screams, she says.

Tell us exactly... (The police are sarcastically patient.)

Emily tries to reconstruct: a scream in the air, screams, it is night and she is alone in the house but she rushes out to the street. (This happens much too quickly for fear or thought to intrude.) She sees the white man with the knife, the black woman screaming, the pregnant black woman screaming.

And then? the police ask.

And then, and then? Emily pounds at the blank that retroactive fear creates. The knife, the blood, the blur.

I guess I ran between them, she says, amazed, her hands shaking.

Emily is inside her house, bandaging the slash on the woman's arm, when the police say: Not a thing we can do, I'm afraid.

Listen, they explain to Emily (kindly, fatherly). A woman like you shouldn't get mixed up . . . *etcetera* . . . bloody lucky you didn't get yourself stabbed.

About the Abo whore, they say. (Excuse our language.) Just asking for trouble. Best to turn a deaf ear. Nobody sees, nobody hears, that's the ticket.

That's the ticket: the same old one that Kitty Genovese held when her number came up in New York, when the knife flashed, when a porridge of her screams filled the air and reached dozens of ears, but nobody saw.

Glittering, curving through air, the knife slices through a life in Boston, March 1987. The blade rests against Emily's throat, whispers to her larynx: I am steel, I am real. You may scream all you want but no one will see or hear. You've been asking for this, you deserve me.

Air! Emily gasps. Air! she pleads. Air! Fresh air!

Personally, someone (an Australian) tells Emily at a writers' conference, *I think writing about violence is in bad taste.*

You see? the knife chortles, triumphant. What did I tell you?

I'll be back, the blade whispers (a sleazy sound, cold as steel against pliant skin). In dream after dream, I'll be back.

Fiona Kidman

The Tennis Player

1988

1

On the leg from Bombay Ellen sat upright beside a cello which had had a seat booked for it because its owner said it was a Stradivarius. The cabin attendants seemed more gracious towards the cello than to the children who had joined the flight at Bombay. The lavatories were jammed with unflushed paper, service came less often than in the early part of the flight, and babies cried. Ellen offered to walk a child whose mother looked like a delicate Asian figurine.

She and the child stood and looked down at Turkey for a long time through the domed glass at the rear of the plane.

'Are you a missionary?' asked a woman across the aisle, when she returned.

Ellen shook her head and smiled politely. She had been travelling for nearly thirty hours. She had begun to think that she would like to be a cello.

2

In London she lugged her huge suitcase up five flights of stairs and found herself in a bedsit under the eaves of a building in Eccleston Square that looked elegant from the outside and was a dump on the inside. There was a fire escape out to the roof just like in *The Girls of Slender Means*.

Only Ellen was forty-five and the war was over.

3

She walked down the street until she came to a Mr Wimpy food bar. She was still unhealthily full of airline food, yet the cardboard-and-onion smell of packaged hamburgers was irresistible. It was like Friday night in Newtown, close to home. The restaurant was full, with black faces and white in about equal proportion, and she was certain that the black faces were friendlier than the white.

Afterwards, she went to the women's lavatory at Victoria Station and queued behind the barrier. The large black woman in charge shouted out, 'Which one of you ladies been and gonna done a wee wee on my floor?' Nobody answered and Ellen knew she thought it was her.

Her cheeks burned. She stepped over the puddle.

4

On the way home (for, for the moment there was no other, except Eccleston Square) she stopped to buy grapes from a fruit barrow, and fumbled with the unfamiliar coins.

'Doesn't know the bleeding time of day, does she?' the man who ran the fruit barrow said to a group of schoolgirls with cheeks like beastly English apples. She gave him money, took what he said was her change, and fled without the grapes. She heard the laughter of the girls as she hurried down the street. Stung, she turned and walked back, shouting at the fruit vendor, *fuck you, fuck you, ah fuck you.*

Then she ran for fear the bobbies would pick her up.

She felt better until she got back to Eccleston Square.

She spoke of herself as an ordinary woman. But she was used to living in a house with restored ceilings and pale walls that faced out to sea. She listened to classical music on the radio when she took her morning baths.

In the room, she sat on the bed and wondered if there would be a nuclear attack before she got back to New Zealand and what were the chances of seeing her family again.

5

The best part of every day was saying *fuck you* to the fruit vendor when she passed. You could almost say they were on nodding terms. In Wellington, the city she came from, she had observed a woman dressed in a yellow and red cloak, who ran from behind a door at the railway station to feed pigeons. This activity was strictly forbidden. She did it when she thought no one was watching. Only someone always was. She got chased by a station attendant with a broom. Ellen could not stop thinking about her.

6

She went to a communion service in Westminster Abbey. It was Mothering Sunday and she began to cry. A woman in a good tweed suit and a slouched hat stood up in the middle of the service when the choir had just finished singing the Twenty-third Psalm. The woman shouted out to the congregation that they were all fools and hypocrites, and mistaken and misled. Ellen wanted to cheer when she was led away across the cold stones. Mostly because it might have been her getting caught but was not. Instead she drank the blood of Christ, and resolved to speak more forthrightly to the fruit vendor.

7

The next day she bought an Israeli avocado and a bottle of German wine at a corner store and took them back to the room. On a roof garden opposite to her, three men carried a garden up from the street, and she saw that it was full of flowering daffodils. In the square below, two men unlocked the gate and went inside to play tennis, locking the gate behind them, so that no one could get in.

It amazed her that nobody shook the bars. Rally, they cried, game love set.

On the day following that, she bought two cobs of bright gold corn. She had never eaten such sweet corn. It made her want to cry again, it tasted so much of home, and childhood, only better.

Outside snow had begun to fall, and the three men had appeared on the rooftop garden to take the daffodils away. She wondered how the corn had ripened in weather like this, and realised that of course it must have been imported. She rummaged through the rubbish tin and found the label on the packaging. The corn had been grown in South Africa.

8

She knew she was as nutty as a peanut slab when she got on the train at Charing Cross to go to Paris, but thought that maybe it wasn't showing. The thing was, she was getting out of it. She opened her phrase book. She had passed School Certificate French. She had meant to refresh herself but hadn't found the time. It felt as if it was thirty years since she had recited a French verb.

It was.

Exactly.

9

She sat for a long time watching the railyards turn to open fields, glimpsed grass and trees through mist. She was so afraid that now she would have been grateful for Eccleston Square. She had been running late and missed the *bureau de change*. Effectively, she was bound for Paris with no money. She passed her hand over her stomach where her travellers' cheques were strapped in her money belt. The belt had worked round and the zip chafed her skin. The lack of money was something to worry about, and she supposed it would preoccupy her all the way to Paris. Her husband would have said, if you haven't got something to worry about, you'll invent something.

Which was all very well.

But if there was no *bureau de change* at the station, how would she get a taxi? She must also go to the lavatory on the train, or the boat, or somewhere, because if she did not, maybe she would have to pay to go at the station in Paris, and then if she had no money, and they would not let her in, how would she take off her money belt to get the travellers' cheques out so she could change them anyway? There was so much to think about. Since she had been away she kept trying to cross things off lists she must do, if she was to survive alone in Europe, but instead she continually remembered more things to add. She did not know how she had ever looked after her children when it was so difficult to look after herself.

She pushed her gloved hand distractedly through her hair and avoided the feet of the young man sitting facing her, as they threatened to become entangled with hers. The feet were clad in fine soft leather boots.

10

She had observed the way people did not stare at each other in England, and the way that they did not make random comments to each other. Even though she had not spoken to anyone except the fruit vendor for several days she knew she should resist the urge to speak.

11

The young man pretended to be asleep whenever she looked at him. She knew he pretended by the way he moved his feet. He had started being tidy with them.

After a while he pretended to wake up and took out a book. She saw that it was a collection of Andrew Marvell's poems. She felt ashamed that she was only reading a novel, even though it was by Barbara Pym who was now rediscovered.

The young man wore designer jeans. He picked one of his feet up off the floor and placed it on the seat so that his very long leg was cocked along it, and his shapely crotch exposed towards her.

It was as good as a smile.

'Are you a student?' she said, looking at his book, and recalling English I.

'No,' he said, but he did smile. He had strong white teeth, and his face was lean and tanned. He turned the book a little so that she could appreciate the cover. 'It's a good read.'

'Have you been to Paris before?' she blurted.

'Not since last week,' he said.

He pointed to the luggage compartment. She saw then, two tennis racquets in frames. They looked shiny and expensive.

'I'm a tennis player. I play in tournaments. Most weeks I play somewhere in Europe. This week and last, it's been Paris.'

'How exciting,' she said, and heard herself breathless and a little tremulous. 'Are you famous? Should I know you? I'm from New Zealand, you see, we don't see all the games, well only the finals at Wimbledon, I might not have seen, you understand...?'

'No, not so exciting, no truly. Of course, in New Zealand I can see you might not have... sometimes on television, yes, but in New Zealand, well I can understand that. I do win some.'

He smiled again. She recognised false modesty when she saw it.

12

He was kind though, generous with details. They told each other the story of their lives, listening carefully to one another. He came from Devon. His parents had thought he might do better than be a tennis player but he didn't understand their problem. It was a good job. It took a long time to tell her this. She, having had a longer life, took even more time.

They hurtled past fields she could barely see because the mist now hugged the edge of the railway tracks like white fur.

They discussed the agrarian patterns of Great Britain. In the fifth form, she had been taught about grain production in East Anglia. She could not understand its relevance to her life. She had wondered if, coming here to England for the first time, she would discover why it was important to her to learn about its grainfields when she had only a rough idea of where wheat was grown in New Zealand.

His tone was almost sharp. 'Of course it's important,' he said. 'It is a central factor in the British economy.' He paused, frowned. 'And New Zealand depends on Britain, doesn't it?'

How curious, she thought, if, after all, an ear or two of wheat were to come between her and the consummation of what was clearly shaping up to be the most classic interlude in her life. A young man, in Paris, where despite the portents on this side of the Channel, it was officially spring and bound to be fine. A small subterranean voice begged her to remind herself that it was simply fucking in a general sort of way that she had in mind, rather than with this particular young man. She dismissed the voice. For the moment, she thought that if her husband were here, right at this minute, she would probably prefer the tennis player.

'Would you ever play in South Africa?' she asked him, holding her breath.

'Never,' he said with fervour. She breathed a long sigh of relief, forgiving him East Anglia. She saw his head on the pillow beside hers, and the index finger of her right hand sitting inside its new glove, purchased in Oxford Street the day before, traced his profile in her mind's eye. She knew already that she was bound never to forget him.

'In the mornings we eat breakfast outside at the sidewalk cafés. You must do that,' he was saying. 'It is the only way to have breakfast in Paris.'

13

At Dover she thought the white cliffs were a hill covered with birdshit. They had disappeared behind the hovercraft before she had time to appreciate them.

'Is that all?' she said to him. 'Is that all?'

At the terminal people had turned to look at them. He had bought her coffee and croissants, and refused to allow her to pay. 'In New Zealand,' he said. Already it had been decided that he must play the New Zealand circuit some summer soon.

She felt herself walking with the special pride of someone who has recently become one half of a new couple. It occurred to her that he might be very well known indeed. Look at him, she imagined the eyes that followed them were saying, he has a new woman. Perhaps it would get into the papers. Young tennis player woos mystery woman. Antipodean sweetheart – how long can this romance last? In praise, again, of older women.

'You'll be speaking French in a minute,' he said, and too late she realised that the English Channel was behind her.

She opened her phrase book at Arrivals and Departures. 'I have two hundred cigarettes, some wine and a bottle of spirits,' she said, frivolous in her mood.

'The children are on my wife's passport,' he said, running his finger down the list.

She laughed out loud, '*Non. Je ne suis que de passage.*'

He nodded approvingly. 'Passing through, eh? *Bon.*' He opened his hands, a mock Gallic gesture. '*Je n'ai rien à déclarer aussi.*'

He put his hand on her phrasebook. 'Don't worry about it so much.'

14

The train stopped often in the French countryside. The small towns all seemed to have rubbish tips for backyards. Their conversation became erratic. It was still raining.

'You must be privileged if you play tennis in England,' she mused, and aware already that he was. But she had been thinking of Eccleston Square.

His head was slipping sideways towards her shoulder. She could smell him. He smelled like a new racquet, gutsy and clean.

'Probably. Tell me some more about New Zealand,' he said drowsily, without minding whether she did or not. She watched him. She thought of something special she would do for him.

15

The lock in the bedroom door worked by a number of turns in either direction. She could not work out the sequence. Not only could she not get in, but once in she could not get out either. She had to call reception three times before she had mastered it, and on the last occasion she was near to hysteria. The young man on the desk came upstairs on his own to explain it to her the first two times. His English was bad. The third time he brought another man, who spoke good English. He explained the lock in a slow and patient way as if she were simple. She considered leaving the hotel and going to another, but night had fallen and she did not know where to go.

When it seemed as if she understood the mechanism of the lock she sat in the room and shook. Several hours had passed since the tennis player had last bought her food, and the hotel had no restaurant. Even if it had, she was afraid to leave the room.

Still, at least she liked it. After Eccleston Square it was like a return to some other life where ease and comfort were again possible. The king-sized bed was covered with a frilled quilt with a pattern of pink and green peacocks, and there were rose-coloured lights on the wall. There were gold-coloured taps in the bathroom and a deep bath.

The louvre doors led out onto a wrought iron balcony overlooking Rue Pasquier. The life of the city stretched below her had she chosen to walk out onto the balcony, though for the moment the sound of traffic had caused her to close the doors so that she could hear herself think.

She knew she would not sleep if she did not eat, and maybe drink as well, and that the longer she left it the more difficult it would be to set out.

Carefully she tried the lock and this time the combination worked to perfection. Emboldened, she left the hotel and walked quickly along the boulevard in the direction of St Augustin. Her handbag was comfortably full of francs. 'You'll be all right now, won't you?' he had said when he left her at the counter of the *bureau de change*. 'I'm sorry I can't see you to a taxi.' He had become tense and athletic, fretting with his tennis racquets. He had explained on the first train, in England, that his game was on the other side of Paris. As it was, he would be cutting things fine to get there on time.

Traffic swirled past her. She could not see where the centre line of the road was, or indeed, if there were any true sides to the roads, as a car mounted the pavement and ran its left-hand tyres alongside her ankles. She leapt out of its path and watched it subside into the path of an oncoming car, which swerved in its turn.

Right up until the last moment she knew that she had been shamefully hoping. Even in the taxi, re-counting her money, which she had been short-changed the first time it was given to her, and she had had to demand in a loud high voice that it be counted again, she wondered if he had heard her tell him the name of the hotel, and regretted that she had not had the courage to repeat it when he was leaving.

It was after the second time that the lock on the door would not open that she admitted his expression. It was, she remembered, decent and perfectly nice, marred by a slight but growing sense of impatience.

She found a restaurant. The waiter was young. He did not speak any English at all. She pointed out a phrase in her small blue book. *Je ne parle pas bien le français. Je viens de Nouvelle Zélande.* He brought her a carafe of wine without being asked. When she drank it thirstily he brought her another, and indicated to her what he had decided it would be best for her to eat.

Vous êtes très aimable, she wrote on her paper napkin when she left. She felt undone by such simple kindness.

Like the kindness of the tennis player. They had not talked about his aunts, but she knew without such a conversation taking place, that he was kind to them. He would be good to them if they were ever foolish enough to go to Paris alone. He might even try to dissuade them from going.

16

Inside the room she felt free, with a sudden odd delight that she was alone. She leaned against the door with her back to it. It was April, and she was in Paris. She had come from the other side of the world for this. She had transacted money. She knew the combination of her lock. She had bought a meal. In a minute or so she would run a large hot bath.

She had not drawn the curtains yet, and outside the night sky shone with reflected light.

Ellen walked to the doors leading out onto the balcony and opened them, breathing deeply and calmly. She stepped outside, and a fine rain was falling. She gripped the edge of the wrought iron balcony, and was happy.

As she stood there, a curious thing happened. The astonishing traffic began to grind to a halt beneath her. Two cars hit each other with a sickening thud. The drivers leapt out of the cars, and without looking at each other, raised their fists in her direction, as if it was she who was responsible for their misfortune.

More cars began to stop. Within moments Rue Pasquier was

clogged with cars askew where their owners had abandoned them with their motors running. Behind the cars that had stopped, drivers in the oncoming wave who could not see what was happening began to sound their horns.

Ellen was increasingly bewildered by the commotion. But it was surely a phenomenon which, if studied, must give insight and meaning to the character of the French. She prided herself in a lively curiosity. The men who had first waved their fists at her were now shouting at each other. But other drivers, less hapless, still appeared transfixed by something at the point where she stood. She thought that it must be above her and looked upwards, putting her hand on the wall over her head.

A man headed towards the balcony then, laughing and shouting at the same time. She drew back, afraid. She was not so far above the street that a man could not scale the wall to where she stood.

She caught a word. She was sure it was not in her phrase book.

But she understood.

17

When the door to the balcony was double locked behind her she ran her bath. She took off all her clothes. She looked at herself in the steamed-up glass.

The wife who might pass for a maiden aunt or a missionary who might pass for a whore looked back though it was difficult to say whether she looked any more like one of these than the other.

Most likely, she thought, she resembled the cello.

Rosa Safransky

A 'Happy Little Vegemite'

1988

The washing is a monument to neatness, to order, to precision. My father's socks are pegged symmetrically to the line. The art of the bedsheet, the art of the tablecloth. My mother mutters to ghosts in the backshed; a low barely audible stream of words, as she scrubs sheets on the washboard or stirs clothes in the copper. My words cannot reach her because no word has yet been invented which she hears while she sews, while she scrubs, while she cooks. What use are words? A look is enough. Her lips pressed tight, she hypnotises the bedsheets.

My mother sits at her treadle machine on a painted wooden chair, giving the wheel a twist with her hand, then applying pressure with her slippered foot, making the machine hum and the floor vibrate. The needle races through cloth till it becomes a blur. Dresses and coats lie in heaps on the floor. She hems each one, then lays it across the back of a nearby chair. My mother sews her confusion into the dresses. Where is she? She stitches the years together. She sleeps with her eyes open. She listens to the dark.

I study my mother as she prepares dough, pounds it, pinches it, rolls it tightly between her hands. The word 'no' does not exist in her vocabulary.

'Do you want an orange? A pear?'
'No!' It's peeled and in my hand.
'Are you hungry?'
'No!' The table is covered in food.
My mother brings cherries from the market.
'Cherry earrings' she laughs as she hangs a pair over my ears.
I walk along fences holding her hand. When it is cold, she lets me slip my hand in her pocket, where it is warm.

'Get off my fence!' a woman shouts at us. My mother grabs me and we hurry away.

I wave at strangers from the tram. Mustn't wave to strangers. Mustn't talk to them. Mustn't look at them. My mother is a mystery. In the bath, I study the bright blue veins in her legs. Tragedy hid under the bed, in her clothes, in her eyes. Tragedy lives in her sighs. That sigh of my mother's. Everything in that sigh.

I kick the side of the sink while she peels potatoes.
'I want something to do'
'Help me clean up'
'No! I want to play'
'You're lazy!'
'I don't care'
I detest my mother's constant cleaning.

A familiar battle rages in the kitchen as my mother retells an old story. Alternately the heroine and tormentor of my fantasies, she hides in a barn concealed from the Nazis in a bale of straw. Machine gun bullets strafe the wall. A little boy lies murdered on the ground.
'In Poland, people starved because they didn't have enough to eat. What's the matter Princess Margaret? Isn't this luxury enough for you?'
'Leave me alone. I hate the noodles. I hate you!'

The specially prepared luxuries of Poland are battlefields between us. My heart is set on one thing. I want to be 'A Happy Little Vegemite'. I know the song on the radio off by heart. So does everyone else at school. My thick rye bread sandwiches stuffed with garlic salami, sour pickles and my father's favourite Russian caviar, are no match for paper thin sliced vegemite sandwiches with no crusts.

A beaming Australian grandmother called 'Granny Davis' holds the key to social success. Her face is painted on all the trucks that deliver her bread to the milk bar. She even does home deliveries.

'Granny Davis is a fake.' My mother equates Granny Davis bread with advanced malnutrition. Granny Davis is a member of the Ku Klux Klan. She dresses in a white bedsheet and victimises all eaters of rye bread sandwiches in Australian schoolyards.

But what do Australians know about food? Choosing a fish, fruit, took ages. It had to be the right one. I tag along beside my mother in the market. She stops to talk. It feels like months. I pull some paper away from her string bag and come face to face with the glassy eye of a fish.

Her tomatoes. She coaxed them from the earth. Giant sunflowers, sweet peas. The nectarine tree with curly leaf disease. The pumpkin aimed strategically at our heads when we opened the back door. Our rose bush is held together with a 'shmatte' a rag. I inhale the heavy perfume. Bee sting. Backyard vibrates. I howl. Cicadas shriek. Summer. I watch my mother pluck her eyebrows in the sun. Her appearance is striking. Jet black hair, erect gait. I listen to the stories she tells of her mother who refused to cut her hair but pinned it up and concealed it under a wig, contrary to Orthodox law which governed her life in Poland. My mother removes the pins from her hair and unwinds it in front of the kitchen mirror. She combs it, then equally carefully, pins it back up again.

One day, Glenda leans over our front fence and grabs fistfuls of my mother's hair. No sound comes from my throat as I stand petrified beside her. Everything is frozen. My legs, my arms, my feet. Rain streams from the sky while my mother tears Glenda's hands away from her scalp, unlocks the door, pushes me inside then bolts it shut.

That night, as the fire burns, I lie on the sofa watching shadows dancing on the wall. The tiny window just beneath the ceiling, sometimes traps the moon. A tapestry of a lion hangs from the mantelpiece, glaring into the kitchen. I can hear it growl.

Jennifer Paynter

The Sad Heart of Ruth

1988

Jesus Christ was coming to dinner, and Ruth Jackson had extended the leaf in her reproduction Regency dining table and set out six Ken Done Opera House placemats and fashioned six red table napkins into bishops' mitres. She had put red candles in her Proud's candelabra and washed and dried her floral centrepiece of red bisque porcelain roses.

'Doesn't it look colourful, hey Bob?' she asked her husband, who was an alderman on the Ku-ring-gai Council and often pretended not to hear Ruth when she asked him things. He pretended not to hear her now because he was resetting his federation Kookaburra clock, and he was cross with her about the menu. He'd told her to serve fish, but she'd gone her own sweet way and bought a leg of lamb and made a kiwi fruit pavlova.

Apart from Jesus, their other guests were the Very Reverend Keith Creevey and his wife, Sylvia, and Jesus' interpreter, a Mr Naji Jabour.

The doorbell rang. 'That'll be Him!' said Ruth, but it was only Mr and Mrs Creevey.

Bob poured out some sherry, and they all sat down to wait.

Keith Creevey was very nervous. He kept pressing his upper lip white and saying silly things. 'Isn't this incredible?' he kept saying. 'Isn't this incredible, Bob?'

Bob kept on pouring out sherries and pretending not to hear. He'd organised several little dishes of olives and ripe figs, but he didn't want to pass them around until Jesus arrived.

Sylvia Creevey started to laugh. 'Do you suppose He's lost, Ruth? Do you suppose He's gone to the wrong address? Does He know Pymble at all? Does He know how to get to Pymble, Ruth?'

Ruth made a married signal to Bob to put away the sherry. She got up and went to the kitchen and opened a tin of orange and mango juice.

Sylvia Creevey followed her, still laughing. 'Aren't you nervous though, Ruth? Aren't you worried He'll think you're too rich? I mean, you have such a divine home, Ruth. All the Venetian glass you collected on your overseas trips. And Bob's clocks. And this kitchen. What's He going to think of this Customtone kitchen, Ruth?'

Ruth was basting the lamb. 'He won't be looking at this house, Sylvia. He'll be looking into our hearts.'

Sylvia sipped her orange and mango juice. 'I think I'd rather He looked at this house, Ruth.'

'It's not as if we've done anything we need be ashamed of,' said Ruth.

'Have we done anything?' said Sylvia.

A little bit of fat hissed up and stung Ruth's cheek. This was the sort of talk she disliked, silly negative talk, and Sylvia was rather prone to it. Sylvia was a nice person, but she had absolutely no idea. Whenever there was a church function, a fete or a fundraising drive, someone had to cover for her. She could not be relied on. And Keith was the same. They were very nice people, but they didn't have a clue.

Ruth closed the oven door and said, 'Shall we go back to the lounge then, dear?'

But Sylvia had perched herself on a bar stool. 'He won't look like His pictures, you know, Ruth. He'll have a sallow complexion and lank black hair. Semitic looking. And probably quite short. I've tried to prepare myself, but I can't. I still see Him like my Harry G. Theaker picture book.' She was laughing again. 'Sitting Upon an Ass.'

Ruth wondered, not for the first time, if Sylvia was a believer. Bob had once told her that Keith had problems with the immaculate conception.

'How about you, Ruth? Have you prepared yourself?'

Ruth took Sylvia's empty glass. 'Unfortunately I don't have your imagination, dear.'

Returning to the lounge, Ruth saw straight away that Bob had ignored her sherry signal. Keith Creevey's face was flushed, and he was talking about Aborigines, silly negative talk about how the church had failed the Aboriginal people. The sherry bottle was almost empty, and Bob's face was also flushed. He was cross because he'd been unable to prevent Keith from hoeing into the olives.

'He's late, Ruth,' said Bob, indicating his infallible Thomas Tompion bracket clock. 'He's twenty-three minutes late.'

'May I?' Sylvia helped herself to two olives and sat down beside her husband.

Ruth picked up the sherry bottle. 'What we need is some nice music.' She crossed to the hi-fi to select an album, but Bob was there before her. He hated her to touch his hi-fi. 'What'll it be then?' Without waiting for suggestions Bob extracted 'Allan Wicks at the Organ of Canterbury Cathedral'. He blew off an imaginary speck of dust and placed it on the turntable. A loud knock sounded on the front door as he was lowering the playing arm. Sylvia gave a tiny scream, the needle careened across the disc, and Keith leapt to his feet, knocking over the last of the olives.

Ruth went to the door, still clutching the sherry bottle. She was an experienced hostess, but her heart was beating in her neck. This is silly, she said to herself. He would not want me to be nervous. She heard Keith say in a high silly voice, 'Am I prepared to meet my Maker?' She placed the sherry bottle on the marble topped mahogany washstand and opened the door.

A short man with shoulder-length black hair was standing on the mat and smiling at her. He wore a blue shirt, black cotton trousers and Adidas running shoes.

'Jesus?' said Ruth, faintly. But it was the interpreter, Mr Naji Jabour. Behind him still in shadow stood the Man of Sorrows. Ruth peered, almost swooning. She could smell cloves and mimosa. Jesus was smoking a cigarette and carrying a bunch of flowers. He wore steel-framed glasses, a pinstripe business coat with matching Fijian skirt and sandals. Oh, my godfather, thought Ruth. Everything was confusion. Mr Jabour and Bob were performing introductions. Keith Creevey was kneeling in the hall. Sylvia was laughing. She too had mistaken Mr Jabour for Jesus. Bob's French singing bird clock was sounding the hour. Jesus just managed to catch Ruth in His arms before she fell.

When she came to, the lounge room was in chaos. They had placed her on the sofa and just abandoned her. There were squashed olives on the carpet and a pile of bathroom towels on the hi-fi. She could hear Sylvia laughing in the kitchen. The TV was on, tuned to 'Sale of the Century'. Ruth tried to sit up, but someone was pressing her back against the cushions. It was Jesus. He was standing behind the sofa watching the TV. He stroked her forehead and murmured words she could not understand. 'Naji!' He called.

Mr Jabour ran in wearing Bob's barbecue apron. Sylvia followed him, still laughing. 'Everything's under control, Ruth. Mr Jabour is an experienced chef.'

'No worries, Ruth Jackson,' said Mr Jabour.

'But the lamb,' said Ruth.

Jesus said something then, and Mr Jabour and Sylvia laughed. Ruth closed her eyes. They could all understand Him except her. Jesus went on stroking her forehead. The scent of cloves was overpowering. Ruth suddenly remembered how her father used to cuddle her while talking to someone else. She remembered his sportscoat with the acorn buttons and how he had smelt of beer, except she hadn't known it was beer then. She opened her eyes and saw Keith Creevey with no shoes and socks on and his trousers rolled up, carrying her old brown plastic washing up bowl. It was full of water, and Keith was walking carefully but unsteadily and sloshing water on the carpet. 'Oops,' he said in a silly voice. 'Oops a daisy.' Bob was behind him, carrying a loofah.

Ruth struggled to sit up, but Jesus pressed her back again. Keith placed the washing up bowl on the floor in front of the sofa, and Jesus said something to Bob and took off His coat.

'He wants to wash your feet, Ruth,' said Bob.

Ruth thought of her puffy ankles and the corn growing between her toes that smelt like blue-vein cheese. And it had been years since she'd used a pumice stone. The soles of her feet were as tough as old boots. She got up off the sofa, panicky but determined. 'Thank you very much but I don't want Him to.' She turned to Keith. 'Please tell Him that I don't want Him to.'

'Naji!' Jesus was rolling up His sleeves.

Ruth ran, heading for the stairs, but Mr Jabour shot out of the kitchen and cut her off in the hall. She doubled back into the lounge, skidded on an olive, and now Bob was after her with the loofah. They were all after her except Jesus. Keith was lumbering about. The burr walnut display cabinet with the Venetian glass was trembling. This is ridiculous, thought Ruth. I'm being hunted in my own home. And she stopped suddenly, breathless and resentful, and allowed Bob and Keith to take her and bring her back to Jesus.

They sat her down on the sofa again, and Jesus turned off the TV while Sylvia helped her off with her Sup-hose.

Then Jesus sent them all away. 'There's no need to be afraid, Ruth.'

And He began to wash her feet, first her left foot, then her right, massaging her toes, working away with the loofah and whistling.

She was so dizzy and uncaring she didn't realise she had understood Him. She was standing in shallow water at Jervis Bay in her green bubble bathing costume with her water wings under her arms. Her father was calling to her from deep water, wanting her to swim to him without her water wings. 'I'm not afraid,' she said. Jesus was drying her toes one by one. 'This little piggy went to market,' He said.

'Grub's up!' called Mr Jabour. He had put one of the red table napkins on his head. Sylvia had copied him, laughing. Jesus took Ruth by the hand and led her to the table. Someone had removed her porcelain roses and replaced them with Jesus' mimosa. Keith started to say grace. 'For what we are about to receive, oh, Lord,' but Jesus had already sat down, motioning Ruth to sit on His right hand and Sylvia on His left. He placed a table napkin on Ruth's head and one on His own head and said, 'Give us a song, Naji.'

Mr Jabour began to sing 'Bless This House' as he served up the rice. They all joined in, and Bob and Keith put their napkins on their heads, and Jesus lit the red candles with His cigarette lighter. 'Bless this house, oh, Lord, we pray. Keep it safe by night and day.' Ruth wiggled her bare toes as she sang. This is just like a kids' party, she thought.

But Mr Jabour had done something very strange with the lamb. He had cut it into little pieces and mixed it all up with yoghurt. And what had happened to her baked potatoes and pumpkin? And Bob's Ben Ean. Mr Jabour was pouring out glasses of a pale bitter-tasting fluid. 'Drink up,' he said. 'Drink up, everyone.'

'Don't you like it, Ruth?' said Jesus.

'Oh, yes,' she said. 'It's very nice, thank you. Very nice indeed.'

Was He laughing at her? Her happiness began to recede, and she forked the lamb around her plate, trying to make it look less. Everyone else was eating heartily. Sylvia was absolutely wolfing it down. She forced herself to drink more of the bitter fluid, and Mr Jabour immediately refilled her glass.

'Five big meals for four big people from one leg of lamb and ten tomatoes, no worries.' Mr Jabour was talking with his mouth full to Bob and Keith about cooking.

'Isn't that incredible?' said Keith. 'Isn't that incredible, Bob?'

'Dear, you've got divine hands!' Sylvia was flirting with Jesus. She was actually running her fingers over the backs of His hands, over the raised scar tissue, and He was just letting her. Just sitting there and letting her. And smiling. 'It's the first thing I notice about a man. His hands.'

'Eat up, Ruth Jackson,' said Mr Jabour. He had already finished his lamb and was mopping up the juices on his plate with a piece of disgusting looking dark bread. 'For dessert we have Oo'whamat. Dough balls in syrup.'

'Yummy,' said Sylvia.

'But what about my pavlova?' burst out Ruth.

'I warned you about that, didn't I?' said Bob. 'I told you it was unsuitable.'

How she hated Bob sometimes. He never supported her, never stuck up for her when she most needed it. He let people insult her in shops and pretended not to hear. He had never really loved her. The only things he cared about were synchronising his silly clocks and detecting flaws in his hi-fi. She tried to eat more lamb, but it stuck in her throat. She was as unhappy now as she'd been happy ten minutes before. Jesus was deep in conversation with Sylvia. She was telling Him about her silly Harry G. Theaker picture book. Mr Jabour stood up and began to stack the plates. Everyone had finished except her.

'Come on, Ruth Jackson,' said Mr Jabour.

'I don't think I could eat any more.' She was practically in tears.

'No worries.' Mr Jabour took her plate. He was going back to the kitchen to fry up his dough balls. 'Then we have coffee. Sweet coffee for party. Bitter coffee for sad occasion. But this is party, hey Ruth Jackson?'

'Naji!' Jesus got up from the table without excusing Himself and followed Mr Jabour out to the kitchen.

'What's the matter, Ruth?' said Sylvia.

'Have you got one of your headaches?' said Keith.

'She always goes to too much trouble,' said Bob. 'And then she wonders why she doesn't enjoy herself.'

Ruth removed the red napkin from her head. These were the moments, wretched wretched moments, that hollowed out your heart. It was the accumulation of such moments that had made her marry Bob, make chocolate fudge for church fetes and collect Venetian glass. Her father had come downstairs on Anzac Day carrying a tartan suitcase and his tennis racquet and her mother had said, 'Good riddance to bad rubbish.' Ruth began to cry desperately into her table napkin. Her Saviour was still in the kitchen talking to Mr Jabour.

It was then that it happened: a farting, spluttering, rushing sound and a tomcat scream from Mr Jabour. Before Bob could reach the kitchen, Mr Jabour shot out with a frill of fire all down his right arm. 'Help me,' he cried. 'Help me, Ruth Jackson!'

They were all running about. Sylvia grabbed one of the towels off the hi-fi, and Ruth raced for her brown washing up bowl.

'Roll on the floor, Mr Jabour!' shouted Keith.

Bob had picked up the vase of mimosa and run smack into Sylvia. The two of them fell, winded, just as Keith managed to floor Mr Jabour in a flying tackle. All four of them were shouting and flailing on the carpet. Sylvia had broken her denture. Keith was slapping Mr Jabour's still-smoking arm. Ruth flung her washing up bowl water at Mr Jabour. Suddenly the house was in darkness.

'Naji.' Jesus was moving among them in the darkness, flicking His cigarette lighter. 'Let's have a look at the damage.'

Ruth stood perfectly still. Nobody was moving or speaking except Him. She could smell cloves again, and her poor sad watertight heart was pulsing like a tree frog. Mr Jabour's arm glowed briefly, bright and unblemished, right as rain. The lighter was moving away from her, but she could still see herself in His glasses. 'Don't leave me, Father,' she whispered.

And all at once Bob's clocks began to strike, all striking together for the very first time, the Brighton Pavilion skeleton clock and the Thomas Tompion bracket clock, the Austrian cuckoo clock and the French singing bird clock, the Big Ben picture clock and the federation Kookaburra clock, and the early eighteenth-century brass lantern clock with the half-second dead-beat escapement.

The noise was deafening, and Jesus had to shout to make Himself heard.

'Come along then, Ruth!' He shouted. 'Follow me, my little lamb!' Mr Jabour had opened the front door. 'Give us your hand, Ruth Jackson.'

And they walked down the front path together, Ruth in the middle, with Mr Jabour on her left, and Jesus on her right, out the front gate and into Bungalow Avenue, turning right into Telegraph Road and then right again and out onto the Pacific Highway.

It was a mild and starry night, and Ruth enjoyed the feel of the road beneath her bare feet. 'Give us a song, Naji,' she said.

Stephanie Johnson

The Glass Whittler

1988

She changed cities. She had actually changed countries but the people around her looked the same, only more aggressive in their speech and gestures. It was to be expected. The city she changed to was bigger, the country harder, invaded a century earlier by more desperate men.

She slept in a room without windows and sweated at night. When she woke the sheets were damp. She would touch the man and he would be wet too, the nearest part of his body slippery. It felt like she imagined a baby's head to feel, the slime still on it. It frightened her.

She spent the days reading maps and walking. The two activities rarely had any relation to each other. The city was immense. There were strange patches of green inhabited by ancient species of animal – ibis, marsupial – and in the fountains gleaming macho men immortalised in stone. She noticed the places in the green patches where the green didn't grow properly. It was a disappointment to her – the dry earth, the sense of failure, of not being quite strong enough to survive in the opaline gassy air. She would walk quickly through these parts of the park, watching how they attracted an element. One day there was an old man, rolling in his pyjama pants, grasping at the fly, his threadbare jacket showing evidence of other daybeds. He reminded her of her night sweats. It was conceivable to end up like that. It could happen while you weren't looking.

At night the man was kind. He pretended he was responsible for the night sweats. It was an unspoken agreement between them. In the dark room the sheets never dried properly, and the flowers she put on the mantelpiece lasted forever. The scented bottle he dabbed on his face left fragrant shoals in the chilled air, a reassuring smell. If she shut the door on to the landing at any time of the day the white flowers glowed in the dark, and she could breathe in the smell of him.

When they went to bed the man would sometimes make love to her, absentmindedly. Then he would sleep, drugged with his pleasure, and she would lie alert beside him. Sometimes she would begin the slow slide to sleep, but would be jolted awake by myriads of people stacked like larvae in their cells, wrapped in white sheets like shrouds – cocoons of life that would metamorphose in the morning to the people she saw walking purposefully through the streets. At night their breathing and anxious dreams pervaded the windowless walls of the room. Sleep, when it came, was a damp door shutting them out.

In the morning the man would polish his cameras, heave his equipment into his car, and go to work. She didn't know where he went, or what he did, except that when he came home he was tired of light and welcomed the dark room. The photographs he brought back were of women – endless strips of tiny women holding bottles of shampoo, or canisters of lavatory cleaner. He would tell her stories of the women who did the make-up, the women who posed for the pictures, the go-getter people from the advertising agencies, and the sums of money involved. She shrank from them, never remembering the details. They worked a kind of violence in her.

The man interpreted her lack of interest in his work as arrogance. Sometimes he shouted at her to go back to where she came from – the tiny islands shaped like a question mark at the bottom of the world where people retained a kind of dignity, and mostly held their souls inside them at night. She considered returning, but she carried an obligation from the place of the question mark. The obligation was to see the rest of the world, or at least this ancient red continent, and report home.

Every day she looked in the paper for a job, but nobody needed a glass whittler. Nobody even knew what a glass whittler was. In the park she would roll up the newspaper and stuff it in a wastepaper basket. She would only do this after the park keepers had been around, so that it would still be there as a blanket for one of the old men. As she sat on the park benches she would feel them around her, the voices of their dead companions who didn't know they were dead, mingling sadly with the live ones. Then she would return to the dark room and sleep, the city's sleepers up and about, their wandering souls firmly involved in operating steering wheels and gear sticks, or lifting cups of coffee and cigarettes to their active mouths, or counting money with their sunburnt fingers.

One night the man returned angry and late. He showed her a photograph of a woman with warm eyes in a rumpled bed on the other side of the continent. He said she was interested in his work and that she wasn't afraid of harsh light or the huge inland expanses where the green didn't grow properly. She looked at this photograph of a woman who had a knowledge of the man shining from her eyes – and hungered for a piece of glass to whittle.

There was a kitchen downstairs which they shared with three men and a woman. After the man left, out into the night and slamming the door after him, she peeled back the moist sheets and went there.

A single wine glass stood on the bench, among the bread crumbs and dirty cups. She held it to the light bulb and saw the colours refract on the rim. In the bowl of the glass a cockroach waved its legs. She smashed the glass in the sink and gathered up the glistening fragments. The cockroach righted itself and fled beneath a saucer.

Upstairs she moulded the glass with her hands. The candles she'd lit about the dark room waved their golden heads in the breeze from her working arms making the glass glitter and blaze. Trickles of blood ran down her arms to the sheets of the bed, where she crouched intent on her craft. Her fingers twisted and kneaded the glass, her blood working as mortar, thick and scarlet.

Finally the globe hung from the ceiling, a mass of flickering emerald, indigo and vermilion, a perfect replica of a perfect world.

Below it she lay drained on the bed, splinters of glass cold in her cooling flesh. That night she slept alone, giving neither pleasure to the man nor comfort to the souls of the city.

Of course we have all visited the glass works where the men shovel the glinting shards into the flames and blow the resulting morass into objects of beauty and practicality. But I have told you this story because she was the only glass whittler the world has ever known, and in this estival city she created her world of gentle light, without a knife.

Jan Hutchinson
Romance, Gardening and Feminist Theory
1988

Old enough to be your mother

But Gemma, she's old enough to be your mother, was the first thing Gemma's friends said to her when they found out about it. And French too. Gemma, how can you, not after what they've done in the Pacific.

But Gemma didn't care. She didn't listen. Gemma was in love.

At fifty-two, Odette looked barely a decade older than Gemma herself. Her fine French features betrayed little of her pre-war childhood in the olive groves of Arles. Her eyes shone with a hint of the gypsy. Her hair was the colour of cut coal.

Ah, oui, she had said on that first day they spoke. I can see you have a love of the gardening.

Gemma had looked straight into those eyes. Yes, she'd said, I have.

Two tubers

The prevailing climate and north-easterly aspect of Gemma's front garden were perfect for chokos. It was free from frost and provided the maximum sunlight necessary for their long growing season. The fact that her front garden was small did not matter unduly, since the vines required little land space in which to grow, so long as they had a sufficient area on which to climb. The Victorian wrought-iron railings and leaden-grey slates of the front veranda of Gemma's semi-detached were more than adequate, and at the height of summer curly bright tendrils could be seen twining in and out of the elaborate, indeed intricate, lacework.

Although hardy, the plants required ample water, especially during dry weather. They grew well in the well-drained loam of Gemma's place. Even though single plants could be quite successful, Gemma knew it was better to plant a pair at a time, and thus had planted two tubers, one in front of each post of the veranda.

Gemma had dug the soil deep, incorporated a good layer of well-rotted manure and about half a bucketful of ash. Since the soil tended to be a bit clayey in wet weather, she'd mixed in an equal part of river sand before nestling the already shooting tubers about seven centimetres below the surface of the soil and with the shoot end pointing upwards.

Choko vines require very little attention, but Gemma made sure that the weeds did not get out of hand and, until the plants were well-established, had guarded against the young shoots breaking by providing a wire netting surround.

But a story just about gardening is perhaps not everybody's cup of tea. If it's romance you're after, though, you'll have to hang on a bit.

More often than she used to

Imagine Gemma's front garden, then. It is Sunday afternoon. Gemma has just watered her choko vines, transplanted a punnet of tarragon seedlings, thinned out the lemon thyme, cut back the borage.

You can save the flowers, she hears.

Gemma looks up. She's seen this woman before. She walks by this way sometimes. Perhaps more often than she used to.

You put them in a mixture of household borax and dry sand and that way they will keep that beautiful colour.

Gemma looks back to the penetratingly vivid blue stars and puts the cut stems to one side.

April fool

The choko vines fruited every year towards the end of March, and by the first week in April had reached their peak. This was a fortunate coincidence, because it meant that those pale green fruits of vegetables were at their youngest, tenderest, in short at their very best in time for Gemma's annual cocktail party and choko exhibition, held every year on April Fool's Day at sundown, by which time a prank could no longer, according to the rules, be considered such.

This annual event was regarded quite seriously and looked forward to as marking the beginning of the round of parties for the cooler season by that select set of people known in some circles simply as Gemma's friends.

Not another bloody ghetto story

The phone rings. Odette comes in from her back garden, wiping her muddy feet on the doormat and propping her spade against the architrave.

What have you been doing? asks her friend on the line.

Gardening, she says.

Have you got any plans for the afternoon? he asks.

I was going to do some writing, says Odette. I'm working on a new story.

Not another bloody ghetto story? her friend asks.

No, no, she protests. It's a lesbian love story.

You haven't had one of those for a while, he says.

Haven't had any kind of story in a while, she says.

What's it called?

Romance, Gardening and Feminist Theory.

Sounds complicated.

The romance and gardening are all right. It's the feminist theory I'm having trouble with. And this story is being written in a quite different way to any others I've written so far.

How do you mean? her friend asks.

It's all in dribs and drabs. All the bits just keep on coming to me and I go and scribble them down as they come, and hope that sooner or later they will all add up.

So how's that different? he asks.

Usually it all happens in a rush, she says, like a fast orgasm after a long period of celibacy. As if it's all just been lying there in wait, the what I want to say and the how I want to say it. It usually all comes out in one go. Voilà, and the draft is done. The first line, the last line, the title, the structure, the tone. Everything. With this one it's different. It all has a different feel to it. It's slow, tentative. Like being in bed with a new lover, one who feels as no other lover has felt before. And so you see

I can't say what's going to happen. Because I don't know. I have all the ingredients but I don't know how the recipe will turn out.

I thought you were trying to stop writing about food all the time, Odette, either in reality or in metaphor.

You're right, she says, I am. How's this then? I've got a packet of seeds, a surprise mixture. I have a fair idea of what may be in the packet, but not exactly. I dig my ground, manure it, then scatter the seed, not knowing how many will germinate, which will find the chosen spot perfect and so flourish, which will fall fallow.

Much better, he says. Well, have fun with your lesbian. And your story.

I intend to, she says.

A herb for every man

It was the right time of year to divide the chives, snip off the starry heads of basil, uproot the spent coriander. Gemma had done all that and was now digging carefully around her plants, turning the soil over with her little fork. She dug in some three-in-one manure, not too much as she didn't want her herbs to lose flavour through over-fertilising. Her hard work was paying off. The garden was doing well. Everybody said so.

Every woman should plant herbs. They are so necessary for the cooking.

It is that French woman again.

Yeah, says Gemma, I throw them into everything. And they're great companion plants for the chokos.

Chokos? What are chokos?

Vegetables, these vegetables, says Gemma, fingering the tendrils.

Ah when I was young, says Odette, I grew vegetables. In Provence there was plenty of land. But when I moved to Paris I had only an apartment. Vegetables were not possible. I had only some terracotta pots on my balcony. Oh, I had geraniums like everyone else, but I also had herbs. I had, she says, a herb for every man I had loved.

There were many by the time I left.

Oh, says Gemma.

What do you do with chokos?

Mother used to say that in the war they made apple pies with them. Peeled and sliced and in with a bit of Granny Smith and you'd never know the difference. Boiled or baked, that's what she did with them. Always with parsley sauce, lots of it. They'd be drowning in it. She'd never grow it herself, the parsley that is. Grow parsley and you'll get pregnant, she used to say. But she did have a knack with the chokos, all over the palings, with the passionfruits fighting for their breath and a look-in on a bit of sunlight.

So, what do you do with chokos? any one of Gemma's friends would persist.

Chutney, you can always make choko chutney. Or choko and apple jam, like in those wartime pies.

Look, Gemma, I don't know, I thought you were sick of cooking.

Thought you'd had enough of it.

I have.

Well, forget about how you're going to dish up all those fucking chokos and for heaven's sake throw them in the proverbial compost. Soup, what about cream of choko soup? Choko scones. Stuffed chokos. Scallopine alla choko. Squid braised with chokos.

Gem-ma

OK, into the compost they go. But you know what will happen? They will shoot anew. Vines, new vines will spring up out of the compost, they will thrive in the warm richness and I'll have more than ever. Then what? Compote of choko. Fricasseed chokos. Choko cocottes. Choko soufflé. Pretend they're a new and rare variety of avocado and serve them freshly halved à la vinaigrette.

No, no, you've said quite enough. Now get out of my kitchen, girl, and back to your garden. But, just before you go, what do you do with chokos?

Give them to your friends.

You've made your bed

Gemma, you can't possibly grow vegetables in the front garden. Mother, why ever not?

It's just not done, dear. It's like hanging your washing out there, knickers and all.

Come now, mother.

Well, if you insist, at least stick to something low and unobtrusive.

Like silver beet, or rhubarb. But I suppose you've made your bed, Gemma.

Beds, mother, corrected Gemma.

It was what her mother had said when Gemma first and finally had got around to telling her mother she was a lesbian.

Well, you've made your bed, Gemma; her mother had attempted to bring the conversation to its unnatural conclusion.

Mostly it's unmade these days, mother, Gemma had resisted the temptation to say.

Gemma had to hand it to her mother, though. She had changed over the years, become more accepting, grown accustomed to Gemma dropping in unexpectedly with one of her – what was the right word? – girlfriends. She'd greeted them all with polite propriety, remembered to ask whether they'd like herbal tea, kept a supply of wholemeal cookies double-wrapped in plastic supermarket bags to keep them fresh.

And then they'd stopped, the women coming with her. Gemma would visit alone. Gemma's mother could no longer admit that she was relieved. No longer could she think, with more than the usual hopefulness that mothers have of their daughters, that Gemma had come to her senses, seen the error of her ways, recognised it as just a passing phase. They had all been quite nice. And no man had ever appeared. Gemma's mother was a patient woman. Her own marriage had produced that quality in her. She sat it out.

Forgive me, Gemma, she finally started one day, but isn't it a long time – she paused searching for a suitable expression – since you've been with anyone?

Gemma looked startled. Her friends too had started to needle her. What was she waiting for? Was she becoming a radical celibate? If so, it didn't suit her. You should go out more,

Gemma, they said. And why do you spend so much time in that garden of yours?

It was a long time since Gemma's mother had said, I don't mean to pry, Gemma, but surely what you do with those women couldn't be altogether satisfactory, could it?

Back-breaking work

Gemma looks up from her weeding just as the French woman passes by again. That must be twice today, she thinks.

It is a hot day for such hard work, Odette says.

Yeah, back-breaking work for sure, says Gemma, I can tell you.

But it will be worth it. Your garden, it will be very beautiful.

Hope so, says Gemma, avoiding the woman's eyes.

Excuse me for asking, my dear, but why do you not grow any flowers?

Couldn't be bothered really, says Gemma. Not all that much you can do with them, is there? You can't eat them. But I do have a few succulents down the back in pots.

Oh, says Odette, a garden without flowers is like a woman without lovers. I could not live without my lavender, my marguerites, my primroses, my crocuses. Perhaps you would like to come and see them some time? I do not live far away.

Les fruits de la passion

In your ordinary run-of-the-Mills-and-Boon type of romance, what might our protagonists be doing by now? Falling in each other's arms, sighing in a moment of total ecstasy, melting with the heat of passion? Perhaps. Maybe their love, their final consummate love, has been thwarted by parents, or by a previous lover. Maybe their own innate, human blindness has prevented them from seeing that they were so right for each other, that this would be the love that would surpass all others.

Let us look at Gemma and Odette now. Odette is walking along the footpath, towards Gemma's place. Gemma is in the lounge room, or the sitting room as she has of late preferred to call it. But, contrary to its current name, Gemma is not sitting. She is standing, and has been standing for quite some time now, at the bay window. For quite the better part of the morning, in fact, she has been peering through the matchstick blinds, unseen from the outside but with a perfect view through the naked green of the choko leaves to the front gate. She has been more than a little impatient, impatient in that way that comes only with a sense of impending excitement. For Gemma has decided, contrary to the best advice of her friends, to invite Odette to her party. Indeed, she has decided to ask her personally, rather than drop one of the invitations printed in dark bottle ink on pale-leaf, linen-look paper into Odette's letterbox in the next street.

Odette now approaches. Gemma watches as she pauses at the gate, glances uncertainly at the garden, nods delicately at the vines, then continues on her way. Gemma's inner clock starts ticking. She knows exactly how long it will take Odette to walk to the end of the street, cross the road to the corner shop, buy her few daily necessities, and head back.

Gemma waits no longer at the window. She dashes out the back, into the courtyard, nearly trips on the doorstep. She grabs two square grey punnets, each containing a bright, shiny, irregularly leaved green seedling with a plastic marker saying Norfolk Island Black. She picks up her rustproof garden trowel, her canvas and cotton garden gloves. Back she goes through the house, down the dark hallway to the front door. She must appear cool, natural, as if she'd been there a while. Gemma takes a deep breath and begins to dig.

Ah, Gemma, she hears Odette's voice, there you are. I was wondering why you weren't in your garden these last few mornings. She pronounces Gemma's name with a softened 'g' so it sounds like the sweet stickiness of caramel fudge or the velvety lining of a hoya in full flower.

Ah, Gemma, what are you planting now?

Gemma lowers her head minutely, blushes slightly, then raises her eyes so they look directly into Odette's.

She refrains from embarking on an explanation as to how she'd tired of chokos, of how she wanted to grow something altogether more voluptuous, richer, mouth-watering. She does not go into details of how if she cares for the new plants properly she will get a second crop, of how she longs to see the sensuous purple and cream flowers with their long golden stamens, of how she has in fact, for once in her life, taken her mother's advice. But of all this she says nothing, not wanting to lose any of the impact of that single, three-syllable word.

Passionfruit, she says.

Ah, les fruits de la passion, says Odette.

Oui, replies Gemma, just a little self-consciously. And so you see this will be the last choko party I have one every year and everybody comes I know it sounds silly but they all love it they all say so they all rave about it. She is losing her calm now, her poise has tangled. So, I'm putting in these new plants and as soon as the season's over I'll whip out the chokos and voilà, no more chokos.

Oh, says Odette.

And what I really want to know is, well, if you'd come.

To your party?

If you'd like to.

I should be delighted, says Odette, touching Gemma's hand which is resting on the gate post, sending small shivers of delight through Gemma's arm. She can see the trowel shaking.

So, says Odette, at what time should I come?

You've got to be joking

Gemma, whispers Odette, still at the front door on the evening of the party. Are all your friends women? Are there no men at all?

Yes, I mean no, I mean yes, I know only women, says Gemma.

Ah, says Odette.

They, my friends, and me, we are woman-identified women, stammers Gemma, not used to such a challenge.

You've got to be joking, Gemma's friends had said when she told them she'd invited Odette.

I've never been more serious in my life, she'd said.

All these women making separatist mountains out of sexual molehills, says Odette now. What has feminism done to us?

Gemma is now regretting her invitation to Odette. She is thinking this will be the end of it. She's blown it, missed her chance, been nipped in the bud, so to speak. It must have all been in her imagination that there was something between her and Odette, something that she could not yet put her finger on. Well, there was no use in pursuing it now.

Green fingers

Odette does stay at the party. But let's not elaborate on Gemma's friends bitching about her in the corner in the kitchen. Let's skip the details of the choko carved like elegant jade in the shape of a swan, of the winner in the hairiest choko section, of the biggest organically grown choko and even of the delights of the choko and crême de menthe punch, Gemma's own concoction, which practice over the years has produced to perfection. Let's hurry to the end of the party, knowing as we do how impatient readers, like some lovers, can be to get to the good bits. Here we are at Gemma's front door. Odette and she have talked on, long after the others have left and gone home to their ideologically paired beds.

You know the sort of thing.

Cups of tea, another glass of wine, how about some port. Gemma has put on softer music, turned the lights down.

You've all been there, done that. There are some easy things about writing romance.

And now, dear Gemma, I'm afraid I must go, says Odette. It was a lovely party.

Knew it, thinks Gemma.

Unless, of course, says Odette, you had meant to ask me to stay.

I don't know what the others will say when they find out about this, says Gemma later in bed as she lies in Odette's arms, the sweet taste of the older woman still in her mouth.

It does not matter, Gemma my love, what they think, only that we are together at last.

But, starts Gemma.

I know what you're going to say, says Odette, that to be truly woman is to be feminist, to be truly feminist is to be lesbian, to be truly lesbian is to be separatist, and to be truly separatist means having nothing to do with women who have anything to do with men. Don't think I haven't heard it all before.

But, tries Gemma again.

I love you, Gemma, says Odette, nibbling now at the furry mango seed of flesh between the younger woman's thighs.

I'll never understand what you see in me then, says Gemma.

That is easy my love, my one and only love, it's your green fingers. And I want them inside me now.

Post-lesbian

The next morning Gemma can still not quite believe it. And yet here Odette is, under Gemma's doona, in Gemma's arms, placing light kisses on Gemma's breasts, sucking surely at Gemma's pale nipples.

So, this is what young feminists get up to these days, says Odette stroking Gemma's belly. Choko parties, indeed.

Actually, says Gemma, still flushed from the early love-making, I consider myself post-feminist.

Oh, says Odette, with the utmost seriousness, and I suppose that makes me post-lesbian.

The stuff of real romance

It'd make a great story, says Gemma over breakfast.

What do you mean? asks Odette, dipping bread into her hot, milky coffee.

Oh, you know. Young woman who likes gardening grows vegies out the front in hopes of meeting new lover. Older but still attractive woman with past. Wicked sisters. A bit of French. Food. Love grows in spite of all. The stuff of real romance.

Barbara Anderson

Up the River with Mrs Gallant

1989

Mr Levis invited them to call him Des. And this is Arnold he said.

Mr Kent said Hi Arnold.

Mrs Kent said that she was pleased to meet him.

Mrs Gallant said Hullo, Arnold.

Mr Gallant said Good morning.

Mr Borges said nothing.

Des said that if they just liked to walk down to the landing stage Arnold would bring the boat down with the tractor.

Mrs Gallant said wasn't Mr Gallant going to leave the car in the shade.

Mr Gallant said that if Mrs Gallant was able to tell him where the shade from one tree was going to be for the next six hours he would be happy to.

Mr Kent said that he was going to give it a burl anyway and reparked the Falcon beneath the puriri.

Mrs Kent told Mrs Gallant that she and Stan were from Hamilton.

Mrs Gallant told Mrs Kent that she and Eric were from Rotorua.

Mrs Kent said that she had a second cousin in Rotorua. Esme. Esme. She would be forgetting her own head next. And that she supposed she should wait for Stan but what the hell.

Mrs Gallant smiled at Mr Borges.

Mr Borges nodded.

At the landing stage Des said that he would like them to take turns sitting in the front and perhaps the ladies?

Mrs Kent remarked that the landing stage looked a bit ass over tip.

Arnold said that the landing stage was safe as houses and would the lady get into the boat.

Mrs Kent said Where was Stan.

Mr Kent said Here.

Mrs Kent asked Mr Kent where he had got to. She hopped across the landing stage, climbed onto the boat and into one of the front seats. She said that it wasn't too lady like but that she would be right.

Mrs Gallant followed.

Mr Kent and Mr Gallant climbed into the next row.

Des said that Arnold was on the Access Training Scheme and doing very well but it was difficult to fit in the hundred hours river time in a business like this and that he hoped that the customers would have no objection if Arnold came with them and drove the boat back because of the hundred hours.

Mrs Kent said that she would be delighted anytime.

Mr Kent said Well.

Mr Gallant asked how many passengers the boat was licensed for.

Des said that it was licensed for seven passengers.

Mrs Gallant smiled.

Mr Borges said nothing.

Arnold said Good on them, climbed into the boat and sat in the back row with Mr Borges. Mr Borges smiled.

Des started the motor and picked up the microphone. He said that the river was approximately ninety miles long and had been called the Rhine Of New Zealand. It had been used as a waterway since the time of the first Maoris. Perhaps the busiest time on the river, he said, was the end of the nineteenth century and the beginning of the twentieth until the Main Trunk was completed. River boats plied, freight and passengers were transported in thousands and in all that time there were only two deaths which must be something of a record.

Mr Gallant said that he hoped that it would stay that way.

Des invited him to come again.

Mrs Kent said that Mr Gallant was only kidding.

Mr Gallant said No he wasn't.

Mrs Gallant said Eric.

Des said that he was born and brought up on the river. He had lived on the river all his life and he knew the river like the back of his hand and his aim was for every one of his passengers to learn more about this beautiful river which was steeped in history.

Mr Kent said that Des would do him.

Mrs Kent said Hear Hear.

Mr Borges, Mr Gallant and Arnold said nothing.

Mrs Gallant said that it was a lovely day.

Des said that she wasn't running as sweet as usual, probably a few stones up the grille.

Mrs Gallant asked What did that mean.

Des said Stones you know up the grille.

Mrs Gallant said that she realised that.

Mr Gallant smiled.

Mrs Kent said that they had a lovely day for it anyhow.

Des said they certainly had and to take a look at the flying fox across the river. He explained that the alignment of the posts was very important indeed.

Mr Gallant said that it would be.

Des said that otherwise she could come across but she wouldn't go back. On the other hand if it was wrong the other way she would go back but she wouldn't come across.

Mr Gallant said Exactly.

Mr Kent said it was all Dutch to him Ooh Pardon,

Mrs Kent said that the young man wasn't Dutch and that Stan needn't worry.

Mr Kent said Then what was he?

Mrs Kent said that yes the day certainly was a cracker.

Mrs Gallant smiled.

Des said that the cooling system wasn't operating as per usual either. Usually she stayed at twenty. That was what he liked her at. Twenty.

Mrs Gallant said that it was at seventy now was it not.

Des said Yes it was.

Mrs Gallant said Oh.

Mr Gallant laughed.

Des said that they certainly would like Pipiriki.

Mrs Kent said That was for sure.

Des moored the boat at the Pipiriki landing stage. Everyone climbed out. Des put a large carton on an outdoor table and said they could help themselves to tea or coffee.

Mrs Gallant said that she and Eric would only need one teabag between them as they both took tea very weak without milk.

Des said that Mrs Gallant needn't worry as he had provided two tea bags each per person as usual.

Mr Gallant said that she was only trying to help.

Mrs Kent asked if there was a toilet.

Arnold pointed up the path.

Des said that after lunch they should go up and look at Pipiriki. Pipiriki House had once been a world famous hotel. It had burned down in 1959. He said to have a good look at the shelter and to go around the back as there were some flush toilets.

Mrs Kent said that now Des told her and they both laughed.

Mrs Gallant said What shelter.

Des said A shelter for tourists you know trampers, that sort of thing.

Everyone liked Pipiriki very much. After an hour they climbed back into the boat.

Mr Kent said that he wished some of those activists could see all those kids happy and swimming.

Mr Gallant said Why?

Mr Kent said to look at that one jumping there. That he hadn't a care in the world.

Mr Gallant said that that was hardly the point.

Mrs Gallant said Eric.

Mr Gallant said Hell's delight woman.

Mr Borges smiled.

Mrs Kent said that they used to live near Cambridge but that they had moved in to Hamilton when the boy took over.

Mrs Gallant said Was that right, and that she wished they had been able to land at Jerusalem.

Arnold said that he could go a swim.

Des said that he had been going to have a good look at her yesterday but that he hadn't had a break for so long and that he just hadn't felt like it.

No one said anything.

Des said that anyway he had had another booking in the end as things had turned out.

The boat leapt and bucked high in the air.

Mrs Kent said Ooops.

Des said that that showed you what happened if you let your concentration slip even for a second with a jetty. She had hit a stump.

Mr Gallant laughed.

Arnold asked if the Boss would like him to take over.

Des and Arnold laughed.

Mrs Gallant said to look at that kingfisher.

Mrs Kent said Where.

Mrs Gallant said There. That Mrs Kent was too late. That it had gone.

Des pointed out many points of interest and said that no she certainly wasn't going too good.

Mrs Gallant said that hadn't the temperature gauge gone up to eighty or was she wrong.

Des said that no she was not wrong and that he had better give her a breather and stopped the boat. He said it was probably the temperature of the water, it being a hot day.

Nobody said anything. The boat rocked, silent on the trough of its own waves. The sun shone.

Des said that should have cooled her down a bit and started the boat.

The temperature gauge climbed to seventy.

Des said that was more like it and that there had been a Maori battle on that island between the Hau Hau supporters and the non-supporters.

Mr Gallant wondered why they had chosen an island.

Des said that Mr Gallant had him there and swung the boat into a shallow tributary of the river. He told Arnold that they had better check the grille and how would Arnold like a swim.

Arnold said that that would be no problem. He climbed around onto the bow of the boat and said that they would now see his beautiful body. He removed his shirt and told Mrs Gallant and Mrs Kent to control themselves.

Mrs Kent yelped.

Arnold faced the vertical cliff of the bank, presented his shorts clad buttocks and shook them.

Everyone laughed except Mr Gallant and Mr Borges.

Mr Borges stood up quickly, took a photograph of Arnold's back view, and sat down again.

Arnold jumped into the water and swam to the back of the boat. Des fumbled beneath his feet and handed the passengers various pieces of equipment for Arnold to poke up the grille. The male passengers handed the things on to Arnold with stern efficiency.

After some time Arnold said that he had found three stones up the grille.

Des said that that was good.

Arnold said that they were not big buggers though.

Des said Never mind.

Arnold handed the equipment back into the boat and did a honeypot jump from the shallow water into a deep pool.

Mr Kent said See?

Arnold swam to the bow of the boat and heaved himself into the boat.

Mr Borges took a photograph of Arnold's front view.

Mrs Gallant said that they were lucky that Arnold had come with them.

Mrs Kent said that Mrs Gallant could say that again and would the boat go better now that Arnold had removed the stones.

Des said that he hoped so.

Mr Gallant laughed.

They stopped several times on the return trip for the boat to cool down and as she was not going too well Des sometimes had to make several sweeps before she could pick up enough speed for her to lift up over the rapids. Des said that normally at this stage, when she was less than half full of gas he could fling her about all over the place no sweat.

Mr Gallant said that they must be thankful for small mercies.

Des swung the boat in a wide spraying circle and pulled into the jetty at the old flour mill. They climbed the hill, Des carrying the afternoon tea carton. After tea Des said that he would tell them about the old flour mill and the river in general. Everyone expressed interest. They trooped into the warm shadowy old building and Des began.

After half an hour Mrs Kent asked whether Des would mind if she sat down.

Des said that although perhaps it was technically more correct to call them river boats he still thought of them as steamers though strictly speaking they weren't steamers for long.

Mrs Kent sat down.

Mrs Gallant sat down.

Mr Kent looked as though he was going to cry.

Mr Gallant closed his eyes.

Arnold sat outside in the shade.

Mr Borges joined him.

After three quarters of an hour Des said that he hoped they had all learned something of the river.

They climbed down to the river in silence.

Des said that as she wasn't the best perhaps if Mrs Gallant and Mr Kent would like to sit in front.

Mr Gallant muttered something about sensible arrangement of ballast.

Mrs Kent asked Des why.

Arnold said it was because he liked the good-looking girls in the back with him.

Mrs Kent told Arnold to get away and climbed nimbly into the back seat.

Mrs Gallant said nothing.

They set off with Des at the wheel. The temperature gauge rose above eighty. Des asked the passengers to look around their feet for a tool which would enable Arnold to take another poke up the grille without getting out of the boat.

Mrs Gallant said that there was a pipe thing here if that was any help.

Mrs Kent gave a startled cry and said What was that smoke.

Mr Gallant said that that was steam.

Mrs Kent said that it was red hot that pipe thing there.

Mr Gallant said that he was not at all surprised.

Arnold said that she would be right.

Des said that she had better have another cool off and stopped the boat.

The boat limped to the original landing jetty two hours later than planned. The passengers collected their belongings without comment and trailed up the hill.

Des told Arnold that he could bring the boat up.

Arnold said that Des was the Boss.

Mrs Gallant remarked that it had been a very interesting day and that wasn't the river beautiful.

Mrs Kent said that yes it was but that she had felt so sorry for the poor chap.

Mr Gallant said God in Heaven.

Mrs Gallant remarked that she saw that Mr Kent's car was in the shade.

Mr Gallant said that it probably had not been for the first six hours.

Mrs Gallant said that that remark was typical absolutely typical.

Mrs Kent said that they used to have Jerseys but the boy had switched to Friesians.

Mr Kent said that he had been happy enough in Jerseys but that there you were.

Mrs Kent said that they just want to be different and that it was quite understandable.

Mr Kent said that he had never said it wasn't.

Mr Borges said nothing.

Arnold appeared on the tractor, pulling the boat on its trailer. He parked it in the shed and appeared with a Visitors' Book. He invited the passengers to make their crosses.

Everyone laughed except Mr Gallant and Mr Borges.

Des said that he would give her an overhaul tomorrow that was for sure.

Mrs Kent signed the book and wrote Lovely day under Comments.

Mr Kent signed and wrote Ditto.

Mr Gallant signed his name only.

Mr Borges signed and wrote Sweden.

Mrs Gallant missed the signing. She stumped across the bleached grass and stood gazing at the river.

It said nothing.

GLENDA ADAMS (b.1939) was born and educated in Sydney. In 1964 she travelled to New York to study and has lived there ever since, teaching creative writing at Columbia University and other colleges. 'Wedding' comes from her first collection, *Lies and Stories*, published in New York in 1976; it was reprinted in her first Australian collection, *The Hottest Night of the Century* (1979). She has since published two novels, winning a number of prizes for the latest, *Dancing on Coral* (1987).

BARBARA ANDERSON (b.1926) was born in Hawkes Bay. Anderson began writing after working for most of her life as a teacher and lab technician. She has published stories in a number of periodicals and brought out a collection *I think we should go into the jungle* in 1989.

ETHEL ANDERSON (1883–1958) was born in Leamington, England, while her Australian parents were travelling. Educated in Sydney, she married a British army officer and lived in England and India before returning to Australia in 1926. She published three collections of stories, three of poetry and three of non-fiction. 'The Rector's Wife Tempts the Bishop with a Brew of Nyppe' comes from *At Parramatta* (1956), interlinked stories most of which also relate ironically to one or other of the seven deadly sins.

JESSICA ANDERSON was born in Queensland and educated in Brisbane. She later spent some time in London but has lived in Sydney for most of her life. While working for the A.B.C., she wrote plays and adaptations of novels for radio, but did not begin writing novels herself till she was 40. She first came to prominence when her fourth novel, *Tirra Lirra by the River* (1978), won several literary awards. It was followed by *The Impersonators* (1980), also a prize-winner, and *Stories from the Warm Zone and Sydney Stories* (1987), source of 'The Late Sunlight'.

ISOBEL ANDREWS was born in Scotland and grew up in New Zealand. She wrote over fifty plays, winning a number of awards, poetry, stories, two novels, articles and reviews. A collection of stories *Something to Tell* was published in 1944.

THEA ASTLEY (b.1925) was born and educated in Brisbane. She taught at primary and secondary schools in Queensland and later in Sydney; then lectured at Macquarie University, Sydney, from 1967–1980. Since 1958 she has published nine novels, many of which have won major awards, as well as two collections of stories. 'Right Off the Map' comes from her most recent book, *It's Raining in Mango* (1987), interlinked stories relating the history of one North Queensland family since the nineteenth century. In 1988 it won the inaugural Steele Rudd Award, given annually for the best collection of stories by an Australian author.

MARJORIE BARNARD (1897–1987) was born and educated in Sydney. After gaining First Class Honours and the University Medal in History at Sydney University, she won a scholarship to Oxford, declined at her father's insistence. She worked as a librarian and, as 'M. Barnard Eldershaw', published five novels, one of the first collections of critical essays on Australian fiction, three historical studies and a play, all written jointly with a university friend, Flora Eldershaw. Under her own name, Barnard published a further eight works of non-fiction and *The Persimmon Tree and other stories* (1943), source of 'The Party'.

A. E. BATISTICH (b.1915) was born in Dargaville and wrote for most of her adult life. Her collection of stories *An Olive Tree in Dalmatia* was published in 1963. She also wrote two novels, one in Croatian.

CARMEL BIRD (b.1940) was born and educated in Tasmania but now lives in Melbourne, where she teaches creative writing. In 1988 she published *Dear Writer*, advice for would-be writers. Her other publications are the novel, *Cherry Ripe* (1985) and two collections of stories, *Births, Deaths and Marriages* (1983) and *The Woodpecker Toy Fact* (1987), source of 'Buff Orpington and the Disasters of Middle Life'.

BUB BRIDGER (b.1924) was born in Napier (Ngati Kahungunu descent). Bridger started writing in the mid seventies and writes poetry and stories, published in a number of periodicals.

MARION CAMPBELL (b.1948) was born in Sydney but subsequently moved to Perth where she now teaches. She has published two novels, *Lines of Flight* (1985) and *Not Being Miriam* (1988), which reflect her interest in feminism and cultural theory. 'Peepshow', first published in *Westerly* in September 1977, reappears, somewhat revised, as the second chapter of *Lines of Flight.*

SARAH CAMPION (b.1906) was born in England and lived in South Africa and Australia before settling in New Zealand. She has published twelve novels, including a trilogy set in North Queensland, *Mo Burdekin* (1941), *Bonanza* (1942) and *The Pommy Cow* (1944). 'Amble' first appeared in *Southerly*, 1, 1953.

LYNDAHL CHAPPLE GEE (1908–81) was born in Timaru. She wrote stories, poetry and children's verse. 'Double Unit' was published in *Speaking for Ourselves*, ed. Frank Sargeson, 1945.

ANNA COUANI (b.1948) was born and educated in Sydney. She is a qualified architect, art teacher and teacher of English as a foreign language (her own background is Greek and Polish). She has also been active in organising writers' workshops, especially those involving women, and in small press publishing. Her own three collections of stories, *Italy* (1977), *Were All Women Sex Mad?* (1982) and *The Train* (1983), were all published by small presses. 'Xmas in the Bush' and 'The Train' were first published in *Island in the Sun: An Anthology of Recent Australian Prose* (1981).

JOY COWLEY (b.1936) was born in Levin. She has published a number of novels beginning with *Nest in a Falling Tree* in 1968, and a collection of stories, *Heart Attack and Other Stories*, in 1985.

ELEANOR DARK (1901–85) was born and educated in Sydney, daughter of the writer Dowell O'Reilly. After marrying Eric Dark in 1922, she moved to Katoomba, in the Blue Mountains of New South Wales, where she spent the rest of her life. She published ten novels, many of which won literary awards and most critical acclaim. 'Serpents' comes from her last book, *Lantana Lane* (1959).

BEVERLEY FARMER (b.1941) was born and educated in Melbourne. She has worked at a variety of jobs, including school teaching and waitressing, but now writes full-time. Her publications include a novella, *Alone* (1980) and two collections of stories, *Milk* (1983) and *Home Time* (1985), whose title story is included here.

FIONA FARRELL POOLE (b.1947) has written numerous radio plays and plays, stories and poetry. A collection of poems *Cutting Out* was published in 1987.

THELMA FORSHAW (b.1923) was born and educated in Sydney. She served in the WAAF during World War II and has since worked in advertising and as a freelance reviewer. 'The Grand Passion' comes from her only collection, *An Affair of Clowns* (1967).

JANET FRAME (b.1924) spent her early life in Oamaru and Dunedin. New Zealand's major novelist, Frame has also written numerous short stories, poetry, and autobiography. 'Jan Godfrey' comes from her first publication *The Lagoon* which won the Hubert Church Award in 1951.

YVONNE DU FRESNE (b.1929) was born in Takaka. A teacher and a writer, du Fresne has published numerous stories in periodicals, two collections of stories, *The Growing of Astrid Westergaard* (1985) and *Farvel and Other Stories* (1980), and two novels. 'Christmas (Shirley Temple is a Wife and Mother)' was first published in 1977.

HELEN GARNER (b.1942) was born in Geelong, Victoria, and educated at Melbourne University. She worked as a school teacher and journalist before becoming a full-time writer. Her first novel, *Monkey Grip* (1977), was a controversial winner of the National Book Council Book of the Year Award because of its frank portrayal of inner-city living and drug-taking. Garner has since published *Honour and Other People's Children* (1980), *The Children's Bach* (1984) and *Postcards from Surfers* (1985). Its title story, included here, first appeared in *Australian Short Stories* in 1983 as 'Postcards from Surfers Paradise'.

KERRYN GOLDSWORTHY (b.1953) was born in a South Australian country town and educated at Adelaide University. She is now lecturing in English and Australian Literature at the University of Melbourne and was for several years editor of *Australian Book Review*. 'Female Friends' was first published in the feminist anthology *Frictions* (1982) and appears in a revised form in her first collection, *North of the Moonlight Sonata* (1989).

PATRICIA GRACE (b.1937) was born in Wellington (Ngati Toa, Ngati Raukawa, Te Ati Toa descent). Grace published the first collection of short stories in English by a Maori woman writer (*Waiariki*, 1975) and also the first novel (*Mutuwhenua*, 1978). She has published two more story collections (*The Dream Sleepers*, 1980 and *Electric City*, 1987) and an award winning novel *Potiki* (1986).

KATE GRENVILLE (b.1950) was born and educated in Sydney, later completing an MA in Creative Writing at the University of Colarado. 'No Such Thing as a Free Lunch' comes from her first collection, *Bearded Ladies* (1984). Her novel *Lilian's Story* won the 1984 Vogel Award; she has since published two further novels, *Dreamhouse* (1986) and *Joan Makes History* (1988).

LYNDALL HADOW (1903–76) was born in Kalgoorlie, Western Australia, where her mother Florence Stuart had organised the first Women's Labour League and her father edited the *Westralian Worker*. She worked as a commercial traveller, for a time edited the magazine, *Our Women*, and wrote numerous uncollected stories, articles and reviews. 'Act of God' comes from her only book, *Full Cycle and other stories* (1969).

MARION HALLIGAN (b.1940) was born and educated in Newcastle, NSW, and later lived for several years in France. She now lives in Canberra where she recently organised the 1989 National Word Festival. She has published a novel, *Self Possession* (1987) and two collections of stories, *The Living Hothouse* (1988) and *The Hanged Man in the Garden* (1989). 'Blood Relations', reprinted in the latter, originally appeared in the *Australian Literary Quarterly* in 1986.

BARBARA HANRAHAN (b.1939) was born and educated in Adelaide. Early in the 1960s she began printmaking and painting, which she later studied in London, and has now held over two dozen exhibitions. She began writing late in the 60s and has now published nine novels and a collection of stories, *Dream People* (1987), source of 'Lily'.

JANETTE TURNER HOSPITAL (b.1942) was born in Melbourne but educated in Brisbane. Since 1971, she has lived in the USA and Canada. She studied and later taught English at Queens University, Ontario, and now teaches for part of the year at MIT, Boston. She won Canada's prestigious Seal Award for her first novel, *The Ivory Swing* (1982) and has since published three more novels, *The Tiger in the Tiger Pit* (1983), *Borderline* (1985), *Charades* (1988) and a collection of stories, *Dislocations* (1987). 'Isobars' was first published in *Overland*, 112, 1988.

KERI HULME (b.1947) was born in Christchurch (Kati Tahu, hapu Ngaterangiamoa Ngaiteruahikihiki descent). Hulme is best known for her celebrated novel *the bone people* (1985) but has also written poetry, and short stories, collected in *Te Kaihau/The Windeater* (1986).

JAN HUTCHINSON (b.1952) was born and educated in Sydney, where she now teaches part-time at the University of Technology. For several years she organised the 'Writers in the Park' readings at the Harold Park Hotel. 'Romance, Gardening and Feminist Theory' first appeared in *Meanjin*, 3, 1988, and is collected in *Desire and Other Domestic Problems* (1989).

ROBIN HYDE (1906–39) was born Iris Wilkinson and wrote professionally as a journalist and writer all her life, publishing four collections of poetry, five novels and other works of non-fiction. 'America Won the War' was published in *Tomorrow*, and is one of a number of Hyde's short stories which have never been collected. Hyde died in England.

STEPHANIE JOHNSON (b.1961) brought out a collection of verse in 1987 and her stories *The Glass Whittler* in 1988. She now lives in Australia.

ELIZABETH JOLLEY (b.1923) was born in Birmingham, England, and educated at home and at a Quaker boarding school. During World War II she trained and worked as a nurse. In 1959 she moved to Perth with her family, following her husband's appointment to the post of Librarian at the University of

Western Australia. Though she had been writing for most of her life, her first collection of stories, *Five Acre Virgin*, did not appear until 1976. She has since published two further collections and nine novels, many of which have won literary awards. 'Woman in a Lampshade', the title story of her third collection (1983), originally appeared in *Westerly* in 1979.

GWEN KELLY (b.1922) was born and educated in Sydney but now lives at Armidale in northern NSW. She worked as a school teacher and as a university and college lecturer and has been writing fiction since 1950. Her publications include five novels and a collection of stories, *The Happy People and Others* (1988). 'Country Show' originally appeared in the anthology *Transition* (1970) and was later made into a film.

ANNE KENNEDY (b.1959) is a freelance writer for television, and has worked on two films, as well as publishing stories in a number of periodicals. *100 Traditional Smiles* appeared in 1988.

FIONA KIDMAN (b.1940) was born in Hawera. Kidman's writing includes over 60 radio plays, four novels, several collections of poetry and two collections of stories *Mrs Dixon and Friend* (1982) and *Unsuitable Friends* (1988).

SHONAGH KOEA was born in Taranaki. A journalist, teacher and writer, Koea has published stories regularly since the late 1970s. A collection, *The Woman Who Never Went Home*, appeared in 1987 and a novel in 1989.

JOAN LONDON (b.1948) was born and educated in Perth and now lives in Fremantle. She has worked as a school teacher but is now writing full-time. 'The Girls Love Each Other' comes from her first collection, *Sister Ships* (1986), which won the *Age* Book of the Year Award.

OLGA MASTERS (1919–86) was born at Pambula on the NSW South Coast and worked for many years as a journalist on country and suburban newspapers. The mother of seven children, she did not begin publishing fiction until they were grown up and she in her fifties. Her first collection of stories, *The Home Girls* (1982), source of 'On the Train', won a National Book Council Award. Two novels were published during her lifetime and a further novel, a collection of stories and a play posthumously.

FINOLA MOORHEAD (b.1947) was born in Melbourne and educated there and at the University of Tasmania. She has worked at various jobs, including school teaching and taxi driving, as reflected in her novel, *Remember the Tarantella* (1987). She has also had several plays produced, though not published, and has written many stories and short prose pieces. 'Where Are You, Ellen Spalding?' originally appeared in *Refractory Girl*, 10, 1976, and was collected in *Quilt* (1985).

OODGEROO NOONUCCAL (b.1920), formerly Kath Walker, was born on Stradbroke Island, of the Queensland coast near Brisbane. She worked as a domestic servant and served in the AWAS during World War II before becoming actively involved in the movement for Aboriginal rights. In 1972 she established the Noonuccal–Nughie Education and Cultural Centre on North Stradbroke Island and in 1988 changed her name in protest at the celebrations of the white invasion of Australia. Her first collection of poems, *We Are Going* (1964), was a best-seller. She has since published three more books of poetry as well as a collection of stories, *Stradbroke Dreamtime* (1972), source of 'Mumma's Pet'.

RUTH PARK was born and educated in Auckland. In 1942 she moved to Australia and married the writer D'Arcy Niland. Though she has written in several genres, she is best known for her novels and children's books. Several, including *The Harp in the South* (1948), *Poor Man's Orange* (1949) and *Playing Beatie Bow* (1980), have been adapted for film and television and won major literary awards. 'Regatta Day' first appeared in *Coast to Coast* in 1944.

JENNIFER PAYNTER (b.1944) lives in Sydney. Her play, *When are We Going to Manly?* was produced in 1984 by the Griffin Theatre Company. 'The Sad Heart of Ruth' won the ABC Bicentenary State of the Art short story competition and was printed in *Fictions 88* (1988).

WENDY POND (b.1943) is a writer, researcher and scientist. Her stories have been published regularly over the last few years.

'Conversations with the Elders' won the BNZ Katherine Mansfield Award in 1987.

SUE REIDY is an illustrator and a writer. She won the BNZ Katherine Mansfield Award in 1985 for 'Alexandra and the Lion' which was subsequently collected in *Modettes* (1988).

ROSA SAFRANSKY was the winner of the Open section of the ABC Bicentenary short story competition. 'A "Happy Little Vegemite"' was published in *Telling Ways: Australian Women's Experimental Writing* (ed. A. Couani and S. Gunew, 1988).

HELEN SHAW (b.1913) was born in Timaru. A writer and teacher, Shaw wrote stories and poetry from 1945. She published two collections of stories, *The Orange Tree and Other Stories* (1957) and *The Gypsies and Other Stories* (1978).

HELEN SIMPSON (1897–1940) was born and educated in Sydney. She left Australia in 1914 planning to study at Oxford; instead she served in the WRNS during World War I. After marrying, she lived permanently in England. Despite her early death, she was a prolific writer, publishing 14 novels (three written with Clemence Dane), as well as poems, plays, non-fiction, children's books and many uncollected stories, essays and reviews. 'A Posteriori' originally appeared in *Modern Short Stories* (1935).

CHRISTINA STEAD (1902–83) is at last gaining recognition as one of the twentieth century's finest novelists. Born and educated in Sydney, she spent most of her adult life outside Australia, living at various times in Europe, the USA and Britain. 'The Triskelion' comes from her first book, *The Salzburg Tales* (1934), a collection of stories supposedly told by a group of people gathered together for the Salzburg Festival. It was followed by eleven novels and a collection of stories; a further collection and a novel, *I'm Dying Laughing* (1987), have been published posthumously. A collection of her letters is now being prepared.

J. C. STURM (b.1927) was born in Opunake (Taranaki). A librarian and writer, Sturm's first published story appeared in 1951. She was the first Maori woman writer in English, and published stories, poems and reviews through the fifties. Her stories were collected in 1986 as *The House of the Talking Cat*.

MARGARET SUTHERLAND (b.1941) is a writer and a nurse who has published several novels, children's stories and a collection of short stories, *Getting Through and Other Stories* (1977). She has won the Katherine Mansfield Award.

KYLIE TENNANT (1912–88) was born and educated in Sydney. She worked at a variety of jobs – journalism, in radio, as a barmaid – in part to gain background information for her novels, which won a number of awards. She published nine novels and two collections of stories, as well as much non-fiction, including an autobiography, *The Missing Heir* (1986), and several volumes of plays. 'The Case of the Blond Beast' comes from *Ma Jones and the Little White Cannibals* (1967), interlinked stories featuring that most unlikely, but most effective, of detectives, Ma Jones.

GREVILLE TEXIDOR (1906–64) was born in England. She came to New Zealand in 1941 and, encouraged by Frank Sargeson, began writing. Her work was published in periodicals and anthologies but not collected until 1987, as *In Fifteen Minutes You Can Say a Lot* edited by Kendrick Smithyman. Texidor died in Australia.

MARGARET TRIST (1914–86) was born and educated in Dalby, Queensland, but moved to Sydney when she was seventeen. Her fiction – two collections of stories and three novels – remained, however, predominantly focused on life in the country or small town. 'The Bridesmaids' originally appeared in the 1951–52 edition of *Coast to Coast*, an anthology of stories by Australian, and many New Zealand, writers published by Angus and Robertson from 1941 to 1973.

VICKI VIIDIKAS (b.1948) was born and educated in Sydney, though left school at fifteen to work at a variety of jobs. She was one of the few women involved in the Sydney 'new writing' scene of the early 1970s. Has since travelled widely in Asia. Her publications include three volumes of poetry and a collection of stories, *Wrappings* (1974), source of 'The Snowman in the Dutch Masterpiece'.

ANIA WALWICZ (b.1951) was born in Poland and moved to Australia in 1963 when she was twelve. She studied at the

Victorian College of the Arts and now lives in Melbourne, working as a visual and performance artist as well as a writer. She has published two collections, *Writing* (1982) and *Boat* (1989), and had work included in many anthologies. 'Big Tease' and 'Big Red' were first published in *Island in the Sun: An Anthology of Recent Australian Prose* (1981).

JUDITH WRIGHT (b.1915) has for many years been one of Australia's most celebrated poets. Born on the family property near Armidale in northern NSW, she later lived in Queensland for many years and now lives in southern NSW. She has published fourteen collections of poems, as well as children's books, critical and historical studies and collections of essays. More recently, she has been concentrating on non-fiction, particularly that which supports two causes to which she has long been committed: nature conservation and greater justice for the Aboriginal people. 'The Nature of Love', originally published in the *Bulletin*, 16 May 1964, became the title story of her only collection (1966).

Acknowledgements

The editors and publishers are grateful to the following for permission to reproduce stories in *Goodbye to Romance*:

'The Triskelion' by Christina Stead. Reprinted courtesy of Angus & Robertson, Australia; and Laurence Pollinger Limited, London.

'America Won the War' by Robin Hyde. Reprinted by kind permission of Derek Challis.

'The Party' by Marjorie Barnard. Reprinted courtesy of the copyright holder Alan Alford, c/- Curtis Brown (Aust.) Pty. Ltd. Sydney.

'Regatta Day' by Ruth Park. Reprinted courtesy of the copyright holder Kemalde Pty Ltd, c/- Curtis Brown (Aust.) Pty. Ltd. Sydney.

'Every Saturday Night' by Isobel Andrews. Reprinted by kind permission of the author.

'Double Unit' by Lyndahl Chapple Gee. Reprinted by kind permission of Maurice Gee.

'The Bridesmaids' by Margaret Trist. Reprinted by kind permission of B. S. Jenkins, Executor of the Estate of the late Margaret Trist.

'An Annual Affair' by Greville Texidor. Reprinted with permission from *In Fifteen Minutes You Can Say a Lot* (Victoria University Press, 1987) © The Estate of Greville Texidor, 1987.

'Amble' by Sarah Campion. Reprinted by kind permission of the author. With acknowledgements to *Southerly*.

'Where to, Lady?' by J. C. Sturm. From *The House of the Talking Cat*, 1986. Reprinted courtesy of Hodder & Stoughton, and The Spiral Collective.

'The Rector's Wife Tempts the Bishop With A Brew of Nyppe' by Ethel Anderson. Reprinted from *At Paramatta* courtesy of Penguin Books Australia Ltd.

'Singeing the Cockerel' by Helen Shaw. Reprinted with permission from *The Gypsies and Other Stories* (Victoria University Press, 1978) © Frank Hofmann Estate.

'Serpents' by Eleanor Dark. Reprinted courtesy of the copyright holder Michael Dark, c/- Curtis Brown (Aust.) Pty. Ltd. Sydney.

'The Nature of Love' by Judith Wright. Reprinted by kind permission of the author.

'Jan Godfrey' by Janet Frame. Reprinted from *The Lagoon*, Caxton, 1961.

'A Place Called Sarajevo' by A. E. Batistich. Reprinted by kind permission of Longman Paul Ltd. Auckland.

'The Grand Passion' by Thelma Forshaw. Reprinted by kind permission of the author.

'The Case of the Blond Beast' by Kylie Tennant. Reprinted courtesy of the Estate of Kylie Tennant, c/- Curtis Brown Australia.

'Country Show' by Gwen Kelly. Permission courtesy of Australian Literary Management, Victoria.

'Mumma's Pet' by Oodgeroo Noonuccal. Reprinted from *Stradbroke Dreamtime* 1972, by kind permission of the author.

'A Wedding' by Bub Bridger. Reprinted by kind permission of the author.

'The Snowman in the Dutch Masterpiece' by Vicki Viidikas. Reprinted by kind permission of the author.

'A Servant of the People' by Margaret Sutherland. Reprinted by kind permission of the author and *Islands*.

'Where Are You, Ellen Spalding?' by Finola Moorhead. Reprinted by kind permission of the author.

'Wedding' by Glenda Adams. Permission courtesy of Angus & Robertson Ltd. N.S.W.; also Australian Literary Management, Victoria.

'Peepshow' by Marion Campbell. Reprinted from *Westerly* No. 3, 1977, courtesy of *Westerly* and also by permission of the author.

'Woman in a Lampshade' by Elizabeth Jolley. Reprinted courtesy of Penguin Books Australia Ltd.

'Xmas In the Bush' by Anna Couani. Reprinted by kind permission of the author. Also published in *Island in the Sun 2, Italy & the Train, Transgressions.*

'It Used to Be Green Once' by Patricia Grace. Reprinted by kind permission of Longman Paul Ltd., Auckland.

'Big Tease' and 'Big Red' by Ania Walwicz. First published in 'Writing', Rigmarole Books, 1982 (Australia); reprinted as 'Travel/Writing', Angus & Robertson, 1989 (Australia & New Zealand). Reprinted by kind permission of the author.

'Apple Wine' by Joy Cowley. Reprinted from *Heart Attack and other stories* by kind permission of Hodder & Stoughton Ltd.

'Christmas' by Yvonne du Fresne. Reprinted by kind permission of the author from *Shirley Temple is a Wife and Mother – 34 Stories by 22 New Zealanders*, edited by Christine Cole Catley, Cape Catley, 1977.

'On The Train' by Olga Masters, from *The Home Girls*, published by University of Queensland Press 1982.

'Female Friends' by Kerryn Goldsworthy. Reprinted by kind permission of the author.

'Postcards from Surfers' by Helen Garner. Reprinted courtesy of McPhee Gribble Ltd. Australia.

'No Such Thing As A Free Lunch' by Kate Grenville, from *Bearded Ladies*, published by University of Queensland Press 1984.

'Alexandra and the Lion' by Sue Reidy. Reprinted by kind permission of the author. From *Modettes and other stories*, Penguin Books 1988.

'Home Time' by Beverley Farmer. Reprinted courtesy of McPhee Gribble Ltd. Australia.

'The Girls Love Each Other' by Joan London. Reprinted from *Sister Ships*, Fremantle Arts Centre Press, 1986, by permission of the publisher.

'The Road to Damascus' by Anne Kennedy. First published in *Islands*, No. 37. Reprinted by kind permission of the author.

'The Knife and the Stone' by Keri Hulme. Reprinted with permission from *Te Kaihau/The Windeater* (Victoria University Press), 1986 © M. A. Bodger/Keri Hulme.

'Blood Relations' by Marion Halligan. Reprinted from *The Hanged Man in the Garden* courtesy of Penguin Books Australia Ltd.

'The Dancing Master' by Shonagh Koea. Reprinted by permission of the author from *The Dancing Master* (New Zealand *Listener*, 5 Sept. 1987); *The Woman who Never Went Home and other stories*, published by Penguin, 1987.

'The Late Sunlight' by Jessica Anderson. Reprinted from *Stories from the Warm Zone* courtesy of Penguin Books Australia Ltd.

'Footnote' by Fiona Farrell Poole. Reprinted by kind permission of the author.

'Buff Orpington and the Disasters of Middle Life' by Carmel Bird. Reprinted courtesy of McPhee Gribble Ltd. Australia.

'Lily' by Barbara Hanrahan. Reprinted by kind permission of the author, c/- Curtis Brown (Aust.) Pty. Ltd. Sydney.

'Right Off the Map' by Thea Astley. Reprinted from *It's Raining in Mango* courtesy of Penguin Books Australia Ltd.

'Journal of a Hanger-on' by Wendy Pond. Reprinted by kind permission of the author. First published in *New Women's Fiction*, edited by Aorewa McLeod, New Women's Press, 1988.

'The Tennis Player' by Fiona Kidman. Reprinted by kind permission of the author from *Unsuitable Friends*, published by Century Hutchinson, 1988.

'A Happy Little Vegemite' by Rosa Safransky. Reprinted by kind permission of the author.

'The Sad Heart of Ruth' by Jennifer Paynter. Reprinted by kind permission of the author.

'Romance, Gardening & Feminist Theory' by Jan Hutchinson. Reprinted courtesy of McPhee Gribble Ltd. Australia.

'Up The River With Mrs Gallant' by Barbara Anderson. Reprinted with permission from *I Think We Should Go into the Jungle* (Victoria University Press, 1989) © Barbara Anderson, 1989.

Every effort has been made to establish copyright in these stories. Any information leading to further identification of the writers in this volume would be welcomed by the editors and the publishers.